ODDS & SODS

IT'S A RACE FOR REVENGE...

ANDY CATLING

T

The manufacturer's authorised representative in the EU for product safety is Authorised Rep
Compliance Ltd, 71 Lower Baggot Street, Dublin D02 P593 Ireland
(www.arccompliance.com)

Odds & Sods is set in locations that are real.
However, what happens there is fictitious,
along with the characters that inhabit them.

Troubador Publishing Ltd
Unit E2 Airfield Business Park,
Harrison Road, Market Harborough,
Leicestershire. LE16 7UL
Tel: 0116 2792299
Email: books@troubador.co.uk
Web: www.troubador.co.uk

ISBN 978 1836282 105

British Library Cataloguing in Publication Data.
A catalogue record for this book is available from the British Library.

Printed and bound in Great Britain by 4edge Limited
Typeset in 11pt Minion Pro by Troubador Publishing Ltd, Leicester, UK

For
Michelle and Jean

Without the encouragement, support and input from my dear friend Diane Rich you would not be reading this today.

Thanks to Derek Collie for his valued feedback, and to all friends who read very early drafts and gave their feedback too.

Thanks to Keith Gorman whose outstanding illustrations have brought the characters to life.

CONTENTS

LIST OF CHARACTERS
in order of appearance *(sort of)*

Gabby
McQueen *(also known as Mac)*
Lennox Docherty *(Edinburgh gang leader)*
Mlada *(Savoy staff)*
Simon *(Savoy staff, and more)*
Aurelia *(Savoy staff)*
Mo *(also known as Maurice; London pub landlord)*
Françoise Toussaint *(horse trainer)*
Elspeth *(secretary to Françoise, and more)*
Noel *(neighbour of Françoise; horse vet)*
Roche *(member of Le Manx Gang)*

TEAM MCQUEENERS

Team McQueen: London
   Al Dennett *(brother of Dubs)*
   Dubs Dennett *(brother of Al)*
   Likely Di *(also known as Diana)*

Team McQueen: North – Liverpool
   Phil
   Binky
   Woollyback
   Wacker

Team McQueen: Midlands – Birmingham
   Blaggit *(also known as Bermondsey Blaggit and Birmingham Blaggit)*
   Tonker

Relatives
    Callum *(Elspeth's cousin, and more)*
    Gabby's sister *(known as Gabby's sister)*

Locals
    Doris *(Suffolk villager)*
    Andy *(Suffolk villager)*
    Elaine *(Suffolk villager)*

Deceased
    Grandad *(RIP. McQueen's grandfather)*
    Limehouse Len *(RIP. London villain)*
    Bagby *(RIP. Scottish former gang leader)*
    Raphael Toussaint *(RIP. husband to Françoise)*

Animals
    Herd Ringer *(a horse)*
    Sweet Pierre, Toto, Usher *(dogs)*

List of illustrations by Keith Gorman

ONE

1997

"Leg it! Leg it! *Do a legger!*"

Gabby's voice was always in McQueen's head, but he'd never heard her say those words before, or sound so desperate, and he'd never seen her move so quick.

*

Today's city of choice was Edinburgh, the furthest so far from their London roots. They were expecting it to be as lucrative as it had been in all other cities they'd fleeced.

He'd watched Gabby earlier, making her move. McQueen knew the signs, having seen it so many times now, but today he'd wondered if Gabby was making the right choice. Him? Really? Why was she was hitting on that one? A spotlessly dressed, well-manicured brute of a guy, oozing wealth, which was what they needed, but there was something about him that made McQueen uneasy. Gabby normally sensed these things, didn't she? Was she really flashing her green eyes at him?

McQueen had always left it to Gabby to pick the punter for their badger con. This was how she'd said she wanted it when she put forward the idea of them doing a city-by-city badger con tour. And as she would be the one getting up close and personal, to some degree, once she'd got their attention in the hotel bar and lured them up to her room, he agreed that yes, it would always be left to her to make the choice. Then he'd step in, on her signal, before things got too hot; Gabby was a confidence trickster not a sex worker.

Down would go his camera shutter: *Click*. The damage was done and a hefty down-payment due.

"Oh dear! I seem to have snapped you in a compromising position, sir." Or sometimes it was madam; Gabby didn't care – she just selected ones who seemed rich and would want any sordid secrets kept quiet. She always managed to pick those willing to pay top whack for the pictures and their silence. McQueen admired that about her. Up to now, the only time she'd called for help was when a punter fell asleep, and she got her dress stuck in his zip. How they'd laughed over that. There was no denying that they worked well together.

Today, McQueen hadn't been able to shake off his bad feeling about the Scottish punter she had gone for. There was something too slick about his manner. Or was it the way he fussed over choosing his whisky like he was a pompous laird? Or was it his expensive choice of a hair-of-the-dog? Flash bastard. Or his passive-aggressive knuckle-cracking that Gabby tried to join in with when the bar staff were too slow? Or was it just McQueen being his ultra-observant, overthinking self? Gabby would say it was. *Trust me, Mac, can't you? You do your bit, and I'll do mine.*

Yes, her voice was always in his head.

He followed them upstairs at a discreet distance and waited for her signal, slowly rubbing each loafer shoe in turn against the back of his calves to keep them shiny. He felt his grandad with him whenever he wore loafers; Grandad had bought him his first pair. "This is the only loafing around I want to see you doing, boy," he'd said, and McQueen had tried to keep it that way. He'd bought loafers ever since and was always proud to be standing in the shoes of his grandad, even though he sometimes thought running shoes might be a better option.

Waiting. Waiting. Waiting.

He checked his fake Rolex watch and tapped the face of it. McQueen hated this chapter of the badger con. He itched to burst in and get it over with before Gabby gave the signal, because he wanted to keep her safe; she always was, of course, and how she'd fume if he went against what they'd agreed. He looked at his watch again then pulled out his camera and checked it, to keep occupied.

*

Inside the hotel room the man was raging. "I can smell ye devious London types a Royal Mile off. Ye'll get paid when we're finished, nae at the start, sweetheart."

Toned muscles flexed as he struggled to get free from the bonds Gabby had seductively tied with more expertise than her target demanded. "Get these off me!" he roared. "Ye've no right, coming up here to Edinburgh, extorting us innocents!"

Gabby froze. How could the way he said his words ooze so much evil? She'd made the wrong choice; she knew that now. She'd insisted she tie him up too early; that was a mistake. And she'd asked for money then too; what a rookie error. She had to get out quick.

"Set me free. *This instant!*"

She backed away towards the door, watching him writhe and flail, convinced he would break out before she reached it.

"Ye'll live to regret this, ye vile bitch," he said, raw with anger. "Set me free, I say! Ye don't know who ye're dealing with!"

Hands groping behind her, Gabby found the handle. She pulled it down and hesitated. She threw a key for the handcuffs into a far corner then burst out of the room.

*

Was this the cue for McQueen to step inside the room and snap sordid shots?

"Leg it! Leg it! *Do a legger!*" hollered Gabby shooting past him. No camera needed. Like Gabby said, it was time to run.

He bolted, trying to keep up. How could Gabby run that fast and talk at the same time? And in heels? He clutched his camera so tightly it dug into his palm like a biting rat.

"*He sussed me, Mac! He sussed me!* But I Scotch-walloped him! He was dazed for a bit."

Had he heard that right? There was no chance for her to tell him – she was off, like a demon Catwoman fleeing from a nemesis, her sleek black bob bouncing, not a hair out of place.

Both struggling to catch their breath, they shot through an emergency exit, pelted down a flight of concrete steps and out into a congested street, keeping up the pace until there was an alleyway. Gabby leaned against a wall, holding her sides, gasping as she tried to explain all. McQueen bent at the waist trying to focus on the tassels of his shiny loafers. Painfully breathless, he gripped his knees, desperate not to throw up. He should never have let her convince him she was up for the badger con. She was too good for that, and she wasn't a courtesan. At least her quick action with a well-aimed half bottle of Johnnie Walker when their mark turned into a menacing psychopath, had bought her enough time to handcuff him to the bed and take flight. Ha! The poor sod, whoever he was, would be stinking of whisky for a week.

His lungs burned. He waited for his partner to recover enough to get her words out and took the chance to slide his redundant Minolta camera kit into his backpack. Ever cautious, he tucked his defence spray up his sleeve, ready for action, just in case. McQueen was a defence man. His attacks weren't physical; he had other ways to bring people down.

"He twigged it, Mac. Right at the last moment. He even called me a thieving blackmailing slag an' all!"

McQueen straightened up. He tried not to sound stressed, but this was the last thing he'd wanted to hear. "Yep. Twigged it all right. I should say so. Sussed it too, like you already said."

He fiddled with the zip on his Harrington jacket, sliding it up and down, then stopped when he realised it would give away how worried he was. *Less of the sarcasm, McQueen, if you can manage that.* He took an intake of breath. "You picked a wrong 'un this time, Gabby. Who was he?"

"Some rich bastard who lives in town. That's what the cleaner whispered to me when she saw him in the bar earlier. She said she knew him."

"Right. And she's the hotel's authority on day guests and where they live, is she? Marvellous."

"She said she used to clean for him, in his big posh flat in Cockburn Street, actually."

"Cockburn Street? This is no time to wind me up, Gabby."

"No, really. She did used to clean for him there. Shot off quick when she saw it was him. I assumed she was getting out of the way cos she didn't want him to see her working at the hotel. Not sure why, but I can imagine. Perverted, mean and sadistic he seemed."

"Who though? Who was he? Did she tell you that? No. I suppose she helpfully buggered off. Did you get to find out who he was during your clandestine massage?"

Gabby spoke quietly. "During a, erm... he'd introduced himself as Mr Docherty and as things got going, he, well, he... tried to force his way out of bondage and he was furious with me."

"Oh, Jeez." A brief wave of nausea overtook him. He leaned forward again, closed his eyes, and shook his head. "Docherty? Mr Docherty? We could be well and truly in the shit now, Gabby," he whispered. "And there was me using up my precious brain power on thinking 'poor stinking sod'. What the hell was I worrying about that for?" Upright again, McQueen's voice grew louder. "This is serious. It isn't just that Docherty worked out you were going to be blackmailing him—"

"*We*, Mac. *We* were going to be blackmailing him!"

"Yes. Right." He struggled to keep his voice low and calm. "But I reckon that was *Lennox* Docherty. Someone said that hotel's most likely on his patch. We never should have been there, not even to have coffee, let alone doing the badger con in one of the rooms." He tapped the face of his watch. "And you gave the Scottish bastard a Scotch-wallop! Oh, Gabby." He closed his eyes. Slowly, through clenched teeth he said, "*The* Lennox Docherty. This. Is. Grrrrrr-im."

She looked at him blankly and shrugged.

"You're saying you don't know who he is, are you?"

"Gimme a clue."

"Well, he's not one of your average Scottish Jimmy, middle-management convention attendees."

Gabby shrugged again. She ran her fingers through her hair. Bright red nails like giant beetles matched her bright red lips like… He didn't want to think about that right now. He had to keep her safe.

"Oh, come on! Surely you've heard of Lennox Docherty? Everyone in our game bleedin' knows about him! We can't hang around here."

Gabby straightened her ultra-short, tight, black leather skirt; there wasn't much to sort. She looked at him sceptically, then at his rucksack. He dug inside to pull out a pair of tracksuit bottoms and threw them at her. He knew she was getting nervous when she instantly bent down to remove her slinky stilettos, then grabbed the joggers and wriggled into them. She tied the waist strings tight without comment or protest. Being a slight man had its advantages if you wanted women to wear your clothes.

Seconds later, as if Gabby was shot through with another fix of fear, they were off again, zigzagging through the thoroughfare towards the taxi rank, attracting curious looks. No queue. That was good. McQueen slowed to a walk.

"What about our stuff at the B and B?" said Gabby, slipping her shoes back on.

"Sorry, I only have a few of my own bits in my bag. Your stuff is still in your room. But I think you can manage without

Leggin' it

lacy lingerie and lippy, Gabby, if you want to save your skin." He gave her what he hoped came over as a 'trust me' gaze when they jumped in a cab.

"Glasgow please," he said.

"Glasgow?"

McQueen caught the driver's concerned expression. Did he think they were jesting with him? He had this problem sometimes when he wasn't in London. People thought because he spoke in a Cockney accent that he was joking, and they didn't take him seriously. But that couldn't be the reason for suspicion today. Had Docherty got word out so soon? Did this man know that villain? *Oh Gabby, what have you unleashed?*

"Whereabouts in Glasgow, sir?"

He tried to sound sincere and stay calm when he replied. "The Hilton. It's the one in the centre."

"Right ye are." The cabbie flashed glances in his rear-view mirror, continuing to scrutinise them. McQueen felt uneasy.

"Saw you running before I pulled in. Looked like ye've both been training for the East Lothian half marathon."

"Er, no. We're just extremely late for our important presentation, so if you wouldn't mind stepping on it."

"Right ye are," said the cabbie. "As my American customers like tae say, I shall gun the engine. Yee-haaah!" He smiled into his mirror, looking pleased, and they were on their way.

"So. What do you think of our new prime minister?"

McQueen winced; he wasn't ready for taxi driver banter and didn't want to get pulled into a political debate. He wondered how many times he'd asked the same question to passengers that year and did his best not to disappoint with his answer.

"Blair's chancellor is one of yours, so for Scotland, I reckon 'Things Can Only Get Better'."

The cabbie laughed. "I love that song. Wannae hear it? It's on my cassette player ready tae go."

"Erm. Not just now. But thanks. Might have a nap or think through our presentation. No offence if I…" He closed the Perspex divider and squeezed Gabby's hand twice – a signal that if the situation spiralled out of control, she absolutely must follow his lead. His mind raced as small talk drifted into silence. Gabby leaned her head on his shoulder. From the way her eyelids flickered, it looked to him as if she was feigning drowsiness. But what did he know? He'd never slept with her. Business and pleasure – not a good mix unless you're in a pub, which they were a lot. Anyway, why stay awake when they couldn't say what they needed to? The back of a cab, even with the little partition, was too risky for conversation – Docherty could have ears anywhere, especially in this neck of the woods.

He stayed alert, hoping for inspiration, with his finger tapping time away on his watch-face as it always did when he was anxious, or planning the next steps. A quarter of an hour out of town, he saw a chance to talk to Gabby alone; the most welcome motorway sign Scotland's M8 could offer. He rubbed Gabby's thumb and spoke loudly. "Darling, there's a toilet coming up. I need to use it."

"Me too," she said, yawning.

"Driver, we need to go to the loo. Could you pull over at the next service station? We won't be long."

"Fine, sir." The taxi pulled in. "You said, 'step on it', but take your time, the meter's running. I'm nae the one who's late fer a meeting, and I'm nae the one who's paying the fare."

They followed signs to the public toilets. As soon as they were out of earshot McQueen let out a sigh, as if releasing a bear that had been trapped deep inside him.

"Mac, what the hell's going on?" hissed Gabby.

"You still don't really know who you were tying up, do you?"

"All I know is what I told you already: this morning the cleaner told me he was some mad jock. Oh. Wait! You panicked me. She might have said he was called Lenny or something, worth a few bob."

"So, it was him! *I Knew It!* Oh, Gabby." He spoke slowly, doing his best not to let on that he once believed just the mention of Docherty's name might conjure up evil if overheard. "Let me spell it out. Lennox Docherty is a brutal, nightmare landlord, hoodlum, corrupt racehorse owner, and overlord of most of the murky capital. We wouldn't have got a shiny sixpence out of him."

"Ooops."

"No. Not fuckin' ooops. This bloke's a bleedin' monumental nutter. You've just seen that for yourself, haven't you? Rumour has it, the man had his postman killed just because he mistakenly posted a letter of his to next door. If word gets out about this humiliation, he'll be the laughing stock of the city's underworld, and he's not gonna let that happen."

"Rumour has it. Rumour! You're just being your usual paranoid."

"I'm not, Gabby. Remember Limehouse Len?"

"Can't say I ever met 'im."

9

"No? And you never will, poor sod. Here's why. Listen. I remember hearing about Docherty venturing south a few years back, with his brood to confront Limehouse Len over some moonshine distillery. We thought Limehouse and his boys were invincible. A week after Docherty's trip, Limehouse and ten of his lads were found wedged in the Thames Barrier, their bodies were all bloated, lips had been cut off, and eyeballs eaten out by fish, so they weren't fresh, poor sods. Hands and feet tied, and legs well mutilated. He never got done for it, but we all knew it was down to Docherty. It had all his hallmarks. Limehouse was a rogue, but he didn't deserve that."

"Thanks for that, Mac. As ever, too much detail. Mate, I know your grandad had a thing about details, and so do you, but those gory details I could have done without. I honestly think I'm gonna puke. Shouldn't have put my shoes back on. I might splash sick on 'em."

"Stop with the jokes, will you? Why do you always do that? *Trust me* – Docherty'll be like a bird-dog on the trail. He won't let up, Gabby. This cuckoo's got contacts in every major city in the UK, and the word is sure to be out to hunt down a London couple, with full description – of you! We need to get back home, pronto."

"So why didn't we just get the next express out of Edinburgh? Why go all the way to Glasgow?"

"Too risky. Waverley Station would be his first thought, obviously, and with just a couple of calls, he'll have his boneheads intercept us on the platform. Or, failing that, his haggis-ticker-tape welcome committee will be there to greet us at Kings Cross. No. We need to throw Lennox Docherty and his thugs north and south of Hadrian's Wall right off the scent."

"Who's this Hadrian? Another dodge-pot mucker of yours?"

"It's *not* a joke, Gabby. Why? Why joke now?"

He lowered his head and stayed silent, breathing in deeply to calm himself and gather his thoughts.

"Sorry. Sorry, Mac. Sorry. And anyway, d'you know how to get them off our scent?"

"Yes. Lucky for you I've come up with an idea. It starts with me going for a slash."

"You are coming back, aren't you?" she said, suddenly pale-faced.

Those eyes. Those eyes. He searched for the lucky green in them and wished he hadn't snapped. He tapped his watch. "Don't worry. I'll see you back in the cab. You get back there. And be sure to keep quiet. You never know who Docherty has on the payroll."

TWO

Gabby was usually calm under pressure, but with McQueen being longer in the Gents than she'd expected, she grew restless, and even alarmed by the thought that he may have scarpered. He wouldn't do that to her, would he? Not Mac, surely? He'd promised to be back. She craved for one of her snouts like she'd never craved for one before but was too tense to fumble about and roll one up. And anyway, she knew he hated her smoking. If he didn't ever come out, she would smoke all she liked, and not give a damn.

"Come on, McQueen. Come ooo-nnnn. Hurry up, will you?" she mutter-whispered to herself, watching the service station exit doors. Was she ever going to see him again?

*

This was no time to daydream about the first time they met, but the memory came back, and she found it comforting.

One sunny afternoon, two years after her last term of school, she was in the food department of Oxford Street's Marks & Spencer when a voice behind her said, "I think you'd better come with me." She'd never forgotten the seven words that changed her

life and since that day had often repeated them to herself with a
satisfied smile as a list.

1. I.
2. Think.
3. You'd.
4. Better.
5. Come.
6. With.
7. Me.

That was then; this is now. She couldn't bear to face the here and
now, so she stayed in the past.

Fearing her game was up and churning over the repercussions
that lay ahead, she shifted round to face the voice head-on. Her eyes
met those of a well-turned-out youngish man. Early twenties, she
guessed. He looked like he was trying to hide a grin when he asked
to see the contents of her Harrods carrier bag. She blushed and
stuttered something about needing to feed her starving baby before
discreetly opening the bag to reveal a booty of stolen sandwiches,
drinks and crisps. Her interrogator winked, laughed and opened
his own Fortnum and Mason bag to expose similar M&S goodies.

And she had never forgotten the biscuity smell of his body as
he leant over and whispered into her ear, "Right. Let's get the hell
outta here! Fancy a picnic?"

They spent the next couple of hours in Soho Square, an oasis
off the main London hullaballoo, munching their grub, laughing,
swapping stories of their easy nabs and near misses. They had a lot
in common: both were reluctant to secure a job in the real world;
both were signing on; both had been let down at school; and both
had difficult family lives. He'd introduced himself as McQueen, or
Mac to his friends and gave no more away when she pestered him
about his first name. "Mac. Just call me Mac."

The evening rush hour was about to kick in. They watched the pavement fill with commuters knocking off from work. He asked her favourite colour, and she told him: "Crimson."

"Back in ten. Sit tight," he said before heading off to the shopping centre.

She sighed, coming out of her dream world, briefly. Some things don't change. Here she sat all these years later, still waiting for him, not sure what the hell was going on, or whether she was doing the right thing.

True to his word McQueen had returned, ten minutes later, dead on time. Would he be coming back this time? She remembered the way he nonchalantly handed Gabby two designer dresses, in a glorious crimson shade.

"You can go to the ball now, Princess," he quipped. "I didn't know what size you were, so I nicked a size eight and a size ten too. Hope that's okay. Give it a couple of days before you take the one you don't want back. Say it doesn't fit and you've lost the receipt, and they'll refund you the ninety-five pounds."

"Buy one get one free!"

"Easy money, honey!"

"I think we should meet again, Mac."

"Yep. I would like that. As buddies. I reckon we could work well together."

"Buddies it is."

"How about here, next Saturday? Ten o'clock. Can you do that, Gabby? It will be right busy then – good for distractions! Get your glad rags on and I'll introduce you to my world of short con misdemeanours, if you wanna help out."

"I can see it now, Mac: Team McQueen here we come. And, no, we can't use my surname for our team because it's a ridiculous one, and I'm not telling you what it is, so don't even ask me."

She remembered being so excited, and hopeful, and jumpy, the way she had been ever since whenever they set off on a joint scam. She still felt like that, but sitting in the taxi, with the waiting seeming endless, she felt sick with nerves. What was he doing? *Come ooo-nnn, Mac.* Should she do a legger? *No. Trust him.* Knowing him, he'd come out smiling, with candyfloss on a stick for each of them.

After her first encounter with McQueen, Gabby learned how to execute The Coin Smack, The Melon Drop, Find the Queen, The Pigeon Drop and so many more cons. She loved it. Every day was like a performance, but she wasn't on stage, she was in among the audience, improvising and getting away with it. She had found her vocation, and in McQueen she'd found a mentor, a business partner, a soulmate, a friend. The two tricksters branched out to bigger things.

Like her, McQueen had wanted to find a pot of gold.

Now it seemed they never would.

*

"Oh, plee-ease come out, Mac or I'm gonna go in there and drag you out!"

Right on cue, the automated doors opened, and he strode towards the waiting cab.

"About bleedin' time too," she said, in a shrill voice that betrayed the anguish she was trying to hide. "I thought you'd fallen down the bog."

She felt less alarmed when he took her hand, without speaking.

*

Apart from McQueen constantly checking and tap-tapping his watch, the rest of the journey was silent and uneventful. When the light was right, he caught sight of his reflection in the Perspex driver-passenger separator. Just turned thirty, and despite his bachelor fast food lifestyle and fervour for a late-night kebab at the aptly named Madonna restaurant, McQueen had retained his slim, youthful, impish guise. His wistful Oliver Twist hazel eyes hid a yearning for understanding, and only a fleck of silver at the temples of his retro haircut hinted at his true age. Today's attire was representative of his modish boy about town wardrobe. Mums always cuddled him. Girls could never fathom him, but Gabby sometimes could. He liked working with her. Right now, he had to get her out of Scotland. And fast.

When the driver offloaded them outside the hotel, McQueen rounded up the fare. "Here, mate. Take a bullseye." He handed over a fifty-pound note. They waited until the taxi disappeared, then turned in the opposite direction, towards Glasgow Central station.

"Mac," said Gabby, with her eyes on a nearby café, "we've got twenty-five minutes till the Euston train leaves. I'm grabbing us coffees. I'll meet you in the ticket queue. You're paying for the tickets."

They boarded just as the train was about to depart. He was certain they'd not been followed as Gabby made straight for a quiet carriage. It was almost empty. She chose table seats opposite each other and set down their drinks. He watched her make ready for the four-and-a-half-hour journey. McQueen stayed awake and alert, glad that for Gabby weariness had replaced the thrice-time adrenaline surge that came with quick getaways of this type, and finally she'd been rewarded with slumber.

*

Back in Edinburgh, the supervisor bounded over as soon as the cab pulled into the rank. "Oi, Hamish! Why did ye nae answer your phone?"

"Sorry, boss. I must need to charge her up. Is there a problem? Ye've a face like a melted welly."

"Problem? Maybe. Mr Docherty has been on the blower to the big wheel."

"Docherty? Should I worry?"

"It's something about a couple of Sassenachs attempting to pick-pocket his wee dear mum's handbag in the market today. He's not a happy bunny and wants us to keep an eye open for a man and woman he reckons are in their mid to late twenties. No details of him, but the hen's about five foot five, pretty, with bobbed black hair, although I doubt if she'll retain her looks if Mr D catches up with her."

The cabbie whistled. "Boss, I need to speak to him now. It's vital. I think I saw them. I know where they are. Listen to this."

Alarmed after hearing his tale of events, the apprehensive supervisor dialled Docherty. He spoke a few words, seemed to shrink, then put his palm over the receiver. "Be sure to stop your voice from shaking," he whispered as he handed it across.

The cabbie relayed his journey to the Glasgow Hilton, convinced that from Docherty's description, the female passenger was almost certainly the one he was after. He added a spec of the bloke she was with, remembering she'd called him Mickey, or McQueen, or something similar.

*

Lennox Docherty thanked him and clicked off. He tipped his head back. Remaining still and expressionless, he let his focus linger on his new target. Snapping to, he hastily called a number with a Gorbals prefix, and instructed the listener to tackety boot up six of his finest for a Hilton visit. He stressed that the dynamic duo he sought must be 'gently persuaded' – Lennox Docherty style – that their scrawny wee butts were required back in Edinburgh, pronto.

*

Gabby cursed herself. Why had she ever wanted to do the badger con?

Yes. It was her idea.

Yes. She knew it would be a good money earner. And yes, they both needed money.

Yes. She knew the risks.

Yes. McQueen had been against it, worried for her safety. He hadn't forced her or bullied her into anything. No one bullied her: not since school.

Gabrielle Gilderthorpe, or Gabby, as she preferred and tried to get everyone to call her, always loathed school and being told what to do. From day one of her secondary school, she was shunned by her year group and labelled as a weirdo, not just because her sister went to a school for children in wheelchairs, but because she was a city kid who loved horses. Instead of having a bedroom wall filled with pictures of 1980s *Top of the Pops* heartthrobs, hers was plastered with any horse picture she could get her hands on. She was mocked by older pupils who relished any chance to make fun of a newbie, shatter their identity, and behind teachers' backs, make their lives hell. This is what they tried to do to Gabby.

"Gabrielle Gilderthorpe! *Gee-Gee*," they'd say, along with, "Is Mummy pony picking you up later? Or will you be galloping home all on your own again, cos you ain't got no friends? Giddy-up, *Gee-Gee*. Giddy-up!"

Sometimes they'd follow behind her in the school corridors making the sound of a neighing horse, or they would overtake her then horsey trot away, giggling like teasing toddlers. But it didn't stop Gabby loving horses, and it didn't make her change her posters.

As if that wasn't bad enough, her piercing green eyes caused problems too: she was nicknamed E.T. and Alien, and constantly heckled with yells of, "E.T. go home!" or worse.

She resolved never to respond to the caustic catcalls, and did well to resist retaliation, until one day, during a lunchbreak, an older girl confronted her, close to the toilets. Urged on by an excited and growing crowd, the tormentor began poking Gabby in the chest, accusing her of being a horse-loving alien-lesbian, and starting up a chant, "Gabrielle will go to hell."

Despite being a good five inches shorter, Gabby gave a swift kick to the bully's crotch, and a slam across her neck. In seconds, the older girl was on the floor with a bloody nose, whimpering like a thrashed puppy. She didn't mind if she went to hell. Revenge was worth it. Nobody ridiculed Gabby again and she was left to her own off-centre introverted ways.

Her school reports always included: '*Must try harder.*' '*Lacks concentration.*' '*Seems to be in a world of her own.*' One smart-arse science teacher, trying to be popular with the kids, wrote: '*Seems to be on another planet most of the time.*'

The only subject she got a better than average grade for was drama, but even then, her teacher commented, '*Drama outstanding but her imagination could one day take her down the wrong path. She might need reining in.*'

Years later these comments hurt Gabby, and she realised how cruel her teachers had been and how little they did to support her or bring out her true talents, but at the time teacher comments made no difference. She could never grasp why it was deemed so important to strive to get a string of O-levels or waste time with CSEs when most of her class would be on the dole, stacking shelves, or within a couple of years half of them would be pushing prams down the high street. None of this was a route she intended to take; she lived in a city of bountiful chimney pots, and she knew – not just from the famous Dick Van Dyke song – that even a sweep on the bottommost rung could find a pot of gold. She wanted some of that and clung to the vibe that there was one lucky sod born every minute; she was going to be one of those, somehow.

THREE

The Euston train pulled into Preston with a jolt that was hard enough to wake anyone snoozing. McQueen, famished and spitting feathers, would bet on his own life that Gabby felt the same, but then she was always up for a picnic.

"Buffet car?"

She laughed and tapped their empty cups. "Your turn, Mac."

He pulled out his train ticket and waved it. "It's always my turn when it's not the cheapest round!"

"Well, you're senior management, in this partnership."

He didn't argue. He knew she was strapped for cash. Her sister was needy. She was younger than Gabby, and even though they didn't always get on, a lot of her spare cash went in that direction.

Five minutes later, he was back, armed with two mawkish sandwiches, crisps, and a couple of chilled cans of their favourite lager which he Cockney rhymed as Winnie Mandela, she as Paul Weller, while everyone else called it Stella. They ate and drank in silence, then turned their attention to the day's events, agreeing that in the circumstances they were fortunate to be on their way back to London in one piece, and that this would definitely be their last badger con for a while – they'd drop it from their repertoire lickety-split, until things settled. He knew that Docherty would be seething, and with such a notorious reputation, he and Gabby were nowhere near out of the woods. Docherty's band of merry miscreants would be scouring the capital for them for the next six months, if not more. He had to break it to Gabby, but she'd dozed off again. He let her sleep; she'd need to keep her incisiveness about her; the day wasn't over. He tapped his watch as the train sped on.

*

Docherty answered his mobile. "What d'ye mean, they never checked in?" he said, blood boiling and mad as a hornet.

The caller assured Docherty that the Hilton's duty receptionist had seen no one matching their description. "That's the bad news, Mr Docherty, sir. On a whim I went to the station, to help you, sir. A ticket seller confirmed that a slightly flustered English couple, he with a red Harrington, eejit, she attractive with black hair, had purchased two singles to London Euston. I guess that means they'll not be coming back."

"Dinnae try and be smart," bellowed Docherty. "When does their train arrive?"

"It's due in this evening, at seven minutes past seven."

Docherty glanced at his office clock. It read just after five. There was enough time. He cracked his knuckles then thumped his fingers into the keypad of his phone, making ready to bark orders at one of his London roughnecks in Camden. Once done with that, he poured a large Macallan single malt into a Waterford cut glass tumbler. He swirled it slowly as he added drops of water from his crystal pipette. He watched them fall – drip, by drip, by drip. Raising the glass southwards, towards London, his mouth twitched into a tight smile. Words broke through it: "Nae so crafty Cockneys after all!" He stood silent, then lifted the glass to his lips and knocked back the lot as if he had snuffed out those he sought to avenge. "*Slàinte Mhath*, I dinnae think so."

*

Another fifty minutes and they would be back in London, but McQueen remained tense. Although they'd outsmarted Braveheart in Scotland, all the what ifs gnarled in his gut, churning his reasoning. The more he chewed things over, the more he realised that he shouldn't underestimate Docherty's grip on Edinburgh's gangland and the influence he'd have in London. An onerous sense of ruin began to close round him. What seemed like a Boy's Own dare at the start could well terminate in a grisly fashion if Docherty caught up with them. McQueen cursed himself for not buying returns to keep them off the scent. Details. Details. They would be scrutinising every detail, right now, to track them down. *Damn.* He crushed up his Stella can and held it tightly in his fist, annoyed at his stupidity. *Damn. Damn. Damn!* What to do? What to do? He brushed crumbs from the sleeve of his jacket and froze, staring at the red sleeve. *Idiot! Oh, Grandad! How could I be so stupid?* He took it off and stuffed it in his rucksack. Nobody on a con should be so conspicuous. That was one of his problems; he often chose fashion over practical.

Now awake, Gabby seemed mesmerised by the smooth rhythm of the high-speed train, her eyes flickering fast as she looked out of the window. Long gone were the shady granite Edinburgh tones. The last of the Hertfordshire countryside whizzed past in green flashes as they neared their familiar grey roots. A tannoy interrupted the calm. "We will shortly be arriving at Watford Junction. If you are leaving the train here, please take all your personal belongings with you." It spurred McQueen into action.

"Gabby! Gabby!" he said, standing up. "Grab your stuff. We're getting off here."

"Why? It's not Euston."

He sounded assertive but inside he felt the pain of pleading when he said, "Trust me," not for the first time that day.

*

Along the twenty-minute brisk walk from the overground station to the Tube, Gabby listened as McQueen explained his reasoning.

"I think you're getting really paranoid again, Mac. You're overthinking it. It's what you always do. You honestly think that Docherty's goons will be waiting at Euston?"

"Maybe, Gabby. In fact, I'd say the odds are quite high. But whatever they are, we definitely need to lay low for the rest of the year."

"Cut back, maybe, like we said, but for the year? That's crazy."

"I don't think so. Hopefully, Robert the Bruce will have cooled down by then."

Gabby went to answer, but he'd made a detour into Boots. What was he doing?

"You're havin' a giraffe, mate," she said, when he finally came out and handed her a box of ginger hair dye. "You want me looking like Geri Halliwell?"

"I'm deadly serious, Gabby. I've got one too. *And tonight, Matthew, I'm going to be... Mick Hucknall!*"

"Don't tell me: *Money's Too Tight To Mention.*" She laughed but stopped abruptly. "Oh, I know we shouldn't be laughing, should we? Sorry, Mac."

"You're right there, Gabby. Docherty will have all his southern informers and sneaks gunning for us. He may look as thick as a brick, but he's shrewd; we both need to take precautions."

Her hands trembled as she took the package, and she made a stab at laughing it off. "Okay, Mac. I'll give it a try. I guess that means I only have dyes for you."

They went their separate ways once they'd reached Oxford

Circus: she westward, he to the south. "I'll call you in a couple of hours just to make sure you got home," he said, not wanting to sound as if he might be fretting about her.

"Thanks. Keep safe, McQueen."

"And you, Gabrielle."

She winked and pecked him on the cheek, then turned. He kept his eyes on her as she walked along the platform, tapping his watch with each step until she faded away.

*

News from the London press gang hit Docherty hard. Word on his team got round quickly: *Watch out. Mr Docherty is going apeshit.* An apeshit Docherty was the thing they always dreaded even down a phone line. They braced themselves for his interrogations.

"No, Mr Docherty, sir. The couple were not on the train."

"Yes, Mr Docherty, sir. We waited at the gates."

"Yes, Mr Docherty, sir. We were at the right gates."

"Yes, Mr Docherty, sir. We were meeting the right train."

"Yes, Mr Docherty, sir. We thoroughly checked all the coaches, and all the toilets, and the guard's room, and all the first-class carriages, and the buffet carriage, and the dining car."

"Yes, Mr Docherty, sir. I am totally certain they were not there, sir."

"Just disappeared into thin air, eh?" Docherty spat the words into his phone, as if he was shooting poison through a blow pipe. "Right. Get Adams and Hill on the case. I want these fuckin' clever spielers. Nobody gets the better o' Lennox Docherty."

He shut off his phone and threw it down, then let rip at his punchbag, snarling, "Revanchism will be meted out. There will be nae stickit."

*

Ten days in, McQueen was getting accustomed to his DIY clipper number three scalp and his unkempt gunslinger beard. He'd only ventured out locally for essential shopping. He was having to live off his savings, along with the fifty-odd quid social security paid into his bank account every Thursday. He sometimes wondered how Gabby was, always promising himself that he'd give her a bell soon.

Two days later, she beat him to the punch. He opened her message, imagining the new-look Gabby, with a silky, ginger hairdo at the end of the phone. She'd looked gorgeous. He read her text:

hi mac. benefits down by half. thanks to gov cuts. tried to get a proper job so put on mini skirt for intrvw with real perv. start mon. admin assistant 4 merchant bankers canary wharf. ME!!! x

It was a bittersweet moment. McQueen was happy for her, but this was tinged with regret when he thought the end of their grifting days may have come. He sent a message back, telling her to knock 'em dead, and promising to keep in touch. He signed off with *keep safe* and a trio of kisses, pressed send, then stared at the screen as the message faded. He let out a sigh. What now?

FOUR

Three years later – October 2000

McQueen liked taking risks, so he strode out and crossed Savoy Court, towards the famous Art Deco façade, dodging the black taxis driving on the wrong side of the road. His lucky day? So far, so good. The shamrock-green neon signature atop the entrance, embraced all, except The Strand's discarded turn-of-the-century pauperised. Moments ago, he'd slipped a couple of quid to a few of these unfortunates, knowing it would fund their preferred tipple: a bottle of overproof fortified wine – Thunderbird – the drink enjoyed by bums all over the world. Ha! That should be its advertising hook, he thought, eyeballing the hotel sign again. 'SAVOY' it announced to the world; not '*THE* SAVOY': far too mundane and doubtless frowned on by Count Peter of Savoy, sculpted in the gleaming gilded bronze statue looking down on every hotel guest as they make their entrance whether humble or grand.

The weighty oak-framed revolving doors transported him into another world: no huddled hobos, lank beards, or the stench of their unwashed bodies. Instead, the warmth and tradition, like old money greeting new, appealed greatly to his knavish spirit.

McQueen at The Savoy

A concierge strolled over, giving the potential habitué a quick once-over. His highly polished name badge, half an inch too wide, screamed *Lorenzo*. McQueen's thoughts turned to his grandad, as they often did. "Know who you're talking to, sonny," he used to say. "Always know who you're dealing with, boy."

"Good afternoon, sir," he said. "How may I be of assistance?"

"Thank you, Lorenzo, but no. I'm just here for a spot of pre-theatre supper in the bar and grill. I hear the performance of *West End Tory* is a real hoot."

"I understand that is so, sir," Lorenzo replied, gesticulating towards the dining room. McQueen saw Lorenzo's curt manner and blank expression as a sign of wanting to be rid of another overburdening, well-heeled tosspot. He took it as a compliment.

At the foot of the carpeted stairs a receptionist tried to discreetly stuff a mobile phone into her pocket, and not look inconvenienced by the presence of a new customer. She failed at both. He noted the name badge: *Mlada.*

"Yes please?" she said, without looking at him directly. Mlada's heavy Eastern European accent suited her dour, desultory manner.

McQueen wondered what had happened to 'sir'? He thought everyone visiting the Savoy was worthy of a sir or madam. He'd had one from Lorenzo and was delighted. Was it simply her lack of Savoy savvy, or bad training, perhaps? Determined not to let anything spoil his visit, he shrugged it off and imagined a role reversal where he greeted her, in subservient guise, and with a falsely sincere, "*Yes, m'lady.*" A lot of effort went into not smirking, so that he could enjoy the thought that she'd make a good Gerry Anderson puppet. She had trademark high cheekbones and dusky bushy eyebrows, all hinting at vulnerability. She was tall, at probably six foot two in her stockings and had a surfeit of preppy red lipstick. Mlada was definitely not his sort.

"Table for one, please," he said.

She looked at the day diary balanced on the lectern. For a split second, he was back as a ten-year-old in church with his grandad, half expecting her to quote Matthew 17:20 *Our faith can move mountains,* the way the vicar once might have. Instead, Mlada asked whether he had booked.

"No."

"Mmmm," she said, examining the pages more.

After his long day McQueen was in no mood for a one-upmanship pantomime. Leisurely turning on his new quarter-tipped, oxblood, tasselled loafers, he made ready to depart, even though he really didn't want to go through with it. He loved the decadence of places like this. It was a far cry from his usual one-bedroom flat complete with a microwave ready meals daily regime.

"A moment!" said Mlada, omitting the sir again. He turned back. "We do have one table available, providing you can vacate by seven."

He glanced at his watch: ten to five. "No problem at all. I will certainly be gone by then."

Mlada led him to a circular table. "Someone will be with you shortly," she said, before dawdling back to the reception area.

He rested his small case beside the table and gazed cheerily round the room. Its burnished conker-coloured panels, winking chandeliers, views over the courtyard, and the spouting fountain impressed him. He sucked in his cheeks to suppress a smile. *Lovely stuff!* he thought, confident that afternoon tea for any old blue-rinsers would be a bounder's paradise here.

A maître d' approached. His foppish wavy grey hair brought to mind a touch of Quentin Crisp. Definitely not his type. He was a *Simon*, according to his badge. "Hello, sir," he said. "Welcome to the famous Savoy Bar and Grill. I trust you will enjoy the experience."

McQueen nodded to acknowledge the greeting, relieved that someone knew how to address guests. Simon limply gestured towards the lines of framed, signed photographs on the wall. "You follow in the footsteps of the rich and famous. All regular diners over the years, sir."

Many faces were familiar, even from a distance: Bacall, Bogey, Norma Jeane, Churchill, and others too. "Si, tell me, is that a young Mick Jagger and Marianne Faithfull?"

Simon leaned forward and whispered into McQueen's ear: "Apparently they only ever stayed for the first two courses and had their desserts upstairs." They chuckled in unison, then Simon stood tall. "Can we fix you a late-afternoon aperitif, sir?"

"Thanks. An old-fashioned, please."

"Excellent choice, sir!" McQueen looked at Simon's wizened face. Old, and well-fashioned. *Like you*, he thought.

"Aurelia will be your waitress."

McQueen made a note of the names, adding the usual details. *Mlada on front desk: offish.*

Maître d', Simon, speaking now: soft voice and gentle manners.

What would Aurelia bring to the table, he wondered.

"Aurelia will bring your drink over, along with your menu," said Simon.

McQueen smiled. *Crikey! A mind reader.* He'd better be careful, dealing with this one.

"May I take your sports jacket and attaché case to the cloakroom, sir?"

"Ah!" said McQueen, rubbing a hand over his inside jacket pocket area. "I'd very much like to leave this bulging wallet in my jacket, but I believe you can't trust anyone in the Savoy cloakroom these days, not the way you once could, so I'll keep it, thank you."

"On the contrary, sir. We pride ourselves on the most secure and trustworthy cloakroom service in Christendom!"

The way Simon emphasised the *st* in 'trustworthy' and 'Christendom' amused McQueen; he'd definitely rattled him. "Oh, all right then. Take my jacket. But this case never leaves my side," he said, tucking it securely between his legs. He rubbed the handle as if guarding an important international trade agreement.

"Is there anything else I can do for you?" said Simon, his composure resumed.

McQueen shook his head.

"If you think of anything more I can do for you personally, or any extras that you require, sir, be sure to ask for me." He stroked his name badge and winked discreetly. "You know who I am. Bon appétit." Simon left with the jacket and a polite flourish.

His invitation unnerved McQueen, but he shook off the feeling and checked his watch, betting Aurelia would be back in no more than four and a half minutes. He scanned the restaurant as the clock ticked. Despite Mlada's earlier fully booked claims, it seemed that guests were thin on the ground. His grandad would have loved it here. He'd be in his usual manic meerkat mode, noting everything about everyone, happily quaffing his jungle juice, not missing a thing: "*The devil is in the detail, boy. Attend to the details and flush out the devil or choose to dance with him. But make sure you always know where he is.*" That, along with "*God loves a sinner*" is what he remembered his grandad saying often. As a child, it both confused and terrified him. Not a day went by when he didn't think of Grandad McQueen. He looked around, noting details.

One noisy couple near the bar looked to him as if they were the wrong side of three bottles of shampoo. He reckoned the male must have at least twenty-five years on the female, but what would she care? Not a jot, by the way she was fingering a rock the size of Birkenhead. He nearly let slip a *blimey!* when he saw how big it was. Next, he noticed the keys she was jingling, and imagined they were probably for one of the poncy new-build apartments across from the Houses of Parliament which, from what he could see of the old boy's behaviour, he would have secured for her. *Ha! Well, if you've got it, girl, go flaunt it.* He pictured Ms Flaunt-it-Bling's old nan wagging a gnarly finger and telling her exactly that. In his opinion, this doll had certainly got it! Not his type though.

Another couple occupied one of the window tables: a pair of plummy types. They sat leafing through the *Hanna Andersson, Best for Baby Clothes Magazine*, together. Nothing under a ton good enough for them. No more Sauvignon Blanc for the Charlottesque, soon-to-be mother though, and just the odd bottle of Bud Light for boring Nigel.

Someone was at a table behind one of the pillars, but he never got to see them as Aurelia appeared, with ten seconds to spare, balancing a tray loaded with his cocktail, wine list, menu and a bowl of plump, mixed Mediterranean olives. She smiled and said she would return when he was ready to order.

He took a small swig of his drink, closing his eyes to savour the honeyed Woodford Reserve, which slipped down easily. Settling into the leather seat, he perused the *carte du jour* and reflected on the day; it had turned out to be a belter.

FIVE

Earlier that day, McQueen had walked to William Hill, Curzon Street, a bookies he hadn't placed bets in before. It had taken nearly a year to formulate his profitable circuit and get to know it inside out. He deliberately selected the busier shops to mask his movements and chose ones where the machines were best obscured

McQueen on the road to ruin?

from the counter. Meticulous planning was his signature. Having done his research, he was confident this one would offer everything he needed to join the ranks.

He'd arrived a tad before noon. Inside, a bank of large TV screens didn't disappoint. They broadcast sports from around the globe: greyhound racing from Melbourne; the sport of kings from Singapore; a mixed doubles badminton final in Moscow, and judo from Budapest. The entire world seemed to be right there with him. Except for Gabby. He imagined her saying, "*Well, this is Mayfair, don't you know! You name it, you can lose money on it!*" She'd use her Eliza Doolittle posh voice. He wondered, as he often did, where she was now. Probably married some rich mug, with one on the way. Ooooh! She'd give him such an earful for thinking that!

Maybe she was lumbered with her frail mum and sister. Or even banged up in Holloway, perish the thought.

He missed working with her.

He missed her chirping away like a Cockney sparrow – peck, peck, peck.

It wasn't just that. He missed her.

Move on, mate. Onwards and upwards, son. That bird has flown.

He picked up a copy of the *Racing Post*, checked the date, then turned to the nearest member of staff and joked with her. "I don't want to be reading yesterday's form! Ah! This is the one. First of the month. And…" he checked his watch, "there's just time to say the customary first of the month 'rabbits', so I'm bound to be lucky!" Her stifled smile told him that she didn't know what he was on about. They spoke no more, and each got on with their important work.

For the next half-hour McQueen studied the paper, formulated his selections for the day, and filled out the necessary paperwork. Once done, he handed his Lucky 31 slip, with five horses written in bold and his nine pound, thirty pence stake, to a beaming cashier. Could this be his new lucky shop?

He knew only too well that betting on horses was a mug's game for most run-of-the-mill punters. Unless someone was privileged with inside information on a sure thing, they were destined to lose, in the long run. McQueen had no hot tips, but his small bet, spread over the afternoon, gave him the opportunity he wanted: a chance to blend in with other gamblers who'd be arriving shortly. He had much bigger fish to fry; not just fish – whopping great whales!

Between one and two o'clock, the sucker-suits would arrive, with their bluster and bullshit. They'd start pumping notes into the fixed odds betting terminals, the vast majority favouring roulette. He would need to be as sharp as a tack from now on. Hovering close, without drawing attention, he planned to note which machines weren't paying out, and which numbers were hot, hot, hot. In his experience, when a machine was bloated with money from such itchy-palmed dealers', that was the time to strike.

There was no shortage of prime candidates, or berks, as he preferred to call them. The one he chose had done close to a grand, and only twenty minutes ago was a couple of hundred up, which he should have pocketed. Now the dullard was chasing his losses. Down to his last twenty quid he put it all on seventeen. Moments later, he left, muttering Latin obscenities. It was McQueen's turn. This was his moment! He replaced the birdbrain on the swivel stool and reviewed his options.

Gaming machines paid out around ninety per cent of money in. Although you could never be certain of a pickup, today the odds slightly favoured him. The lemon seemed to be siding with high numbers, sucked in, spin after spin, so he placed some fifty pence losing bets on the same high number band, then switched, splitting to lower numbers. The results were monumental. Covering from one to nine, meant paying out forty-five pounds a pop. This was a considerable wager for him. Trusting his gambling instincts, after three goes he'd turned one hundred and thirty-five pounds *into* five hundred and forty. Tempted though he was to keep at it and extend his winning streak, he knew better, so he printed the winning voucher and handed it to Miss Smiley Chops at the till.

"Congratulations, sir. I'll get your winnings from the safe at the back. Won't be a jiffy." She returned, armed with a tasty wad of purple Edward Elgars, before he could time her. He peeled off two and handed them back.

"Treat yourself to something nice, sweetheart," he said. Her eyes welled up, and her face reddened. He left without giving her time to compose herself and thank him; the blush was enough.

What a relief to see an Italian deli nearby where he could sit with a decaf coffee, chill, and reflect. Yes, this was his second biggest yield after the near two grand pull-off at Ladbrokes, Westminster last year. On average days, after travel expenses into town, he'd be lucky if he cleared a ton; and then there were the inevitable losing runs to consider – that would damage the money clip, and his confidence to boot.

Bookmakers in affluent areas usually operated from Monday through to Friday. Their busiest days tended to be towards the weekend, so McQueen knew he only had a narrow window of opportunity with these particular outlets. And then there was his worst nightmare: a suspicious, clued-up manager who would pass his description to all the bookies within a five-mile radius. After that, everything he'd worked for would be well and truly up, gone the same way as the Edinburgh badger con. And Gabby.

*

Aurelia's polite cough jolted him back to the present. "Are you ready to order, sir?"

"Yes thanks. Can I go with half a dozen of the Carlingford poached oysters and for the main your Dover sole grenobloise, with a side of honey roasted celeriac?"

"Certainly. Any wine?"

"Yes. A bottle of *Muscadet de Sèvre et Maine sur Lie*."

Aurelia looked a little embarrassed. "Sorry, sir?"

McQueen understood. He laughed and changed tack; speaking French wasn't his thing. "Number two-zero-three-four."

"Fine, sir," she said, smiling.

He checked his watch as she left and drained the last of his cocktail. McQueen was never happier than on a Sunday lunchtime when Grandad insisted that he abandon all homework to join him at the local boozer and be treated to a bowl of jellied eels and get his very own pint of wallop. Grandad would then go on to explain the art of the short con, and the grifter's code of honour, or some such. Then home for a roast, a snooze, and wake up in time for six o'clock evensong. This came close. What would he make of his grandson eating this posh grub? He wished Grandad could be here too.

A satisfying buzz enveloped him until Aurelia returned, in record time, with the dry white. She offered him the label, opened and poured. He gave one long sniff and one sincere swallow. "Wonderful," he said, fixing his eyes on the glass, willing her to continue. He fought the urge to say, *It should be bloomin' wonderful for ninety-six notes a go!* and instead managed, "Where are you from, Aurelia?"

"Finland, sir."

"Helsinki?" He guessed everyone said that when her lips pinched as if she was holding back frustration.

"That area, sir. Kamppi." She explained that she'd been in London for the past six months to improve her English and was happy with her move. Despite her bubbly manner, he noted an aura of wistfulness. He'd never know the intricacies of her life but, trained as ever by Grandad and unable to resist, he started to imagine how her life might be. Was she yearning to go back to her homeland and try to eke out a living there, perhaps selling vintage clothing in daily flea markets, with her boyfriend? Not knowing every detail was burning him up. Sometimes he cursed Grandad for teaching him this habit. He returned to thinking about his food order and looked at his watch. If he was right, there would be sweet cicely as a garnish. He'd take that as a sign.

His oysters arrived on a bed of crushed ice, with fresh limes, a bottle of Tabasco, and yessss! *Thar she blows!* A scattering of sweet cicely. *Lovely jubbly*, he thought and attacked each one with gusto, followed by the entrée too, pleased to know that Aurelia, his new best friend, was on hand to replenish his goblet. With a monkey in his skyrocket, and the grape kicking in, he felt invincible. If only Gabby could see him now.

He noted two squawking orange Nagasaki-tanned garish secretaries, looking like they'd finished runners-up in a Cher lookalike competition, now occupied the adjoining table. They giggled as they ordered a brace of Porn Star Martinis. Flanking his left was a group of staid, middle management civil servants. McQueen took his phone from the pocket of his button-down Ben Sherman, making it obvious to anyone looking that there were no messages of interest. He dismissed the groaning sweet trolley when it arrived, ordering a double espresso and the bill.

He acted as if his phone vibrated and answered it in an irritated tone. "Hello. Hello? Who is this, please?" He stood up. "Sorry, we have a poor line. I'm in a basement area. Hang on. I'll move." He strode through the chattering dining room, into the hotel lobby. It teemed with a troop of testy ten-gallon-Stetson-wearing Texans, all attempting to check in concurrently.

Fifteen seconds later, outside in the courtyard with the bellhops and bowler-hatted greeters, he carried on talking. "Hello. Hello? Are you still there? Can you hear me now?" And he carried on walking, moving slowly away down the courtyard.

"Thank you. That's better for me too. Who's calling? Guy's and St Thomas' Hospital?" He squished the phone to his ear. His strained expression would tell everybody he was listening hard for a reply. Anyone craning their necks to listen in would have heard every word he said.

"Yes. Yes. I can come to see Dr Mergusson within the hour.

Can't you give me the results of my liver function test now? Okay. I know the drill. I'll see you shortly."

As he walked, he turned his head and saw a fleet of taxis unloading more booming Yanks with their entourages. He kept going, increasing his clip, walking away from the hotel, turning right, about to melt into the multitude of sightseers and commuters when he felt a hand on his shoulder.

Someone whispered, "I think you'd better come with me!"

SIX

The Cross Keys in Endell Street was McQueen's favourite Central London watering hole, just far enough north of the Covent Garden tourist traps. The outside was adorned with a cornucopia of jazzy window boxes; the interior always spick and span, filled, but not cluttered, with highly polished brass curios hanging from the beams, walls covered in oak-framed prints, cartoons, and paintings. They served the best pint of the black stuff this side of Mulligan's on the Liffey, in barrel jugs on request, and they offered a perfect brew of sociable locals and passing raconteurs relating their cock and bull stories. McQueen had spent many impetuous sessions there. Some with Gabby.

From his table, he could see the chick behind the ramp wasn't his type, even though she was an expert in pouring pints of Guinness, always finishing them off by trailing a lucky shamrock in their creamy heads. She passed her latest two to the maverick Gabrielle, who oozed confidence as she navigated the crowded bar, and gently placed the full glasses, perfectly centred, on beer mats in front of him. He tapped his watch and she fiddled with tobacco, making herself a cigarette, while she quizzed him.

"So, McQueen, how long's it been? Three? Four years? You don't write, you don't phone, you don't fax."

"Sorry, Gabby," he said, lifting his glass and sipping the smooth, white froth.

"Thought you'd have a double chin by now, but no. Bet you've still got a six-pack under that shirt."

"If only!" He took another mouthful. "Never mind me. I see you haven't kicked that disgusting roll-your-own habit, then? It'll do for you, you know that?"

Sparking up her battered Zippo, she took a drag, then blew smoke in his direction. "Oh, Mac. I didn't know you cared."

McQueen tapped his watch and stared at her baccy tin. Someone had painted a smoking Tintin on the lid. "Portobello Road Market?" he said, opening it. "Gawd. What are these? Don't tell me these Rizlas are legal."

"Liquorice flavour." She stroked her chin with an index finger and looked at him. "Probably not your type, eh? But I like 'em."

He shook his head. "I suppose it takes all sorts, I guess?"

"*Allsorts?* Your jokes haven't improved."

"I thank you," he said. "Let's drink to that!" And they did.

Half a pint in, Gabby said, "I see you're still operating the Lambert Walk, then."

"It's the Lambeth Walk, stupid."

"I know, Mac. I just love winding you up!"

She was right: it had, but he tried not to let on. "Anyway, how did you suss me?"

"Lemon squeezy!"

He put down his glass and looked at her with an eyebrow raised in exaggerated confusion.

"Behind a Savoy pillar!" She laughed. "I knew exactly what you were planning. I've seen it all before. You and your Lambeth Walk!" She laughed again, emphasising the TH.

"Yeah. I knew you were there!"

"You did *not*, you lying git!"

"Language! Can't say things like that in the Savoy, my dear, so don't say it here!"

"That's why you had to leave, is it? Foul language?" She laughed once more and shot McQueen a playful, quizzical look. "I saw you, making friends with Simon."

"Oh yeah. We're best buddies now." He paused, as it dawned on him that he hadn't fully realised what Simon was really saying when he'd asked if there was 'anything else' he might need. Gabby obviously had. *Hmm... No matter.*

"Anyway, Simon's definitely not your type," she laughed again, "I think it would have gone something like this, Mac," she said.

He pretended to yawn. "Is this going to take long, Marple? Are you gonna do one of your drama queen, dream-the-impossible-dream monologues, and try and tell me what happened, even though you don't really know? Should I get more drinks in?"

Gabby ignored him. He'd forgotten how good she was at that. "I'll bet, ten minutes after the tab arrives, your attendant girlfriend is starting to get concerned – where has her bobby dazzler gone? And five minutes later, in conversation with Simon, she tells him you took a call and how you looked troubled by it and moved to get a better signal. You leave the coffee, along with the one-hundred-and-ninety-pound bill, plus jack all on the table, oh, and your very, very important attaché case is still there. The evening starts to get busier, and the flustered maître d' can't wait any longer, so he takes the case, along with the bill, to the cloakroom, where he opens it and finds... let me think... it contains the latest edition of *Private Eye?*"

"Go on, Ms Smarty Pants," he said, folding his arms, amused and smiling.

"He begins to glow, but at least he has your wallet as security. He reaches into your jacket pocket to remove same, but when he opens it, it's stuffed with cardboard, and where there should be Gold American Express and Diners plastic, there's a load of expired travel cards. It's not worth a tinker's cuss! Close to tears, he's shouting at the girl to 'phone the police immediately', and off he goes to report things to the manager, and hey presto, Mac! The night of the filched Savoy feast is yours! And if I guess right, you got that jacket for a couple of quid from Help the Aged Reach-me-Down this morning. I'm right, aren't I, Mac? And those nice attaché cases are two-a-penny down Petticoat Lane on a Sunday!"

He leaned forward to speak, but Gabby kept going. "Didn't know you was a flat fish sorta guy. Had you down as more of a sirloin steaker." She went into the Doolittle mode he loved:

"How would you like it cooked, monsieur? Just rip its horns off and wipe its arse!"

Laughing, he managed to butt in with, "I fancied a change."

Gabby still hadn't finished. She told him how, for the past few years, she'd got into a routine of treating herself to a couple of Savoy Dry Martinis on the first Friday of the month, to remind her what being on the other side felt like.

After that confession, McQueen ordered another round, and they settled into catch-up mode.

She was now living in a two-bedroom council maisonette in Hammersmith, caring, alone, for her semi-disabled younger sister, who wasn't that poorly after all, but the benefits and allowance kept their heads above water. He hesitated, wondering whether to bring sad news to the table, then went for it: his mother had passed away, two years back. She'd gone into hospital for a minor op, caught pneumonia and, within three weeks, he was delivering the eulogy in a near empty room. There was, however, some good news – she'd left him her two-up, two-down terraced house in Tottenham. Unfortunately, she'd remortgaged it so many times, to fund her bingo and brandy binges, that after he'd sold it on a buyer's market, he only copped twenty-five grand. Grandad McQueen would have been gutted to see the family home gone, but at least he'd got to put down a deposit, and a month's rent upfront on a one-bedroom flat in Finsbury Park. This was a much

43

better base for wheeling and dealing than his previous Home Counties digs had been. The rest went in his savings account.

He didn't want to linger on himself any longer. He tapped his watch. "I thought you'd be… I dunno…"

"What, Mac? You thought I'd have got tied up with a sugar daddy and got one on the way by now? Don't tell me you were gonna say that."

"The thought never entered my head."

"I don't want kids, Mac. I'd have got the wealthy bastard to buy me a couple of horses instead! That'd be nice. Patter of tiny hooves," she said, adding, "Clip-clop, clip-clop," he guessed because she knew it would irritate him. She was right, as usual.

Her phone rang. She stood up, smoothed down her tight jeans, and checked the screen. "Just gonna nip outside to take this."

"Who is it? Mr Money, I suppose."

"For that you can get 'em in again, Mac. Maybe it's my sister, maybe it isn't. That's for me to know and you to guess. I never ask who phones you, do I? But then no one who's not dodgy ever does phone you, cos no one's your type, are they, Mac? And as you don't like me smoking, while I'm gone, I'm having a quick rollie, with Mr Tintin."

"Same again?" he said, passing Tintin over.

"Natch."

He caught the barman's attention and ordered as Gabby went out, then stared at specks of loose tobacco left on the table, lost in thought. She looked ravishing. He'd never tell her, but she was aging well: radiant skin, petite nose and simper smile. A couple of small crow's feet had appeared around her haunting, emerald eyes. She now had pink, not red, well-manicured nails, and maybe a half an inch on the hips, otherwise it was how he remembered her: raven-black smooth hair cut perfectly level all round in her usual Gabby bob. It had been bouncing as they'd run for their lives that day, down Edinburgh's Royal Mile.

When she returned, she asked about his current employment.

Gabby takes a break

He decided to start off cool. "You know – a bit of this, a bit of that."

She snickered. "What, a mini-scab driver?"

"Piss off!" he said, then blew his cool and described his latest turf accounting winklings.

"Seems a bit risky, Mac, for the return. But hey, guess it keeps the pot boiling."

He shrugged. "Not far off. You?"

"Customary crap. Mainly plying the mustard sauce dip,

outside Harrods. Trouble is, less and less of the targets are holding big foldings. It's all plastic these days, and the only ones interested in the cards are the Serbian gangs, which I've no intention of getting mixed up with."

"I meant to ask you what happened to your yuppie leanings in Canary Wharf?" he said. "Come on. Give us some blurb on those bankers!"

She looked at him and swirled her drink. "Lasted for nine months. Bastard line manager! Kept hitting on me, and I caught them up-skirting me. Well, Mac, you know me. One thwack later, I'd busted her nose. Claret everywhere, and guess what?"

Keen for an answer, he didn't have to wait.

"I was sacked straight off, with no hope of a reference," she blurted.

He tried to suppress a laugh. "Always been one for the ladies, eh?"

"After that, I was embarrassed to contact you. I went back to hoodwinking in the West End."

"I should have called you, Gabby. Sorry."

"So should I you." She held up her glass so they could clink.

"Maybe we were destined to be just bit players," he said.

"Oh, stop wallowing, you wombat. We were dynamite back then. You can't have forgotten the pyramid foist when you snared that smarmy wing commander?"

"Woodrow Finch."

"That's it! How much did we take him for?"

He shook his head and smiled. "That seems an age ago."

"I really did miss you, Mac."

"Cheers!" they said, savouring their reunion.

"We're a good team. And you know what? With all the shit that's been going on, I reckon there must be a horse around for you somewhere."

"Yeah! Clip-clop, clip-clop." She laughed, clinking their empty glasses together in the rhythm of a gallop. "And it's your round!"

He slid over a twenty, picked up his pint and downed it while Gabby waited at the bar. Was working the badger con, in Edinburgh, really going to be their last joint shakedown?

"Here we go, Mac," she said. "A double Courvoisier. No ice, if memory serves. Cheers to us, Mac!"

"Cheers to us!" He nodded at her as he drank. "So, what's the word on the street, Gabby?"

"Not much. I hear the Jones Gang are looking for some foot soldiers. Something involving a blackjack racket at the newly opened Luxor casino in Brum."

"No way!"

"Yes way, Mac. Anyway, film security in these new joints is tighter than two coats of paint."

"I wouldn't trust that fink, Billy the Blue Nose, as far as I could smell him."

From the way Gabby was twirling her hair she already seemed tipsy. McQueen guessed she was drinking on an empty stomach, probably surviving on the complementary Savoy cashews because normally she could match him drink for drink.

"You know what, Mac? I still smile to myself about that story you told me about your last two weeks at school."

McQueen looked interested and puzzled. She giggled and went on. "The slightly mutton careers officer, Mr Robins, asked your plans for leaving. You said you wanted to be a hustler and old redbreast spent the next day phoning management companies asking if anyone was looking for a wrestler."

"Deaf old fool."

"Pardon?" said Gabby. "Sorry, Mr Robins, wherever you are. Couldn't resist."

"Don't worry. He won't have heard you."

"Mac, wouldn't it be fab if we could pull off the long con? You know, the big one that could set us both up for years?"

"That would really show Robins. But nobody pulls that sort of flanker anymore," he said, wishing he had an idea to put on the table. "And even if we came up with an angle, we'd need plenty of dosh, and probably a couple of new bods in the team, neither of which we have."

"Typical stick in the mud, you," she said, her pot-valiance soaring. "Can't you come up with something, Mac? For more than just us two – what with all your needing to know who's who, what's what, where's where, and when is when. It could be one of your full-blown Team McQueeners. Think on it. Oh, say you will."

Despite his show of misgiving, McQueen felt a pang of excitement in the pit of his belly. All their talk of horses, and her egging him on to think up another Team McQueener, ignited a spark that set off the genesis of a ploy and he liked it.

"Listen. I may just have something, but I need a while to formulate it, make a couple of contacts, and think on it some more."

"Pray tell," Gabby said. The lucky green glint was back in her eyes.

He tapped his watch. "All in good time. You know how I like to work. I'll bell you as soon as I've thought things through."

She laughed. "Will you? The last time you said that it took a few years! I better check you've got the right number!"

Later, outside, she pecked him on the cheek, the way she always used to, before they went their separate ways.

That night, McQueen dreamed he was sitting on a church pew, staring at the altarpiece, crying his heart out for reasons that he could not fathom. He blamed Grandad.

SEVEN

The next day

Simon sat at the breakfast bar in his velvet smoking jacket drinking his Earl Grey. He ran his fingers through his thick quiff of hair to keep it back, sliced the top off his boiled egg and dipped a soldier into the runny yoke. He was still smarting from the rollocking he received from the general manager over yesterday's non-paying guest, and cross that he would not agree, when he protested, that the waitress should have been more observant and on the ball. It may happen a lot in other restaurants but for the Savoy it had to be a well-planned job, not impromptu, and it irked him that someone had set out to deceive him. But he mustn't let grievances spoil the day, or his breakfast.

He tried to put it to the back of his mind. It was rare that he had a day off on a Saturday and was looking forward to meeting his partner for a spot of lunch on Soho's Old Compton Street.

It was nearly two years since their first meeting in the backyard Turkish bath club. Some men would spend hours there, chewing the fat in between dips in the plunge pool. Most of the patrons were too boisterous for his liking, but one day he got talking to a man around his age and he was surprised to find that they shared a passion for the Wars of the Roses. They bounced Tudor facts and figures off each other. Their relationship thrived. It was never a toilet trader sexual thing; holding hands in the cinema was as far as it would go in public. He would love to snuggle up to him in his pink pyjamas, noting a hint of rouge on his cheeks. Proper old-fashioned fairies they called each other and never wanted to join in with the modern-day trend for parading in an annual Gay Pride Week.

They both had busy schedules, so they usually only got to see each other once a week, which seemed to keep their bond intense. After the starters and a carafe of wine, Simon unburdened himself by outlining yesterday's commotion at dinner, and how the manager gave his arse a kick. His boyfriend laughed and rubbed Simon's thigh sympathetically.

"Simon, my dearest. You'd never see publican Maurice fall for something like that!"

Simon was chuffed to be one of the few who called him Maurice and not Mo. He was also one of the few who knew how much being called Maurice meant to his special friend.

Early November

Gabby hadn't been idle while McQueen was doing all his planning and thinking. The Salisbury on St. Martin's Lane, in the heart of Theatreland, was a lucky discovery, and ideal for her plan. The historic 'ye olde pub', with cosy nooks and crannies, brought worldwide travellers flocking, and she had no trouble developing a good rapport with Maurice, the landlord. Every day she dropped in for her eleven fifteen in the morning red wine livener. Being an impoverished budding novelist in search of inspiration, and he a sycophantic toady creep desperate to please his customers, she couldn't see how her plan could fail.

Pick up, Mac, she thought, her senses working overtime.

"Wotcher, mate. What's it to be, Gabby? Don't tell me –

you've had an idea that I should be selling Big Ben to a Japanese consortium or half-inching the crown jewels again?"

She laughed, relieved to hear his voice. "No. Much more tricky than that, Mac. Can we meet this week?"

"I'm intrigued. Is Friday any good?"

"Fine, Mac. Friday is fine. South exit, Leicester Square. Eleven o'clock. Sharp, please."

"You've got it. I'll be there."

That was easier than she thought it might be. This was promising. She put her phone away, fiddled with her charm and smiled. Why had she been worrying so much about working with him again? If things went to plan, she'd soon know if it was going to work out.

Friday

McQueen bounded across the road. She wasn't convinced by his attempts to seem breathless. "Sorry I'm a touch late. Ten minutes, twenty-six seconds, to be precise. Poxy Piccadilly line," he said as he got close enough for her to hear.

Gabby waved away his excuses and held up a battered plastic record case. "I see you, eyeballing this!" She didn't wait for his questions. "Listen, Mac, I know it was my idea for you to come up with a Team McQueener, but I've got anxious about it all, and so first can we run a tester? Just you and me? We haven't worked together for a while. I need to know that we've still got it. If we ain't, then any grander plans you've thought up can't include me, okay? I've come up with an idea." She didn't wait for him to object, in case he did and got straight into outlining her ruse, as they walked towards the Salisbury. When she finished, she stuffed a copy of the current monthly nerd music mag, *Shindig*, into his hand. "Think of it as the old dog in the bar number, but with a twist. Up for it?"

He seemed to have taken it well. She waited for him to respond.

"Sounds good," he said.

"Wait outside the antiquarian booksellers in that narrow street opposite," she said, relieved. Pointing, she added, "See?"

"Got it."

"I'll be out in about fifteen, Mac. Set your watch!"

Taking slow, deep breaths to quell her nerves, Gabby walked towards the pub, record case in hand. It had been an age since they'd last pulled off one of these sort of stunts. If they were too ring-rusty, this could be the end of everything.

The air was musty inside, cigarette smoke and stale ale slops from the night before lingered, like the blear of a hangover that won't shift. "Usual, darlin'?"

"Not today, Mo. Have to chip off in a bit. Having blood tests at the hospital, so better stick to a cappuccino. Don't want to turn up reeking of booze, do I? I'll neck a few when I come back."

Mo brought the steaming brew over to Gabby's usual table. As he approached, she expected him to be distracted by the low-cut silk blouse she'd specially selected. She knew most landlords found this scenery desirable in their pubs at opening time, or at any time, landladies too, and there was no doubting that they could be swayed by one hot broad. She also knew Mo had never really warmed to her condescending manner, and highfalutin' *I am writing a bestseller book* bollocks, but as a landlord he'd put up with any sexy regular paying customer, early doors, if they were likely to attract more custom. She'd watched him sometimes, playing the letch because he believed some customers liked that sort of attention, but surely he'd have picked up that she wasn't convinced? Either way, his lack of genuine interest for her in that direction made things simpler and she was relieved.

Unclipping the case, she opened it and nonchalantly thumbed through the records inside.

"What you got there, babe?"

She wanted to holler, "*Don't call me babe, you knob!*" but settled for, "Just some old dusty LPs my mother gave me last night. I'm taking them down to Berwick Street to try and flog them."

"Oooh. You got any by The Who in there? Asking for a friend."

"Not sure. Your friend a fan?"

"We both are."

"If there's one in here, it'll be no good to me – I don't have a player. Mum said there may be a couple of rare ones. We'll see." She slipped her jacket on and finished the last of her coffee. "Time I was off for my date with the needle, Mo."

"D'you mean Dr Bloody Vampire or Dr Music DJ?" he said with a laugh.

She winked and leaned forward provocatively as she picked up the LPs. "A cheeky favour, please. Can I leave the records behind the bar? I don't fancy lugging them all the way to the infirmary and back."

"Sure, babe. Pass them over. I'll put them under the counter."

"Cheers, Mo. Don't think I'll be gone long, couple of hours tops if I'm lucky. Toodle-pip."

Gabby strolled over to the waiting McQueen. "Right, Mac. You're on in ten, kid. Try not to screw this one up, eh?"

"As if," he said.

*

McQueen studied the real ale pumps. Nice collection: many he hadn't come across before. He didn't want anything too strong at this time of the day so asked for a pint of Pedigree. Mo poured the foaming ale and they waited for it to clear. "One for yourself, fella?"

"Bit early for me, sir. But, hey ho, it's Friday, and I guess it's five o'clock somewhere in the world, so yes." Mo, reached for a glass to pull another. "I will join you." He raised his pint in McQueen's direction. "Your very good health! I never like to refuse a drink from a down to earth bloke. Better than from some of the Miss Goody-Two-Shoes types that come in. Just had one." Mo tutted and rolled his eyes. "Reckons she's the next Lynda La Plante."

"A wannabe gardener?"

"No. A crime writer. Funny though, what you said, cos La Plante was born a Titchmarsh. It came up in a pub quiz."

"You live and learn," said McQueen mounting a bar stool. He slid the music mag out of his jacket, took a gulp of his Burton, then started reading. He needed to keep the landlord talking before any early tourists turned up. "You must oversee an excellent cellar," he said, taking another sip of beer. "This is one of the best pints of Pedigree I've had. Have you managed the premises a while?"

"Coming up to fifteen years."

"I bet you've seen some changes?"

"Yeah, and most not for the better. All the old regulars are brown bread; the brewery charges a fortune now, and for the bulk of the trade I'm reliant on those bloody backpacking sightseers, with their pints of Pepsi, burger and fries orders."

McQueen fondled his chin to look sincere. "Yep. Every profession's suffered, don't you think? Apart from those money-grabbing fat-cat bankers."

The next few moments were crucial to Gabby's plan; McQueen didn't want to blow it now. The landlord had to reply, else the bunko would fizzle out. He looked at his watch, and for good measure, counted in his head too. *One Mississippi, two Mississippi, three Missis…*

"So, what are you in, mate?"

Bingo! Relief washed over him. "I'm an online sporting and music memorabilia collector and dealer. You know, signed football shirts, Muhammad Ali's boxing gloves, Ian Botham's joint-rolling machine. That sort of thing."

"I get your drift. You're the sporting type, eh?" He winked at McQueen, smiling.

"I've bought and sold some weird oddities in my time, but the real money over the past few years has been in music. Not CDs, it's the old vinyl the market is going crazy for, especially the uncommon labels of the sixties and early seventies. I sold the first Black Sabbath album on the Vertigo label last week for two hundred and ten pounds. I picked it up at a car boot sale for a fiver. You never know what you're going to find next."

Mo walked towards McQueen and held out his hand. "My name's Mo."

"Pleased to meet you, Mo. My old mum calls me Derek, but to everyone else, I'm Del. I'd give you a business card but they're being reprinted. Tell you what, I'll write one out, specially. You won't get the benefit of the design features though. And I can't remember the exact website address. It's a new one."

Mo handed over some paper and a pen then pointed to the empty glass. "Fancy another, mate? My round."

"Thanks, Mo," he said. He wrote on the paper and left it on the bar where Mo was pouring his fresh beer, then carried on flicking through *Shindig*. Mo set down McQueen's pint and picked up the bait. He read it out loud.

Del's music and memorabilia
Buy and sell
It's always swell with Del

Phone 07493 11666

Mo didn't bother reading out the phone number, but McQueen could tell he was thinking about it. He had him down as a music luddite so knew he'd never get the Cozy Powell reference to 'Dancing with the Devil' in the phone number. He couldn't resist throwing that in for Grandad.

When Mo tucked the paper in his trouser pocket McQueen was ready to bet a pound to a pinch of shit he knew what was coming next.

"Del, sorry to be a nuisance – could you have a look at some albums a friend asked me to take care of while she was at the hospital? As you said, you never know. I think she was going to bin them."

55

"Sure, Mo. Let's see what you've got." Mo put the case on the bar and McQueen opened it.

"The most important thing about vinyl is the condition," he said, flicking through the collection. "You can have an extremely rare record, but if it's only in fair order, it's probably only worth five per cent of the very good nick value."

All the usual suspects were there: Abba's *Arrival*, ABC's *The Lexicon of Love*, Max Bygraves's *I Wanna Sing You A Story*, Leo Sayer's *Endless Flight*. Gabby had obviously picked them up from her local charity shop. "Sorry, Mo. Nothing of interest here, but don't chuck them. The hospice shops are always happy to take this stuff."

There was only a handful left strewn on the bar.

"Jesus!" roared McQueen and Mo nearly jumped out of his skin. Adding a "Holy Jesus!" he removed an LP from its sleeve and inspected the vinyl close-up, aware of Mo's eager stare.

Record scam

"Del – what is it, Del? You look like you're shaking, mate. You all right?"

McQueen placed the record back in the cover, exaggerating the gentle way he was handling the goods before saying, "Mo, I have never seen this before. It's The Beatles, their 'butcher' sleeve. The one that was withdrawn immediately after the protests."

"I can see why," said Mo, putting on glasses to scrutinise it. "Just look at those decapitated baby dolls and pieces of raw meat. So, is it worth much?"

McQueen looked at him, square-on. "Twenty-five, maybe forty on a going day," he said.

"Forty quid? Big deal."

"Grand, Mo. Grand. This is rarer than rocking horse shit."

Mo looked flushed, as if his mind was in overdrive. "She'll need a ciggie when she hears this! Even I need one, but I've given up!"

"When's the owner due back?"

"Later on, this afternoon, I think."

"Bollocks! I'd love to have met them, but I'm going to a rugby rarities auction in Wembley and need to be there by two thirty. I've already bid on some high-priced lots and if I'm successful I'll have to be there in person to pay. I can't afford to be blackballed. But hey, Mo, when they return, can you let them know if they ever wanted to part with this holy grail, I'd offer a fair market price. No less than twenty-two thousand, cash." He went to leave but paused. "Oh, I gave you my number, right?"

Mo patted his pocket.

With a hand on the door McQueen said, "And Mo, there will be a nice finder's fee for you."

Outside, Gabby was waiting. "You took your time."

"Patience, me dears. He's hooked. Go reel him in."

"In my own time, Mac. In my own time! See you in Scott's Bar later."

EIGHT

Mo started to panic. That Miss Niminy-Piminy-Bookworm could be back shortly, customers had begun to arrive, and one of his early afternoon bar staff had just called in sick; he must rise to the occasion; be professional.

Twenty minutes later, Gabby showed up. She removed her denim jacket and showed off her plaster. "Took four attempts for the blue dress to find a good vein. Bloody aching, it is. At least the queue wasn't as long as I feared. Better have a glass to ease the pain."

Mo brought her wine over. "This one's on me, babe. You've had a rough morning."

She caught a trace of freshly smoked cigarettes. "Thanks, Mo. Appreciate it."

He gave her time to settle in, then came back. "By coincidence, my sister passed by for a chat. She's bonkers for eighties and nineties music, and I took the liberty of showing her the contents of your case. Hope you don't mind. She's one of those oddball completists – must have the Italian export picture sleeve or the bonus track twelve-inch edition. Anyway, turns out that there were a few of yours that she didn't have, and she asked me to make you an offer for them."

"Go on."

"Seems silly money to me, but seven hundred and fifty pounds."

"Bloody Nora! With that amount I can enrol in that creative writing course that starts next month."

"That's great news, love. I'll get the cash."

"Hold on, Mo. Maybe I should still see what valuation the second-hand record shops would give."

Mo was ready for this. "The dilemma you have with those sharks is that they need to make over fifty per cent profit on a deal, to cover their overheads. Plus, you look rather peaky after your sticking. Should you be yomping around the streets with that weighty case?"

Gabby's "Mmm" laid heavier in the air than the usual fug of pub smoke and Mo felt anxious again.

"Look, I like you," he said, patting her knee. "Let me call my sister to see if she's willing to up her offer."

"Would you, Mo?" Gabby pulled out her Tintin tin and started to prep a ciggie, but he could see she was watching him make his way upstairs. He gave it a full five minutes, hoping to make her sweat, before meandering back down with an envelope he'd removed from his safe. "It's your lucky day! I got her up to a grand. Take it or leave it was her instruction." He slapped the fat brown packet down. Gabby looked genuinely astonished, and he watched as she counted out the twenties, saying nothing.

When done, she thanked him. "Cheers, Mo. I owe you one."

"Another wine?" he said, pouring a glass for himself.

"You know what, Mo, I think I'll pass. Beginning to feel a bit crappy. I'll head home and have a nap."

He walked with Gabby to the door, opened it for her. "I've taken out the ones my sister wanted," he said, handing over the case with the remaining LPs.

"It definitely feels lighter," she said. "I tell you what, keep the lot. You might know someone who likes them. If you make any money, put it in a charity box." She set the case down on a nearby table and patted it. "See you tomorrow, Mo, all being well."

With his spirits higher than the optics above him, Mo surveyed his glorious pub. That was the easiest twenty grand he'd ever be making. *What a chump!*

*

McQueen sat in the far booth, sipping a bottle of Peroni. 'A Whiter Shade of Pale' drifted through the air, and he hummed along. Gabby joined him at his table. "Hey, Mac. How did you get away so quick? Everything go all right?"

"I just told him I had to catch 'The Last Train to Clarksville' and had a 'Ticket to Ride'."

"You little monkey!"

He wasn't sure how or why the thought popped into his mind, but he realised that he liked the way she never mentioned Docherty. He didn't bring the subject up either.

"*Don't say,*

To keep it at bay."

Good advice, Grandad. But keeping it at bay didn't mean that he had put all thoughts of Docherty's right to reap revenge out of his mind.

Gabby ordered a bottle of Bollinger and two glasses, and they broke out in beaming grins, like two happy Cheshire Cats.

"So, what did we hit him for? A monkey?" said McQueen, downing his beer.

"Nope. Double bubble."

"A thousand notes? You little diamond! Just like old times."

"Couldn't have pulled it off without you, Mac. Bonnie and Clyde ride again!"

The waiter brought a tray and they waited, listening to Barry Manilow's 'Could It Be Magic', as he fussed and poured. "Love this stuff," said McQueen, tapping his watch.

Gabby picked up her glass. "I'm not sure if you mean the music or the bubbles."

"I like your shit taste in sounds, Gabby. I keep expecting Val Doonican's *Rocks, But Gently* album to raise its ugly head. Bet you know all the words!"

"I've got a copy of that at home. Saving it for your Christmas present, to go with your pipe and slippers."

McQueen ignored her tease. "Was The Beatles cover difficult to replicate?"

"Nah, not really. My sister did it. These days it's amazing what you can do with a bit of cut and paste from fan sites."

Nice to know her sister had her uses. He wondered if he'd ever get to meet her.

*

They drank and talked about how things would pan out for Mr Greedy, reckoning he'd leave it until Monday, then call the record dealer, to explain that the owner had returned from hospital with bad news and needed quick cash. Relieved things had gone to plan, Gabby enjoyed a chance to steal the imagination of the writer she'd pretended to be. She acted out the way Mo might embellish his story, insisting that he'd be playing for sympathy and would tell Del that out of moral duty alone he'd bought the case at a fair price to help a fellow human being because they had to find money for an urgent op. All week Mo would be having a devil of a time getting an answer from Del's hoax number. He'd assume Del was away on business or on holiday, Vegas perhaps. Then he'd wish that he'd asked for a landline number as well. Gabby was adamant that he'd be missing gawking at the beautiful Miss Fit Bird, who hadn't been in since that Friday. Del's phone would just keep ringing, and by the end of the third week, Mo would start to get panicky. He'd wonder if he should pay a visit to Berwick Street and trade the album there. At least he'd get ten grand plus. He'd leave it for one more week and then, if no joy, seek out Reckless

Records. According to adverts, they claimed to pay top dollar for anything obscure from the fifties and sixties.

Gabby reeled McQueen in with her enthusiasm and they conjured up an image of Mo approaching some hippy-looking dude, who'd be wearing a psychedelic Hawkwind T-shirt. The manager would come out and inspect the sleeve. He'd look up at the rum customer standing before him, who was claiming to be a Beatle fanatic. Mo would lie and tell him that he'd recently discovered it in his attic, and when he surfed the net, found he'd uncovered a little nugget. The owner would sigh and clarify the position: a bona fide package would certainly be worth up to fifty thousand pounds, but this cover was a crude replica, and the record inside was not worth more than a tenner.

Mo would trudge back, feeling as sick as a Ganges snow trout when it slowly dawned on him that, like a record, he'd been played – track by track. A scheming couple out there had conned him out of his hard-earned, and there was sod all he could do about it.

"Hey, Mac! I can't stop rocking but gently with laughter!" said Gabby, hoping McQueen had never noticed the way her nostrils always quivered when she laughed a lot. She whacked his arm, trying to get the words out between hoots. "The poor *babe*... the poor *babe*! *Babe* will be thinking... 'Cocksuckers!'."

"From what I saw of him, I don't think he'll ever work out we were a double act."

She pulled a tissue from her sleeve, dabbed at her eyes, and carried on laughing. "Even if he does work it out, he'll never want to see an LP cover again!" she said, struggling to add, "Cheers!" before sitting back in her chair to enjoy the fizz and the buzz.

Her partner in crime sat tapping the face of his watch as she composed herself. What was he thinking when he did that? Sometimes Gabby was never really sure.

"So, McQueen, I think we passed the test."

"It was fun, Gabby. I'd say we're ready for the big one."

She felt proud. That was high praise, coming from him. "Let me know once you've come up with your final plan for Team McQueen. I can't wait to hear it."

"I will. I will. Just a few things to iron out, and details to check, but you'll hear from me soon. In the meantime, keep your ears open for anyone reliable you think might be up for our dream team, will ya? Hustler types."

★

Simon felt cheery. Things had calmed down at the Savoy and his boss had moved on, and so had the less than tip-top front of house, Mlada. It meant that Simon could see more of Maurice some weeks. "We like this," they'd say, doing their best camp impersonations of their favourite double act, Paul Daniels and his wife, Debbie McGee. "Not a lot, but we like it."

Simon headed off for the weekly slot at the Turkish bath, to meet his adorable friend, as usual. When they met, he seemed down. Simon knew that if he waited for the baths to do their magic, Maurice would eventually calm and reveal all. He was right. Before long, Maurice had spilled the beans about being duped by an LP promise, and how he was desperate for revenge.

"If I ever set eyes on that bastard, Del, I'll do for him. I will. Trouble is, I don't know what I'll do."

Back in Maurice's flat he showed Simon the case of LPs. Simon studied them keenly. "There's some good ones in here, Maurice, dear. I can't believe you don't play them." He walked to the record player and put on the David Essex album, selecting, 'Hold Me Close', then sat back with Maurice and snuggled up to him. "Shame there was only one by The Who." He held up The Beatles cover and inspected it. "And shame this is a repro copy. Del reckoned this would be worth a lot, did he? And that bloke you took it to was ready to pay top dollar if it was for real?" Maurice nodded back, sombrely. "Whoever made this did a good job, Maurice. Don't be too hard on yourself. I can see how you were had. Even the LP label inside is good. We'll play it later, see what's been subbed as a record, shall we?"

"Probably Des O'Connor," said Maurice, laughing. "It's only the cover that's worth the money, though."

"Are you talking about Des, or the LP?"

Relieved to see Maurice less tense when they laughed together, Simon put the record back, closed the case and stood behind his partner to massage his shoulders. "That's better. Laugh it off if you can, sweetie, or…"

"Or what?"

"Or… let's make plans for revenge for if you ever do come across him. We don't know all about the Wars of the Roses for nothing, Maurice!"

They laughed again. Simon was pleased Maurice seemed happier and was keen to get plotting. "We can make two plans. One for if you want to just punish him. And one for if you want to get the law involved."

"What I want is my money back."

"That too," said Simon, standing up to fetch a notepad and get started.

"And to get away with murder."

Simon wasn't sure whether Maurice was joking. He hoped he was.

NINE

Mid-November

Lennox Docherty was pleased to be out in the crisp afternoon elements as he made his way to the whisky bar of the Balmoral Hotel, Edinburgh. Once inside, he sat in his favourite leather chair. His eyes, as always, were drawn to the bar's hand-crafted oak-panelled cabinet displaying more than five hundred whiskies, a few of which he had sampled. The kilted barmaid approached.

Lennox Docherty on his patch

"Good evening, Mr Docherty. How are you, sir?"

"Good thanks, Isla," said Docherty, wishing he could stick his hand up the kilt of this big girl for a root and rummage around. "D'ye have a recommendation for me?"

"I don't believe you have tried the Glenfiddich Grand Cru 23. It's matured in ex-sherry, French oak casks. Tasting notes include pear sorbet, freshly baked bread and apple blossom. A drop of water complements the dram."

Docherty was sold. "Pour away, m'dear."

He was looking forward to this evening as his favourite new rent girl, the posh Scottish and very seductive Shona, was in town with her magic pills, musky unguent, and luscious probing tongue. Two thousand pounds was well worth a night of debauchery with this siren. He tingled at the thought, happy in the knowledge that the concierge was handsomely paid to turn a blind eye to such proceedings. Shona was better value for money than that Cockney slag had ever been, not that he'd really got started with her. And there was no risk of being in a blackmailing swindle with sexy Shona.

Delighting in the smell of his malt, Docherty reflected on his life and the lofty position he now held. He'd done well, and he'd done it all himself. Born out of lust and not love, in a Glasgow fifth-floor sandstone tenement block, his mother was a seamstress with a penchant for gin and giving him verbal abuse. His father, an alcoholic labourer, woke him every night when he returned from the pub, to take the belt to him. Docherty never once cried, and his schoolteachers rarely showed concerns over his many cuts and bruises. They had seen it all before.

On his sixteenth birthday his father had given him a broken nose as a present, and his mother wailed at him, saying that she wished he had never exited her womb. Docherty was no lightweight, and in a flash his parents were hurtling down the steep concrete stairwell. Both died instantly. He located the meagre home savings and hot-tailed it to the capital.

Life in Edinburgh was a little easier and he found lodgings with Mr and Mrs Campbell and paid his way as a pot boy, collecting empty glasses in various taverns. In no time he gained a reputation as a fierce bare-knuckles fighter. He joined the Bagby crew, infamous for their protection racket. Their leader, Fergus Bagby, was always belittling him in front of others, calling him an empty-headed dimwit. Docherty knew that Bagby had the backing of his boys, so he would need to bide his time to get revenge. A chance came later that year when the filth got a whisper that the gang were to raid a jewellers later that day. The whole bunch of them were cornered but after a brief skirmish, they broke free and were running like blind mice down the alleys and turnings. Docherty and Bagby ran together towards Dean Village and the Water of Leith river. Stopping under a bridge to catch his breath, Docherty hadn't known that the next few seconds would change his life forever: he head-butted Bagby, cut off his finger, and flung him into the fast flowing water below, towards the mill and his certain death. Bagby had broken the surface once to scream for help, all in vain. The police found the body some days later, glad that he would no longer bother them, but dumbfounded by the missing finger.

The gang met up later that week to discuss Bagby's death and elect a new leader. Stewart McVie said nice things about Bagby and how upset he was to lose him, and what it meant for the team. He assured them that Bagby would want them to move forward. He proposed that as second in command he should be the new leader. When he officially put himself forward and asked for their vote, all hands were raised in agreement. All hands except one.

"I dinnae need a hand to vote," Docherty had said. He smiled, remembering the looks of horror and astonishment when he pulled from his pocket Bagby's ring finger, adorned by his gold wedding band.

Docherty swirled his whisky as he thought of how they had gasped when he told them it was no accident and confessed to having killed the bastard. He sneered menacingly when he recalled the way he had confidently said that if anyone disagreed with him, he would muller them too. Of course, McVie had made a move but a few seconds later, he was on the floor with a broken jaw and swollen testicles. And when Docherty had bellowed, "Anyone else want tae be a hero?" there was silence, apart from a whimpering McVie. The last voice he heard before his throat was slit would have been Docherty's triumphant boast. "No one, *no one* humiliates me an' gets away wi' it."

With great pride Docherty mulled over how he had moved what he thought of as a two-cent Edinburgh outfit to have influences south of the Palace of Holyroodhouse. So, the embryo of Docherty's reign of protection, money counterfeiting and gun running had begun, and those profitable trips down south were put in place.

He relished his whisky, and he relished his achievements.

Soon he would join Shona, and he'd be relishing even more.

*

The seeds of McQueen's plan lay in anecdotes his grandad told him as a child of great 1960s horse-racing coups on the southern circuit tracks of Fontwell Park, Lewes, Brighton and Folkestone. Some, with switched horses and backhanders, landed the instigators many thousands of pounds, a tidy sum today. This is where he resolved to concentrate his efforts.

Maybe what he planned might mean Gabby felt she had her own horse. He'd like that. What he couldn't bring himself to tell her was that Grandad McQueen had been killed at Epsom Racecourse. Even though he'd known her for several years and she sometimes recited his grandad's sayings, the thought of it always upset him and he just couldn't burden Gabby with the distressing story or show himself as hurt and vulnerable. Having won five hundred pounds in the Lucky Last, Grandad got a bit lippy when he collected his winnings, and a lookout on the bookmaker's team punched him in the head while he was taking a wazz in the urinals. He fell and smashed his skull against the handbasin. He died the same day. His murder made the front pages.

It's possible the bookies got wind of Grandad's twenty-pound note fiddle; McQueen would never know because the murderer fled the country and wasn't ever brought to justice. McQueen had grown up detesting bookies as a result. Since Grandad's death, their intelligence network had become almost foolproof to such embezzlements, so he knew he'd need to operate outside the box to have any chance of his plan working.

It had taken him five days of solid hard graft, studying the *Racing Post* online and *The Riviera Reporter*, to finally unearth what he was looking for and get enough background to go ahead and develop his angle. He'd focused his toils on one key couple: Françoise Toussaint and her husband, Raphael, known for running a burgeoning horse-racing stable in the picturesque town of Villeneuve-Loubet, two kilometres west from the fashionable track at Cagnes-sur-Mer.

*

Françoise had loved horses since she was five. Growing up on the family farm, her involvement with equine affairs naturally progressed to becoming a trainer. Her horse-whispering qualities were greatly admired in the racing community. Raphael had none of her traits and cared little for the mounts. The only horse that interested him was a little horseplay with the patrons at the lawn tennis club in Nice and he could not get enough of it in his last years. A suave businessman renowned for his gift of the gab, he towered, bronzed and tight-muscled, lauding it over everyone in the circles in which he moved, effortlessly selling half shares to playboys and playgirls, enticing them with his cheek, and irresistible charm. It shamed Françoise to remember the way he set up deals with sickening remarks – remarks she felt prostituted her horses.

"We've got a nice firm young colt that I am sure would tickle your fancy, Celeste," he often said.

Or, "And you, Henri, you must visit us for dinner. I've got this delightful young filly just itching to make your acquaintance!"

Thanks to the expertise of Françoise, many of their horses were winners for the opulent clique, but it was always Raphael who got the plaudits, along with the champagne. It appeared she did not give a hoot, as long as her string was safe and well.

Over a twelve-month period, her life turned inside out: Raphael was shot dead by a balaclava-clad scooter driver, while waiting for a taxi outside the Palais de la Méditerranée Casino. Backstreet tittle-tattle divided between an enraged husband who had got wind of an affair going on with his wife, or out of control overseas gambling debts. The police never got to the bottom of it, despite two arrests and releases. For the next six months, Françoise soldiered on. Her adulation for horses helped soothe away her mournfulness, to a degree, but the winners and new owners started to diminish, along with her income. There were the odd firsts that helped keep her spirits uplifted, otherwise she was cloaked in abandonment.

One fateful night she woke with fumes filling her nostrils, a stifling heat and deafening whinnying. "*Feu! Feu!*" she had yelled, and her head lad came to help. Between them, they rescued nine geldings from the blazing stable, but four had perished in the flames, and those who survived were so traumatised, it was improbable they would ever race to their full potential again. The rumour mill churned again, this time the majority siding with the idea that it was a nervous breakdown resulting in the dreadful accident. The premises ended up a write-off and after investigations, the insurance company confirmed it was arson. Due to a small print clause regarding a lack of fire extinguishers, they only honoured two-thirds of the claim. Françoise paid off the head lad in full. She wrote to the owners, advising them that due to the circumstances she had transferred their charges to a local trainer,

Hugo de Montfort, who they should contact in future. She rented a small house on the outskirts of town and a week later, a letter arrived. Inside was a book of matches from an extortion mob – Le Manx Gang – operating out of Marseilles; their way of letting her know they were responsible for the fire storm and for the death of her husband. Despite many previous veiled threats from Le Manx Gang, and unlike other small French trainers, she had ignored demands to inform them when her horses were due to run well, never imagining her actions would bring such horror. She threw the envelope into a bin, wept bitterly for her slain friends, and packed. Two days later she was lodging with a trusted friend from her mademoiselle days, in a small flat in Cambridge, England, to start a new life. She thought about changing her name, and going for a new identity, but it would take an age to get a new training licence, so she kept a low profile while she carefully considered her future.

A few months later, one of her flatmate's contacts offered Françoise a lease on his twenty-box stable in Newmarket, with a small cottage as part of the deal. She wasted no time in purchasing three very fine two-year-olds and forming *Langlois Cadieux*: her own racing syndicate. She advertised in all the best journals and racing papers, inviting the public to invest, and take a five per cent share in a horse.

*

McQueen double-checked her stats. *Un-ber-luddy-leevable!* All the colts under her charge had won first time out. Starting prices ranged from 16 to 1, up to 40 to 1, and overall, Françoise had a very impressive win-to-run ratio. He carried on probing the papers, but the press had hardly picked up on her achievements. She was well under the radar. He would definitely call her in the morning and arrange a meeting; it would be a joy to visit Newmarket.

TEN

Late November

McQueen opened the old wooden gate and surveyed the country garden, admiring its well-ordered beds and borders, with everything in its place and dormant plants labelled. There was a horseshoe-shaped bed cut into the middle of the lawn. Happy memories of his grandad's allotment came back to him: the hours he'd spent there helping to pot on, weed and remove stones from the beds before planting. *"If you want to reap rewards and get an enriching harvest, it's all in preparation and planning ahead, sonny,"* Grandad had said.

Grandad plied his trade selling his fresh vegetables at Borough Market and generally ducking and diving. To help make ends meet he also worked with the Stan Flashman posse selling overpriced tickets outside prominent football stadiums. His belief was: *if you steal, be Robin Hood.* Many was the time McQueen saw him pressing a tanner he couldn't spare into the hand of a local grubby rascal.

McQueen kept to the shingle path, avoiding mud and puddles. It had rained earlier, and he regretted wearing his favourite shiny black loafers. He paused to look out at the grey late-November sky and walked to the end of the garden, convinced it would be possible to see action on the Rowley Mile beyond the fields that spread out before him, each one edged by a hedgerow border. The Suffolk air hung with anticipation: spring would bring forth fruitful growth and rich rewards.

As he walked towards the door he paused, stepped back and bent down to pull a wooden plant marker from the soil. He read it, stood still for a moment, then pushed it back.

A dog barked as he strode towards the door. The brass horse-head knocker gave a satisfying *klunk-ker-lunk-lunk* when McQueen rapped on the cottage door. From inside the cottage, he heard someone shout, "I will get it." Then, "Arrête, mon chien! Quiet!" Then footsteps. He didn't mind waiting. His spirits were high. He was certain he had seen a sign. He was certain all would be well.

When the door opened, he took a step back. "Madame Toussaint?" It felt right to give a half bow.

McQueen visits Françoise

"C'est moi! Monsieur McQueen?"

"My friends call me Mac."

"And mine, Françoise."

He wasn't sure whether to kiss her cheeks, so opted for shaking hands, and it seemed acceptable.

"Please, come in," she said, leading him into a drawing room. "I am so sorry we could not meet last week. Life with horses is sometimes so busy. Entrée, entrée."

He looked down at the outdoor gunk on his much-loved loafers. "I'll leave these here," he said, removing them both. "There's, erm… mud on them." He lined them up neatly in the hall.

"Mud?" Françoise laughed, friendly but brusque. "You should see how much mud I bring back with me when I return from the stables! That is why I always wear Hunters, these very fine wellingtons. I could lend to you a pair. Size eight, are you, non?"

"No need. No need for that today, thank you," he said, making a mental note to check out some charity shops on the way home for himself and Gabby.

The dog scratched at a door and whined to meet him. "Do you like dogs, Mac? Sweet Pierre here seems keen that you do. Can he just say hello?"

"That will be a delight."

Françoise let him sniff his way to McQueen. A more well-behaved dog he had never met; such a beautiful, healthy-looking black Labrador, with a sleek, smooth coat. His tail wagged frantically, but he did not jump up. McQueen rewarded his reservation with a hearty rub, kneeling to fuss over him and play.

Françoise motioned towards an easy chair and sat herself opposite on a worn, chintz sofa. Her dog lay at McQueen's feet. "He is a good judge of character. Très bon," she said.

The room was sparsely furnished – a pair of occasional tables, an undersized teak Welsh dresser, and a couple of wall-mounted framed pictures of her favourite winners from Cagnes-sur-Mer.

He hadn't expected her to be so informally dressed, and wished he'd opted for something more casual, maybe jeans instead of his chinos, but her jogging bottoms, and loose-fitting sweatshirt look, made him feel at ease. A high ponytail of auburn hair, which he found amusing, added to her natural comeliness; her captivating brown eyes had a warmth that drew him in. He could see why horses trusted her, but sensed deep, dolorous murmurings.

A clang from the kitchen brought a young woman to the doorway. "Sorry to have made a noise," she said.

Françoise beckoned her to join them. "Entrée, entrée."

"It's okay, come in. This is Monsieur McQueen – pardon, sorry: Mac. And this is Elspeth, my secretary." The treasured Labrador flapped his tail, and it thudded on the carpet, but he stayed with McQueen.

Elspeth seemed to note that the dog was settled and calm. She looked McQueen up and down. He looked back, feeling for a sliver of a second that she may have thought she knew him. Elspeth? Nothing registered and she'd obviously dismissed the idea of any acquaintance. She was early twenties, if that, he reckoned; not his type, and he definitely wouldn't be hers.

"I teach her French, and she teaches me English ways. Is not that right, mon ami?"

Elspeth smiled, and half-shrugged. McQueen felt obliged to laugh and gave her a friendly, but low-key, "Hi."

"I moved your shoes, sir. Sometimes your new friend there steals them," she said. "Nice shoes they are. It would be a shame if they were chewed. Françoise knows where they'll be."

"Thank you," said McQueen and Françoise at the same time.

"Elspeth has been with me from the beginning. She does not miss a trick. I really do not know what I would have done without her. She is a godsend." Françoise addressed Elspeth. "Mac will perhaps be a new owner with us, Elspeth. My Sweet Pierre seems to think that is a good idea. Do you see how he likes him?" She turned back to McQueen. "Un café?" she said, not waiting for his reply, which would have been, *thanks*. "Bien. Deux cafés au lait. Can you sort that, Elspeth? I think there are some fresh beans in the cupboard."

"Oui. Sure."

Small talk wasn't McQueen's thing, but he'd put up with it until the coffee arrived and was relieved to hear Françoise laugh when he told her about his first encounter with escargot in a Mayfair restaurant. A so-called friend had persuaded him that the correct way to eat snails was to swallow the whole lot, shell and all. His story was going well, but when he got to the bit about needing the assistance of a fast-acting customer, and how, without their Heimlich manoeuvre technique, he would probably not be speaking to her today, he felt awkward. Talking about death was the last thing he'd intended. In a bumbling way he apologised for starting to sound morbid and he offered his condolences for the loss of her husband and horses. Sweet Pierre walked over to her, put his head in her lap and looked up at her face. She stroked his ears with one hand and placed two fingers from the other to her lips as if there was nothing more McQueen needed to say. It seemed that his blunder had forged a bond and a confidence between them; he'd mentioned the unmentionable, and he was glad to have done so. Glad too when Elspeth returned with their coffees.

Françoise took over, bidding Elspeth au revoir, then turned back to her guest. "So, Mac, you mentioned you and a friend are interested in purchasing a horse and would like me to train it for you, is that correct?"

McQueen rubbed the face of his watch. It was time to make the decision he'd been wrestling with during his journey up. Should he tell Françoise the whole truth, or part? As far as he could ascertain, she wasn't the gambling type, just exceptional at training horses to win races. She might tell him to sling his hook and then he'd have to tell Gabby that it was back to the drawing board. Decision made, he drained the last of his coffee, and began to explain everything, starting with the cruel demise of his grandfather at the hands of the murderous bookmakers, and how his ardent desire to one day get one God almighty stupendous triumph over them had led him to discover the story of her success as a trainer and all her tragic losses. To lighten the mood, he ended by mentioning her expertise as a brass-door-knocker polisher and told her how much she'd love the shine on the old brasses in some of his favourite London pubs.

Françoise wiped a tear from her eye and shot out a laugh, then went into the kitchen and came back with two tulip glasses and a bottle of Bas-Armagnac. "Mac," she said, pouring generous measures, "what I am about to tell you has never been recounted to anyone, comprendre?"

McQueen listened as she spoke of the horrifying night of the fire, and the post from Le Manx Gang. When finished, she sobbed almost uncontrollably. He and Sweet Pierre moved nearer to offer comfort. Her tears seeped into his polo shirt. "I'm sorry, Mac. Pardonnez-moi," she said through sniffs, slowly gaining composure. "When I revisit those days, the wound, it unfolds itself and taunts me."

A spasm of guilt knuckle-sandwiched him in the gut. It was a blow he hadn't planned for. Françoise was too wholesome to be mixed up in any of his dubious dealings. It was time to leave before he hurt her anymore. He stood up.

"Where are you going, Monsieur Mac? Home? Non! Non! Non! Not yet, Mac. I think we both have *un compte à régler*." She paused. "Erm. How do you say it? *The score to settle*, non?" She reached for a tissue. "Now what did you have in mind?"

ELEVEN

Mo glanced at his pocket watch: six thirty. So far there was not a mod or their signature pork pie hat to be seen. Two brothers, Al and Dubs Dennett, had been pestering him relentlessly over the past few months to let them launch music nights at his pub. Maybe they could have a residency there and play regularly. 'The Substitunes' they were called; a The Who tribute band. Quite a clever name if you knew your Who, which Mo did.

Their business card read, '*The Substitunes: The Who tribute band. You name it we'll smash a guitar to it!*' They promised him a sell-out crowd of West Ham boys and West End girls if he'd let them play there.

It was tempting, but it was a risk. There were so many music venues in his neck of the woods. Apart from what other pubs were offering, the area was famous for the once well-established Rock Garden, just up the road, now a successful nightclub, and the Royal Opera House too. How many music pubs had that as competition? And then there were the licence issues. Despite all this, Mo relented. The next day the eager Dennett brothers brought him posters and flyers promoting the night. They told Mo to charge three pounds a head on entry and advised him to bring extra staff in to go on the door, sturdy lookers, they'd stressed. Mo set it all up for the night, and Simon was primed, willing and ready to help behind the bar. Mo's hoi polloi would be quite a change from Simon's usual Savoy clientele. Mo had told him not to flirt with The Salisbury customers like he did at work, because he wouldn't get any big tips.

*

The band arrived two hours before they were due to kick off. They unloaded their gear from a battered old transit with bullseye targets on the sides. Al introduced the other two band members, who doubled as roadies and sound engineers. He ordered four pints, on the house, as per their contract, brought them over and got stuck into preparing for a sound check.

Mo watched them set up and warned, "Steady on. Don't want you pissed before curtain-up time, do we?"

"Don't worry, mate. The more rat-arsed we get, the better the performance!"

The set-up was impressive. The sound check went well. Mo was loving it. Dubs used double bass drums, and Dennis, the guitarist, had three of them on stands. Once the spotlights were turned on, their shiny chrome features shone brightly as if the guitars were saying, "*Hey, we're full of magic. You better listen, and you better listen good.*"

By seven o'clock a trickle of fans waited, ready for action. Then followed a steady flow of customers with money ready, and thirsts in need of quenching. Even a few old mods in their parkas made it over from Shepherd's Bush on their Lambrettas. Come showtime, The Salisbury was packed to the rafters. Mo stepped outside and proudly chalked *Sold Out* on the new events board. This would be a night he'd remember. The bar was full; the beer was flowing; Simon looked happy; the band was poised. Right on time they bowled onto the stage.

"Evening all. Thanks for coming to see us," said Al. "We are a nice little band from the East End of London."

There were cheers. Mo assumed from East Enders, or fans of the band, or just punters desperate to enjoy the night.

"We are The Substitunes, and this… is… 'Substitute'." Cheers and whistles gave way to silent anticipation, then the band launched into their opening number.

Both Mo and Simon had seen The Who for real, watching from seats in the gods at Wembley Arena, but being in his bar so close to the live music was awesome, even though he wasn't watching Daltrey and co. This meant the residency The Substitunes sought was a done deal; Mo knew it there and then. He stopped serving and stood back briefly to enjoy the show.

Danny the vocalist's trilling voice; leaps and scissor kicks from Dennis on guitar; Dubs playing his drums like a child splashing in a swimming pool, was all held together by super-impressive, Al-the-rock on bass. Mo, already in seventh heaven, was swept into level eight when he bent down to pick up a fresh vodka bottle and Simon pinched his butt. There was no substitute for that.

The audience bopped enthusiastically from the start, willing the band to play louder, harder. To Mo's delight they were also drinking like lords. He watched an animated dancer, cigarette constantly on the go, the little lady was giving it her all, near to the front and encouraging others to join her. At the end of the fourth number, Al introduced her to the crowd. "Down here is our biggest fan."

"Who are you calling big?" snapped back the pencil-thin fan, clad in red leather trousers. "I'm not even five foot!"

"Apologies," said Al, winking at her fondly. "She's Gucci and she's coochi. And we love her!"

The Substitunes played a solid one-and-a-half-hour set, all bar their short break for beer top-ups. They included all the usual fan favourites. When they played selections from their rock operas *Tommy* and *Quadrophenia*, the crowd cranked up their singing to gusto level. Mo couldn't hold back; he joined in, convinced that with him belting out the words, his section of the crowd sang louder than any others. He was a proud man.

Dennis held up his guitar and saluted him; he thanked the audience and announced, "This is where it all ends. We give you: 'My Generation'."

The crowd, with drinks in their hands, burst into an enthusiastic rhythmic dance frenzy, blissfully oblivious to the beer they were spraying over themselves as they jumped to the music. Wet hair dripping, they nodded to the beat and danced on. Mo was ecstatic. It hadn't been like this at Wembley. Just as he thought it could get no more intense, Dennis put down his guitar and picked up another which he bashed across the microphone stand. Danny joined in, plucking off the mike, crashing it against Dubs's cymbal. He managed to jump back just before Dubs step-kicked his drum kit and pushed it off the stage. It tumbled into a mesmerised front row of excited revellers. Cool dude Al looked on, unphased and impassive. Mo guessed he'd seen it all before.

By the end, there wasn't a dry person either side of the bar; even their sweat dripped down the walls. A cluster of fans crowded round the band congratulating and thanking them for a great evening; others queued for last orders at the bar.

It was past midnight when the boys returned from loading up the van. Mo offered them a well-deserved final drink. Their crazy dancing fan was with them, and Dubs explained they were dropping her off. Mo didn't catch the name but knew he would always think of her as Crazy Dancer, or Fag Ash Lil, on account of her chain-smoking.

Simon did a double take. "Your face looks familiar. Have we met before?" he said.

"Yes, darling," she replied, laughing. "I get mistaken for Marilyn Monroe all the time."

Mo was keen to get to the point. He spoke to the band. "Look, guys. That was bloody fantastic. Great audition! I think we can say you got through. How about you do a Friday residency here? You can take the door money. I'm happy with the bar takings. What do you think, boys?"

Their biggest fan broke in before anyone from the band could reply. "According to my diary here, you're supporting Oasis on Friday week. You'll need that night off."

They all cracked up. "She's our biggest little fan and our biggest little wind-up!" said Dubs.

"Sounds good, Mo," said Al, giving him a few more business cards. "Giz a bell tomorrow, and we can get it sorted."

They said their goodnights and the band set off.

After a final clear-up, and with their ears still ringing, Mo and Simon retired to bed with a medley of songs bouncing around in their heads. They were both convinced they'd seen the fan before. Simon said she was called Di, and they tried to figure out where it could have been. Not one hundred per cent convinced, but in need of sleep, they settled on agreeing she must have visited The Salisbury at some point.

TWELVE

Early December

Phil and Binky sat sipping ale in the White Star pub in Liverpool's city centre just around the corner from the world-famous Cavern Club. Phil looked dejected. For the second time that year they'd been fined in the magistrates' court for unlawful dealings; one more and they could be doing a stretch.

"Don't look so down. We're not banged up yet," said Binky.

"It's all right for you. You haven't just got rid of yer life savings and saddled yerself with lumping it all on a dilapidated house at the auctions! I need plenty of smackeroos to refurbish it. And pay the monthly gas, leccy, booze and such. Where are we gonna get our money if we can't operate the way we need to?" He knew Binky wouldn't totally get it. Binky still lived with his mum and dad. The only thing Binky ever fretted about was if he'd one day have to pawn his piano.

Both born at the city's maternity hospital within two weeks of each other, they'd been tight ever since. Phil had memories of bruised and dirty knees from playing down the brook, and swapping mottled birds' eggs, then some years later, sharing the experience of their puberty-induced wet dreams.

Sweltering summer evenings found them playing three-and-in on chalk-drawn goalposts on the library wall, followed by a round of knockdown ginger and, as darkness fell, they'd pinch empty quart bottles from backyards to take to the local off-licence, in exchange for a Pepsi each.

He often reminisced fondly about the way he loved the penetrating stillness of dark winter nights, when they would light matches from boxes they'd nicked at the corner shop so they could look at *The Observer's Book of Astronomy*, keen to discover the wonders of Orion's Belt, the Pleiades and Taurus the Bull.

Despite their love of soccer, they never made the first team, but, as Binky always said, they made the first team cringe. To this day he used the same joke with Phil, saying, "There's only one thing stopping me playing for Liverpool."

And Phil would dutifully bite with, "What's that then?"

Binky's reply was always the same: "Not good enough!" It was their running joke. Phil loved a running joke with people he treasured.

Seniors had nicknamed them the Benders Buddies, but they cared not a ha'peth as they were well ahead of everyone, and by seventeen they'd already had full fumbles with plenty of girls from the hockey club.

Phil sighed, unable to foresee a bright future. Unemployment in the north-west had been widespread after they'd left school. It was soul-destroying, even if you had qualifications, which they did not. Back then they both lived with their parents and were learning to live by their wits. Saturdays saw them vending monkey nuts at Liverpool and Everton home games, short-changing punters whenever they could. In the second half, they would sneak into the away end for free, and dip the pockets of a few unwary souls.

Things were rosy when they were both enlisted into Ronnie Spalding's forged-ticket deceiver boys at Anfield. It was a nice earner until the stadium became an all-seater. After that, Spalding teamed up with a southern smoother and called them up to assist in the profitable imitation lottery rip-off, but then the authorities got wind of it, so they went back to manipulating any gullible tourist with mock-up Beatles garbage.

*

What to do now? Phil stared at his half empty glass for inspiration. His mobile rang. He checked the screen. "Not a number I know," he said to Binky, who signalled that he was off to the men's room.

"Yes?" he said, braced and ready to knock a scripted sales pitch sideways.

"Is that you, Phil?"

"Who's this?"

"It's Mac. Remember me? You call me your Jammie Dodger."

"Fuck me! The Paul Weller lookalike! McQueen! I thought you'd be in a shallow grave in Epping Forest by now. How are you, mate?"

"All the better for speaking to you. Listen, I've got a pot boiler of a hoodwink on the go and if you're free I'd like you and Binky in on it. This is gonna be the big one. A classic Team McQueener."

"Really? Sorry Mac. No can do. Bit busy at the moment." He waited for McQueen's response. He could hear him tapping his watch at the other end of the phone, remembering the way he did that when he was thinking things through. He left it as long as he could then said, "Nah, just joshing with you, Mac. Sounds intriguing."

McQueen's tapping stopped. "Great. I'll call you nearer the time with a meet-up plan. We'll speak again then."

Binky returned as Phil was closing up his phone, sliding it into his back pocket.

"Anybody interesting?"

"Only our *get out of jail free card*, mate!"

"Free? That sounds all right to me," boomed Binky before rolling out his version of 'All Right Now'.

Sitting in Scott's Bar, McQueen was regretting not talking through his plan with Gabby sooner. He'd wanted to get certain things sorted first and Françoise on board to make sure it was a goer. Gabby didn't seem convinced.

"Yikes! Have you lost it, Mac?" said Gabby. "You're yanking my melon, right? Going to blow all your dosh on some nag Mrs Ooh-la-la's gonna purchase from The-Whip-and-Ginger-Man in County Colcannon, and within two weeks of arrival, Bob's yer uncle – we got our own little Shergar tearing up the gallops? Much as I love horses, Mac, it's insane!"

"Look, Gabby, it's not like that. It's an authentic sales day, governed by Horse Racing Ireland. Not all horses get sold, and if Frannie can't secure what, in her opinion, is an unexposed animal with untapped potential, she'll wait for another day."

"Oh, so it's Frannie now, not Madame Tou-croissant, or whatever her name is?"

"What do you want me to call her? Madame Pony Baloney?"

"Oh, get you! Anyway, what's ten grand gonna buy? Padraig the Pit Pony? Wait! I get it. You reckon you've finally found someone who's your type!"

"Your sarcasm is withering, Gabrielle. Anyone would think you were jealous!"

"Touché," she said, dryly.

McQueen rolled his eyes. "She's a horse whisperer, with a wonderful talent. And I know, before you say it, there's no such thing as a certainty in racing. And yes, I know the risks involved, and they are many, but this could be our last prospect of finally hitting the jackpot."

Gabby fiddled with the base of her flute, making it look difficult to centre it on the drink mat. "Sorry, Mac. I didn't mean to throw a wobbly. Think the bubbles have landed."

"I shall turn the other cheek, as my grandad used to say."

"No. Don't turn away," said Gabby, sounding vulnerable and on edge, before checking herself. "Oh, you mean the cheek-turning bible thing! I get it. Look, I'm sorry if I stressed you. I just want to be certain you're going in with your eyes open. Ten large is a helluva lot to drop and, as you know, I ain't got a pot to piss in at the moment, and I'm comfortably starving, so I can't help. And it was my idea for you to come up with something big. I feel bad."

"Ladies room for me," she said, making to stand up. "I need time out for a Hergé's adventure. Shame ya can't stick some Thompson Twins music on the jukebox to keep you company in this bar, Mac." She walked away with Tintin in her hand and left him grappling with the seeds of doubt she'd sown. Maybe she was right. They'd never attempted anything nearly as complex as this. One cog misfiring, and the whole caper would be knackered. Perhaps he should call Françoise and apologise for wasting her time.

When Gabby was back, he'd almost convinced himself that he didn't have the moxie to pull off the big one anyway, but she seemed to have shaken off her reservations.

"Mac, remember it was me that wanted the whole caboose," she said, "and here I am pooh-poohing it." She touched his hand lightly as she pulled a notebook and pen from her bag. "No. I am with you all the way, mate. Right. Let's get down to the nitty-gritty. I'm ready. Tell me more details of your plan so far. I want to hear it all."

"At last!" he said. "Start the clock." He tapped his watch. Gabby double-clicked her pen and leaned in to listen.

"The three cities in England with the most bookies in close proximity are London, Liverpool and Birmingham. That's around a thousand shops in total. By my reckoning, we're going to need to hit four hundred on the day."

"Wow! That's a lot."

"I know. But if we want to pull off the biggie, that's the numbers. Françoise will be looking to place our pony in a competitive race, where we should be able to get odds of 33 to 1, so if we place four hundred bets at seventy-five pounds a pop, at double carpet, that's nine hundred and ninety thousand pounds. That's before all the tax the thieving Dick Turpin chancellor'll claw back. Plus, I'll be opening online accounts, which should net plenty more for us. And I might even nick a few grand on the exchanges."

"What? You're saying the Labour Exchange will help?"

"Stop taking the piss!"

"Sorry. You're giving it away, Mac. And a right proper Carol Vorderman you've turned out to be," she said, scribbling down notes and smiling.

"Anyway, have a butchers at these." He passed her three inner city maps which she unfolded and spread out. Tintin proved useful as a paperweight. She brushed her fingers over the red dots. "Bookies," he said. "That's all of them. We concentrate on the dense areas, which are mostly the poorer boroughs."

"There's loads of 'em. It must have taken you ages."

"Yep. Over ninety alone in the Stratford, Plaistow, Upton Park triangle of Newham. I paid a visit to a handful of them last week, and placed a number of fifty-pound wagers, without anyone blinking an eyelid."

"Bloody hell, Mac! Your spadework is phenomenal. I shouldn't have doubted you just then."

He ignored her last remark, trying to forget that he'd doubted himself too. "They're all in *Yellow Pages* and online, so that was the easy bit; it's getting the right ground troops I'm grappling with now."

"Yeah, that'd crossed my mind."

"The day has to work with military precision for it to succeed, and we need the best tricksters on board the good ship, *Who Wants to Be a Millionaire*. Is Greyhound Clive still operating? Do you know?"

"No, the jammy git married into money. The last I heard he was running a flourishing seafood restaurant in Devon."

"Hmm… Suffolk Joannie?"

"Ah! Good old Lady Fingers? I understand she's making a mint on the Mediterranean cruises, handling the ultra-illegal Texas Hold 'em dupe."

"So, we won't be seeing her for a while!" he laughed, "how about Freddy boy?"

"You'll like this one, Mac – he managed to negotiate his way into becoming a senior lecturer at Oxford's Magdalen College."

McQueen felt stunned. "Fred? Why does that not surprise me? He could nail jelly to a wall, that one!"

"Well, I guess that will help with his bar bill! It doesn't help us though."

"The Colonel? What about him?"

"Threw a seven, last year. The big C."

"What, he drowned?"

Gabby slapped McQueen's wrist playfully. "That's not funny, Mac. You'd tell me off for saying that, and you know it. But seriously, my ideas."

"I'm ready."

"Diana! I barged into her recently, on Regent Street."

"What? Old Kent Road Likely Di and her designer wardrobe?"

"Yep. That's the one."

"Was she flashing her Vivienne Westwood?" He waited for Gabby to stop laughing. "I hope you remembered to call her Diana, and not Di."

"Are you kidding, Mac? You bet I did. I've seen the look she gives anyone who calls her Di! No one walks away from that look without thinking they're most likely gonna die a lot sooner than they expected."

McQueen chuckled. "I've been worrying about Walthamstow Walter for years ever since his slip-up! It makes me shudder just to think of it."

"Me too! She's not called *Likely Di* behind her back for nothing!"

"Likely Di would write us all off pronto if she knew."

"Yeah, Mac! And without a blink, let alone one of her killer looks, bless her."

They drank more and pulled *likely-to-die* faces, laughing, until McQueen got back on track.

"Still going to pub gigs, is she?"

"I think so. The oldest raver in the mosh pit!"

"What was she up to when you saw her?"

"Acting as the shill in the Three-Card Monte ruse – an education to behold, let me tell you! I reckon I could cover the London triangle with her, and her runners."

"Got her number?"

Gabby nodded. "I have now."

"Good. Good. Give us it and I'll bell her and tell her we're overdue a meet-up. That'll sort it. She'll want in."

"And I reckon good old Blaggit'll be interested," said Gabby. "Moved from London up to the Midlands. Birmingham. That could be handy. We can call him Brummie Blaggit now, instead of Bermondsey Blaggit. Mainly operates in internet dating romance hoaxes these days."

"Blaggit? Romances? Well, I'm stunned once more! I take it he doesn't meet them face-to-face?"

"I knew that would shock you. Ha! Suits you, that alarmed Vulcan look, Mac! He'd never make so much as a shilling if he did!" She held up a hand and separated her two middle fingers into a V the way *Star Trek's* Spock did when he met one of his kind. "Hey, remember the time when the three of us cut into that obnoxious Canadian? We persuaded him to part with five thousand dollars cash for the royal parchment, remember that, Mac? He thought he was gonna get a fortnight timeshare package for him and the family, to stay in the west wing of Hampton Court Palace! I'll bet he flew back to Toronto with his Blue Jays tail between his legs!"

"Yeah!" said McQueen, shuffling forward on his chair. "There's one born every minute! The wide boy, Blaggit, even had me believing his spiel!"

Gabby sat back. She tossed her pen across the table and drummed her fingers on Tintin. "That's about all I got, Mac: Likely Di for London and Blaggit for Birmingham. What you got?"

McQueen grabbed at the pen before it rolled away. He twirled it in his fingers, clicked it twice, and announced smugly, "I've got Binky and Phil in Liverpool, that's what I've got. So, now it's your turn to look Vulcan!"

Gabby looked delighted. "What? Not the pair of scallies running that Liverpool Football Club crooked ticket hokey-pokey?"

"The same. Yonks ago I was in on their lottery ticket prank, till they moved on to other schemes. One day I was reading through the *Liverpool Echo* on a train, and I spotted an article reporting that said Messrs Briscoe and Mavers were up before the beak. They got fined two hundred and fifty smackers each for 'misleading the public'. Binky and Phil had been plying the Jam Auction in The Cavern Quarter, sucking in the Japanese tourist fans to part with their money for fake Fab Four junk, and levelling the Scouse tax. Can you believe it?"

"Erm… yes."

"They're always up for a bit of mischief so I was sure, hands down, they'd jump at the chance of nicking a few readies."

"Good one, Mac."

"I phoned them to confirm, and they're in." He clicked his pen.

"Why didn't I think of them?"

"Cos I'm the brains and you're the beauty in this partnership!"

"At least you didn't say brawn," she said, playfully punching him on the arm in slow motion. "So, what's the next step?"

"Françoise's invited us both for tea next week, and I'll be parting with a big fat kite." McQueen winked. "And you might get to see some thoroughbred horses!"

Gabby swallowed hard. "And so it begins."

THIRTEEN

Mid-December

Françoise looked up from replenishing the bird feeders in her front garden and waved at McQueen and Gabby as they opened the ornate iron gate. She looked the picture of an English rose, which amused Gabby. She noticed her long ponytail with a squirm of envy and felt ashamed that McQueen probably hadn't mentioned it because he knew she might say something crass, which she would have.

Sweet Pierre bounded over to greet them, and Françoise hopped over a flower border with enthusiastic welcomes.

"Hello, Mac. This must be Gabriella. Bonjour, madame."

"Bonjour, madame!" said Gabby. She hoped she looked calm but felt flustered. It was ridiculous, when all around her the scene was perfect peace: fields and paddocks stretching to the horizon; just one little chocolate box thatched pink cottage nearby. Suffolk was so flat, with overwhelmingly big skies, and air so fresh it could knock you over. How could she not have known this before? What heaven.

She tried to shake off her feeling of unease, but ever since McQueen had told her Françoise's sad story, she'd been troubled with guilt for being so unkind about her and wanted to make things right.

McQueen wasn't behind her. Where was he? And the dog was gone. She spied him over in one of the flower beds crouching and looking at a plant label. The inquisitive dog seemed interested in it too, or was it the wellies McQueen had left on the path beside him? Navy for him, green for Gabby. What was going on?

He stood up. "Françoise. Tell me, is this patch going to be sweet cicely?"

"It is," she called over to him. "I did not have you down as a gardener, Mac. Sweet cicely grows well in these parts. I am sure you know that it is good to eat the leaves, and the roots are very good too, if you enjoy the taste of aniseed."

"Well, I'll be," he said, looking happy. "I thought I spotted the label on my first visit."

"It will be blooming in the spring. You must take some then."

He threw a stick for Sweet Pierre to fetch, picked up the Hunter boots he'd told Gabby were for wearing at the stables, and walked back to join them, carefully avoiding the mud.

"Yes. This is coarse loamy soil, you see, Mac," said Françoise, stooping to grab a small handful. She sifted it through her fingers. He looked serious, as though his interest had been stirred up. "Good nutrients, moisture, and humus in this lot."

Gabby raised an eyebrow and darted a perplexed look at McQueen, which he seemed not to notice. The dog came back and she wrestled the stick from him and threw it. Off he bounded, joyful.

"Be careful, Gabby. One look from Françoise and he'll have your fingers off!"

"If I was a bloke, it wouldn't be my fingers I was wanting to protect," she said, throwing the stick again as McQueen turned back to Françoise.

"I'm guessing all that means better drainage and infiltration of water and air in this Suffolk soil? London's is very clay rich. Heavy to dig, that's for sure. A real sod sometimes!" he said.

Gabby had never seen him discuss gardening with a gardener. How interesting could soil be? She was out of her depth. "Sweet cicely sounds quite nice-erly," she said with a laugh, trying to join in.

"You like aniseed?" said Françoise, seeming to miss the rhyming joke.

"I certainly do, but I have no garden. A Pernod and water always goes down well, though."

"Ah! We do that in France. And do you speak French?"

Gabby had practised her reply. "Yes. My roommate, Antoinette, at the Institut Alpin Videmanette finishing school, in Switzerland, was a Parisian and an extraordinary teacher."

"Je comprendre La Princesse de Pays de Galles assistee il ya."

"Eh?"

McQueen laughed. "She's jesting with you, Françoise. You'll get used to it. The only finishing school Gabby's attended was finishing her lines in detention!"

"No, Mac, I did French lessons in school," Gabby protested. "Actually, I did *bunking off* French lessons, so it technically was not *in* school at all!"

They stood in the cottage garden, laughing. Françoise pulled off her gardening gloves so they could finally shake hands.

"Non, non, non!" said Gabby, kissing Françoise on both cheeks.

"Oh Gabriella, so you are a tease, eh? A beautiful tease. I wish I could wear those skinny jeans. On you, they look *magnifique*. I am afraid horse riding has given me a big, wide derrière!" She patted her hips, steering her guests inside.

Such flattery got in the way of Gabby correcting her hostess every time she got her name wrong. She shrugged it off; she'd been called worse things than Gabriella. Trying to please Françoise, she insisted they use the doorstep boot scraper before they go in. Sweet Pierre joined them, and she stroked his smooth, shiny coat, as black as her own hair.

"Well spotted," said McQueen, "I missed this scraper on my last visit."

Gabby gave him an 'I'm a smarty pants' look and got on with her important cleaning.

"Please come in," said Françoise. "I have brewed us some coffee, make yourselves at home." She called Sweet Pierre to her side. Once they were settled in, as before, he sat at McQueen's feet.

Françoise had set out a selection of sandwiches. "Voila, mes amis! I hope neither of you are vegetarians. I only have ham, beef and tuna here."

"I'm veggie," said Gabby.

"Pardon! I just assumed that… mais non! Do you eat cheese?"

"You are not veggie, Gabby! She's doing it again, Françoise. Ignore her jokes," said McQueen, shooting Gabby a look as she tucked into a beef and horseradish doorstep.

Gabby disregarded him. She was sure that all her teasing had broken the ice and helped Françoise get to know her ways. What McQueen had said about this woman was right – there was something unconventional about her, something almost bewitching, and Gabby didn't mind being under her spell. Her beautiful dog was pretty amazing too.

"So, Mac mentioned that if you're not satisfied with any of the horses at the sale, you'll go again – is that correct?"

"Yes, Gabriella. If it takes a few visits, then so be it, but without, erm, how do you say it? *Vantardise?* I normally pick a good one first time round."

As Françoise went on to explain more, Gabby tried to hide that she'd never heard that word before. Was it French or English?

"I have been looking at the fixtures of next season and there is a suitable race here on the Rowley Mile, mid-April." She gestured towards the window and across the fields. "It normally attracts a big field of well-regarded three-year-olds. It would seem the ideal race for our bookmaker coup de grace. And also, I am off to the Limerick auctions next month, and at this time of the year there are normally a few bargains to be had."

Gabby could tell from McQueen's expression that he was

working out the timing and what this meant for the money situation as Françoise went on. "I will call you from the sales, Mac, if I can secure a horse within your budget. We can get him transported over within two weeks, then bedded in. Some light cantering the next month, then the full gallops, so the timing of the spring contest would be realistic. But many a slip between the lips and cuts, as you English say, non? And now, un autre café, and then I shall show you my stables, my bébés."

"Yes please," said Gabby.

*

As they walked across to the stables, wellies squelching, she pulled up her coat hood to ward off a biting east wind. Mid-December was colder in Suffolk than it was in the city. She felt in her deep pocket and pulled out her Tintin tin, hell-bent on having a smoke now they were outdoors.

"No! Non, Gabriella!" said Françoise, her face all sadness and terror. "No smoking in the stables please. Ce n'est pas permis ici."

The dog's barking stopped the instant Françoise stroked him. A stable hand looked up from sweeping straw and horse debris.

How could she have been so stupid? So insensitive? So bloody self-obsessed.

Françoise changed her tune and made light of it, as if it was her mistake, not Gabby's, but Gabby was briefly crushed and felt she would never forget that moment and how generous Françoise had been in taking no offence by her utter thoughtlessness.

Once in the stables she stared, drawn in by the allure of the steeds with their eyes as deep with understanding as any human, transfixed by their intoxicating odour and the sound of their snorting. Without any sign of complaint, Sweet Pierre waited at the door as if this was standard practice.

"You like horses, Gabriella?"

"I do. Very much." She held out a flat hand for a horse to explore with its muzzle as she spoke. "Not as much as my sister

96

though. We only ever got the chance to ride the sand ponies on day trips to the seaside. A holiday in Bognor did it for her. That's where she fell. Some idiot was acting as a bookie, and thought it was smart to take bets on children who weren't even jockeys. She always wanted to win at anything, so when she twigged what was going on, she shouted giddy-up and dug her heels in like she'd seen on the telly. She can walk now, up to a point, but I don't think she'll ever ride again. All we ever wanted as kids was our own horse. No hope of that though. And the man ran off with a pocket full of money. He didn't even stop to see if she was okay."

Françoise took Gabby's free hand and held it still. She looked into her eyes as if searching for hope in a mist. "Bon coeur, mon cheri. Kind heart, my dear," she said.

Gabby wanted to feel more of the calming strength that Françoise oozed. In the silence that followed she studied Françoise more closely. Her hair was not just long, but the same thickness and colour of the horses that stared out from their stable bays – brown with a lemon-ginger hint. Her eyelashes were long too: longer than Gabby had seen on any other person; captivating lashes like the ones she and her sister had stared at and envied on the ponies at Bognor. McQueen broke the powerful stillness by glancing at his watch, the way he often did when he felt emotional or when it was time to get going. He thanked their host for her excellent tour.

It was early evening and dark outside when they walked back to the cottage. A bright crescent moon hung low in the sky. "Cor! Look at that. It's like a fairy-tale moon. I've never seen it that low. There's so many buildings round where I live, you can't see the moon till it's up high, and that's if you stand on a chair to look out the window." An owl hooted. "Woah! That's so cool."

Françoise excused herself once they were inside.

"I knew you'd love her, and love it here," said McQueen as they left their boots on the doorstep and changed back into their city shoes.

"Shut it, Mac," said Gabby, not sure why she hadn't wanted to acknowledge he was right. Should there be shame in feeling that this world suited her more than her London roots? She used a cloth Françoise had left and got busy wiping muddy paws, loving every second.

Startled by a loud thud in the hall they looked up as Françoise reappeared, struggling to bring in a large box. "Let me help you with that," said McQueen, rushing forward to grab it from her. Sweet Pierre was all tail-wagging and sniffs.

"What the?"

"Christmas tree, Gabby. Must get the decorations up tomorrow," she said. She held out two sprigs of mistletoe. "This is an old French tradition."

Visions of an unsavoury ménage à trois flashed through Gabby's mind, until she realised with relief that Françoise was merely offering them each a sprig to take away.

"These come from the trees nearby. Hang them on your front doors, and you will be blessed with good fortune for the New Year."

"Good fortune from Newmarket mistletoe? That's exactly what we need!" said McQueen taking his sprig. "Thank you, Françoise. I hope you hang some on your door too."

Gabby grabbed hers. "Thanks. Maybe we need more than one sprig each! Does it work like that?"

"Rest assured I shall hang many sprigs."

Embarrassed that she'd let out an audible 'Ooooh!' and had only just managed to stop adding 'la-la!' Gabby knew it was time to leave.

Françoise pulled gently on McQueen's sleeve as he adjusted his woollen scarf, making ready to get going. Sweet Pierre joined in, gently tugging at the hem of his trousers. What was going on? Another French pre-Christmas custom?

"Mac, have you forgotten something?" said Françoise, signalling for her dog to stop.

"Ah! Idiot me!" McQueen shouted, spinning round, and stuffing his mistletoe sprig into Gabby's hand. He pulled a cheque from his back pocket. "Sorry, Françoise. So sorry. It's not an old English tradition, I promise."

"Genuine mistle-take there, Mac?" said Gabby, making light of it.

"I have been reading up on your lot," said Françoise. "Once a crafty Cock-er-ney, always a crafty Cock-er-ney, eh?" Her frown broke into a smile and then much laughter with some happy canine barks too.

FOURTEEN

McQueen perched at his kitchen table, nursing a hot toddy, feeling sorry for himself. His fever had broken and left him languid but glad that for the first time that week, he wasn't bedridden.

When Gabby phoned him, she was her usual unsympathetic self. "It's just a cold, Mac, man up."

"I tell you I'm running a high temperature."

"You couldn't run a hot bath! Call me when the Grim Reaper's buzzed off."

He stared at the blank A4 paper in front of him. Feeling the way he did, how could he ever get his befuddled head into gear enough to crunch some numbers into the calculator? He made a start, jotting down notes.

getting all the bets on at the agreed stake = £30K
team players to be paid £5K = £20K
from the start of January between them they'd need = £50K
time to come up with the readies = 14 weeks
£50,000 ÷ 14 = £3,571
PER WEEK = £3,571

His little screen mocked him: three thousand, five hundred and seventy-one pounds was what they'd need to reel in each week. He checked it on the calculator again. Yep. That was the amount they'd have to accrue each and every pre-race week; nothing less would do. He winced at the thought of it all and the heebie-jeebies started sprouting. It would be shit or bust.

This wasn't his only worry; there was also the matter of getting the timing right for when to explain everything to the cohorts in Birmingham, Liverpool and London, once they were all ready. Meeting too early might start Chinese whispers circulating and that would jeopardise the whole shebang. Meeting too late was a risk to the smooth running of the scam. He studied his diary. Four weeks before his horse's race looked logical, once he had a horse, that is. Team McQueen London had the lion's share of shops, so he'd approach Likely Di first.

The next day he phoned Gabby. "Done a Lazarus?" she scoffed.

"I'm feeling better, if that's what you mean."

"Told you."

"Right. I've done the final figures and timescale; the good news is that you'll have time to pick up a bargain pair of walking boots in the Boxing Day sales. The not so good news is that by my calculations you and I need to raise over three and a half grand, every week, from the start of January for over three months."

Gabby whistled down the phone. "Can't be done, Mac."

He'd been dreading her saying that, but it wasn't a surprise. "If you say we can't, then we can't, Gabby. If that's what you really think, then let's go back to playing *pin the tail on the donkey*. I might as well get my Gregory Peck back from Françoise and forget all about it. But I think we owe it to ourselves to at least give it a crack."

Gabby took her time coming back with an answer. "Okay, Mac. You're the big cheese, but if it goes tits up, don't come crying to me."

"Cheers."

"By the way, changing the subject, my sister, being the old softie that she is, has invited you over to spend Christmas with us. She said something about, even spent grifters shouldn't be alone during the festive season."

"Erm… I'm touched. What can I say? Erm…Tell her thanks, but there's plenty I need to straighten up in my mind, so I'll pass."

"All right, Scrooge."

They agreed to hook up the day before New Year's Eve, in Covent Garden.

On Christmas Eve, Françoise phoned to wish him Joyeux Noel and to confirm she would be flying to Shannon Airport in a few days. She promised to keep in touch if there were developments. When he put the phone down, a lonesome, pensive feeling took hold. Maybe he should have accepted Gabby's invitation. *Naaahhh!*

He finished the last of his Chinese takeaway, polished off a bottle of Soave and, despite the early hour, turned in for a deep dreamless sleep.

30th December

The Cross Keys was quiet. One traveller sat squinting at a Japanese tourist guide to London, and four old timers in the corner played cribbage for two bob a point. He assumed people were saving their livers for tomorrow's New Year's Eve celebrations.

"So, what did Santa bring you, Mac?"

"A Bernard Matthews turkey crown and a bottle of Cockburn's," he said, swallowing the head of his stout.

"Nice day then?"

"Yeah. Thanks." He handed Gabby a small box. "Santa dropped this off for you down my chimney. Sorry it's late."

She opened it and stared at the silver bracelet inside.

"Friendship bracelet," he said. "I figured we'd been friends long enough for you to warrant one. And it's got a…"

"I see it, Mac. A horseshoe charm. I love it. Thank you so much. Clip-clop, clip-clop!" She put it on, and he hovered ready to help, but independent as usual, she could do it. "I'll always wear it."

Chuffed that she liked it and hadn't read anything more into his gift, they drank to friendship and got back to business.

"Think we can raise the ante in time?" she asked, rubbing the charm between her finger and thumb.

"Are you still thinking we can't?"

"Maybe. A bit. Can we?"

"I hope so. It's going to be a bumpy ride that's for sure. I'll continue in the bookies, but I'm upping my stakes. It's risky, but the time frame dictates."

"You'll get it sorted, Mac. All the details. You'll have it planned to the last footstep, I'll bet. What's my first step?"

"Can you join a couple of swanky West End casinos? There'll be rich pickings for an accomplished cutpurse like your good self, and if anyone's fool enough to have jotted down their pin number, that'll dispense plenty from the ATM. The roulette table is your best bet. When the punters lean over placing chips, it leaves them wide open. Try between eight and ten, after the marks have enjoyed a few sherbets."

"I'm on it like a car bonnet."

"Good. Françoise is all set. She reckons once we get our new Pegasus, it will return our money. Things will kick off the day after next."

"New Year's Day?"

"That's the one. We should meet here every Friday at four, for updates."

"Let's. But with these blinkin' holidays it'll be closer to two weeks until we next rendezvous. I might bell you if I need to."

"Make sure you do."

They Happy-New-Year-hugged, and wished each other luck, then ventured into the wintry night.

One hundred and six days and counting; every one of them crucial to his plan.

"Tick-tock!" he shouted back as he walked away.

He thought he heard her say, "Clip-clop, clip-clop," in return. It was starting to grow on him.

He loved working with Gabby. Should he really have let Docherty keep them apart for those four years?

January 2001

The fortnight flew by; McQueen's plan was no longer a pipe dream. Gabby sat with him at their customary table. Both were animated and keen to spill the beans on how things had progressed. Gabby got in first, barely stopping for breath with news that it had been a doddle joining the Grosvenor Barracuda in Baker Street, and the Cromwell Mint in Kensington, where it took a couple of visits to acclimatise to the surroundings and suss their security was inadequate, and that at the Barracuda, she was already on first name terms with four or five croupiers. On the fourth night, she pilfered an offensive German's wallet, gobsmacked to find when she opened it in the toilet cubicle, nearly five grand. The following night, the Mint coughed up over a thousand, courtesy of a bimbo leaving her bag unattended. She couldn't pull those strokes every day at the same casinos though, so she broadened her horizons and joined eight more gambling houses including Maxims, the playground of the high rollers.

McQueen leaned back, clearly impressed; he was on a roll too, but on the machines. He'd bagged two thousand and a further one and a half thousand when a side horse multiple wager had copped. They raised glasses in a salute to Grandad and took a swig.

Elated, Gabby burst out, "Nine and a half large in our first two weeks, Mac. That's over our target. At this rate, we'll be done and dusted in no time! From what you've told me about your grandad, I reckon he'd be well impressed with these details, Mac."

"Softly, softly, Gabby. Let's play to our strengths. It's still early doors, and we can't afford to become a busted flush."

"Is that another of his sayings, Mac?"

McQueen gave her a succinct, tight smile. "Anyway," he said, "I've news from Françoise."

Gabby's heart raced. "Don't tell me! She couldn't find a nag under fifty grand and she's flying back today?"

"Not at all. We've got ourselves a horse, and the best bit, it was a little under budget." Now he looked as excited as Gabby, who was dealing with a cocktail of raging emotions: elation, panic, anticipation and trepidation all vying for her attention.

"Well, get you, saving the best news for last! What's he called?"

"Herd Ringer."

"What? Her Dringer! 'Anyone seen Her Dringer?' That's a bit rude, isn't it?"

"Trust you, Gabby. It's *Herd* Ringer."

"Well, it's a crap name."

"Yep, but all the best horses have hogwash titles – just look at those Middle Eastern owners." As he spoke his face changed and he had one of his mischievous looks, the sort of look that would make her mother want to embrace him.

He took a sip of beer before saying, "Françoise has asked us over in a month to meet our little money spinner. "It's all coming together, Gabby."

"Yep," she said, fixing a smile on her face to hide the worry building up in her mind: could the negatives start to battle out the positives?

The next week wasn't good for Gabby, and she only managed to collect close to a thousand pounds. Having been chased off by a doorman at Harrods who saw her trying to double dip an Aussie couple, she got lucky in Maxims when a sozzled geezer's wallet fell out onto the floor, and she managed to kick it under the table to pick up later.

McQueen's total was half Gabby's; the machines were cold all week.

*

The minute Gabby set eyes on McQueen the next Friday, she knew she was going to hear bad news. "Fffff-ffflippin' 'eck! Look at that shiner, Mac. What happened?"

"I got flash and started playing two machines simultaneously. Apparently, that's against the rules! Anyway, I hit a purple patch and was about to cash in, when this bloke hollers, 'Out!' I turn round and I'm temporarily blinded when the camera snapped me close up. I swing an *I'm a lover, not a fighter* haymaker, which misses him by a country mile. Next thing, I've taken one for the team and went down on me arse like a sack of spuds."

"Oh cripes, Mac. You all right?"

McQueen held his hand out horizontally and shook it in a so-so gesture. Was she turning into her mother? Seeing him like this, she wanted to make sure he was okay. She'd always thought of him as youthful and able to care for himself, but this injury signalled the old McQueen that was to come. Would he cope in the future on his own? Was he coping now?

He carried on. "Next thing, the manager strides over, coldly confirms he knows all about my little game, and says he was watching me the day before at a different branch. He then gleefully informs me that my mug shot will be in all the shops by close of play. And that's that. I'm barred from my little honeypots for the foreseeable. My nightmare's coming true! My circuit; my patch! Wiped away at precisely the wrong time."

"I don't know about that, but you've got a right purple patch, for sure. I always said you was a pirate." She nudged him with her elbow. "Geddit, Mac? You need an eye patch, aa-harrgghh!"

"Don't joke about it, Gabby. It'll take me till doomsday to create a new circuit I can work, let alone make any profit."

"We could try the badger con round here. Stump up a lot of bunce I reckon, but you'd have to be the masseur this time and I'll take photos."

"Are you mad? This is no time for one of your funny quips. And I don't want to think about our Edinburgh fiasco. It might bring us more bad luck."

"Sorry, Mac." She hated herself for always making jokes whenever she felt uneasy about a situation. "You must feel gutted, mate," she said, knowing her own news was going to make him feel worse. And she'd already goofed by nearly mentioning the dreaded Mr D.

She opened her Tintin tin, took out a pre-rolled rollie and went to light it, but when McQueen glared, she put it back. One minute he was like a defenceless boy, the next he could easily be her estranged father reprimanding her for smoking. McQueen was hard to work out. Reluctantly she started to explain how her week had begun well, with a six hundred pound winning finger at the Barracuda, but on Tuesday at the Mint, she misjudged the depth of a mark's inside pocket and was almost caught, red-handed. Of course, she'd apologised profusely but to no avail. Apparently, he was some bigwig, and demanded his pound of flesh, so security marched her to the manager's office. The mark claimed that she had tried to thieve his wallet, and he wanted to press charges. She told the manager that she'd slipped and slid into him, with no intent of stealing anything. He explained that while a court summons was bad publicity for any casino, and normally, as manager, he'd pacify any accuser, this matter would have to be looked into because only a few months back a woman's handbag had been rifled through and she lost over a thousand pounds. Gabby knew she could be for it when they viewed the CCTV footage, but luckily for her the images weren't clear enough to be conclusive. The mark still got dinner in their three AA Rosette restaurant, while she got warned off, barred, and then turned away from wherever she went. The circuit was tightly knit, and word got round that Lady Muck was a bad pony.

*

The heebie-jeebies were back with McQueen. It was all going wrong; they'd never accrue what they needed in time to make the impact he wanted on the bookies.

When he totalled up the kitty, they had ten grand; that was forty short. They were screwed. Even if he risked putting in his savings, they'd still be twenty-five light. There was nothing for it, but to throw in the towel and hole up for a bit before they met to divvy up the wedge, then they'd visit the new colt, Herd Ringer, and break the bad news to Françoise. He wasn't looking forward to that.

He spoke to her and arranged a trip, trying to keep any tone of despondency out of his voice, but he knew she could hear it was there.

FIFTEEN

February

Françoise poured them all coffee from her cafetière. "I am betting that you both cannot wait to see your gee-gee," she said once they'd finished. "Come on, let us go now." She clapped her hands. Sweet Pierre stood up. He darted to the front door where he sat waiting, with his tail tapping on the mat keenly.

"Boots on! Bring your mugs. Allez, allez!" ordered Françoise and they made to follow the expectant dog.

As before, Sweet Pierre did his own thing; this time he chose to stay near to Gabby. She was quiet and reserved as Françoise led them to the stables. McQueen sensed she was glad for the company of the dog, and he left her to it, taking a chance to try and break things to Françoise as they walked on. A thick February fog smothered the surrounding fields, blocking them from view. It hung heavily around like the foreboding gloom that surrounded him.

"I checked out his form," he said. "Two runs at Cork, both nearer last than first. Not meaning to be rude, but that's hardly inspiring achievements, wouldn't you agree?"

"Do not worry, Mac, the ground was bog-like in those races. We will not encounter anything like that at Newmarket in April."

When Françoise unlocked the stable door, Herd Ringer casually poked his head out: confident, inquisitive, magnificent. The description Françoise had given hadn't done him justice. It stung him to see the way Gabby looked on in awe, like a lovestruck child. The chestnut colt was a beauty, with chiselled features, firm flank and a perfect white diamond marking between his eyes.

"He's got a star," she said.

"Bravo, Gabriella. So many people call it a white diamond because that is what they see."

McQueen felt foolish for being proud of Gabby; she must have remembered that from her childhood horse obsession.

As they got closer, Herd Ringer viewed them with a quizzical stare. His ears pricked forward as he studied Gabby and McQueen, then they returned to the side as he relaxed with them. When he nuzzled into Gabby, as if demanding affection, McQueen saw tears in her eyes.

"Not only is he handsome, but your Herd Ringer is also a speed machine," said Françoise. "When first I saw him, I said to

Herd Ringer: wondrous beast

myself, he is a strong and athletic horse; he is a very lovely-looking horse, and I was certain he had *stayer* written all over him. I was not mistaken. I believe he will do well for us, Mac. Have the confidence that he is *tres magnifique* and so for that I will not be charging for training fees before the first race. He will win for us. We will be as you say, *in the money*."

McQueen shook his head but didn't speak. He was about to let go of the certain promise this wondrous beast offered and it hurt. And he sensed he was breaking Gabby's heart. That hurt too.

*

Back at the cottage, Elspeth cleared away their cups. Taking Sweet Pierre with her, she retired to her room, leaving the three of them to settle down to business. Françoise prepared stronger drinks. "I saw you notice the perfect white diamond of Herd Ringer and I was pleased. I bought these to celebrate. I hope it is to your liking. Diamond White cider, although technically we should call this his Star White cider. Shall we, Gabriella?"

Before she could go further, McQueen shuffled in his chair and coughed into his fist. "Françoise, I need to tell you something."

Five minutes later, she knew all the facts. Her face was stern, but she was not shaken by the news. "I thought something was amiss when you called, Mac." She leant over her chair, picked up a canvas bag and lobbed it at him. "Voila! Some of this might be useful to you. As you say, *come in handy*."

Gingerly, he unzipped it and looked inside. "What the…" he said, flicking through bundles of ten and twenty-pound notes. "There must be twenty grand here."

"Thirty actually, Mac."

"What did you do? Hold up a bank?"

"A bank was involved, yes. My late husband's life insurance policy paid out a reasonable sum."

He glanced at Gabby. "We can't accept this, Françoise, it's not right."

"The rights and wrongs do not come into it, Mac. You and Gabriella were unlucky. This is now un plan de secours. Écoute attentivement." They leaned in to listen. "You said you have twenty-five, I will loan you the other twenty-five, and some to spare. When this is all over, the money is to be returned to me, and you shall entertain us all at a restaurant of my choice. Fair enough?"

"You would do this for us?" said Gabby.

"Yes, my dear. You put your trust in me when you gave me money to purchase a steed, now I am trusting you. Anyway, we are too far down the path of this extravagance to be the quitters. Let us now raise our Diamond Whites to toast and honour our white diamond, our real white star, Herd Ringer."

"To Herd Ringer," they said, before clinking glasses and drinking a toast. For the next hour they drew up a joint schedule. It was still two months before the race. Despite her pledge to trust McQueen, he sensed that Françoise still needed to be more convinced that the *jolly miscreants*, as she called them, that he had engaged, were still on board, and up to the job. He'd come to realise that she wasn't one to hold back when she wanted to know something, so of course she'd asked for news on his teams and of their commitment.

He answered her cheerily. "Deffo. They're onside, for sure. Good people. Good people. Perfect for the job. The lure of a diddle's in their blood."

Was he trying to convince himself, too? Now she was their sponsor as well as trainer it was even more important to keep her assured, so he promised to report back regularly, even pay her a visit if she wanted, after his meet-up with the three Team McQueens in four weeks' time.

"Good. Good," she said, nodding so fervently that Sweet Pierre thought it was a game and started running around, barking. She calmed him, saying, "Then I suggest you both keep a low profile for a while, and no épineux dealings. D'accord! Everything straight for now. Keep in touch."

With the welcome cash injection, the pressure was off, but McQueen remained anxious and kept up with his meticulous planning. *Details, details, details! Yes, Grandad. I know.*

He and Gabby spoke on each of the fourteen days before the Team McQueen London meeting, exploring any new avenues and concerns that kept coming up. Their foremost worry was how much time would be needed to place a wager, and whether they could get enough wagers done, without raising concerns in the mind of any betting shop cashier. Rushing in and out could make staff suspicious enough to raise the alarm, but staying too long in a shop would throw the timing out. Gabby started calling him Sir Hewlett-Packard whenever he ran through it. He wasn't offended.

"Three minutes is the optimum choice to allow for a nose around the shop, a brisk page turn of the *Racing Post*, time to casually write out the bets, approach the counter and then stroll out."

She agreed, but it didn't stop him going through specific details for each area, of course.

"There's ninety shops in the Newham area."

"*Ninety?*"

"That's right, Gabby. Keep your hair on! Covered by four in Team McQueen London, it'll be fine. I have it sussed. By allowing three minutes in house, then allowing for walking time between shops, that's a minimum of an hour and a half. Bookies open at nine, and this area should be covered by eleven. Herd Ringer's race is last on the card, at a quarter past five, so that's plenty of time. And same timings for the East End."

"Then?"

"Like we've already agreed, the four in Team McQueen London – you and Likely Di as leads, and whoever she recommends for the other two. You'll use the Tube and split the remaining one hundred and ten shops in Acton, Kilburn, Camden and Brixton between you."

Gabby didn't respond. She had her thinking face on. McQueen waited for her to mull the timings and practicalities over. Finally, she said, "Yeah. Yeah. That'll work, Mac."

"But it's not London that bugs me. It's the North: Liverpool and Birmingham."

"Stop worrying. You've the basis of two great teams – Phil an' Binky, Liverpool. I'll bet Likely Di rates them. And she'll rate Blaggit too, in Birmingham. Phil an' Binky will have lots of contacts to choose two great foot soldiers from, and Brummie Blaggit will too for his extra one. They'll be top quality, Mac. No one'll want to let you down."

He appreciated Gabby attempting to convince him that all would be well, but it didn't stop him continuing to go over things. "Hmm... yes. But what if the price collapses too quick, and they can't get the bulk of the money on?"

"Just tell 'em to get their arses in gear! They'll know the best people to recruit locally. And they'll get 'em signed up and briefed."

"Hmm... yes. They'll have to. I want to win as close to nine hundred thousand as possible on the road alone." He thought he heard Gabby gulp, and she may have whispered, "Ssshhhh-iiiiittt," but he ignored it. "And I'll be at home betting online and watching the odds shift. I'll be vigilant online when the price shortens, to get the next-best prices, and any exchanges would be a bonus."

"Are you telling me? Or giving yourself a pep talk, Mac?"

"Sorry, Gabby. I'm just checking details."

"I know, Mac. But on the day, it either will or it won't. Just make sure you do good team briefings. It'll be Team McQueen on the day, and it'll be Team McQueen all the way to the winning post. That's what matters!"

SIXTEEN

March

Every Friday afternoon Likely Di enjoyed a large barmaid's blush at a favourite corner table in her local, the quaint, Edwardian, Lord Nelson on the Old Kent Road, with its quirky décor, and engraved mirrors. This Friday was no different.

Gabby and Mac meet Likely Di: Team McQueen (London) begins

"Well, stone the crows," she said when Gabby and McQueen walked in. "If it ain't Mulder and Scully!" Likely Di lifted her chin so slightly that only those looking for a welcome would have noticed. Gabby gave a fingertip wave in return. Likely Di noted that Gabby's eyes had scanned her black velvet jacket. Did she know it was Gucci? Probably not. She'd tell her later.

"McQueen!" said Likely Di. "Last time I saw your boat race must have been down the Stow. That's when you started to go to the dogs, Mac! Don't think I don't know you was feeding the odds-on favourite, a pre-race string of bangers, to slow it down, while you backed the second favourite and had a chance to collect some winnings. You've always been one for pulling the rug out from under the bookies, Mac. They'll have you some day, mate, but not if I have anything to do with it."

"You're probably right. I'll keep all that in mind," said McQueen, parting the curtain of cigarette smoke that surrounded Likely Di's table and sorting chairs so they could join her. "It's truly good to see you, Diana."

"And you, Mac. Come on, splice the mainbrace bosun, mine's a double port and lemon and some pork scratchings. I'm Hank Marvin. The market was heaving today, and I guess you're not here to enquire about my health. What's the scoop?"

"You still act like royalty then, Princess!"

She pointed to the wall above her head and McQueen laughed. "Ruddy hell. You're even sitting under a picture of the old baked bean!"

Likely Di removed a cigarette from her pack and lit it, theatrically. She took a drag and made sure a tunnel of smoke followed McQueen as he walked to the bar for drinks. "Hey, someone put 'Smoke Gets in Your Eyes' on the jukebox," she said.

"Don't you mean 'Smoke Gets Up Your Arse'?" said Gabby, laughing while checking out McQueen's.

Likely Di's full name: Diana Roper-Lovering was a name she was proud of. Roper-Lovering was how some circles knew her, and in others she was known as a relative of the celebrated Parisian milliner, Caroline Reboux. As a result, she had some classy cast-offs and, as she'd done today, she sometimes wore them on her market stall, just because she could. Her designer clothes, even though they were family cast-offs, said: this chick don't shop at C&A or British Home Stores; this chick ain't no East End nobody; this chick has class; this chick is somebody. She'd thought about putting ads in the paper to sell them, whenever times were hard, but she couldn't do it. She'd rather be hungry and go without her ciggies than say goodbye to them.

She didn't mind approaching fifty, or that although no one would say it to her face, she sensed they thought she looked older. She saw it for herself every day in the mirror, and so what? Despite her extrovert manner, she was sometimes blighted by bouts of melancholy. She usually hid them behind cigarette smoke and a glass of red.

Coming from a long line of costermongers and hawkers, she was legendary for smelling out a pound note. Over the years she'd played most of the short and long cons, some with McQueen. She'd made bundles peddling repro Victorian iron fireplaces to the hoity-toity trendies moving to Whitechapel and Bethnal Green in the late eighties and was held in high esteem by all east of Bow Bells since 1995, after she bamboozled a party of affluent visiting Scandinavian businessmen into parting with twelve thousand pounds to sponsor the following year's Pearly King and Queen week with all the takings dished out to the underprivileged of the borough.

Tough as old boots on the outside, but inside she shone like a diamond, and to her delight, everyone loved her. She never married, and when asked would reply, "Doyenne spinster of this parish, always too busy to fall in love, love." She knew people wondered if she nursed a broken heart, but she wasn't letting on. Nosey buggers. Unfortunately, money burned a hole in her pocket; most of it ended up in bookies' pouches at the dog tracks of Catford, Walthamstow and Wimbledon.

She took a last drag from her cigarette and twisted the butt into an ashtray, then she pulled the final one from her packet of twenty and offered it to Gabby who waved it away. Likely Di lit it up: her fortieth of the day. She stood the empty pack upright on the table, like a Capstan non-filter monolith.

"How's yer sister doing these days, Gabby? Still into her artwork, is she?"

"She is. She's even moved into making art on a PC. She could do you some lovely publicity stuff and flyer designs for your stall if you ever needed it, or maybe you know someone who does. I'll give you her details. She's got a website."

"Lovely. That could be handy. I'm a bit like Mac though. I don't do all that emailing website stuff. I'm still a phone and letter person, me."

"Don't tell me! Sometimes, I think Mac is convinced that opening an email is like opening Pandora's box. He's a confirmed phone or handwriting man, you're right there!"

Just as Gabby had written the number on a beer mat for Likely Di, and she had tucked it away, McQueen was back with drinks.

"Go on then, Mac. Outline your plan."

*

All through the telling, Likely Di didn't take her eyes off him; neither did she wait to be invited to comment. "It's no Yiddisher fiddle, I'll grant you that. In my day it was called 'The Milk Round' but it's fundamentally flawed. What if the horse gets beat? You're banjaxed! God knows how many times I've bet on a good thing, a cert, and seen it get turned over, even your frog mate would agree."

"I know it's not bomb-proof, but my trainer has a gift with those young horses. Gabby thought it didn't have a snowball's chance in hell at first, but she's been won over. She's always wanted a horse. And we won't ever get an opportunity like this again."

"And you're offering me five grand, win, lose, or draw?"

"Yep."

As Likely Di spoke, her cigarette stuck to the Vaseline on her bottom lip, and it wobbled with every word. "Well, count me in, Mac. But if you pull off this dodge, don't come back to me and say it's not enough! Ha!" She cackled for a bit, then got back to business. "Now, if you've no objections, I'll mobilise the Dennett brothers, Al 'n' Dubs, for this skulduggery."

"The Dennetts? I've heard of them. You sure? Aren't they in an Oasis tribute band?"

"It's The Who, Mac; different league. Al 'n' Dubs, that's who. Trust me. Those two little scamps know the land like the back of their brass bands, and they're light on their dew beaters."

"Still a rock chick then, Diana? Your very own *Likely* Lads, eh?" said Gabby joining in, but not helpfully. This wasn't good for his anxiety.

Oh, Gabby must be loving this. But why now? This was not the time for her to play-up behind Likely Di's back.

"My lads are Londoners, not northerners like them two on telly," snapped Likely Di.

McQueen moved quickly on to keep Gabby's jokes at bay. "That sounds good, Diana," he said. "Gabby makes your fourth. You two can lead it jointly."

Likely Di took one final long inhale on her cigarette. She squashed it in her usual way, eyes fixed on Gabby. "She'll do nicely. So, Team McQueen London is me, Gabby, Al 'n' Dubs Dennett. That'll work well. Who you got in the Midlands and North?"

"Phil and Binky are Liverpool, and Blaggit in Birmingham. I'll leave it up to them to pick their own extras to work with them on their patch."

"Good choice. They're kosher. Just ensure Blaggit don't go on the piss the night before. Understand he likes the odd pint, namely the thirteenth and fifteenth. He can neck a bottle of Henry Westons eight point two per cent Storm Trooper faster than you could sign a cheque." She turned to Gabby. "Cat got your tongue, sweetie?"

"No. Just planning ahead."

"That's my grifter!" said Likely Di, ruffling Gabby's hair. "Watch yerself! That planning ahead gets you sucked in when you spend too much time with Mac."

He said, "You're brave, Diana. Some have had a knockout punch for doing similar, isn't that right, Gabby?"

"Don't I know it! Not to worry, Mac. Gabs 'n' me, we're all right," said Likely Di, smoothing down Gabby's hair and laughing. "Anyway, she has to bend down to take a swipe at me and that's not good for anyone's power punch!"

McQueen scheduled in a call with her for the next week, after his meetings with the teams in the North. He pulled a two-hundred-and-fifty-pound wodge from his wallet. "On account," he said, handing it over, along with four compact maps of the area, on which he'd marked the borders. "Get the boys to number and dot the bookies on the map. They can decide who's hitting which shop, and sort it with Gabby."

*

Likely Di kissed them both before they left and caught a whiff of Wright's Coal Tar soap on McQueen and L'Air du Temps mingled with Old Holborn tobacco on Gabby.

"Funny ole day," she said to the barman when they'd gone. "One minute you're trying to flog tawdry hand towels from a stall, next you're planning a Mediterranean cruise for the week after Easter."

"Another one, Diana?"

"What's the time, Frankie?"

"Nearly seven, love."

"Go on then, one for the hedge before the charge of the light ale brigade ride in."

SEVENTEEN

Mac arranged to meet his Team McQueen Midlands leader Brummie Blaggit, and North leaders Binky and Phil at a midway point between Birmingham and Liverpool. He chose Stoke and travelled there alone on a mid-morning train, checking into the Best Western Hotel. He'd planned enough time to relax, shower, practise his pitch and watch some sport. He switched on his hotel TV, selected Sky Sports, made a pot of strong tea to keep a clear head, and then settled to watch the Edinburgh derby: Hearts v Hibernian. As ever, it promised to be a traditional feisty affair.

Without expecting it, his thoughts turned briefly to Docherty. Would he be watching the match too? Maybe he was in among the capacity crowd, flanked by his oafs and relishing a snifter from his hip flask? Who would he support? Not Hearts, of that McQueen was certain: a neanderthal like Docherty didn't possess one. To be on the safe side he flipped the channel to keep further thoughts of Docherty at bay.

Before meeting the team in the bar at five, he spent twenty minutes gearing up for it. Getting them to grasp the opportunity of easy moolah for a day's graft was one thing; making sure they understood the task and took it seriously was another.

As he walked into the lounge they were huddled together, laughing and already on their second pint. Wondering if he'd selected the right bunch, he stood before them. "Gentlemen," he said.

"Yippee ki yay!" said Phil, looking up.

McQueen reached across their table and shook them all firmly by the hand.

"If it isn't the changing man, Mr Paul Weller. McQueen, you old tosher," Phil added, looking pleased to see him. McQueen had always been flattered that on his very first encounter with Phil, he'd likened him to Paul Weller and called him a genuine Jammie Dodger ever since.

Binky joined in. "You're looking sharp in your two-tone suit, Mr Mac. They'll come back in fashion one day. How d'ya get up here? On your Vespa? How the devil are you, dear boy?"

"Not too shabby, you pair of Aintree irons," said McQueen. He shifted his gaze onto Blaggit. "I see you're still shabby though, Blaggit!" He didn't like to point out that Blaggit had put on weight as his extended firm belly hung over his belt.

Blaggit absent-mindedly twirled his greasy, greying ponytail. "I do my best to please. That's one reason why I rocked up early. Another was to have a couple of nerve straighteners before the start time of the meeting."

McQueen hoped this wasn't true and wondered if he should have given Blaggit a later start time. He dismissed the idea, knowing Blaggit was reliable, and his constitution was solid enough to cope with a few pre-meeting bevvies. He turned back to Phil. "Still going to Anfield, Phil?"

"Naah, Mac. The terraces aren't for me anymore, not since the blade thing. Bastard hooligans, that Tottenham crew turned out to be." He rubbed a scar on his cheek. "I'm really into me Britpop music though. You wanna see my record collection."

"Do I?"

"You do!" piped up Binky, looking enthusiastic. "There's stuff in his record heap I can't even sing. Yet." He turned back to his pint.

"I should introduce you to my mate, Del, in London one day," said McQueen, smiling. "He does very well out of second-hand records."

"Thanks, Mac. Binky and Blaggit might even like to meet him too."

He laughed to himself, thinking that without Gabby's ruse, just a while back, and his alter-ego, Del, he wouldn't be here at all.

"So, you all like music? I wasn't aware you three were that well acquainted."

"Plenty you don't know, Mac," said Blaggit. "Remember all the ballyhoo in the press about that art student's flim-flam a few years back? Bigging up worthless artworks and making a killing." Blaggit winked. "Had worse."

Binky collected four fresh bevvies from the bar.

"Steady on, lads," said McQueen. "Don't want you to get too Schindler's List. We're not on a paperback writer today, and no other human drinks as fast as you lot!" He took a gulp and eyed his old muckers. It had been a while.

The three-inch scar, courtesy of a Stanley knife slash at a Spurs match, hadn't faded from Phil's cheek but otherwise he looked snappy, sporting boot-cut Levi's, Fred Perry top and Adidas classic trabs. He still seemed as wise as a Shankly docker. And Binky, as shrewd as ever, wearing drainpipe callards, with a mod haircut, and sprite-like earlobes. And then Blaggit, the oldest of them all, as usual resembling a recently graduated toper vagabond, with his snide, diamond pinkie ring, greasy thinning hair, tied in a rat's nest of a ponytail, and his crooked discoloured front 'ampsteads, always broken, like the Ten Commandments. Today he smelt of sour cabbage water and as ever was still fighting a losing battle of the bulge. Blaggit would definitely never be asked to play James Bond.

"So, Mac, what's so dramatic that we all had to drag hundreds of miles for a cloak and dagger powwow?" asked Binky. "Couldn't it be sorted on the blower?"

McQueen inhaled, then coughed, which wasn't part of his plan. "I want everyone on board to understand this mission inside out."

"Mission Impossible?" said Binky. "I'm up for that!" Ducking into a crouch, he sang the theme tune and peered round as if on high alert, until Phil shot him an exasperated look and he stood up, giving McQueen an apologetic shrug, and Phil a feeble smile.

McQueen remembered what an annoying idiot Binky could be, and how he liked a song. Grandad's *keep calm and carry on* post-war way of life, was all very well, but only when you didn't feel you'd been cast in a *Carry On* film. Despite the operatics, McQueen hadn't forgotten that Binky always came up trumps on the day. He remembered too, that Phil had an inexplainable tolerance for Binky's musical outbursts.

Sitting back in his chair he calmly carried on as if nothing had happened. "It means a lot to me," he said, and briefed them, outlining the minutiae exactly as he had done for Likely Di and Gabby.

Phil was the first to comment. Bright as ever, he got straight to the point. "Dicey, balls of steel needed on this one, Mac, but it's sound that you persuaded Likely Di to rally some troops and join the party in London. From what I hear, she's the dog's."

"She rates you all too," he said, hoping flattery would help get them on board.

All three shared Likely Di's misgivings. Their concern and attentiveness convinced him they were the right ones for the job, and he assured them the risk was all his, that he was going in with his eyes wide open, not flying by the seat of his pants.

"Just to reiterate, guys, the overall success of the day rests on how much we can get on at the biggest prices. The odds will, of course, shorten at some stage, but if they get wind of things early doors, then the winnings are gonna be greatly reduced. It's all about timing."

"And luck," said Binky, launching into singing the chorus from 'Luck Be a Lady Tonight'.

"Yeah, and that too, Binky."

"Forgot how musical he is, did you, Mac? Beatles nut, him," said Phil, rolling his eyes. "It's in the blood for all us Scousers. He had them rockin' at last week's karaoke night at the Grafton Club. He was belting a six-song medley. Binky's got a gob like the Mersey Tunnel. Any cue for a song and he'll take it."

That started Binky off. "Hey there were others egging me on," he said, and he was singing again. This time it was 'With a Little Help from My Friends'.

What would Grandad make of this lot? *Know who you're dealing with? Jeepers!* He was dealing with a musical theatre amateur. He hadn't factored this irritant in.

McQueen waited. What else could he do? Once Binky was done, he continued with the briefing.

"I'll be at home monitoring the market moves online. I won't miss a trick and if there's the slightest hint that the price is about to tumble, I'll lump on."

Without warning, Blaggit flung his arms around him. McQueen had forgotten that Blaggit was prone to hugging. He should have been ready. Up close, the first whiff of Blaggit's odour made his eyes water. He blinked and pulled away. "Watch the cloth, moth," he joked.

"I think I can say on behalf of us all," said Blaggit, "without your encouragement over the years, we'd probably still be running a poorly executed pigeon drop, or a hoax bleedin' online dating site." He laughed, then got serious. "Or worse, taking air and exercise."

Phil and Binky lowered their heads, nodded solemnly, and shuffled in their seats. "We'll get this done for you, kiddo," said Phil.

"Oh, shut up," said McQueen, wiping his eyes. "You lot'll have me in bleedin' tears."

"Wey hey!" they cheered and took to their beers until McQueen was ready to carry on.

"By my calculations, the Liverpool area will need four on the ground to cover. Can you arrange for a trusty couple of scallywags to up your numbers, Phil?"

"The whizzer bomb-heads, Woollyback and Wacker, will be made up to partake in a little high-jinks. What think you, Binky?"

Scratching the top of his pointy ear, Binky didn't hesitate. "Yep, boxed off, they'd be. They're always brassic," he said. "But you'll need to have a stern word with them, Phil, cos they've been overdoing the devil's dandruff recently and we can't risk having them wired-up on the day, charging around Merseyside like a runaway circus act."

McQueen pretended not to have heard. He trusted Phil and Binky well enough to let them sort out the problem. He moved straight on to stave off another musical interlude and another unwanted thought that had come to him: did Docherty have to put up with this kind of behaviour?

"Blaggit, you need just the one extra working with you. Any ideas?"

"Tonker Newley's a good man and always up for a tilt at the layers," he said, flicking his ponytail and rubbing the straggly ends between his fingers as he spoke. "Worked with him plenty of times since his stint as a professional rugby player got scuppered, poor sod. Mind you, it didn't stop him loving the game. If this little project of yours was earlier in the year, Mac, you'd have no chance of getting him; he never misses a Five Nations. Ooops, Six Nations I should say these days. He'd have me for that slip-up! Rugby mad, he is. I tell you, Mac, he's not a man to cross when he has a cobb on. Brummie as they come, he is and with a heart of gold. It will save him going all around the Wrekin if he works with me. And those, Mac, are Brummie terms I've learned since moving there."

126

"Well done, Blaggit," said McQueen, feeling he ought to seem impressed and perhaps grateful. "I'll let you sort that out then, mate."

He moved on to handing over street maps for their areas. "You'll need to buy a couple more of these and pinpoint the exact locations for all your team. You've got a postcode list of the betting shops to help. It shouldn't take more than a day to mark 'em up. We'll all of us meet back here one week before the race, to tweak any last-minute problems. That's when I'll explain everything fully. I'll hand over the wager money and give out betting bags for you guys to sort ready for the day."

After they'd agreed on an April meeting date, he went on. "I'll tell you the name of our horse then, but don't inform your runners until race day." Looking each one of them in the eye in turn, he waited for them to mumble their agreement, before he said, "Right, my shout. Anyone fancy a steak sarnie?"

*

Once back home he called Likely Di and Gabby to confirm that the others were on board, and things were going to schedule. Now he needed to draw up plans for the other London boroughs, and that took much longer than he'd anticipated. Locating Camden and Brixton shops was relatively straightforward, but planning Acton and Kilburn, with bookmakers spread over a much greater distance, was a different kettle of fish; he'd designate these to the fleet-footed Dennett brothers, as recommended by Likely Di. He also placed a seventy-five-pound bet on some outsiders in each of the four areas, to take in any reaction. None of the cashiers batted an eyelid, not even when one nag actually won at 12 to 1. Delighted, he spent his winnings on supper at Bentley's Oyster Bar and Grill in Piccadilly.

Back in his flat, he never stopped readying things for what he started to call *Operation Golden Fleece*. He'd bought three laptops, for flexible access, opened several online bookmaker's accounts, and deposited money in each. He planned to place some mug-style bets, so bookies saw him as an ordinary Joe Public punter, who could never win in the long run. This would soften their defences for the big day.

Spread over his lounge carpet were ten zipped bags, each one stuffed with the correct number of eighty-pound wedges secured in bundles, as well as spare pens, water, plasters, glucose tablets, disposable rain ponchos, a wallet for placed betting slips, and travel cards for the capital crew. He hoped he'd thought of everything because there was barely room to walk. He tiptoed round the bags to his mantelpiece and stroked the chunky, shiny, brown-glazed horse ornament. His heart ached. He'd nicked it from Woolworths when he was a child as a silent protest, the day Grandad had been wrongly accused of keeping dog-eye in a high-profile mugging. He got a six-week suspended sentence at HMP Hollesley Bay. He always assured the worried McQueen that if he went, it would just be a little holiday in Suffolk, and said he reckoned he'd be on gardening duty the whole time, so he'd be happy.

"We'll stab 'em in the purse, where it hurts them most, Grandad. We'll fleece 'em golden, the bastards," he whispered.

When he called Françoise to reassure her of his confidence in Team McQueen, she filled him in with news that, according to the vet, his charge was in rude health and catching pigeons on the gallops, in fact, she couldn't be happier with his progress, so he was confident that his little Herd Ringer would be cherry ripe on the day.

That evening he had a laugh with Gabby on the phone and briefed her on the latest state of things. As ever, she took the piss out of his obsession with double-checking the meeting schedule for next week and listing the contents of the bags.

"What Mac, no name badges? I know you love staring at a name badge. I bet that's cos you never got to be a milk monitor at school."

He didn't mind her pulling his leg; it was good to hear her

laughing, so he went along with it. "Yeah. Well. I can't get them shined up enough, and 'Woollyback' doesn't fit on a badge."

"You fool! We'd all have to have aliases, Mac. What would yours be?"

"Vin," he said, without hesitation.

"Huh?"

"Steve McQueen. Vin. *Magnificent Seven.* My hero from yesteryear."

"And your namesake too: 'McQueen'. I get it. But wear that Vin badge when we next go to see Françoise, and she'll ask if you want magnificent vin blanc ou magnificent vin rouge!"

After the call he stood for some minutes staring at his kitchen wine rack.

Vin blanc ou vin rouge? Naaah!

He laughed and shook his head, as he cracked open a can. Suddenly he was consumed by the unexpected relief that he and Gabby were blessed to have dodged a Docherty vengeance bullet. Things could have turned out so differently.

EIGHTEEN

One week before Operation Golden Fleece, McQueen's holdalls were bulging with all the goods. They were too big for the luggage rack, so he pushed the smallest under his seat and rested his feet on the other. Train travel suited him, especially today, when he had one of his thudding headaches. The pain made him glad that he'd failed his driving test every time he took it, because he knew he would never be able to drive feeling like this, but there was still the regret that he'd missed out on owning the car of his dreams. He'd discarded his yearnings for a red Ferrari long ago, or wanting to join the black Porsche Sloane Ranger brigade, and the four-by-four weekend squires lot was definitely not for him. Nope. What McQueen had always wanted was the blue Mini from the set of *The Italian Job*, so that one day he could blow the bloody doors off. Ridiculous to think of car choices: going by train to meet the new Birmingham and Liverpool recruits for Team McQueen gave him the chance to shake off his migraine.

Running through race day for the umpteenth time was taking its toll. No amount of scrutinising his plan revealed anything amiss, but he was constantly haunted by nagging doubts that he'd overlooked something crucial. The detail, the detail; he must attend to the detail. Was there a devil about? Had he flushed him out, or would they soon be dancing together? He'd have more of an idea once he met the team newbies. Would his Achilles heel be lurking there? He wished he could shake off these thoughts.

Settled in the hotel lounge with coffee, he stared at his watch while he waited, still wracking his brains for a flaw, apart from the obvious one: he was about to hand over fifteen thousand pounds. What if they all took it and then scarpered?

Blaggit was the first to arrive, accompanied by his Birmingham teammate, the gargantuan Tonker. Blaggit was no oil painting, with his broken front teeth badly askew, and his always greasy, long grey ponytail, but the new man, Tonker, upstaged him with a busted nose, cauliflower ears and with, as Grandad might have

Tonker Newley: Team McQueen Midlands (Birmingham)

said, one eye on the pot the other up the chimney. Tonker wasn't the sort of geezer you'd want to meet in a dark alley, but he'd learned from Blaggit that friends knew he was a pussycat at heart. Someone with a physique like Tonker could be an asset to a team should the need ever arise, thought McQueen, hoping it never would. Horses for courses. Yes, Grandad, I know.

"I understand that this ain't no shrapnel beano, Mr McQueen. Bostin days!" Tonker said with a warm smile. "I'm up for it. I'm your man." His Brummie accent was so strong McQueen had to fully concentrate on his every word.

Blaggit's firm handshake put McQueen at ease. There was always a risk that Blaggit's diamond pinkie ring might dig into his hand, but not today. It was a bad breath day for Blaggit, though. Never mind calling him Bermondsey Blaggit or Brummie Blaggit, today McQueen wanted to call him Body Odour Blaggit. He stepped back as Blaggit spoke through his mangled teeth. "Mr T here, was, back in the day, one helluva tight head prop for Leicester Tigers. He even won an England cap, but he's probably best remembered in that game for a tackle so high that it almost broke the Welsh fullback's neck. A straight red card, and his England career lasted exactly eight minutes. That's what you always say, innit, Tonk?"

"Thought it was closer to five!" said Tonker, his broad shoulders rising and falling in a stifled guffaw.

"That's five more minutes than me," said McQueen, hoping he'd heard Tonker right, and wondering if it was at all true. Blaggit had a tendency to big people up if he admired them – as if Tonker needed to be any bigger. England glory or not, he wasn't going to upset Blaggit by challenging a bloke that size whose accent was as Brummie as his was Cockney. If Blaggit recommended Tonker, Tonker was good enough for McQueen. He smiled meekly and said, "Very impressive. When did you finish playing?"

Tonker pulled up his left trouser leg, to reveal a metal knee brace. "Gotta wear this for the rest of me natural. Couple of weeks after me international debut, we were away at Bath, and a scrum collapsed as did me knee, causing me leg to rotate at a forty-five-degree angle. It was the only time in my life I cried. Retired from the game with less money than I started with." He smoothed his trouser back into place and kept his head down. "Look at the salaries they get today: shocking."

The story, and Tonker's sadness, made McQueen shudder. He tried to hide his discomfort, glad for the distraction of Phil, the Scouser's, arrival.

"Oi! Oi! Saveloy! You early, or are we late? All right, fella?" Phil boomed as they bowled over. McQueen greeted him and introduced Tonker.

"You wanna see the other bloke," said Blaggit, laughing while Phil stared at Tonker's dishevelled face and massaged his own scar. Bastard change in the weather was probably causing skin problems, thought McQueen, turning to see Phil and Binky's recruits, Woollyback and Wacker hovering at the door.

"Come on you two," said Binky, standing behind them, ushering them in. "Don't be shy, soft lads. Meet the gang."

Two lily-livered, amphetamine-freak-skinnies stepped forward meekly, both in tight denim trousers that covered legs as thin as any ant's. How could such thin legs hold up any human? McQueen thought of them as Scarecrow and Lion, fresh from the Yellow Brick Road, approaching Oz's great wizard – himself, humble as ever. He studied their forms, concerned he'd need to work magic on them, or at least give them some luncheon vouchers.

Wacker had a touch of the 'calm-downs' about him. With an unfashionable semi-mullet hair-do and pitch-black tash to match, he was a throwback from the nineties in his dark-blue high-waisted denim jeans, shiny black leather belt, soft-blue denim jacket and white Nike T-shirt, while Woollyback in the same, but greys and black, with a shock of mousey hair, gin-blossom conk, chin like a docker's kneecap, and shiny winkle-pickers, produced a real win double; Thatcher's children they were not. They'd do as foot soldiers

Woollyback and Wacker: Team McQueen North (Liverpool)

as long as they had the courage of a lion and weren't hollow tin men, or brainless scarecrows. Woollyback might need to ditch his winkle-pickers for the day and invest in some round-toed trainers though. Their denim gear wouldn't look conspicuous. Good. That was good. At least they weren't wearing a red Harrington jacket, like some idiot he knew once had on a job. What was he thinking? Grandad would have been turning in his grave. Jeez! He'd leave it to Phil and Binky to broach the footwear matter.

The tables in the room he'd hired were small. McQueen sat with big boys, Blaggit and Tonker, who each took up the space of two, so the four Liverpudlians – Woollyback, Wacker (the denim duo), Phil (the scar) and Binky (the songster) sat at a separate table. McQueen ordered coffees for all. He could see through the open door the bar was empty, but it would soon fill up. They fell into small talk, their chatter rising and falling as they waited for their hot drinks to arrive. Tonker turned to Blaggit. "What are those Scousers banging on about?" he said.

McQueen swallowed a laugh, wondering how Blaggit would cope with this question. He himself doubted whether Woollyback, Wacker, Phil or Binky would understand what this splendid Brummie was banging on about. Blaggit had it sorted, good man. "Sod knows. All that '*arl, cob on, la, working a welt, meff*' stuff, could be pissing Martian banter for all I know. Go and ask them. You know how you hate to miss anything. Remember, they probably won't be able to understand a word you say though, Tonks! Just don't start talking about my internet dating fast one. They'll probably end up thinking I'm a right perv if they have to guess what you're saying." Tonker took him up on the idea of tackling things head-on and sauntered over to introduce himself to Woollyback and Wacker. He was wider than the two of them put together and it set them off laughing and measuring.

A waiter brought in their coffees, with complimentary muffins, left over from breakfast. McQueen beckoned Phil and Binky across to join him and Blaggit, leaving the three newbies: Tonker, Woollyback and Wacker, to get stuck into scoffing and jesting.

McQueen discreetly manoeuvred himself to make sure that Binky and Phil distanced him from l'eau de Blaggit, glad the door was open. He drummed his fingers on the table to get their attention then spoke. "Blaggit, Binky and Phil, my Team McQueen leaders, for the Midlands and the North – or BBP, as I call you," he said, grateful of their laughter and even of Binky saying they were the BBP – the British Broadcasting Pissheads. He let them settle, then handed each of them a slip of paper. "This is the name of the spanker. Keep it under your hat." His eyes turned to shoot a glance in the direction of the other table. "And remember," he said, "they're not to be told until race day morning. Understand? I don't want the world and his wife knowing the name of my horse."

The instant he saw them reading the name he started to worry, wishing he'd kept totally shtum for longer. Could he trust them to keep it to themselves until race day? A week was a long time in horse racing. He blinked and shook his head to try and clear away the niggling doubts. For goodness' sake, he knew half of them. Likely Di swore by them, literally, and Gabby trusted Likely Di's judgement and his too, so why the sudden panic? He tried to pull himself together, sound assertive, and make light of things. "I'll contact you next week and, of course, on Friday. And I'll be watching the odds, so I'll know if you've let the name slip out," he said, regretting that he'd added one of his friendly winks.

"Tommyrot name," said Binky. "Who'd want to bet on a name like that?"

Binky's remark stopped McQueen fretting and he worked hard at keeping his face serious, aware that some of them might be thinking far worse to say about the horse's name than the things Gabby had come up with.

Blaggit looked uncharacteristically puzzled. "What does Herd Ringer even mean?"

"It's Gaelic for 'free Guinness tomorrow'," said McQueen, keeping a serious face. He nearly burst when Blaggit bit with a reaction straight off.

"So, we get free stout when they open, right?"

"You muppet!" said Phil.

McQueen felt relieved when his leaders, including the butt of the joke, Blaggit, laughed. Even the diamond in his pinkie ring seemed to glint.

Tonker, Woollyback and Wacker looked over. Tonker stood up. He lifted their table as if it was doll's house furniture made from balsa wood and brought it with him when he walked over to join them. The two Scouser lightweights scuttled speedily to shift the crockery and eat the last of the muffins.

How could McQueen have wished this moment away? All he had to do was get them race day ready. And possibly get some deodorant and a toothbrush for Blaggit.

BBP produced their updated area maps and gave out team copies.

"Excellent work, boys," said McQueen, scanning them to check that all the shops had been highlighted. He got busy lining up the shoulder bags on the tables.

"Bit poncy, them bags aren't they? Who gave you the Marks & Spencer's vouchers? That Judy of yours?"

"No, Phil. And she's not my bird, all right?"

Phil rubbed the scar on his cheek and looked awkward. He reached for a bag. McQueen waited for them each to take one and check it over, then settle, ready to pay attention.

"Now listen up, gentlemen," he said.

Binky nudged Phil and flashed his eyes at Woollyback and Wacker. "Gentlemen. That's us," he said, laughing until Phil elbowed him in the ribs.

McQueen went on, demonstrating everything as he spoke like a keen salesman selling to deaf customers. "The straps on these bags are long enough to go across your body diagonally. You can alter them to fit, see? Don't just hang 'em on your shoulder. You'll be carrying a lot of dosh in here. Keep it safe." He waited for them to fiddle with the straps.

"Here's what else you're getting: see the large, zipped compartment inside? That's where you keep your stash of exact shop bundles of eighty pounds. Always keep just one eighty-pound wad in the outside zipped pocket, and keep it closed."

Sharp Phil interrupted. "I thought the bet was seventy-five?"

"I'll come to that in a minute."

He waited for them to zip and unzip things like children with presents on Christmas morning.

"Before entering a shop, you remove the wad from the outside zipper zone and put it in your pocket. Then, take a new bundle from inside, and place it in the outside pouch, ready for the next bookies."

He looked directly at Phil. "Regarding the eighty pounds you queried, still place the seventy-five on the horse but do a cheeky little fiver-weekend football bet. You'll see the coupons in the wall dispensers. Pick any three teams, go to the counter with it on top of the horse wager. It might look less suspicious than placing one bet. Write out the slip as per mine. There are samples for you, see?" He pointed out each section. "The time of the race is at the top: five fifteen, Newmarket. That's our race. You'll find out the horse's name on the day and you must put it in the middle, see?" He was glad Herd Ringer's name was under wraps for all but he and BBP, because as a full team this lot would take the piss endlessly.

He looked sternly at Binky. "Under the horse's name, put the current price. You'll see this on the screens inside each bookies. You're betting seventy-five pounds win. And put the stake in the bottom box."

Blaggit looked puzzled again. "What's a bottom box?"

"Blaggit's obscene arse!" said wise-crack Tonker.

"Oh, you can talk, Mr Bigger-Than-Me-In-Every-Way," said Blaggit, pushing his belly out and patting it proudly, looking as if he'd swallowed a fully inflated orange Space Hopper down in one and was getting ready to excrete it.

Team McQueen North, egged on by the antics of Blaggit and Tonker who made up Team McQueen Midlands, crumbled into laughter. Suddenly he felt like he'd stepped into the shoes of Captain Mainwaring dealing with the idiot boy, Pike. This was even worse than when Gabby acted the fool. He reeled them back in and went on.

"And don't forget to put the shop's address on the back of the receipt you'll get. Got that?" They all nodded.

"Address on the back of the receipt," muttered Wacker.

McQueen explained the next step. "So, you'll have the shoulder bag, your map, a pen, your wads of money, and… a wallet. The wallet is to keep the betting slips in so you can keep them secure in one place."

"Look at all that lot," said Binky, smirking. "You've thought of everything, Mac. There's enough here to have a saucy weekend away in Blackpool! And you packed it all here for me, Phil and Blaggit to take away. Ah. No. Something's missing. Thought you might have chucked in a Trojan for the weekend, sir? You never know, one of us might get lucky!"

McQueen ignored the remark and the laughter, willing it to subside. His inner self pleaded, *Please don't sing, Binky. Please don't sing. Please don't sing.*

"And I suggest you work as a team," he said eventually, "taking alternative shops: safety in numbers. Go in relaxed, but not overconfident. I've hired the private room above the Argyll Arms, round the corner from Oxford Circus, Saturday week, for team leaders, so I'll see BBP there with Gabby and Likely Di. A week should give everyone enough time to collect all the winnings. We'll split the takings there. Tonker, Wacker and Woollyback, you'll get the agreed cut directly from BBP once they get back from London, but before all that, they'll dish out your bags and betting cash on race day." He checked his watch. "I think that's about it. Any questions?"

"What if it goes wonky?" said Phil.

"It'll be Carey Street for me, mate, but let's not think about that." He looked from Phil to Blaggit. "Instead, let's think about how we can all come out smelling of roses."

He signalled for more coffees and ordered sandwiches. Leaders, BBP, gathered up their team bags and McQueen handed over the wads of cash for them to pack ready for the day of Operation Golden Fleece, telling them to keep it safe.

They sat for some time, sorting out who would do what and when, pawing over a map, churning over the obstacles and the what ifs. He was glad to see them in action, and watched Binky, all serious and without a song in his heart, unravelling the possible flaws and finding solutions. Details, the details, they were going through the details, just as it should be.

He shook everyone's hand, and they wished each other the best. Before he left them to it, Woollyback approached him. "I want to thank you, Mr McQueen. You've made things very clear for us. We won't let you down." Looking McQueen in the eye he sniffed twice and tapped his nose with the tip of his finger as he nodded his head, then walked away.

NINETEEN

Jiggered by the events of the day, McQueen was moved by Woollyback's gesture and felt more reassured that Wacker and Woollyback's cocaine habit wouldn't mar the day. He made his getaway to the pub next door to calm himself and make notes on his team. He ordered a large cognac before heading to the station. In exactly one week they would know their fate. And he would know if he'd made the ghost of his grandad proud.

*

McQueen spent the entire train journey home going over and over things and thinking about each member of Team McQueen in turn.

He had always prided himself in being able to read people and make good judgements. Living his first eight years with a man he called Father, who was ill-tempered, meant he had to learn to see a violent outburst coming and quickly hide or pretend to be asleep if he wanted to dodge one. And it meant that when this violent man vanished from his life, he hoped he would rot in Pentonville.

Did he think his team were all up to it?

The answer had to be *yes*. In spite of their constant tomfoolery, he could see it was all good-natured tomfoolery.

Grandad would probably agree.

He owed his grandad so much. His parents' relationship had always been turbulent. His mother seemed more interested in *Coronation Street* ups and downs and her stash of Green Shield stamps, than being a good mother. He saw the man he called Father less and less. Some nights he would wake him to give his son a beery sweet and sour sloppy kiss. When they divorced, after the revelation of his male infertility, Mother descended into depression, exchanging any semblance of good housekeeping for a vodka bottle. It was Grandad who saved him. They shared his small two-bedroom flat in south London. It was Grandad he owed everything to. Grandad: his champion then, his champion still; his champion forever.

By the time McQueen reached home, he was running on empty, mostly from the emotional effort of reminiscing, but he still couldn't see anything missing in his plan. The only thing he knew he'd missed was Gabby. They hadn't seen each other for a while, and he liked working with her; he liked her wit, and he liked her engaging company. Four years without it, all because of Docherty. Had he overreacted? Had Gabby been right about his paranoia?

After a shower, he microwaved a chilli. While he scoffed it, he spoke to her on the phone, giving a brief update on his meeting, and telling her how she'd have got on well with the Team McQueen North bunch. Her tone struck him as needy. Maybe she'd missed him too; maybe he was flattering himself; most likely her sister had been playing up. He confirmed their meet-up for tomorrow when he'd have to go through it all again, but at least he'd be on home ground. He packed the four bags for Team McQueen London inside his large empty holdall and called it a day.

*

The next afternoon Gabby, Likely Di, Al and Dubs waited for him in the snug. They were all there, looking keen when he turned up, directing his gaze to a tankard which stood waiting for him on the bar, like a glinting Gold Cup trophy with his name on it. Gabby was the first on her feet. She greeted him with a delicate peck on the cheek. Likely Di was carrying beers so she chin-waved him from the far side of the table. Some of her cigarette ash narrowly missed a pint as she put it down, and two alarmed cries of 'Woah!' went up.

"Sorry we couldn't stretch to your usual vintage, Mac. I was just telling Diana about your purloined bottle from the Savoy!"

"Ah! That would be a bottle of their finest 2034 if I remember rightly," he said, smiling.

"Bloomin' wine connoisseurs," said Likely Di. "Don't you just hate them, Gabby? I bet Mac couldn't tell a claret from a Bordeaux!"

McQueen bit his lip, fighting the urge to explain that a Bordeaux is a claret. He was grateful that no one else put her right, but perturbed to think they may not have known.

Likely Di kept up the chatter. "Talking of connoisseurs, or cons as I call 'em, these are the waggish Artful Dodger Dennett brothers." She put the tray down and beckoned them forward. "They like their beer ash-free, fussy buggers!" Laughing, she scraped the frothy tops with a clean beer mat. "Came across these Herberts a while back, operating their public transport ticket control tricks at Victoria Station. Poor tourists: in the country less than an hour, and instant sitting ducks for Penguin and Riddler here." She tapped them in turn on the shoulder. "Mac, meet Al. Meet Dubs."

They nodded and she added, "Within a minute of meeting these two, the poor tourists were forty pounds poorer."

The arch-enemies of Batman: Penguin Al, and Riddler Dubs, held out their hands to shake McQueen's. "Pleased to meet you, Mr McQueen," they both said.

The Dennett Brothers, Al and Dubs: more Team McQueen (London)

"Just Mac, guys."

There was no mistaking them as brothers. Al, a little older and broader than Dubs, both with similar mannerisms: diamond-faced, beatnik barnets, bobbing Adam's apples, and rapier-like prying, blue-grey eyes. "I understand Diana holds you in high esteem. No pressure, but it's likely that a fair part of the day's success will be down to your ability to hit the far-flung shops of Acton and Kilburn before they figure out what's going on."

"Yes, Diana has briefed us. You've got the right guys, Mac," said Dubs. "Lucky you got us. We're just back from Istanbul."

"Doing a gig there, were you?" said Likely Di, winking.

"Yep. The Bull in East Ham." The pair of them fell about laughing. "Geddit?" Likely Di and Gabby joined in. McQueen didn't mind being had, if it raised team spirits.

"Really?" said McQueen, feigning curiosity which gathered interest. "Ah yes. I heard you were in a first-rate Who tribute band with a nice little following on the circuit. I remember seeing them in the late eighties at the Albert Hall. The kids were definitely all right!"

McQueen looked alarmed as Dubs shot his arms in the air and twirled his fingers. "God! Is he having some sort of fit?" he asked.

"No, Mac. Stay calm. Call off the medics. He always goes into his drumstick twirling mime whenever someone praises the band. And so do I!" Instantly, Al produced a plastic plectrum and began air-guitaring, plucking at his polo-neck jumper. "Fender bass plectrum this is, Mac," he shouted, chortling with his air-drumming chum.

A middle-aged couple peered round the door but retreated when they caught Likely Di's glowering look. As ever, it was fierce enough to tempt him to join them and leave the madness, and grinning Gabby too, right there and then, but he resisted and opened his holdall instead, spreading out the team shoulder bags on the adjoining seat, glad when Al and Dubs stopped to look.

"Bit swanky, Mac," said Likely Di.

"Only the best for my minxes," he replied, glancing at Gabby.

"Not designer though, are they?" said Likely Di, laughing and brushing the sleeve of her turquoise silk blouse.

Once Likely Di and Gabby were both armed with a fresh cigarette, things went much as they had in the Midlands, ending up with them sorting out meeting on race day at Upton Park Tube station at eight thirty sharp. That was when The Marvel Boys would pick up their bags loaded with their labelled maps and all the cash, well before the shops were due to open at nine. Al and Dubs left happy, mumbling something about running through a new song, getting bob-squashed at home, and a date with a couple of sorts up the West End.

Gabby got a round in for herself, McQueen and Likely Di, and was soon back with a full tray, in good spirits. "Al 'n' Dubs seem solid," she said. "Reckon you found a good pair there, Diana."

"Yeah, bit Jack the lad occasionally, but I'm sure you were at their age, eh, Mac?" He didn't answer. "Mac?"

"Sorry. Miles away."

"Not 'aving second thoughts, are we?"

"Nah. It's just this thing eating away at me – it's all a bit too smooth. Have I missed something?"

His anxiety and self-doubt provoked protectiveness in both of them. They sidled up to him, Likely Di on one side, Gabby the other, teasing and squeezing him between them on the pub pew, calling him their tasty Big Mac. Gabby playfully rubbed his thigh, and he stroked the face of his watch. "Look, mate," she said, "you've done your bit, and now it's all down to that magnificent four-legged friend of yours and our own Madame French Fries."

Likely Di, catching sight of the thigh-rub, muttered, "Oooh, très bien!"

They were doing their best to cheer him, he knew. He caught his reflection in the bar mirror. The anxiety etched on his forehead, and Frank Sinatra's 'That's Life' going on in the background, messed with his head.

By Tuesday he'd checked on the troops and called Françoise as promised, to assure her all was well. Everyone seemed relaxed and in tune. Maybe this dog would have its day, after all.

TWENTY

April

"You're not expecting anyone today, are you?" said Elspeth.

"No. Certainly not. It is too near to Friday's race for me to entertain."

"That's good as I've to nip into Cambridge. I'll be back later."

Françoise did not see any point in mentioning that Noel would be visiting mid-morning to check on Herd Ringer, and to talk about borrowing Sweet Pierre again for beaters in the local pheasant shoots when the season started later in the year. She did not need Elspeth around for that, and Noel would be more at ease without her secretary hovering. He was a horse person, shy in human company. Given her location, it should have been no surprise to have had a veterinary practitioner who specialised in equine matters as her nearest neighbour, but it was a surprise to have one whose first language was French, although coming from Bruges, he spoke it with a Belgian accent. But you cannot have everything.

They were due to meet down in the paddock and with Elspeth out of the way, maybe he would come in for a drink and a chat, one neighbour to another; one horse lover to another. She thought it might be possible that Noel was even fonder of horses than she was. He had devoted his life to them. He did not seem to be in it for the money, which was so refreshing. He really cared about their welfare. His stables mostly housed rescue horses he had saved from a worse fate once their racing days were done.

"I'll be off then," said Elspeth.

Françoise made her way to the paddock with her happy Labrador by her side. Noel was there already, wearing his funny little trilby hat, slightly too small for his head and sporting his funny little wispy moustache slightly too big for his top lip. He looked up and gave a funny little wave. Sweet Pierre bounded over, and Noel told him to sit, before patting him and rubbing his back enthusiastically. It was Noel she had to thank for this precious dog. He had named him Sweet Pea but let her change it, insisting she take him when she moved into the cottage, telling her Sweet Pierre would be company. She knew the truth was that really, he had wanted her to have a dog to make her feel safe. She would not be without him now. Right then, for the first time in a long time, she did feel safe, with Sweet Pierre by her side, with Herd Ringer, and with Noel as her neighbour. How her world had turned around. She leaned in and patted the horse as if she were stroking her horrors away. Life felt good.

Françoise leaned in and patted Herd Ringer

148

It seemed that no one in the racing world had escaped hearing of Françoise's misfortunes, but no one knew the truth about Le Manx Gang, and except for her confession to McQueen, she was too afraid to tell it. Noel was no exception. At least she did not have to go through explaining all that with Noel. He had his own painful memories. She sensed it the first time she saw him, and she was right. Torn from his parents, mid-teens, when they were killed in a hit and run accident not far from their home in Damme. The date was Valentine's Day; he swore then he would never have a Valentine of his own, and he had stuck to it. 'No Love Noel', he was nicknamed all through veterinary college. He did not mind. He stuck to his coursework and passed with flying colours. Not the doctor his parents had wanted him to be, but he hoped they would have been proud of him for at least following partly in their footsteps and doing well. Animals were more important to him than humans. All that, Françoise had learned on a first meeting when he had come over, concerned that one of her colts was limping and offering his help. Extraordinary, Noel had said, as he had never spoken to anyone about his past before.

She trusted him with her horses, and when he checked Herd Ringer, telling her the magnificent colt was likely to fly home on Saturday, she believed him. There was one caveat though. His own horse was in the same race. He promised to let her know on Friday whether it was worth placing a bet. Such a rank outsider, the odds would be worth a punt, but he insisted she must not waste a penny unless he gave her the thumbs up.

*

Françoise hardly slept on Wednesday night, tossing and turning, with a troubled mind spinning. Her phone had rung that evening; it was a call she had been dreading. She answered and recognised the voice instantly. The sound of it brought back nothing but horror. Roche was speaking in his gritty low French growl. She fought to stay calm, to stay in control, desperate not to break down. She knew it was essential she operate in a level-headed manner. Le Manx Gang had tracked her down. Not wanting a repeat of the French massacre, she reluctantly informed the evil Roche that she was hopeful of good runs from two of her horses, and that both had subsequently won, albeit as favourites. He then let on that he knew she had a runner in the last race on Friday of that week and he proceeded to grill her about its chances. Terror-fuelled, she knew she had no other option than to say that he was in excellent form, but lied to buy some time, and told him the horse was due one final workout at dawn, as he had bled a little from the nostrils earlier that day. She promised to call him after breakfast, with an update.

After that she had no hope of getting back to sleep. Although it was only just past three, she wandered downstairs, made coffee, and sat considering her options. Noel had been right; it was a comfort to have Sweet Pierre with her even though it did not solve her problems. If she played down Herd Ringer's chances excessively, and he romped home, there would be serious ramifications. On the other hand, if she praised him too much, all the fancy prices would be snapped up online before the betting shops opened at nine, and that would scupper the endeavours of McQueen.

When her double espresso hit home, she felt jittery as well as apprehensive. Could she go on? She shook off dark thoughts and took a soak in her hot tub, then dressed, made her way to the stables with her dozy, loyal dog, and headed to Herd Ringer's box. The beautiful horse was awake. He recognised her and she was glad to be greeted with billows of warm nostril air. She lolled her head on his. "I think this is what these Brits call *caught between the devil and the deep blue sea*, Ringer," she whispered.

A few hours later, she sat pushing jam into a croissant on her plate and eating none of it. What little appetite she managed to muster when she prepared it, had waned. Sweet Pierre was grateful for a treat. She blew on her strong black coffee to cool it. There was no point putting it off any longer, she must make the call. She washed her cutlery and plate then dialled.

"So, madame, do I tell our Belfast betting associates to put their houses on it? Oui? Ou non, eh?" Roche taunted.

For a fleeting moment, her thoughts turned to McQueen and his type. She wanted to say, "*Why do you not stick it up your fat fucking Le Manx derrière!*" The words were building up in her larynx but the memory of her burning geldings on the Riviera, and their shrieking, their frantic squealing and death cries were too much. Holding back her anger, she politely replied, "I am not sure that is wise, Mr Roche." She even forced a tiny giggle. "He galloped with all his old zest this morning, and the haemoglobin issue appears to be resolved, but I have studied the other runners. Many are from powerful stables and fashionable breeding lines. It is a hot maiden contest, but I think my chap will outrun his odds. Hopefully he will be in the first three, but I would not stake my life on it."

"Let's hope you never have to," Roche grunted back.

"Let us hope not," she said, before the line went dead.

Eight o'clock was far from early for Françoise, but fragile and mentally drained after her night of Le Manx fretting, it seemed to her more like pre-dawn. The stable lads and lasses would be returning from their morning run-outs on Newmarket Heath in a couple of hours. That gave her a bit of time to grab a nap before getting on with her day. She waited for sleep to drag her under, praying that Roche and his mob would be conservative with their stakes, given her appraisal, so McQueen could get a fair crack at the whip. She felt unsettled, with her soul exposed for all to see. Had she opened a portal to a world of betrayal? Would there ever be closure?

TWENTY-ONE

Early to bed for me, Françoise promised herself. Having made it through the day with heavy eyelids, and acting like an automaton to get through every essential pre-race-day task, she turned in. Once abed, despite her anxieties, she had no difficulty falling asleep.

A heavy knock at the front door disturbed her dreams – *merde!* Please, not another night deprived of sleep. Disorientated, yet aware enough to know it was bordering on being too late for visitors, she called for Elspeth; the only reply was another beat on the door. "Coming!" she hollered, huffing, and groping to find her shoes and slip them on, before darting downstairs. Wondering why there was no barking, she wiped sleep from her eyes, then, flustered, she fiddled to unlock the door.

"Madame Toussaint?" It was a heavy brogue, Highland accent, from a man unknown to her.

"Yes?"

"My name is Mr Docherty. Mr Lennox Docherty. I think we need tae have a wee chat." He pushed her aside and went in. "Nice gaff ye've got here, Mrs T. I had a stroll around the stables; very impressive I must say."

Françoise lost her footing and felt sick. He did nothing to support her. Still no barks. She feared the worst. "Please. My dog. I need to—"

"Ye need to do nothing except listen tae me."

"No. Please. Mon chien. I must check on him. Please."

Docherty pulled a pot from his pocket, and shoved it into Françoise's face, so she could read the label. Squinting, she stuttered out, "*Melatonin.*" She paused. "You have drugged him? You have drugged my dog. How? Why? Where is he? How did you get in? This is madness."

"Your wee doggie is all cosy in his kitchen basket. He'll sleep for some time and be groggy for a day. It could hae been worse. Now, listen tae me."

"Not until I see him."

With exaggerated exasperation, Docherty strode to the kitchen door, opened it and with his arm across the entrance so she could not go in, he let her peer at the deep-sleeping dog. "There. See him?" He shut the door and kept his back to it.

"Elspeth. Elspeth. Have you drugged Elspeth too?" Françoise turned suddenly and darted upstairs, calling Elspeth's name.

He followed. "Have yae lost someone, Mrs T?" he said, from the bedroom doorway.

On Elspeth's bed was a note. He snapped it up and read it aloud. "Staying in Cambridge for a couple o' days. Good luck with race day. Give Sweet Pierre a pat from me."

"I-I... I need to be near mon chien. My dog."

*

"Race day," said Docherty. "Now there's a coincidence. I need tae talk tae ye about that."

"Sweet Pierre," said Françoise, looking dazed. That pleased him.

He let her walk back downstairs and she stood by a chair, twisting her handkerchief in her hands.

Good. She's feeling nervous. Good. "Now, what I am about tae tell ye will determine whether the status quo remains or…" he laughed in her face, "I will explain option two later. And please, dinnae deny anything. Your buddy McQueen and his painted jezebel did me a disservice a while back. By my nature I'm not a forgiving man. However, by the grace of the Almighty, I find myself here, knowing that in little more than twenty-four hours I'll be basking in the afterglow of sweet revenge. I know this cuddy of yours has blistering speed but unfortunately, he will nae be winning tomorrow."

"What do you mean? Who? He?"

"Be quiet, woman! I havnae finished. You see, I also own a nice swift colt who is running in the same race. Perhaps nae as nifty as your fellow, but it matters not, as yours will nae be winning, because ye're going to tell your jockey to take a pull, are ye not? That way mine wins and I scoop the prize money, quite a pretty penny, in addition tae the winning bets my lackeys will be placing at the racecourse tomorrow. And McQueen? Ha! McQueen has tae suffer his loss of what, twenty-five grand? Perhaps more? And of course, your investment." He cracked his knuckles. "Happy days. Non?" He leaned in towards her. She could smell his whisky breath. "Your jockey must, on no account, overtake or hinder my horse. Last place in a race is the only place McQueen's horse deserves tae be for what he did tae me, hen. His horse must nae pass the post before mine at any cost." He spat on the carpet as if sealing the deal.

Françoise felt for the edge of the table and held it as she lowered herself into her chair. He was making her job impossible. How could her jockey do this if he didn't know which horse he owned? His expression told her that he was enjoying her weakness and the sound of her quivering voice. She must pull herself together. She'd managed it with Roche; she could manage it with this brute.

"How do you know all of this? What is your grievance with McQueen?"

He gave her a close-lipped smile. "I am a well-connected man, Mrs T. Over the years, many have regretted underestimating my potency. I'd hate for your name tae be added to that list. Now, while you mull it over, may I have a mug of tea, please? Two sugars." He laughed. "Make one for yerself. You look like you need it. Oh. And try not tae wake yer wee dog while ye're in the kitchen." He stood in the doorway, watching her every move.

*

What has come over me? Françoise thought, her heart pounding with dread and anger. *I must not let this oaf control me. I must pull myself together. But I must stay safe and keep everyone else safe. What to do? Oh, what to do?* Never mind the money McQueen could lose, or her reputation being shattered; what most troubled her was how to keep Le Manx Gang happy and Docherty too, if she didn't know the name of his horse? *Merde!*

She spat in his tea and stirred it, knowing she had little alternative but to face the unbearable truth: she must agree to his demands and face the ramifications later. Through the open door she spied the thick-set, mutton-chopped, malevolent-eyed barbarian. He was now snooping round her room, treading mud wherever he walked. *It will be all up the stairs! Non, non, non!* He was touching her trinkets. This cold-blooded savage had probably committed acts of brutality beyond her worst nightmares, but this was like rape and pillage. *Deux sucre? Beaucoup de merde! Je prefere l'arsenic, but I have none.*

She checked on Sweet Pierre. He was in a deep, but not dangerous sleep. There was little time to work out a way to get out of this impasse. Right now, all she could do was spit in Docherty's drink again and give it another stir. That done, she returned to the drawing room and handed it over, feeling a little bolder, and determined not to seem intimidated.

She gathered her shattered wits and said, "It appears that I have little choice in the matter, Mr Docherty. I will instruct my jockey. I just hope the authorities do not get a sniff of wrongdoings. If they do, I will be banned for life."

"Well, I for one will nae be losing any sleep over your predicament," he said, lifting his little finger as he sipped the tea.

"Out of interest, what is your horse called?"

"Nice try, hen. You give that vermin the name, and he places bets on mine, nae his? Treat me like a dunderhead again, and ye'll make the acquaintance of the Barlinnie Drumstick. Ye'll find it's impossible tae ride with two shattered ankles, and your little doggie will nae wake up. And a word to the wise, if I smell a rat between now and race time, what happened tae ye in France will seem like a teddy bears' picnic this time around, so dinnae try any of your parlour tricks around here. Savvy?"

Docherty stood up as if preparing to leave, but her hope was dashed. "Give tae me yer mobile an' charger. You dinnae want to fall into temptation, do ye?" She scrabbled to get it from a drawer, alert to his movements as he walked across the room, unplugged the landline phone, and waved it at her. "This is a keeper too." He knelt down to check the wiring. "I can see it's yer only one. Lucky for ye or we'd be upstairs again together, because now I've had some tea, I feel more active."

Oh God, please no, she thought.

He held out his hand and, though it sickened her, she handed over the goods. "Ye'll get them back after the race. Promise."

She said nothing, mindful of Docherty's forbidding stare.

A tap on the front door filled the silence as he spun round and rushed to open it.

"Sorry. Didn't realise you had company, Françoise," said Noel, voice muffled, and barely recognisable: he'd pulled up the collar of his roll-neck jumper. It was his trilby that gave him away. He was peering over and around Docherty to get a glimpse of Françoise. Alas, he did not seem to have his hunting rifle.

"Just wanted five minutes. I could nip back later if you're not too busy. Big day for you tomorrow. It's all thumbs up, is it, here?" He raised both thumbs. "It's all thumbs up."

She got the message. Place a bet on his horse if he gave her the thumbs up sign. That was their code. Right. What chance was there for that? His horse was the last thing on her mind. "Yes, Noel. Thumbs up. No need to come back. And do not phone. I will be going straight back to bed once this gentleman has gone. Sweet Pierre is asleep already."

Docherty's right hand clenched into a fist and she expected the worst as the Scottish monster stooped to speak in Noel's face. "That's okay, toerag. Me 'n' my thumb," he said, putting his thumb on the end of his nose and waggling his fingers like a petulant child, "we're just up and leaving. So are ye. Bye-bye." He shepherded Noel away, and he was gone.

"I'll be watching out for ye the morrow, Mrs T. Hae a guid day," Docherty said, patting her phones as if they were sleeping babies. And then he was gone too, into the gloaming.

She wanted to call after Noel, get him back and tell all, but terror overtook her, and the tears started rolling. She couldn't risk his safety as well as her own or the safety of their animals. Washed up, bleary-eyed, her brain a scrambled kaleidoscope of contradictions, she was petrified of the cancerous méchant that had been in her house. She checked all the doors and put chairs against them, knowing she needed to organise her brain and leap straight into action if she was to find a loophole in this labyrinth and a way out.

As she put her hand on the boot-cupboard door to fetch her paddock footwear, she heard a rustle at the back window. Not the familiar scratching branch but something different. Who was there? Docherty? Roche? Truly haggard with the strain of suspense, she looked out. Noel. It was Noel.

"*You all right?*" he mouthed through the closed window.

She could run to him. Leave all her troubles behind and flee. She could. She knew that she should. But did she run? No. Incriminating this dear man was not the way. She wrestled with the window latch, pretending it was stuck, then smiled and nodded to Noel that she was fine, raising her thumbs. Determined to avoid talking face-to-face, she resorted to miming an oaf driving away, desperate to assure him Docherty had gone. To finish off, she yawned, closed her hands as if about to pray and rested her head on them sideways, to show she was in need of immediate sleep. Marcel Marceau would have been impressed. Noel looked relieved, raised his hat to her and waved goodbye.

It was almost ten thirty by the time she returned from the stables. She checked on Sweet Pierre, checked the house for intruders, blocked the door again, and switched on her computer. If nothing else, she at least had this. There was no point in emailing McQueen: he was not an email person, damn him. He did his dealings by phone, text, or face-to-face, from what she could make out. And Gabby? She had to use her sister's computer, so she never bothered with email. Even if either of them had it, after Docherty's threats, she was too scared to get in touch. She must do this alone.

She logged onto the *Racing Post's* Friday declarations page. Including Herd Ringer, there were twenty-two runners for the last race. The next few hours were pivotal; unless she found the name of Docherty's horse, the whole hustle would become a house built on sand; everything would be lost and she feared she'd have Docherty back with demands and threats if she didn't obey him – she had no doubt about that – and repercussions from Le Manx Gang if Herd Ringer wasn't placed. She stared at the list of runners, desperate for inspiration, and poured herself a stiff drink. She would stay up all night if she had to, vowing not to sleep until she'd worked it out, then, early morning, she'd be needing a critical discourse with her jockey. But what if she couldn't unravel the Docherty trail? She tried to bury her fear that she'd have to watch Herd Ringer forced into coming in last on his first race with her, but if you bury a fear, you bury that fear alive. Would she find peace?

TWENTY-TWO

Considering tomorrow's importance, McQueen had spent the day feeling oddly at ease. His checklist had tripled, but he'd got through most of it, including all the calls he needed, except the evening call to Françoise: her mobile kept going to voicemail. She was probably in the stables out of range and hadn't taken it with her. He'd left messages, certain she'd pick them up.

He checked the odds for the race. It was too early for them to be posted online, but the *Racing Post* estimated 33 to 1. Over the past two weeks he'd placed numerous bets with his newly opened internet accounts: win bets on the no-hopers; exotic multiple wagers on the likes of *Round Robin*, *Lucky 63*, *Union Jacks*, *Permed Yankees* and *Goliaths*. That should flag him up as an archetypal hapless punter. Even though his flat was filled with all the IT clutter for tomorrow, it was good to be there, amusing himself by imagining how different the bookies would be feeling in a few hours. He set his clock alarm for five in the morning, switched the phone off, and hit the sack, wrestling with optimistic hope and logical anxiety. Roll on Operation Golden Fleece.

*

Back at his Newmarket hotel, Lennox Docherty raided the mini-bar. Today had gone as planned with Françoise. He'd revelled in her discomfort, but the best was yet to come. As he cracked open another Johnnie Walker miniature her phone vibrated in his pocket. He pulled it out. Someone was leaving a message: *Hi! It's Mac. Just making sure all's fine with our winner. Speak in the morning. Cheers.*

So that's what you sound like, you scumbag, he thought, throwing her phone on the bed. *There is only going to be one winner in tomorrow's Lucky Last, and it's nae going to be owned by some vulgar barrow boy and his trollop.*

*

Likely Di lay in bed waiting for sleep to take her. Tomorrow was a big day. She ran through it in her mind, but her thoughts were stolen as they often were when she was overtired. Sometimes she longed to be told that she had an incurable disease. At certain times of year – anniversaries of key losses in her life – she couldn't shake the idea off. Nothing too painful or drawn out. A form of depression, it was. The Black Dog, Churchill had called it. Did he long for death too? Heaven knows, she'd been trying to smoke herself into oblivion for years, and breakfast for her was not as he'd said, 'a cough and a cigar', but a cough and a ciggie. She often imagined seeing a doctor, and being sent off for the usual blood tests and scans and the way she'd be told coldly and professionally that she had a rare disease. She always called it a made-up name. Martin Scopple Syndrome, or something similar: a disease that meant she wouldn't make another birthday and she'd soon be free to join all those she'd lost. She thought of the way the doctor would say goodbye to her for the last time. And the way she'd had to say goodbye to those she'd loved, especially her special one. The special one who had left her with no one to love or to be loved by; no shoulder to cry on; no hands to hold on the couch; no one with whom she could reminisce about the golden past. Such things were now a distant dream. Most of her time these days was taken up with market stall filler shifts, scrimping, saving and crossing off lists. At least Mac's horse race challenge had given her focus and rekindled their friendship. *Come on, girl,* she thought. *Tomorrow's a big day for you and Mac. Just think about that Mediterranean cruise you'll be going on soon, in first class it'll be. Never know who you might meet at the captain's table.* She reached over to switch off the bedside lamp; the alarm clock ticked over, tomorrow had just become today.

*

Ten miles away from Likely Di's Old Kent Road flat, restless Gabby prepared for sleep in Hammersmith. She climbed back into bed after visiting the bathroom for the third time that evening. She knew it was just nerves, but she'd never felt so on edge. All was still, apart from her sister wheezing in the bedroom next door. Gabby felt the sudden urge to creep in and fall asleep, hugging her, like they used to as children. She stared at the ceiling. Had she forced McQueen into this? He'd been fretting for months; now it was her turn to do a shift. If there was just one slip along the way tomorrow, all his hard work would have been in vain. It must go well.

It was late and she was getting frustrated, but her anxiety had been replaced by something far worse: the annoying irrelevant earworm that was Britney Spears's 'Don't Let Me Be the Last to Know'. She kissed the pillow where McQueen's face had never been, pulled the duvet over her and tried to sleep by making an A-Z list of pop songs in her head, about horses.

A = 'A Horse with No Name', America.
B = 'Ballad of a Runaway Horse', EmmyLou Harris.
C = 'Crazy Horses', The Osmonds
D = '

She finally dozed off thinking of one for D.

Race day

Was it time to get up already? McQueen doubled-checked his watch, then hit the alarm button on his radio, relieved when things went quiet. It would be too easy to have a ten-minute snooze. No chance, because his phone alarm, which he regretted setting to a loud horse's whinny, went off and he had to get out of bed to stop it. He turned on his phone and checked for messages. One text from an unknown number.

Sorry change of plan. put it all on Lorraine and Nancy instead. TRUST ME. F.

He was thunderstruck. He phoned Françoise. *Dammit.* He still couldn't get through. Her mobile was dead. The landline was off too. His head felt like it was in a tightening vice; that was the last thing he needed. Fumbling in his bedside drawer for his pack of Migraleve, he knocked a water glass over. He mopped it up with yesterday's socks, cursing, then dragged himself to the kitchen to take two tablets. As he sat waiting for their magic to work and the kettle to boil, he tried the mystery phone number. It was dead. What the hell was going on? Had something happened to Françoise? Or to Herd Ringer? He switched on the television: no major disasters in Newmarket overnight. He sat down to gather his thoughts, heart fit to burst, and mind hurtling through the possible permutations. He checked the race odds page. Herd Ringer's odds had plummeted overnight from 33 to 1 down to 14 to 1; Lorraine and Nancy's was at 40 to 1. Was he being set up? If so, by whom? Had that text really come from Françoise, or could it be from an associate pulling a double bluff?

McQueen had decisions and calls to make.

First, he'd talk it over with Gabby.

Relieved she was up early, he set out the dilemma and gave her the anonymous number. She was shocked, but practical. It wasn't one she had in her contacts list. She told him adamantly that she didn't think anyone in Team McQueen would have blabbed the name of his horse and offered plausible explanations for the phone mystery.

"Someone's given her a winner's tip. She'll have been desperate to tell you, I'll bet."

McQueen didn't think the betting quip was funny and asked why all her phones were out.

"Maybe she knocked a cable in the house, doing le yoga or some such, and you know how crap the mobile signal is in Newmarket. Or maybe she simply left hers in the house? She'll have borrowed a stable hand's phone, and I bet it ran out of battery."

Gabby's reasoning momentarily quelled his foreboding, and he sipped his tea, relaxing more when she pointed out his three obvious choices:

a. Abort the whole thing.
b. Stick to the original plan and put all the money on Herd Ringer.
c. Do what Françoise said, who she believed the text was genuinely from, and put the lot on Lorraine and Nancy.

She summed things up by saying, "Work the problem, Mac, that's what you preach, all the time. It's time to put it into practice!"

He could hear her fidgeting, probably trying to open Tintin with one hand while she held the phone. "There's always an angle, Gabby. Always an angle."

Her intolerant sigh told him she was adding her last words: "Well, do what you wanna do and let us regional leaders know, pronto. Time is running out."

He took two minutes ten seconds to make up his mind, then called her back.

"Okay, love," she said. "Speak in a couple of hours."

Love? That was a first! The day had begun in earnest.

*

Despite her exceptionally late night, Françoise still rose early. Before breakfast, she crossed the crispy, dew-speckled lawn to check her horses. A sense of foreboding enveloped her as she neared the horse-box, but Herd Ringer was inside and content, in readiness for their departure to Newmarket Racecourse later that afternoon.

Worrying about Le Manx Gang, and about Lennox Docherty too, was bad enough, but not knowing whether McQueen had received her text, or acted on it, put her even more on edge; she could not relax. If he had received it, did he believe it? Or were they both about to lose their significant wedge on an animal that Docherty had already made sure was not going to win? And what did that mean for Mr Roche? She leaned her head on Herd Ringer's. "I have taken on too much, boy. I am sorry. It is horses like you I love, not all this underworld. Mon pauvre cheval."

Back indoors, she checked the odds; Le Manx had waded in at the long odds. *Merde!*

*

Gabby was pleased to get another call from McQueen before she set off to meet the London team outside Upton Park Tube station. He told her that he'd already phoned Phil and Binky in the North and Blaggit in the Midlands, and they were up for whatever the day threw at them and assured him things would be well.

When she met up with her lot – Likely Di, and Al and Dubs, they huddled together, all ears and excitement, tinged with uneasiness as they counted down the minutes to nine o'clock. While they waited, Likely Di reminded them to meet McQueen in The Oxford Arms pub, Camden, at four, to watch the race. On the dot of nine she shot off like a rocket. Gabby and the dexterous Dennett boys gave her an 'okay-roger-that' sign and sped away to place bets in their first shop.

*

Between peering at his watch and scratching his stubble, McQueen sat, perspiring and uptight, viewing the betting odds screens and his bookmaker's pages. The betting shops would be up and running in no less than ten minutes. In need of fresh morning air, he opened a window that overlooked the park. Leaning on the windowsill, he stuck his head out to fill his lungs, cool off and calm himself. It didn't help because when he looked out, a lone magpie strutted across the grass. A shudder ran through him. He thought them arrogant birds, but that didn't stop him being superstitious. He saluted it, straining his neck to catch sight of a mate to ward off a harbinger of ill fortune. The bird beady-eyed him, dispatched a raspy chatter and flew off. Not good.

It was the end of the lull, and a storm was coming.

He'd briefed the team leaders to call once an hour, at staggered intervals, from ten onwards.

Team McQueen race day call – instructions to leaders:
Midlands: Blaggit. Briefed. Check
North: Phil and Binky. Briefed. Check.
London: Likely Di and Gabby. Briefed. Check.

What if the first incoming call was Gabby saying, "*The game's up, Mac. They've blown the whistle on it and they're rejecting our bets.*" He went back to his screens; the odds hadn't changed.

Blaggit was the first to ring. "Piece of piss this, mate. Even Tonker can't balls this one up! It's getting the babby a frock and pinny."

"Don't be too cocksure, kid. Just get on as much as you can, as quickly as you can."

"Sure thing, boss."

Next, Phil reported that all was on course, and that although Wacker and Woollyback had arrived resembling a shite-hawk's breakfast after last night's session, one sneaky line of the Bolivian marching powder had got them quickly into their stride, and all was good. And Woollyback was in trainers.

Gabby was the last to make contact. "Going first rate, Mac.

No hiccups. Likely Di's been cracking the whip, and we are a little ahead of schedule, and her Tweedledum, Al, and Tweedledee, Dubs, are grease lightning!"

So far so good, Mr Magpie. Pica pica winner, he thought, hoping he had.

*

Docherty returned from a hearty full English breakfast, peeved that his favourite morning dish of Arbroath smokies wasn't on the menu but smug that he'd brought the young waitress close to tears when he bollocked her about the omission. He shaved, showered and donned his suit ready for the day's hocus-pocus. His plan was to arrive at Newmarket Racecourse early, secure a prominent table in the Owners and Trainers Bar, and use this as his base for the duration of the meeting. His bogeymen would join him when they arrived from Edinburgh. He checked teletext for the odds. It looked like the French tart had been true to her word; she'd not contacted the maggot, and the odds had already contracted on the Cockney's nag – a sure sign that McQueen was rapidly parting with his never-to-be-seen-again cash. He checked his own horse; it hovered around the 40 to 1 mark. *Yes.* All was as he hoped. Cracking his knuckles, he headed down to reception to check out, keen to get on with the day's misdemeanours.

*

The next round of calls kept McQueen's frayed nerves calm. Everyone continued to report successful placings, and the Londoners were about to set off for their own target areas. This meant Gabby would be on the Underground and out of touch. He made himself a drink and checked the odds again. Lorraine and Nancy's had shortened to 16 to 1 with one bookie. Herd Ringer's was down to 12 to 1 across the board. It was almost time to shoehorn his betting boots.

TWENTY-THREE

Tayla opened her Paddy Power shop, as usual. In the first hour the regular gaggle of flotsam and jetsam trickled in, either to collect any winnings – usually a pittance, or to place a moon-shot small-stake punt, before returning home to daydream in front of a three-bar fire, about what they would treat themselves to with the winnings. It was the same shit routine every day, but as her father continuously reminded her, it paid the bills. This morning had something different. A pleasant, middle-aged, softly spoken woman came in. A new customer. Tayla first noticed her because of the exquisite fragrance. "Excuse me," she said. "I adore that smell. What is it please?"

"Gucci Bloom. I sell it on my market stall at the weekend. Come down and I'll give you a discount."

"Oh, thanks." Thrilled, and hoping for some meaningful company, Tayla offered her a coffee, but the woman declined, saying she was already running late for her hairdo as she placed her betting slips on Tayla's counter. Tayla rung up the football bet, then paused to check the horse wager. She sensed the customer was watching her every move and wondered if she'd ever stop talking.

"I always have a bet on this day," she said. "For my husband, Bernard, may he rest in peace. Last year I won over two hundred pounds. Can't remember what I put it on – the old brain's not what it was like. I just stick a pin in. He'd laugh at that. Wish me luck, dear."

She must be lonely, bless her, thought Tayla, smiling to show she was listening while she exchanged money for slips. Once done, the woman left, leaving her exotic air.

A while later head office phoned. The high street office was two down, and as her shop was fully staffed, she was needed over there now. Tayla set off. She'd worked with Troy, the manager, before; they had a good rapport.

He greeted Tayla with a hot coffee. "Been busy this morning?" she enquired, even though the shop was quiet.

"Nope, just the usual riff-raff. Oh, and one chatty woman placed a fair bet. Something to do with her husband, I think she said. I was glad to get rid of her. She made the place stink like a brothel."

Tayla picked up the processed bets and thumbed through them. Halfway in she spied it – the same handwriting, the same race, the same amount, the same horse. Excited, she phoned the Barking Road branch and the cashier confirmed she'd also taken the same bet, but from a man, who wasn't a regular. Putting down the receiver Tayla bellowed, "Troo-oooy! You need to call head office, *now!*"

*

She'd opted to wear less than flattering attire – baggy tracksuit, trainers, and no slap – but even like this, Gabby was surprised by the amount of attention she was receiving. It came mostly from older punters who couldn't take her placing bets in a bookies seriously. In the first one someone said, "Don't tell me. You're in here to nick the tiny biros for your doll's house, aren't you, darlin'?" It gave her an idea.

In another, someone was more personal. "Cor! Last time we had a looker like her in here, it was Red Rum's third Grand National win, in... what? 1977, eh, Colin? Good luck to you, darlin'!" If she'd been nearer to him, she reckoned he would have tapped her arse. Just for today she'd have put up with it. She even made a plan to do one of her leggers if she needed to, to keep herself from reacting violently.

Other comments coming her way were outright objectionable, some sexually offensive, but she gritted her teeth and tolerated them as she was on a mission, a mission for McQueen, and she knew that answering back would have blighted things. Having a mission didn't stop her despairing at the way some men acted as if they'd never seen a woman in a betting shop before. Halfway through her allotted route it struck her that maybe some hadn't. She even felt sorry for them and their limited lives, stuck in a bookies, hoping for a win. Who was she kidding? She was hoping for a win too! Maybe they and she weren't that different. What a thought. Suddenly she hankered to expand her horizons.

For now, all she could do was block off the unpleasant remarks and concentrate on the day. She couldn't let McQueen down: he meant too much to her. She thought about this as she sat on the Tube train to get to her next patch, and how their chance meeting, all those years ago in Marks & Spencer, had mushroomed into this well-planned day. She wondered if she'd had mushrooms in her swag bag on that day, and smiled at the idea, dreamily mesmerised by the rhythm of the train.

Underground, she was out of contact; she didn't like being out of contact with McQueen, those lonely 'Docherty years without him', as she called them, had proved that. How was McQueen coping alone today? How was the betting going? Her mind wandered. What did he think of her? Did he fancy her? Probably not. Not his type, he'd say! Questions, bloody questions! Answers, bloody answers!

Another station, another exchange of passengers. The new

man next to her stank of cheap aftershave. She smiled, thinking of the one McQueen had worn since 1990: Eternity for Men by Calvin Klein. He still smelt the same. She liked it. She liked him. *Eternity for Mac,* she thought. *Eternity for Mac and me. Stop it, Gabby.* She couldn't. What direction would their lives have taken if they hadn't met? Mac was destined to lead the long con. She was destined to be… well, a petty thief at best. She shook her head as if to oust gloom-ridden thoughts of life without McQueen.

Time to stand up. She weaved her way round awkwardly placed bags, and stepped over passenger feet to reach the door and get through before it slid shut. Whatever the outcome of today, she hoped there would be a happy ending, one way or another.

*

Al leaned against the lamp-post as Dubs jogged over from yet another bookies.

"You okay, mate?"

"Back's playing up a bit with all this pounding the street." Al rolled his shoulders in circles, left, then right, then both together. He lifted his chin to stretch his neck. "You drummers have it easy, sitting down for a gig."

Dubs laughed the way all drummers learn to do when they get that quip. "You wanna try Pilates for that bad back, Al. I read in *The Sun* that bass guitarists swear by it."

"Yeah? I'd do more than swear by it, if I had to ponce around in a leotard. I'd strangle someone with my bleedin' G-string."

Dubs laughed again, wary of his brother's darkening mood and keen to keep him cheery and on task. They were so close to their finish line. "You'd be on page three, bro! It might get some publicity for the band!"

Al didn't seem amused. "And I'm spitting feathers," he said. "Look, the last couple of shops are miles away from here, and we're ahead of schedule, but Mac doesn't know that. Let's knock things on the head for today and get some fodder and a nice cup of builder's. We'll tell him we ran out of time."

Dubs nodded in agreement, even though it disappointed him to be letting Likely Di down. It was always best to go along with what Al wanted. Older brother's rule. It had been that way all through their childhood; it was that way in the band; it was that way in the ruthless underworld they made their living from. "Yeah. All right, Al."

Fifteen minutes later they were tucking into an all-day breakfast with extra bubble and black pudding, sipping steaming mugs of sugary tea. It energised Al, and that was a relief to Dubs.

"You know what, Dubs? I wonder how much McQueen will pay us for today's runaround."

"Monkey? Grand tops, I'll bet."

"Likely Di will be getting five times that, just for getting us involved! She thinks we're the dog's."

"That's because we are!"

"Yeah. We are. And the more I think about it, the more I feel we're getting done up like a kipper." His resentment rose as he spoke. Dubs braced himself. "Bertie big bollocks and his bimbo get all the cream. We should be higher up the food chain, not just shitty sweat crossbreeds."

Dubs shrugged. He was interested. Who in their position wouldn't be? But his brother often had hare-brained schemes for being top dog on the streets, so he wanted to play it cool. "Anything in mind?" he said.

"It's just, you know, as I've said before, us playing bass guitar and drums in a Who tribute band doesn't qualify you or me to be the top 'Pinball Wizard'."

"I'm serious, Dubs." Al added more sugar to his tea and stirred it vigorously. "And we don't have enough gigs to survive on that. The Salisbury does us proud, but it's not enough. And who knows when that Mo and his Simon might pull the plug?"

"So, how the hell are you planning to take over? Go on then.

Tell me. I'm listening." It was always best to know what Al was mulling over.

"I know Tony the Turk of Pimlico is raking it in on the coke supply chain."

Dubs shook his head. "Coke supply chain? Sounds bad. And we'd need muscle and money to cut in there, bro."

"Yes, I know." Al sounded impatient.

They stopped to eat, and Al ordered more tea. Dubs could tell his brother wouldn't be letting this go. He was right.

Al pushed away his empty plate. "And maybe, just maybe there could be a favour I can call in," he said.

"Yeah? You've never mentioned that before. Tell me more."

"I did this geezer, by chance, a service a while back on a lookout job. I think you were away with some bird in Tenerife at the time. Anyway, after it was all done and dusted, he bowled over and gave me a hundred quid and his calling card, and he says if I was ever in his manor and needed anything, I was to bell him. I think that's what he said: broad accent he had but seemed nice. Never really thought about him again. Wait. I've got it with me, I think." He fumbled to pull a dog-eared card from his wallet and paused to read it. "Yeah. This is it."

Dubs took the card. After some scrutiny and thought he looked back at Al. "Never heard of him or his manor."

"Me neither," said Al. "But when this is all over, I think I will call him."

"Really?"

"Really. He had a business card. That's got to be good! The likes of McQueen and his lot have had their salad days, Dubs. It's time for new faces on the block. We'll keep cool in the pub, bro, but know this: we'll be taking our pittance for the last time. I tell ya, we'll be moving into our glory days."

TWENTY-FOUR

As ever, April showers were replaced by blooming flowers for Newmarket's first meeting of the season. The virgin green grass spread out like acres of magnificent, crushed velvet. The growing crowd buzzed and fussed in anticipation of an exciting afternoon.

Newmarket Races: first meeting of the season

All the players were there: the form students looking for the next flying machine; the pin stickers with their 'Gotta back *Stanley's Delight* in the third race – my first ever boyfriend was named Stanley, God bless him'; or 'Green is my favourite colour. I always back a horse if the jockey is wearing it'; and 'Ooohh, that horse looks frisky. Never back a frisky runner'.

There were plenty of old-timers out for the day too – those who had seen it all. Even though their losses might have amounted to many thousands over the years, they were back on track for more action. Onsite food and drink vendors were already doing steady business with their enticing smells of burgers and beers, chips and Chardonnay, cockles and mussels wafting across the course. The old-timers watched as one of the last remaining tic-tac men stretched and put on his brilliant white gloves. He rolled his shoulders, and flexed his fingers, and made ready. How times were changing.

*

McQueen frantically punched numbers on his keyboards as another one slashed the odds. It was a race against time to get the bets on before they caved in. They were flicking to blue on the screen, and prices were shortening across the board, with the layers taking evasive action to cover themselves.

He managed to get all his loot on at various prices and finally his account balances read zero. The bookmakers had cottoned on earlier than he'd expected and now the cat wasn't just well and truly out of the bag – it was chasing a mouse around the garden. He was still upbeat, confident that his field agents had lightened their bags early and availed themselves to bigger odds.

The next communications confirmed his speculations. Blaggit said they were only being offered a maximum of a tenner at the starting price, and some knocked them back completely. In Liverpool someone had got suspicious and called the bizzies, and in London Gabby's lot had the same problem, so McQueen instructed them to get on as much as they could then bail out. No need to rip the arse out of it. The humans had done their bit, and it was now down to the equines to fulfil their part of the bargain.

*

Having crossed the mainland from Liverpool after placing their final bets, Phil, Binky, Woollyback and Wacker sat in the New Dock Hotel in Birkenhead, known to locals as the 'Blood Tub'. The four of them attracted disturbing, unfriendly glares from dust-covered local labourers who looked like they'd already pissed away half their week's wages. Across from them were a dozen or so unsavoury types. Phil recognised the signs: they were itching for a tear-up, so he'd doubled on the bar order and they sat with two pints apiece to stay put in their seats and keep clear of trouble.

"This is your friendly local then, Phil?" joked Woollyback, sniffing.

Phil suspected he'd succumbed to a snort of his beloved wizz on route to the pub, Wacker too, most likely. He let it pass without comment, relieved that at least they'd kept their promise to him and Binky and got the job of the day done clean. "No, Woollyback. Never been here before, mate, and unlikely to return in a hurry. No, my local's The Stork, but you can't watch the races in there. You'll find a much better class of villain though! It doesn't open till five thirty on a Friday, so maybe we can head down there after the race."

"Yer. Sounds good," said Binky.

It was no surprise to Phil when two pockmarked heavies bowled over and challenged them.

"So, you plazzy Scousers, or what?"

Wacker stood up and faced them. "Yer. What's it to you, mate?" Phil's heart sank. He hadn't wanted to be right about Wacker, but it seemed he was. This wasn't how he planned for the day to end.

The men closed in.

Phil pulled Wacker back into his seat. "Yes, mate," he said

calmly, looking right into the eyes of the leader and smiling meekly, as might a submissive animal. He hoped he'd see it that way. "We are the genuine article. Got me place down the road, and the other three are from Tranmere."

He felt them staring at his cheek scar, their eyes almost boring into it, before they replied. "Ah. Yer all right then. Don't want any city rats in here." Satisfied, the heavies returned to their pints.

Wacker went to stand up to them again, but Phil held his shoulder and Binky put a warning hand on his knee. He spoke through gritted teeth. "Phil's right. Cool it, mate. This is one hard boozer. Let's just have our couple of ales and relax, okay?"

Wacker hesitated before agreeing. "Okay."

Phil looked across at Woollyback. He raised an eyebrow at him and waited.

"Okay," he said, crossing his heart. "Me too. I'll behave."

"Right. That's settled," said Phil. "Now let's talk about our epic day and anything we need to feedback to Mac." They chatted quietly, trying to keep their laughter low, comparing escapades and tensions that had escalated as the odds had shifted. As they chatted, Phil watched Woollyback and Wacker and tried to think up a satisfactory Plan B for watching the race, should they need one.

"Well. We've done what Mac wanted. Whatever the result, he can't complain about Team McQueen North," said Binky, leaning back in his chair before returning to his Guinness.

Woollyback asked a question he looked like he'd been bursting to ask since day one. "He seems a good guy that McQueen. He certainly had it all planned right well. Is he really that much of a star though, Phil?"

Phil turned to Binky. "What do youse think, Binky? Don't you think we've never worked with anybody with his gift? You two scallies should be proud to have him on your CV as an employer."

"You're right," said Binky. "Having Mac on a CV for the likes of you and Wacker is better than any bonus he could give you, if this goes well."

Woollyback looked delighted.

Phil went on. "Big X, as we used to call him, could come up with a baby elephant at the click of his fingers! The man is always three steps ahead."

"Sure you don't mean 'One Step Beyond'?" mumbled Binky.

"I do not mean that," said Phil curtly, in case the idiot started on his singing madness. It did the trick.

"Hey! Remember that time, way back, when we bet Mac that he couldn't get you, me, him and Gabby into the Royal Enclosure on Ascot's Ladies Day?"

"I do!" said Phil brightly. "Straight away Mac said, 'By hook or by crook, I'll do it'. But we had no idea how he could. And I remember feeling sort of, I'll be a monkey's uncle, if we're all there on the next Thursday afternoon."

"And did he do it?" asked Woollyback like a kid waiting to hear if Peter Rabbit had escaped from the farmer.

"Yeah," said Phil, as ever feeling proud of McQueen. "I was amazed."

"What? Proper Ascot-posh? Booted and suited, like?" said Wacker.

"Yep. Top hat and tails all dandy like. Gabby in a stunning crimson dress and peacock-feathered hat."

"And Mac's topper always at a rakish angle, the cad!"

"It looked good on him! You're just jealous, Binky, cos you've no head for hats!"

Binky laughed. "I had a blinkin' bowler, remember? There we were, mixing with the likes of Lord and Lady Foringay, and the Duke of Albany and Sir Giles Wotnot."

Woollyback and Wacker's eyes bulged with interest and enjoyment.

"And our name badges, remember, Phil?"

Phil nearly choked on a mouthful of beer. "Mac's was M Adman, Esquire."

It was Woollyback and Wacker's turn to choke on their beers as they laughed mid-mouthful.

"Gabby was Annie Wilkes."

"Who?"

"The crazy fan girl from the movie, *Misery.*"

"Ah. Not seen it, have we, Wacker? Who were you two badged up as?"

"We were Peter Perfect and Rufus Ruffcut from *Wacky Races*! You probably haven't heard of that cartoon. Anyway, as soon as the nobs went out to watch the races from the balcony we got as much of their Moët and Chandon down our necks as we could. Proper pissed we got! So, it comes to the Gold Cup Race and Gabby'd placed a tenner to win on the favourite. You tell the next bit, Phil."

"To start with, she had a cigarette holder with a roll-up wedged in the tip. What a look! And then she's hollering, in her best Covent Garden flower girl accent, something like, 'C'mon, slow coach! Move yer bloomin' arse!'." He took a break for beer, breath, and laughter, then set off again. "The gallery was stunned, but Mac, proud as punch, addressed them. 'Don't worry', he said, 'it's all the rage in Newmarket, don't you know!'."

Phil couldn't carry on for laughing so Binky took back the reins. "I think we even got an invite to the Queen's garden party the following year."

Woollyback's smile dropped, and he looked puzzled. He nudged Phil and nodded to the middle of the room. While they'd been winding down from a tough day, two of the builders had stripped to the waist. They seemed to be preparing for an arm-wrestling bout, while others placed bets on the outcome. One turned to Binky, jesting, "You're up next against the winner!"

Binky flexed his biceps and winked in response. "I can't arm-wrestle, but I can belt out a tune." He pretended to arm-wrestle with himself, while singing a chorus of 'He's Got the Whole World in His Hands'.

Phil started applauding, desperate to stop Binky getting into the verses. "Sorry about my mate here," he said. "He's Sally Army. And related to Paul McCartney. Aren't we all around here?" This could go either way. He waited for repercussions. Nothing came, but what the hell, he thought. Two pints now inside him, and laughter lifting his mood he stood up to go back to the bar. "Just one more round here," he said.

"Just one more for 'The Long and Winding Road'," said Binky. "This could be 'The Final Countdown', after all."

Phil leaned into him. "Shut it, Binks. No more singing. We could get our heads kicked in in here."

"No chance," said Woollyback, muttering to himself. "Not with your rugged Action Man scar."

Phil heard and shot him a withering look then went back to the bar, keeping an eye on the arm-wrestlers who went back to wrestling. He didn't like feeling intimidated on his own manor, but for today he'd let it pass as he was now convinced they had no hope of watching any races in this boozer today, let alone the race their horse was running in, not with the mob that were lauding over the bar today. It wasn't just the wrestlers; he'd spotted a couple of Liverpool-shirted bruisers trying to watch the match review of their next game, eyeing up Binky as if he, and he alone, was to blame for everything that distracted them. Waiting to be served, he mulled over ideas for where to go next and kept at it as he carried back a rusty tray with two lagers, one bitter and one Guinness. "Where's Wacker?" he said, divvying out the drinks. A roar went up to greet the new arm-wrestling champ. Phil, Binky and Woollyback raised a glass in the direction of the victor, and all was well.

"Yeah," said Binky. "He slunk off a bit sneaky, like."

"Gone for a piss has he, our Wacker?"

"Saw him talking to a couple of lads near the pool table," said Woollyback. "Seemed solid."

"It's just we really need to polish these off and head off to mine. It'll get rough in here soon. I don't fancy a ruckus tonight. And not just that. There's the race to catch. No chance of doing that here."

They waited for Wacker and drank in silence, or what passed for silence in a pub with an impromptu arm-wrestling contest going on.

*

Docherty settled into his chair and sipped from his champagne flute, feeling more than a little pleased with himself. He'd treated his bruisers to a round of Mick Jaggers and watched them tuck in. Not only had his heavies made it to the course in good time, but they also informed him that the contract out on the dobber, Dundee Slim, was finally sorted. Another of Docherty's rivals successfully dealt with. On top of that, he'd backed the first two winners on the card and was monitoring the form for the third. This was proving to be a good day.

From where he sat, he could see more than his lot; right now, a group of pished Essex wide boys were on the lawn, attempting to breach a hen party of underdressed and undereducated chookies, but what interested him most was the sight of Françoise heading towards the horse-boxes. He finished his drink and ambled over to her, doffing his hat as he approached. "Good afternoon, Mrs Toussaint. I trust ye're well."

"Monsieur Docherty," she replied, tersely.

"I must say I am gratified ye complied with my instructions. Truly, the last thing I would want ye tae do is witness the slaughter of yer charges and the stable's destruction. Especially any horses ye've brought here t'day."

She turned away, patting her colt as she walked. All he heard was her faint and feeble, "Thank you."

TWENTY-FIVE

McQueen arrived at The Oxford Arms pub a full hour before the others were due. He purchased a stout and located a table close to a TV where he could watch the horse racing. Most of the lunchtime clientele had returned to their offices and it was too early for the Friday POETS mob, with their craft beer, their tequila shot buffoonery, and their habit of pissing off before closing time for a Ruby Murray. He checked his watch then squiggled figures into his notebook. Whichever way he looked at it, his winnings could be twenty grand light and he predicted the ground troops would have suffered similarly. The odds on his phone showed the best price for Lorraine and Nancy was now at 7 to 2, with Herd Ringer at 6 to 1. They seemed to be the only two runners being seriously backed, apart from one other, Sixties Overtures, currently nibbled at 150 to 1.

His mind turned again to Françoise; both her phones were still unobtainable, and he prayed that no harm had come to her. His spirits lifted moments later when she appeared on the screen, being interviewed about her recent run of good form, but she seemed unsettled and lacked her customary lustre. Perhaps it was interview nerves. She didn't strike him as someone who wallowed in TV fame. Or was it something else? A feeling of culpability started to kick at him. He tried to shake it off when Team McQueen North, and straight after, Team McQueen Midlands phoned in to update him on how things were going. Once he'd collated all their information, he started to fret about Team McQueen London, until Al turned up with Dubs following behind, both looking relieved and happy to be in the pub.

"There's no place like home, eh, Dubs?" Al laughed as they handed over their slips and bags containing the last five wads of unwaged money. "Geographically impossible to place these, given the restraints. Sorry, Mac."

After a quick, "Don't worry about it, glad you're here," McQueen left them to compare betting shop experiences and headed to the bar, doing some quick mental arithmetic while he waited; the boys had performed better than he'd anticipated. Likely Di had been right about them. He returned with three pints, and a bottle of red with two glasses, ready for when the ladies turned up.

It was just before four, when Likely Di bowled in, all spruced up, her colourful, hand-embroidered designer hat akimbo, breathing heavily. "Sod me, Mac. I'm plum-tuckered out. Reckon I've done more steps than Fred Astaire and Ginger Rogers today. Got blisters on me bleedin' blisters." She passed her bag across, and he swapped it for a full glass, which she wasted no time emptying and refilling. Gabby rocked up soon after, seeming flustered, but looking elated. Likely Di poured her a large one while McQueen did more tallying up. It was four thirty by the time he was done.

"Listen up, my fellow conspirators," he said. "I was hoping to take the bookies for close on a million, however, it looks like we'll be a bit shy of that when the beast wins. Still, as my grandad used to say, 'Any profit is better than no profit'. And rest assured, what we'll end up with, if things go our way, won't be at all bad for a day's pavement pounding."

Al raised his glass and yelled, "Cheers to that!" which turned into an impromptu toast to Operation Golden Fleece.

For a while they chatted, still buzzing about the day's achievements. They were all impressed that they covered all that they had and looked chuffed about it. McQueen let them revel in it for a bit and drifted into a world of his own. In less than half an hour, it would be either sadness or euphoria, depending on whether they'd bet on the right horse.

"Allez oops, Mac!" bawled Likely Di. "Snap out of it. We're heading for showtime!"

*

It was raining in Birmingham and had been all day. Tonker Newley thought nothing could top the smell of thirty steaming rugby players leaving the pitch after eighty minutes of battle, but he was wrong. The only evidence he needed was the odour emanating from a soaked Blaggit, who sat next to him: evidence that smelt so strong it was enough to overpower an entire jury. But Blaggit was his friend, and he'd put up with whatever he had to, to keep it that way. It didn't stop him necking his first pint in one, almost gagging, and heading off to the bar for temporary respite from the whiff and a refill.

He glanced around the bar in the Old Joint Stock pub. There was no one else there but girl students digging into their club sandwiches and happy hour cocktails. They all avoided eye contact with him. Sad, but true, he thought. *These days I'm more like Tom Bruise, than Tom Cruise.*

The second beer went down easily, so he ordered two more, took a deep breath, and went back to sit with his partner for the day, who looked worn to a frazzle.

"Yow all right, bab?" he said, not waiting for Blaggit to answer. "There yow go Mr B. Another couple of these and yow'll be right as rain."

"You know what, Tonk? I ain't never going to do this again. I'm done with dashing around for wretched hours like an overstretched paperboy. I don't care how much treasure is in it. No, that's me done with this type of foot soldier lark. From now on I'll be keeping strictly to the whirlwind in-and-out short cons. I'm good at that, McQueen or no McQueen. I'm grateful to good old Mac though, for counting me in on this. It's opened my eyes again."

Tonker tried to keep his pint close to his face so he could smell beer, not Blaggit. "Remind me again, how long have yow been in this business?"

"Forever," said Blaggit. "Started off pinching apples and nearly ended up pinching the Queen Mum's handbag, but that's another story. Getting long in the tooth now. Well, mid-fifties, if you call that old. Younger, smarter faces have appeared on the scene. Online fraud, issuing bogus qualifications for a fee, and bank login scams are overtaking me. Even my online dating hoax is old hat. Nope. In a couple of years, I'm going to take my pension pot and buy that little cottage in Cornwall, and I'll write my memoirs as I promised myself."

Tonker could see Blaggit was beginning to get emotional, so he changed tack. "So, do yow think Mac's onto a winner for us, then?"

Blaggit lifted a bit of dirt from under his fingernail with the corner of a beer mat. "Well, if anyone can pull off a caper like this, Mac can. The man's a God-given natural, but nought further he can do now."

"Just wait for the race, like us."

"Yep," said Blaggit raising his glass. "Here's to you Mac, down there in London. May your horse be as true as an arrow and fly first past the post."

"To Mac," said Tonker with the reverence he felt Blaggit sought. They stopped their chat to drink more, then in a grim voice Tonker confessed, "To be honest, Blaggit, I could really do with a cash injection. I spent a fortune getting a ticket for the England game in Paris. Thought we were certainties, so I staked a bag of sand to double me money. The lousy Garlic Roosters beat us by one point with the last kick of the game. Choked I was and broke I'm heading for, so I need this little job to make up for what I lost."

Blaggit fiddled with his scrap of a ponytail. "You sound like Mac, mate, with that hint of rhyming slang. Or maybe you've picked it up from me. Shame you didn't check the bet out with Mac first. He's good with odds. I've never been into betting on the nags, or sport meself – too many stories over the years of bent races, fixed games and paid-off jockeys or players for my liking."

"Yow not wrong there. It's a gamble. Let's hope he's got the odds right today."

They laughed and drank again.

"Anyway, Tonk, how's the old leg bearing up?"

Shifting it to rest on his bag, Tonker grimaced. "Think I'll be resting for a bit after today. It's throbbing like a gout-ridden lord."

They both emptied their glasses and Blaggit fetched more. He set them down carefully then pulled bags of peanuts and pork scratchings from his pockets. "Mind yourself on these, Tonk. You don't want to end up with busted front teeth like me."

Tonker laughed and flashed his teeth. "It's all right. I've got my rugby gum shield in my bag for such delicacies! My teeth are the only bit of me that's perfect." He pointed to his squishy ear, twitched his wonky nose, and opened wide his no-hope-of-being-symmetrical-ever-again eyes. "Between us we have a perfect face. And today we've been a perfect team. Cheers to yow!"

"A few close shaves we won't mention to Mac, eh? What he doesn't know won't hurt him, and all the money went on, just like he wanted," said Blaggit, already half a pint in. He twiddled his gold pinkie ring and stared at the diamond. "So, what you going to do with your winnings if the horse comes up trumps?"

"Been thinking about that while yow were at the bar. Not bet on another rugby game, that's for sure." He laughed, cheered by Blaggit's optimism. "I've only got me cock to keep, so I was thinking about joining that Open University thing, yow know, better meself: get a degree in art or sommink. Make me daughter real proud it would." He blinked to shift a tear.

Blaggit slapped his back. "Don't get maudlin, mate, that's the job of old-timers like me! I can just picture it, Tonk – you fooling them with your arty-farty stuff, and pooling resources with Mac to purloin the *Mona Lisa!*"

"No, Blaggit. I could never stoop so low as to get into stealing a lady's smile."

They both rocked with laughter that was loud, deep and long, while the other patrons looked on uneasily.

"Nearly race time, Tonks," said Blaggit, turning his bloodshot eyes to watch the big screen.

Tonker stretched his leg then went to the bar for more beer. He returned with two each just as the last horse was being led into the stalls. In approximately seventy-three seconds the race would be done and even the seasoned boozy duo would struggle to down both pints by then.

*

Eventually Wacker came out of the Birkenhead toilet. He stood, seeming mesmerised by the arm-wrestling crew. Woollyback and Binky beckoned him over. Phil sighed impatiently. "You took your time, Wacker," he said.

"Okay, lads. My shout," said Wacker, upbeat and bright. "What we having?"

"No, mate," said Binky. "We're off to Phil's now. There's one 'ere for ya. Drink up." He passed it to Wacker who set about downing it between gulps of air.

"Too much atmosphere in here for us to stay, so it's Plan B," said Phil. He strode to the door, tutting as he waited, nodding at Binky to hurry Woollyback along and last of all, a disorientated Wacker, to join him there.

A twenty-minute walk brought them to a smarter part of

Birkenhead. Binky had been singing a famous Proclaimer's walking song most of the way, which Phil was glad of because it helped keep up the pace. Finally, they arrived at his house. It was one he'd recently bought for fifteen thousand at an auction and he was refurbishing it himself. Woollyback, Wacker and Binky dumped their things down in the wallpaper-stripped hall and sat on the floor of the work-in-progress living room.

"Where's your TV?" said Binky while Phil raided his own fridge.

"Sorry. No TV, guys," he said, coming back in the room and handing them each a tinny. "It's coming next week. I've a plan though. We'll phone the William Hill line and listen on my phone."

"You know what?" said Binky, opening his can. "If we do have it off today, I might ask that tidy sort behind the ramp at my local to come to see Greece with me."

"I've seen that," Wacker announced, as if proud. "Not bad."

"Not the film *Grease*, pinhead," said Woollyback, smirking. "He meant Greece the country. Anyway, the only part of *Grease* you've seen was on telly round at my house and my mum threw you out for poncing around like John Travolta in front of the screen and declaring your love for Sandy."

Wacker looked at him, hurt. "Yeah. Well. I knew what you meant. I was joking."

"Calm down. Calm down, youse two. Three," said Phil, darting his eyes to include Binky. "So, we will have to listen to the race on my phone, then we'll be out on the razz if we have a win, and the energy. And you can do what you want in Greece, Binky. Just don't sing about it here." He dialled the William Hill commentary line on his mobile.

"Come on, Wacker!" shouted Woollyback. "They're at the start."

Wacker came out of Phil's khazi, shark-eyed and sniffing. He dusted off his moustache and walked towards them. "You know, guys, I really respect you, and with hopefully a bit of my future winnings, I borrowed fifty pounds from Mac to invest in some grade-A coke. Wanna snort, anyone?"

"*No!*" shouted Phil. "The race is about to start. And never, ever take Mac's money. All right?"

In the background, the voice of a sports commentator reported: "*They're halfway through loading…*"

"Sorry," said Wacker, eyes wide and staring. "It was just like they were a clued-up gang and fifty sovs seemed a good deal, so I let them know about our good thing that can't lose in a minute."

"What?" shouted Binky and Phil together.

Phil kept at him. "You wanker! It's not a cert. You were told that when you met Mac!"

"Anyway," said Woollyback, a touch calmer than Phil or Binky, "who were you blabbing to?"

A contented smile spread over Wacker's face. "Soft-spoken man," he said. "Fitted three-piece suit and walking cane with a duck's head on top."

Phil dropped his head between his knees, knowing and dreading what was coming next.

"Charming man is Mr Scarisbrick," said Wacker.

"*…They're under starters orders. And they're off,*" belted out from Phil's phone, but he wasn't listening. Wacker had flipped his outrage switch, and he wasn't going to hold back. He was on top of the scrawny bag of bones in a flash, hands round his neck, trying to stop the air in his throat. It was Binky who dragged him off and stopped things escalating into anything more life-threatening.

"Christ, Phil. You're a stupid sod sometimes," he said, eyes on Wacker who was gasping for air.

"You wanna know who your new best buddy is? *Do you?*" sneered Phil, salivating, shaking with rage, and snarling like a cornered pit bull.

Wacker looked back with terror in his eyes and gave a nod so slight it could have been a twitch.

"Scarisbrick is one hard bastard. If our horse don't win, you have fucked us, Wacker. The only suit we'll be wearing will be a concrete one."

"Phil's just concerned for you," said Binky, gesturing for Phil to stay back and keep calm. "You don't mess with McQueen's money, Wacker. And you don't mess with me or Phil. Got that? Not if you want to stick around here and get enough work to be able to pay your rent. And not if you want to keep feeding your habit, which I think it's time you broke. What say you, Woollyback? You gonna help with that, as his friend? Cos in my experience coke-heads aren't just joke-heads: they end up broke-heads and then they're very soon dead-heads. So, be good boys and stay away from that crap, and away from dealers like Scarisbrick. You can bump into a lot of them round here, so watch yourselves."

TWENTY-SIX

The brawny Scot always had pre-race nerves. He stared, slack-jawed, at the odds on the massive screen. Lorraine and Nancy was up there as favourite at 3 to 1. Who had backed it down to this price? Not McQueen: his money was surely on his own bag of bones. The French bint had no idea which horse he owned, so it wouldn't be down to her, and he'd made sure his trainer wasn't a gambling man. That meant one of the stable lads must have leaked news of the horse's potential. There would be Glasgow malky when he unearthed who leaked it, and unearth it he would. *Still,* he thought, three *times your lowie is better than none.*

As he handed a bundle of notes to each of his underlings, he gave instructions to wage it all on his horse. He waited, absorbed in odds updates, for them to return and hand in their betting tickets. Collecting them, he savoured their elaborate individual designs while noting the bookmaker's name and number, checking his hoods had written the odds and amounts on the reverse, as he'd demanded. He dismissed them and stole away to work out the total profit projection. At the thick end, Docherty expected no less than thirty thousand and the winner's prize money on top, when Lorraine and Nancy romped home.

*

The hostelry was beginning to fill, and Team McQueen London clustered round the wide-screen TV. The booze brothers, Al and Dubs, queued at the bar for more sherbets. The table they'd temporarily abandoned was littered with bookies pens, all collected by Gabby: red from Ladbrokes; blue from Coral; green from Paddy Power. A rainbow of biros, she'd announced as she'd tipped them out of her bag. Dubs had instantly made a Jenga tower and played with Al and Likely Di until their race was due.

"What's Herd Ringer wearing?" said Gabby.

"He's number five."

"I see him. Blimey! He looks like a summer show extra! Herd-de-Hi! How did that happen?"

"Hi-de-Ho! Design the silks yourself, Mac?" said Likely Di leaning towards them, laughing.

"You can talk, with that Ascot hat you're wearing!"

"Ralph Lauren," said Likely Di, flinging it on the table like she was throwing down a gauntlet.

"Yep. I designed 'em. I love that colour combo," said McQueen, not ashamed to show how pleased he was with his design.

"Thought so. Last time I saw something like that, some mush called Joseph was decked out in it! Trifle over the top, don't you think, Gabby? All it needs is a bleedin' cherry on top!"

Their banter stopped abruptly when the commentator announced: "*They're at the start and about to go behind the stalls for this EBF Maiden Stakes for three-year-olds over the straight six furlongs. The favourite at 5 to 2 is Lorraine and Nancy in the market, followed by Herd Ringer at 5 to 1, Oakwood, and Mojo at 12 to 1, War Eagle is 16 to 1, and it's 20 to 1 bar. The first is about to be loaded, more money for the favourite now 2 to 1.*"

The butterflies McQueen felt in his belly morphed into a

colony of bats, and his heart thumped like a galley slave's hammer. Gabby entwined her fingers with his, squeezing them whenever the commentator said something exciting. They listened to the build-up as the horses settled. "*Goldcrest will be the last in. That's it. They're under starters orders. And they're off.*"

McQueen held his breath. Looking around it seemed that he wasn't the only one who had put their breathing on hold.

"*A fairly level break, with Yale and White Smoke showing good early speed, followed by Moonwalk and the hard-pulling Baltimore. Settling down now, after a couple of furlongs, Blue Note has moved his way to the front from Yale and Ashley Gardens on the outside, with both Lorraine and Nancy, and Herd Ringer being held up at the rear. At halfway, it's still Yale that leads the way, but they're queuing up behind to deliver their challenges, with Waterloo Sunset going well within itself and still no move from two fancied horses on the stand's side. Two furlongs out and passing the bushes, the field spans across track and you could throw a blanket over them all. On the far side Sixties Overtures has taken it up and quickly moves on by a length from Dancing Cloud, and the others are now on the near side. Herd Ringer is angled out for his run along with Lorraine and Nancy.*"

*

Wacker rubbed his sore neck, grateful to be breathing freely, as he listened to the phone with one eye on Phil, in case he went for him again.

"*…And with half a furlong to go, it's Sixties Overtures in the lead. But here, on the stands side, comes Lorraine and Nancy. It's going to be a close thing as Herd R—*"

Bip, Bip, Bip.

"*Shit! Shit! Shit!*" said Phil, staring, along with everyone else, at his spent mobile. He looked up at each of them in turn, crestfallen and frustrated. "Out of credit," he mumbled.

Binky reacted before anyone could get their own mobiles out

and tune in to the race. "Where's your nearest bookies, Phil?" he said. "Plan C."

"Ladbrokes, in Grange Road. Round the corner."

In a second, they were off.

Wacker felt his best mate grab him. "What's going on? Where are you taking me, Woollyback?" he said, surrendering to being dragged along the street beside him, and hearing his friend's desperate mumblings about future rehab and today's race, while they tried not to be fearful about ending up in a concrete suit.

*

McQueen knew in a split second there were horses in the race stronger than the one all his cash was on; the day was lost. But wait! Something wasn't right. Lorraine and Nancy and Herd Ringer were boxed in. The frustrated jockey manoeuvred his mount and went for a small gap next to Herd Ringer, taking some of his ground, causing a snatch-up and loss of momentum to his rival. The commentator was now in full flow.

"*Now passed the dip, a furlong out, it's Sixties Overtures two lengths clear, but here on the rails, eating up the ground, is the favourite, Lorraine and Nancy.*"

Having been quiet the entire race, Gabby, the fair lady of the gathering, jumped from her seat and used what she knew was McQueen's favourite Doolittle line. It was hers too. Starting off in a tense, but very refined voice she said loudly, "Come on! Come on, horsey!"

Then in a tense, but less refined, impatient voice she shouted, "Come on! Come on, horsey! *Come onnnn!*"

And then in her desperate, guttersnipe voice she hollered, as if her throat was being ripped out, "*Come on, horsey! Move yer bloomin' arse!*"

Remembering the very first time he'd seen her do that, McQueen wanted to laugh, wanted to cry, and couldn't bear to watch the race, all at the same time. He focused his eyes on a love heart, carved on the table, wondering who Andy and Michelle were.

"*A hundred yards to go, and it's still Sixties Overtures, but Lorraine and Nancy is closing with every stride. It's Sixties Overtures, Lorraine and Nancy, Sixties Overtures, Lorraine and Nancy.*

"*The winning line coming up. It's…*

"*Lorraine and Nancy, just by a head. Second, the game Sixties Overtures. Third, the staying on Star of Martell, and fourth, the very unlucky in running Herd Ringer. The starting prices are first, 2 to 1 favourite, second, 100 to 1, third, 25 to 1.*"

When McQueen's happy band of winners screamed, "*Yeee-eesss!*" the landlord's face burst into a smile.

"Had a little tickle, did you?" he said.

Likely Di piped up with, "You could say that!" then joined her friends as they whooped and hugged in celebration, flushed and jubilant.

McQueen discreetly extracted himself from the madness and merrymaking. He beckoned Gabby over. "Thank you, for helping me work the problem," he said. "It was down to you that I trusted the text message and switched horse."

"You're welcome, mate." For a brief moment she looked bashful, then tried to pull him towards the celebrations.

He held up his hands, refusing her. "Just a few things left to check," he said. "I'll be with you all in a bit."

"You better be, or I'll get Tonker down here all the way from Birmingham to drag you back!"

She turned to join Likely Di and left McQueen studying the replay of the race on TV and mull over what the inevitable result would mean. He smiled to himself, relieved that he had not been at the racetrack. Details. Details. He'd been attending to the details.

*

Lennox Docherty wallowed in the moment. With a proud, knowing smile, he strolled down to the winners' enclosure to greet his champion. He shook his trainer's hand and waited for the young jockey to dismount before congratulating him on a fine tactical ride. Formalities over, he went back to hand out the winning tickets for his crew to collect on. Off they dutifully went, leaving him to raise a glass to the sky. As he looked up, the jolting sound of a klaxon blasted out: *Ah-oog-ah! Ah-oog-ah!* There was instant silence, and everyone waited for an announcement.

"Steward's enquiry! Steward's enquiry! The public are reminded to retain all tickets until the official result has been announced."

Docherty's men had already joined the queues awaiting payment and he meandered across to meet them. Pumped up, he shouted to the nearest bookie, "Come on, ye tight bastards! The horse won fair an' square, now show me the money!"

"Sorry, sir. You need to wait until the official result is announced."

*

Françoise led a hobbling Herd Ringer back to the horse-box and tried to ground herself in the present and make sense of the past. She hoped that McQueen had got her message and taken the advice seriously, and she wanted it to be that way so he and Gabby were happy, but knowing that without Docherty's menaces, Herd Ringer would have comfortably triumphed, she felt despondent, rather than hopeful.

It wasn't just that; she knew she couldn't cope if there was backlash from Mr Roche. She pinned her hopes on the Le Manx nasties accepting that without interference from Lorraine and Nancy, Herd Ringer was bound to have been in the first three, just as she had advised them.

*

In the back offices, stewards studied the race. From a normal angle it appeared that Lorraine and Nancy had justly taken the spoils, but when they reviewed the incident through a head-on camera, it was clear that the rival horse had bumped Herd Ringer at a crucial stage. They continued to deliberate for a further ten minutes.

When the klaxon sounded again Françoise froze.

"Amended result! Amended result! Lorraine and Nancy has been disqualified and placed last. The full result is as follows: first, Sixties Overtures, second, Star of Martell, third, Herd Ringer. Weighed in. Weighed in."

She burst into tears and hugged Herd Ringer. "We did it, boy!" she cried. "C'est magnifique!"

*

A furious disturbance erupted in the betting ring. The carnage resembled Custer's Last Stand, with punches flailing, and steel toecaps going in. In the ensuing pandemonium Docherty and his marauders tried, unsuccessfully, to retrieve their loot from the bookies' satchels. A posse of security guards entered the melee to aid the bookmakers. Docherty, suspecting that a film crew might arrive when he heard the bobbies had been called, ordered his men to leg it to the car park and scarper. He scarpered too.

Newmarket disturbance

*

McQueen stepped outside to answer his phone. The signal in The Oxford Arms was never good, and although being in the open air made no difference, at least it was free from cigarette smoke. Gabby and Likely Di really should give up.

"Hello? It's a bad signal."

He managed to hear, "It's Françoise."

What a relief. "You're breaking up. Sorry."

"Françoise!"

He put a finger in his left ear and pressed the phone onto his right. "How are you, Françoise?"

"I am on Noel's phone."

"Noel's phone?" He thought he could hear horse hooves in the background. "I saw you on TV."

"What?"

"TV."

"What did you say?"

This was hopeless. He spoke loud and slow. "*How. Are. You?*"

"I am fine, Mac. Did you get my message?" There were definitely horses with her. Was Herd Ringer there, he wondered.

"I got it. Your text. Thank you. What happened to your other phone?"

"What?"

"Other phone?"

"Did you back Lorraine and Nancy?"

"Yes."

"What?"

"*Yes. We. Did. Lump. It. All. On. Lorraine. And. Nancy. As. A. First. Past. The. Post. Bet.*"

This was exhausting. He wasn't sure she'd heard at all, even when he got a reply.

"Ah! Fantastique. It has been some difficult days. I will explain later."

"What?"

"Explain later."

"How's. Herd. Ringer?"

He waited for her reply, but the call cut off. He'd catch up with her at the stables in a few days. They'd sort it by text.

*

McQueen got back from the phone call and the toilet to find his team sitting in silence. "Someone die?" he said. "Dubs, what's up, mate? You look like you've lost a strawberry mivvi and found an ice pop."

Dubs nodded towards the screen. McQueen turned round and stared at the new result.

"So fucking close, Mac," said Likely Di softly. Gabby was too choked to speak.

McQueen tried hard to maintain a solemn, dumbfounded expression. He shook his head glumly then said, "Such a shame that on-course bookies only pay out on the official result." He couldn't manage his dour pretence for more than ten seconds and burst the illusion with the joyful truth and a beaming smile, announcing, "Whereas, unlike racetrack bookies, all the wagers I placed online, and your little shop beauties are settled on a first past the post basis, as well as any adjusted one."

Gabby tried to get her words out. "So, we're... in the money?"

"Yes, Gabby. We're in the money! Ha! I'll bet Binky's singing that right now! So, let's cheer up, everyone!" He twisted his arm in an exaggerated sweep and looked at the face of his beloved watch. "It's not all doom and gloom because... it's... Friday. It's five to five."

Dubs beat a drumroll on the table with his fingers and everyone joined in to say, "It's... *Crackerjack!*" Dubs nodded across to Al, who took the cue.

"We're with you, Binky and crew," he hollered, before leading Team McQueen London in a chorus of 'We're in the Money', with some knee-wobble actions, which Likely Di excelled in. Amid the mayhem his thoughts turned to Françoise, assuring himself that being in the racing game she'd know that they'd still get paid out.

"Can we cut the gee-gees off now?" said Likely Di, calling across to the bar staff. "It's party time over here! Hey, Mac! Get some music on." She flipped a coin over to him and he caught it. "Go on. Stuff that in the jukebox!"

Speedy Al beat him to it, encouraging everyone to go crazy, which they did as 'Crazy Horses' by The Osmonds filled the happy air. Gabby sat upright, wide awake. "C is for *Crazy Horses*. I had that! Got one for D?"

Dubs chose next, with The Who's 'Pinball Wizard'. Al hugged his brother and shouted in his ear. "Excellent, mate! Excellent! This time next year we'll be the bosses, don't forget!"

"Play it cool. Play it cool, bro," whispered Dubs, launching into a spirited sequence of head-banging and table-drumming which set Al off in a frenzy of air-guitaring, energetically windmilling his arm until he knocked over who knows whose pint. He spent the next five minutes mopping it up with beer mats and copious apologies.

"Gawd," said McQueen, keeping clear of the crazed whirling brothers. "I thought Binky was bad enough! Good job he's in Liverpool or we'd be here 'All night long (all night)'."

"Nice one, Mac!" Gabby shouted, dancing to Lionel Richie.

After that he took control of the jukebox, opting for his favourite Queen track: the five of them sang together, like they were champions. From then on, the night was all a kind of magic.

TWENTY-SEVEN

Docherty ground his teeth, mulling over the fifty-odd grand he'd spirited away on the whim of a bunch of some jobsworth chinless wonders and the fact that McQueen's horse hadn't been humiliated as he'd intended. Seething more with every mile, he tensed his fists around the steering wheel and made his way to Françoise's stables. He turned the last corner. Parked on her drive was the last thing he wanted to see, but see it, he did – an old bill's car. He carried on for another hundred yards and parked up until it was gone. Within fifteen minutes he was inside, and for safety, Sweet Pierre was out of his range, shut in the kitchen. He pawed at the door, yelping.

"What did the cozzers want?"

Françoise looked confused. "Cozzers?"

Her naivety angered him, and he snapped back, "Ye'd better not be winding me up. The police. Gendarmes."

"To know if I, or any member of my staff, had witnessed the earlier fracas at the track."

He had to admit, Françoise kept her cool where many had floundered, but God, she was an irritating woman. And pompous, with that stuck-up French accent.

"What did ye tell them?"

"The truth, Mr Docherty. I am a truthful person."

He wanted to laugh. She'd sounded brave at first, but now he could tell she was nervous, and that was the way he wanted it.

"I said that both I and my jockey were loading our horse at the time, and we were nowhere near the brawl."

He fixed his eyes on her and waited, trying not to be distracted by dog howls. The bolder Françoise acted, the harder she'd fall.

"So, Mr Docherty, by irony of fate, nous avons flambé notre argent."

Docherty flinched. "Eh?" he said, damning his ignorance, damning the dog, and damning the triumph that flashed across her face as she translated for him.

"Obviously, we both have money to burn, numbskull."

He drummed his lips with his fingers, keeping calm, saying nothing, smug in the knowledge that his time would come. He reckoned five minutes. That should do it.

Françoise continued. "Or perhaps you prefer what some uncouth British speakers might say? We have both flushed our money down the toilet."

A noise from upstairs brought relief and stopped his urge to retort.

"That is my secretary," Françoise said. "I am not alone here, Mr Docherty."

Amused at the thought that she would be quivering inside, and elated by what was to come, he raised an eyebrow and twirled his fingers, encouraging her to say more.

"Now, as I kept my part of the bargain, may I please have my phones and charger back?" she said.

"But you welshed on our agreement. I wanted McQueen's horse tae come last."

"Non, non, Monsieur Docherty. You said we must not pass the post before your horse. And you said our jockey must, on no account, overtake or hinder your horse. Or is your English not so good, and you meant something else, peut être?"

Her sickening smug smile made him want to strangle her, but he resisted, saying instead, "My revenge is tha' yer beast will never race again."

Françoise looked shocked. "How do you know that?"

"I have my ways," he said. "And I'm feeling generous." He delved into his deep jacket pocket and pulled out the gadgetry. "Here ye go, Joan of Arc. As ye just lost thirty grand, I suppose ye cannae afford new ones. Think of it as my parting gift." He slid her bundle of tangled wires across the table.

"Thank you," she said, reaching out to grab it all before it went over the edge.

How satisfying it was to see her hands shaking, as she fumbled to unravel her charger and attach it to her phone. She looked across at a plug socket by the window but didn't move. He imagined she was longing to phone McQueen. He'd so love to listen in.

"Now," she said, "if there is nothing else, I would like you to leave."

"Oh, there's just one final thing, Mrs T." He swaggered to the bottom of the stairs and looked to the top, calling, "Elspeth, are ye ready, my sweet?"

"Ready!" came her instant reply. Her voice did not match the sheepish way she walked down the stairs, avoiding eye contact with Françoise as she dragged her bulging suitcase.

"Hello, Uncle Len," said Elspeth. She took her coat from the rack and Docherty picked up the case.

"Like I told ye, I have my spies everywhere, including my beautiful niece here." Watching Françoise shrink and flinch, the pleasure was all his. "And to think, ye never once suspected she was eavesdropping on yer conversations, reporting back to me all along. But as they say, 'C'est la vie'."

He hadn't expected Françoise to let rip, but smiled arrogantly, savouring her brief moment of frustrated fury as she shouted, "That's enough! Get the fuck out of my house, Mr Docherty, and take that bitch lapdog niece with you, before I phone the police!"

"Cozzers," said Elspeth, her accent stronger than Docherty had ever heard it. He felt proud; Françoise looked amazed.

Docherty leaned towards her. "I'll bet ye widnae dare call them." He moved in close enough for her to smell his stinking booze-breath the way he liked to, and he made sure she felt it on her cheek when he whispered, "And I dinnae suggest ye try it, Mrs T."

Sweet Pierre whimpered and Elspeth opened the kitchen door to comfort him. "Goodbye, little Dog-Hurty," she said. "I shall miss you, my special little Dog-Hurty."

Françoise looked deeply wounded and was shaking as she spoke. "How could you have been calling him that name for all these months whenever he has been sick or injured? How could you do it? And how could you have let him be drugged? You loved that dog. You know you did."

Elspeth shrugged. "I persuaded Uncle Len to spare him. You should be thanking me."

"Get out, traitor."

As they left, Docherty turned back and said, "Be seeing ye and yer horsey friends before long," then slammed the door.

*

It had been hectic collecting their winnings the week after the race, in time for the Saturday Team McQueen meeting for leaders, at the Argyll Arms. None of the bookmakers had reneged, but Binky and Phil had been warned off in a couple of the Toxteth shops. McQueen was grateful to have had Tonker working with Blaggit, suspecting that was why they'd had no such trouble in the Midlands. London had been generally without trouble as far as he knew.

Now it was all gathered in, the six of them sat around an old oak table in the upstairs room McQueen had booked. He watched them nattering about the day of the race. Woollyback, Wacker, Al, Dubs and Tonker would get their rewards when their team leaders got back to them. McQueen both regretted and rejoiced that they weren't there. There was a lot to celebrate, but in truth, the thought of the musicians Al and Dubs meeting with singing Binky was too much, so he settled on just calling in leaders. Maybe the whole team would meet up one day.

"Don't think we'll be pulling that one again anytime soon," said Blaggit and they all bobbed heads in agreement, laughing.

McQueen looked at the unkempt, wonky-toothed, reliable old sod. What a bloke Blaggit was. He'd been loyal to McQueen for years. He was glad Likely Di sat near him, smoking furiously, as ever. The smell of her cigarettes kept the eau de Blaggit at bay.

Was he imagining things, or had sitting with Likely Di turned his confirmed bachelor friend into a beau de Blaggit? He was definitely eyeing up her Mary Quants. Amused, McQueen tuned into their private conversation, and listened with intrigue.

*

"You know what, Diana? Next time I'm in London, I'm gonna take you out for a top-nosh meal at Veeraswamy."

"Vera's what?"

"It's the capital's oldest curry house. Established a few years after World War One, you know."

"Yes. Veeraswamy. I've heard of it, Blaggit. It's nearly as old as thee and me."

They laughed together, then Likely Di added, "My dear old mum was called Vera, and she was in the army in the 1940s. Vera's Army, she called it. That's the truth!"

"What a woman she sounds." He looked impressed and genuinely interested. "I bet you don't say 'that's the truth' very often."

"Cheeky sod!" said Likely Di, tapping him on his arm with a beer mat. "You'd be surprised what truths I tell."

"Surprise me then."

"What Vera managed to create from a homemade meat curry and a boiling pan of rice, should be on display in the Tate Modern."

"Now that I do believe! My mam was the same. She called it posh stew. Seriously, Diana, if you fancy a ruby at Veeraswamy, please join me."

"Not arf! That's a date for my diary." She held her hand out and as Blaggit took it to plant a gentle seal-the-deal kiss, she eyed up his diamond ring. "Is that the real thing?"

"It is, indeed, Diana." He winked at her. "And if you're lucky, darlin', when we've had our post-curry coffee and stuffed ourselves with After Eight mints, I might even let you kiss it right back." He let go of her hand and she kept it in the air.

"Kiss your ring? After you've had a vindaloo?" she said, voice volume high, attracting everyone's attention. "There's no way I'm going anywhere near your ring, even though having it on your little finger makes you a diamond geezer!"

She looked tickled pink to have an audience. Now acting squiffy, she put her hat back on and rose to salute McQueen with a speech. "Ladies and laddies, it's been a privilege working with you all, in Mac here's little conspiracy. It was a master plan, dreamed up by the legend that is McQueen, our very own, Wizard of Odds. It's proper warmed the cockles of me heart, which proves I'm no tin man!"

Gabby laughed and shot out a well-received heckle. "Hey, Diana! Which one of us two is Dorothy and which one of us is the Witch of the West?"

"Let the magician decide!" said Likely Di, sipping from her glass and spilling a bit.

"Come on, Mac. Don't sit on the fence," said Phil, urging him on.

"Oooh, look at him! He's gone the colour of ruby slippers!" said Binky.

McQueen stood up. "You're all my beautiful little munchkins!" he said, circling his glass to include not just Likely Di and Gabby but all his Team McQueen leaders: Blaggit, Binky, and Phil too. "Jeez, with that lot up north, you're an odd bunch of sods. And ladies," he added, "please don't fight or no one'll get to wear the ruby slippers!"

"Cop out!" Gabby laughed.

"He's a friend of Dorothy, if you ask me. He's keeping the shoes for himself," said Blaggit, chuckling into his beer. "He'll swap his loafers for them."

They raised their glasses and Likely Di led them all in a cheer of "To Mac!"

"Speech, speech!" hollered Gabby, banging her Tintin on the table.

McQueen felt his face redden but obliged. "Without all you iffy line-up of zany desperados – and the five absent ones you gallantly kept in line, that's Tonker, Woollyback and Wacker, and them Dennett brothers Al 'n' Dubs—"

He paused. The relief of reaching this day was suddenly overwhelming. He took a deep breath and fought to compose himself. "Without all of you—"

He must not let his voice waver.

"Without all of you, the bilk would never have been executed." *Phew.* He'd said it. He knew he could carry on. "And we'd never have found our pot of gold. Because of you lot, we will now go down in the annals of grifting as McQueen and the Dream Team. Thank you. I love you all!"

Likely Di made a toast to the pot of gold and then to Operation Golden Fleece. She raised her glass to make another but stopped when Binky started singing 'Somewhere Over the Rainbow'. McQueen knew he only had himself to blame, although he had to admit, Binky's voice was really good.

When he sat down, Likely Di had tears in her eyes. She turned to him with her glass raised yet again. "Well, you beat them, kid," she said.

"You were right, Diana, it's not enough. But it's bloody close!"

Had he avenged his grandfather? Had he done enough? Would anything ever be enough? He would think on that later, and forever,

Loaded with booze – Binky and Phil with Blaggit

he knew it. For now, as promised, McQueen distributed the booty. He gave them all an additional five grand, and a sizeable bonus to pass on to Likely Di's Dennetts, lion-hearted Tonker, Wacker and Woollyback, with his appreciation. It came as a surprise to some that Phil refused the bonus for direct payment to Wacker, insisting that he'd use it to pay rehab fees and help him get clean. Everyone agreed that was the right thing to do.

The happy team leaders bent their elbows late into the evening. When they were loaded with booze, they quizzed McQueen in turn, trying to find out what was so special about the horse Lorraine and Nancy. All he said was, "I cannot say." He kept it up till it was gone midnight, when they all pretended to click the heels of their ruby slippers together – harder for some to do than others – and said their farewells.

When he got home, he still couldn't say.

*

Two days later, Françoise was on the porch when they arrived. She rushed down to greet them with a hug and kiss on each cheek. Sweet Pierre beat her to it, his tail wagging like a hyperactive windscreen wiper. She stood back, laughing. "He is so pleased to see you!"

Once inside, she sorted drinks for everyone, and they all settled down.

"No Elspeth?" said Gabby.

"Her uncle came to take her back to Scotland. She will not be returning." Her blink quickened. "It is no matter."

"I thought I picked out a hint of an accent."

"Oh. It was broad, believe me. She hid it well."

Françoise stopped herself from saying more. She wanted to build up to the big explanation and keep things calm for as long as she could. She had already assured McQueen, on her mobile, that Le Manx Gang had phoned and were satisfied Herd Ringer had just been unlucky, so she was not fearful of repercussions, and she said it all again, now they were meeting face-to-face.

"I should bleedin' think they are satisfied," said Gabby, indignant. "They still copped, as they'd bet on him each way."

Françoise let a couple of moments pass, then cleared her throat. "There is something I have to tell you, Mac." Her voice was hushed when she spoke. "Many things, actually. But this one is très importante."

"Go on," he said, with a puzzled expression.

"I am afraid that during the race Herd Ringer sustained an

injury to his hock. The vet informs me that he will never race again. I am so sorry."

Gabby made a noise that was a cross between a gasp and a whimper, and McQueen stared out of the window towards the stables. "Can I go and see him please?"

"Of course. But you must trust me, he is fine, just no longer a runner. In fact, it is not all bad news. I have a proposition. I would very much like to purchase him from you. I have really fallen in love with him and hope you agree your horse can become my hack. He will have a good life."

"What?" he said, as if jolted from a dream. "Ah. Wait! Money. The money. Your loan. I have it." He took thirty thousand pounds out of his bag and thrust it at Françoise. "Thanks for the loan. Herd Ringer is yours. Let me take… what? Ten back? Is that fair?"

Françoise shook her head. "No, Mac. I do not want any of this. I want you both to take it all. Who knows? A little extra may come in handy for you, no? Let us talk money later. For now, return it to your bag."

TWENTY-EIGHT

Glad to have left behind the cluttered streets of London and dressed for a day in the late April Suffolk countryside, with its fields bursting with green, they walked to the stables, wellies squelching. McQueen asked the questions he had been burning to ask Françoise since he'd first seen her text on the morning of the race. Gabby listened. "You never explained how you knew to switch the bets to that other bloody horse? What was so special about it? Why the secrecy? What exactly has been going on? Please explain."

They listened as Françoise told them about the night of Lennox Docherty's visit and the threats he'd made, and that Elspeth was working for him, and how he'd drugged Sweet Pierre, and how he wanted to get even with them both and ensure his horse did well and get her to guarantee that theirs didn't have a chance. She said that from that moment she knew that to make things work for McQueen, she *had* to know the name of Mr Docherty's horse, and more than anything, she had to give McQueen the name of a horse to pass on to his team that would do better than Herd Ringer.

He was shocked. Stunned. Horrified that Françoise had been through all that on her own. And shaken that Docherty had tracked him down. He had put this trusting friend in danger, and she had tried to do the best thing for him. Stumbling over his words, he said, "And… you're okay, are you?"

"I am," she said softly. "Thank you."

"And look, your lovely dog seems fine, sniffing away over there."

"He is fine. I think he is sniffing for Docherty. He has not stopped since the last visit."

McQueen looked puzzled.

"It is for protection," Françoise explained. "He sensed something was wrong. He has a nose for the bad." They watched the Labrador snuffle, pause, mark his territory, and move on. A dog on a mission. A dog out to get revenge.

Five horses returned from a gallop. Their riders nodded respectfully at Françoise as she stood with Gabby and McQueen waiting for them to pass. Gabby looked thrilled, watching every move as if she wanted to blow kisses when they passed, hooves clattering on the ground. Françoise spoke to one and confirmed their next training session. Stable hands greeted horse and rider cheerily and assisted when they dismounted.

"So, did Docherty's horse do well?" said McQueen.

Françoise seemed reluctant to snap back into the world of Docherty, but he knew she had to at some point, so he persisted as they walked on towards Herd Ringer's stable.

"The result was a very fair one, I would say."

"I can't believe he told you the name."

"He did not tell me."

"What? Then, how?"

"I worked it out."

McQueen stopped walking and they all stood still.

"How?" he asked. "There was no horse in that race with a name that pointed to Lennox Docherty. Not that I recall." He pulled a race card from his inside pocket and checked the list of runners. Gabby leaned in to look at it while McQueen quizzed Françoise some more.

"He's as sly as a fox," said Gabby.

"Exactement! And he is not a… a… what is it you say, Mac? A full-blown imbecile!"

"So how did you track his horse down?"

"Well, Gabriella. It was not easy. It was not instant. It will take a long time to explain."

"We don't mind, do we, Mac?"

"Françoise. My ears are all yours for however long you need them," said McQueen.

"Very well. I shall explain all details."

There, amid the hubbub of her working stables, in the oaty, sweet, dung-scented air, she outlined her night of terror.

"I knew the horse of Docherty was not going to be listed in his name, but I double-checked to be certain. There were no Scottish trainers bringing their steeds down, and no owner's silks remotely hinted at a Highland theme. The more I racked my brain the further I seemed to be from getting to a solution. The rich Arabs had four representatives, so at least these could be discounted. I kept going back to the list of runners. Which one was his?"

McQueen and Gabby listened, staring at the race card, checking every detail as Françoise spoke. They hung on her words as she unravelled the mystery. Close by, Sweet Pierre looked up occasionally as if he was interested too, but then got back to his essential sniffing.

"I had Docherty down as vain, but not totally dim-witted so I expected that, like many owners, he would attempt to be clever in naming his horse. Docherty would be the sort to either use an amalgamation of the sire and dam—"

"Colt and mare is that?"

"Exactement again, Gabriella. The sire is the father and the dam the mother."

"Thanks. Just checking."

"Check away. Where was I? Ah! If not the amalgamation, then Docherty would most likely have some other smart play on words or hidden meaning. What had he gone for? That is what I had to know."

McQueen and Gabby took it in turn to name the runners and comment on likely links to Docherty. Françoise was not giving any clues. "You have to do the work, like I did," she said. Was she laughing at them?

The only thing they usefully suggested was War Eagle. Gabby had come up with the idea, pointing out that eagles are native to Scotland, and that Docherty is like a warring rapscallion. When McQueen added that the name Docherty means 'hurtful', which is him to a tee, Françoise let her guard down and said that the name was one of horse racing's many red herrings and promised to tell more back in the house, insisting they move on to catch up with Herd Ringer, which they did immediately.

*

As ever, the stable was engulfed in an intensely still, warm air, its heavy silence broken only by the snort of horses and the click of hooves on the floor.

McQueen wasn't convinced when Françoise made out his colt recognised them both, but it was a comforting thought. "Just look at the way he was stomping and whinnying as you approached."

"I bet he does that for all the dames," said Gabby, laughing at her own joke. She stopped when McQueen stroked Herd Ringer and leaned in to touch him. He saw in Gabby's eyes that it moved her to see him so tender and so emotionally exposed.

"Goodbye my friend, until next time," he whispered, patting the chestnut head and rubbing his thumb on the white star.

"Clip-clop, clip-clop," Gabby said softly, wiping away a tear that trickled down her cheek. She moved towards Herd Ringer and stroked him lovingly.

McQueen straightened and turned to Françoise. "It's clear to me now, that I owe you so much more than this beautiful fella," he said.

*

Back in the cottage after their spell outside, they warmed themselves by the fire and Françoise brought them large mugs of hot chocolate. She knew her London guests would find Suffolk air cold, even at this time of year. Françoise served her speciality homemade madeleines to soak up the hot drink and promised champagne for when they had unravelled the puzzle she was about to set before them.

She decided the next thing to explain ought to be the time when she and her husband had once visited Lorraine for her cousin's wedding. Of course, the moment she mentioned the name of the French town she could tell from the expressions on both their faces that it was finally beginning to dawn on McQueen and Gabby that the horse they had backed, Lorraine and Nancy, was actually Docherty's horse, and being Docherty, he would not just settle on jeopardising Herd Ringer's chances: the vile man had wanted to secure an outright win.

Without interruption she was able to explain that for as long as she could remember, she had been fascinated by her country's history, unlike Raphael, her husband, who was a football nut. Nearly ten years ago, they had rented an apartment in the Lorraine capital, on the banks of the Moselle River. They had struck a bargain: he would spend a couple of days taking in the sights with her, provided he chose the evening restaurants, and she would accompany him to Sunday's football match. She knew he never let on how much he savoured the arm-in-arm meanderings in the idyllic cobbled backwaters of the medieval old town, with its quaint bohemian bars, stunning architecture, and the hushed chill of Saint-Sébastien Church where they both lit a candle for absent friends. She blinked back tears, thinking of how narcissistic

Raphael had become after their happy days in Lorraine, and the way they had once laughed together about the local motto: '*Qui s'y frotte s'y pique*' – '*Who touches it, pricks oneself*', and how they had wondered what the local significance was. When the teams took to the pitch on the Sunday, they found the answer: embroidered on the home team's shirt badge, was a thistle; the emblem of Lorraine and of course, Scotland too.

"So that's why he called the horse Lorraine. I get it, but 'and Nancy'? Why that? Why not settle for McLorrainerty or something simple, and save you all your trouble, eh?" said Gabby.

Trying to stay polite, Françoise made clear that it was not as simple as Gabby thought, but as she was on a roll, she was not going to let Gabby distract her from it so went on. She explained that having got that far in her workings, she had opened the *Racing Post* again to check for further clues and studied the runners' names. Names for sire – father of a horse; and names for dam – the mother. She was looking for anything that would signal the parentage of Docherty's horse to confirm things. She emphasised again that owners often used this in their naming of a horse and there was too much at stake to settle too quickly on a horse if it was the wrong one. She had to be sure.

When Françoise gave her reasons for being so cautious, she noticed the way Gabby nodded frantically, as if she knew that anyone would be an idiot to jump to a quick conclusion. It made her laugh to herself.

Her research threw up De Gaulle's Cross as a sire, and Light of Frank's Life as a dam. Teasingly, she left McQueen and Gabby to think it through, just as she had struggled to puzzle over it. After some minutes, the excruciating sight of them wrestling with theories led her to tell more of her workings.

Why a cross? This had been her starting point.

Was the late French president cross, annoyed, vexed, upset? Surely it could not be this. She did not remember President Charles de Gaulle in that light.

She went over and over it.

De Gaulle's Cross, De Gaulle's Cross, De Gaulle?

Finally, she explained, she had a further breakthrough! Yessss! Oui! C'est ça! De Gaulle's Cross was not an emotion at all! The apostrophe signalled possession – possession of a cross, maybe? De Gaulle's Cross of Lorraine was the symbol of the Free French during World War Two. That was a link to the sire and Lorraine. So, she stopped the search of more Lorraine evidence, but could still not be totally certain. Not without a link to the dam.

How did the name of Nancy fit in?

Was she investigating the right horse? Or was this trail a waste of time?

She was having more fun telling this story than she had anticipated. Gabby and McQueen seemed to be on the edge of their seats. She wondered if this was how Docherty felt in a position of power when he bullied people, and quickly shook the thought away.

She told them how an idea had come to her in a flash: the dam could be some seedy villain Docherty might hero-worship. Which villain? Might Sinatra be a villain Docherty was likely to idolise?

With that notion in her mind, the solution followed quickly.

Who did Sinatra himself worship? That would be the key, she felt sure of it.

Sinatra worshipped none other than his darling daughter, Nancy. That meant Nancy was Sinatra's ultimate dam, so Docherty poached her name. Very clever.

Gabby went to clap, but Françoise halted her. Even though she was ninety per cent sure she had hit on the horse belonging to Docherty, there was so much at stake. She still needed more proof and kept searching online. She wanted to be absolutely thorough.

"Like a thoroughbred." A joke from Gabby which Françoise and McQueen ignored.

Companies House listed the horse owners as Durban Entertainment Technologies Ltd, a private company, incorporated in July 1991, showing a healthy profit, with various daughter companies. So far, there was no mention of Docherty, and another few hundred pages to trawl through. With time getting on, she was determined to reach a positive conclusion. The dining-room clock struck two thirty as the name Docherty finally emerged: yes, there was the name Docherty, appointed as director.

"Je t'ai eu! Now to contact McQueen," she told them she had shrieked.

"And you did!" he said, jumping up from his chair, ecstatic and in awe of the amateur detective in his presence. "I picked up the text first thing in the morning: had no idea whether it was genuinely from you or not."

"Just in time, I sent it. That was my spare phone, with hardly any battery left and no charger."

"That was a brilliant piece of detective work, Françoise. We will always be in your debt." McQueen strode to the ice bucket, looking so chuffed that Françoise would have believed he had solved the mystery himself. He pulled out the champagne bottle, opened it, poured three glasses and they drank to the brilliance of Françoise, calling her Madame Poirot.

"Mac's right," said Gabby. "You must be some kind of genius. I could never have worked that out. And I'm still not sure I have! Actually, I don't think I ever will understand it all!"

Françoise shrugged. "That is not where my story ends, mes amis. I need to tell you both, I have decided to hand my training licence in. I love the horses, but not the serpents. It was a mistake to think I could be independent and alone in England. Maybe I will change direction, turn this into an equestrian centre for people with disabilities. Your sister can perhaps come, Gabriella."

"Oh Françoise, how wonderful," said Gabby. "I'll be sure to let her know."

"Très bien. And you must, you absolutely must visit too, Gabriella. Please, always think of Herd Ringer as your own horse."

Gabby wiped away more tears, unable to reply.

McQueen cleared his throat. "I wish you luck. What you will be doing is very honourable," he said. "Horse racing will miss you, but I don't blame you one bit. It will be a big undertaking single-handed, though."

"Ah! Do not concern yourself about that. I will not be alone. I have been asked to make a home and a life with my good neighbour. Noel will be on hand." At the thought of Noel, she subconsciously pulled at her ponytail and shook her hair loose.

They drank to Françoise and her new life with Noel, but Françoise insisted that she had more to say. She went on, hardly stopping for breath.

"Noel, I said, will be on hand." She gestured across the paddocks. "That is the Noel, who lives in the pink cottage with the thatched roof. It is the Noel who is the vet. And the Noel who loves sixties music. Also, the Noel whose horse it was flying on the gallops. And yes, flying at 150 to 1. Maybe this Noel will invest in the centre. I do not know. But I do know that it is the Noel who is the owner of Sixties Overtures."

She waited for a reaction, but her guests seemed too astonished to even move as they took it all in. She carried on, hoping they would like her next piece of news.

"And mais oui, he gave me the thumbs up, and I placed a small investment on Sixties Overtures for me, and one for you both also, just in case of ruin in your race. So yes, you must keep the money I loaned you."

"Sixties Overtures!" said a stunned Gabby. "I don't believe it!"

"Françoise, you little dark horse!" said McQueen.

"You placed a small investment for *us?*" said Gabby. She opened her mouth as if she was about to say more, but nothing came out, so she rushed to hug Françoise.

McQueen joined in. "Well, I'll be! I'm so very pleased for you, Françoise. And so very grateful." He stepped back to drink to her again. "And thank you. We shall use the money wisely. Thank you. Be happy. You absolutely must keep Herd Ringer."

"Well, that's amazing news," said Gabby. "I'd stick with Noel if I were you. I've always wished it could be Christmas every day, and I reckon that's what you could get, and it'll all turn out to be Wizzard!"

Françoise laughed politely. "Ah. Très bien! You and your English humour, Gabriella. You mean it will always be Joyeux Noël? But what is 'wizard'?"

"She's jesting with you again. It's the name of a band that sings a kind of modern-day Christmas carol," said McQueen.

"Well, perhaps you will sing it to me now, Gabriella," she said, deliberately keeping a straight face to unnerve Gabby.

It worked. Gabby froze and looked at McQueen who egged her on to sing. Instead, she laughed until once more, tears ran down her cheeks.

"You see? I can jest too, Gabriella."

TWENTY-NINE

May

McQueen didn't need to check his watch, but he tapped it; Gabby was late, and the head of her Guinness had begun to thin. She'd called him yesterday to sort an urgent meet-up but hadn't said why. If she asked, the answer was no; he was most definitely all out of scams. The door opened and there she was, same immaculate thick black hair still cut in a cheery bob, her big eyes peering round the pub until they settled on his.

"Sorry I'm late. Had to pick something up."

"No problem. Where's the fire?"

Gabby spotted her drink. "Cheers, Mac. Hate the froth anyway," she said, taking a slug, then handing him a package. "Go on. Open it then."

He tore at the envelope and stared at what he saw. Brochures. Brochures for a three-week break in a luxury beach house on Harbour Island in the Bahamas, and two first class return tickets from Heathrow, leaving on Friday.

"Friday?" McQueen said, double-checking the tickets.

"Well, you're not up to much else, are you? Read the details. Bet you won't be able to say no."

He flicked through them. When he looked up, she was smiling. "Gabby, this is beautiful. How come?"

"I thought we deserved it; don't you think we do?"

"Yes, but…"

"No worries. I can just about afford it. Ha, ha, ha!"

"I hate to ask, but, erm… your sister's not coming too, is she?"

"No way, Mac! She and her new boyfriend will be visiting Françoise. You've no idea how much me having a bit of bunce in the bank has perked her up. And it turns out, having a love of horses if you're a wheelchair user is a real turn-on."

"Well, good for your sister."

"Maybe we could visit the stables and meet them after we get back? Can we? Françoise says he's nice, but she keeps him at arm's length."

"Quite right too. Remember what we said, Gabby? We'll keep away from there for a few more months. You never know who might be watching that place. I don't want any snooper to find out where we live."

"You still mean Docherty? He'll be long gone by now, Mac, surely?"

"I think that's right. I just wanna be certain, you know me. I want it to stay all quiet on the eastern front." He looked back at the glossy brochure. A niggling worry couldn't be suppressed. "It's not gonna be hurricane season, is it?"

"No, Mac. I knew you'd ask that. This is May. Hurricane season starts in June. And it's not Kansas we're going to." She paused to laugh at her own joke. "So, that all means that if Mother Nature behaves, I'm afraid we'll miss the opening ceremony for hurricanes and houses getting blown down rainbows."

"Just checking." Relieved, he returned to the sights of sea and sand.

"The house looks delightful, Mac. The best photos are in the middle pages."

He turned to them. "Wow! No kidding! Look at the size of the lounge. And it has views over the bay, a stunning kitchen, great bathroom, and king-size four-poster bed. Crikey."

She tapped his watch, grinning. "Maybe you could get yourself a new Rolex now. A real one," she said.

"I don't think so. I like what I know. A new one wouldn't be my type." He looked into her eyes. "But you are, Gabby."

"Well, how about we start a new type of partnership, then?" She leaned forward and kissed him; this time it was full on the lips. "Maybe we'll make more than a million, next time," she whispered. "And if you become my long-term rich mug, how about you buy me that horse?"

"Oh. You're trying that already, are you? I thought Françoise said you could always share Herd Ringer."

She pulled a face.

"You got me, Gabby. Maybe I'll talk to Françoise about that." Now it was his turn to lean in and kiss her. "As long as you promise not to call it Cockney Clip-Clop!"

"That's a very good name." She laughed.

They kissed again.

"Mac, have I ever told you about *my* grandad?"

Early June

Docherty settled down to enjoy his traditional Friday night fish supper with a pint of heavy, congratulating himself on the day's purchase. He'd secured ownership of the town's derelict warehouse at a hugely deflated price, thanks to his low tender bid, and a bent councillor. His under the counter mantra from the start had been: 'Let the local do-gooders rehouse the good for nowt vagrants who doss there', and it got him what he wanted.

He sprinkled vinegar on his battered haddock. Just as he was about to dig in, there was a rap on the door. He swung round and shouted, "Can a man nae enjoy his bleedin' fish 'n' chips with nae interruption?" Irritated, and tutting, he scraped his chair back and got up to open the door.

A gaudy lemon-and-orange-topped DHL driver stood on the doorstep with a flat, square package, too big for a letterbox. "Sorry to disturb you, Mr Docherty, but this needs your signature."

Grunting, Docherty scribbled his name and returned to the table. He was ravenous; the delivery would have to wait. Two mouthfuls later, curiosity got the better of him and he hastily cut the pack open with his razor-sharp silver letter opener. Inside was an album cover. There was no LP inside it, just the cover: *Who's Next* by The Who. Was someone having a joke? No one he could think of would send him a picture of four Cockney wankers who'd just had a Jimmy up a wall – not an ordinary wall: the wall of a large grey monolith in the middle of nowhere. Someone was definitely taking the piss. He knew of the band The Who. Not one he liked, especially that big-nosed tosser, Town… something. Townshend. That was it. Him and that band had some nasty habits, that he knew for sure, and he also knew who'd supplied most of the gear for them. It never stopped them turning into zillionaires though. He'd do everything he could to stop filthy Londoners like them getting rich on his watch.

Leaning the cover on his pint to keep it upright as he ate, he noticed it was defaced. He held it close to his eyes. Someone had scanned or drawn, he couldn't tell, his own face onto one face of the stone. As he put it down his hands started to tremble. He cracked his knuckles to release his growing rage and fire up his thinking. This was not good. Not good. What did it all mean? Who had sent it? There were no details. Why had they sent it?

He felt inside the album cover and found something he'd missed: a photo of that London strumpet on a golden beach at sunset, outside a luxurious waterside apartment. She was holding hands with someone who could only be McQueen. "Fuckers! How could they afford that?"

Flipping it over he read:

>*Mr Docherty,*
>
>*Some of us know about that bandit McQueen's past dealings, and your Newmarket debacle. We know how you like to get revenge. We have caught wind of the Cockney sod and his scrubber's whereabouts on a specific date. For a small arrangement fee, you may like the two spivs' details.*

The note was unsigned, but there was a mobile number scrawled at the bottom. He cracked his knuckles some more, then ate slowly, almost in a trance, pondering and planning until his plate was empty and his mind full. He stroked the image of the two of them for several minutes, shifting his finger from one to the other, before picking up his phone. Very deliberately he dialled the number, simultaneously erasing McQueen's head from the photo with his knife.

*

Freshly back from holiday, Gabby and McQueen set about putting the plans they'd made into action. To prove that her short spell in Canary Wharf hadn't gone to waste, Gabby made a list detailing what they'd agreed. *Documenting*, she called it.

1. Enjoy our pot of gold.
2. Give up scams with bookies.
3. Hide from Docherty.
4. Get out of London. Look in Suffolk and buy a place of our own. (We both like it there and we've got the wellies now.)
5. Stay friends with Françoise and make sure there are no repercussions for her.
6. Get a dog? Dunno. Call it Toto if we do.
7. Stay friends with my sister. (Really? Do I *have* to? Mac says I do. Ha, ha, haaa!)
8. Stay in touch with Herd. *Yessss!*

9. Do other scams if we want to. Don't get caught.
10. Have fun.
11. Keep the wine rack well stocked.
12. Have a party and invite Team McQueen.

"I think that's what we agreed, Mac. Can you spot anything that's missing?" she said, following him round and reading it for the fifth time.

It was no surprise to either of them that they were due to be proud and loving owners of an Airedale terrier called Toto, with Noel lined up as official trainer. Thanks to the genius negotiator, McQueen, in no time they'd paid upfront for a remote thatched cottage, south of Newmarket, moved in, and Gabby was advising him on where to put the brown shiny horse he'd nicked from Woolworths.

Mid-June

The Dennett brothers were happy to find Likely Di seated in the snug, with spaces around her.

"Good. She's on her tod. That's good," said Al as they walked over.

She took off her Ray-Bans and set them on the table then looked up and watched them approach as if they were men on a catwalk. Al had seen her do that before, but never to him. "Afternoon, boys," she said, swiftly swallowing her drink and holding out her empty glass. He took it and held it out for Dubs to take to the bar.

"A large one?"

She lifted a pencilled-on eyebrow and laughed. "Is there any other type?"

Al waited for Dubs to bring their drinks, and they got down to business. Likely Di began.

"So, boys. If it's another gig you're after, it's currently a no, I'm afraid. Nothing doing," she said, pausing to blow cigarette smoke from the side of her mouth before adding, "Sorry."

Al wasn't sure if it was an apology for the smoke or for no hope of a gig. Dubs seemed confused too. He was rhythmically finger-drumming on the table to The La's 'There She Goes'. He stopped abruptly when Likely Di said, "Stop that! Much as I love your drumming, I don't want you to have me bleedin' drink over. Anyway, boys, you've got The Salisbury pub for gigs. People love you, as always. That should be getting you more coming in, surely?" She paused again for the sake of tobacco, then laughed. "I know why you're here: you want me to be your manager?"

Al looked at Dubs. They'd been given a compliment. What to do? Not their usual 'We've been given a compliment' routine here, surely? "No, we're not here about a gig," he said before Dubs could start up. "But… glad you like seeing us there." He was struggling to get his words out. He'd not thought of her as intimidating until now.

Dubs backed him up. "We'll… erm… we'll think about the manager thing, though, won't we, Al?"

"Come on, sons, spit it out," she said, which didn't help.

"Well, it's like this. Dubs and me have been thinking about Mac and all of us hitting the jackpot at Newmarket, and—"

Likely Di interrupted him. "Yes?"

He suddenly felt embarrassed, almost ashamed to be bringing this up, but that's what he and Dubs had met up with her for, so he went ahead. "It's like, well, McQueen had it right off, and we feel we were just yesterday's leftovers, and we deserve more, and we want to move up the food chain. Mac and co are old, and we want to be the new kids on the block, and not just dogsbodies." He took a swig of beer. He couldn't believe he'd got through it.

Likely Di's face hardened. She stared at them both then leaned towards them. "Tell me. How old are you both?"

"Me, twenty-one and he, twenty-two. Thirteen months between us," said Dubs, proudly pumping out his chest.

She drew on her cigarette and lifted her head to blow out smoke into the air and the silence above them. "So, you both wanna be faces, eh?"

"That's the idea, Diana," said Al.

He waited for Likely Di to cheer; to say she'd back them; to ask how she could help, like she did when they talked about The Substitunes. Instead, she said, "You know what? Mac put everything on the line for Newmarket. One small cock-up and he was going to be doomed. Long cons need precision to succeed, and this was no smash and grab job. Mac was proud of your efforts and doubled your wages for the day. He's a top-notch hustler and a true gent."

Her voice grew louder, and she spoke more slowly. "Please don't ever diss him again in my presence."

This wasn't the way Al had expected it to go. He hadn't even got to produce his trump card. He couldn't bear to think what Dubs would say to him later and joined his brother in looking at the floor.

To his relief Likely Di's tone had softened when she next spoke. "Look, lads," she said, "Mac has been doing the rounds since God knows when. Rumour has it that when he was born, he cut his own umbilical cord and half an hour later he was dipping the midwife's pocket. You get me?"

Dubs laughed softly.

"Once you're a friend of Mac, you're a friend for life. Mac will always look after you." She took another drag on her cigarette. "He probably thinks he'll retire now, but he'll no doubt always have an ear to the ground for any big plays, and if they're in the south, I'm sure he'll contact me and, in turn, me to you. Plenty of action will come your way, boys, but *softly, softly, catch a monkey*. Your time will come, but you must give up on pulling McQueen out of his tree."

No one spoke.

"Oh. Don't look so crestfallen."

"Sorry, Diana," said Dubs.

Al wasn't quite ready to make apologies. "It's just so frustrating for us," he said. "I know we're better than mere underlings."

"You're not underlings. You're an important cog in Mac's wheel. Team McQueen, remember?" She sighed. "My advice, for what it's worth, is keep to your own patch, that way someone's always looking after your back. Don't set yourselves up against the hand that feeds you."

Al felt like he and Dubs had just been told off by their mum. In a strange way he liked it.

*

Had she done enough to get them to lay off McQueen? She wasn't certain.

"Anyway," she said, "to move up quickly you need plenty of greenbacks and muscle. You got that?"

"We got this," said Al, producing a business card.

"What's this? Your joker I suppose? Let me have a butchers," she said, snapping the card from him.

Her world stopped still when she saw who they seemed to have been dealing with. She tried to gather herself and do her best to appear calm. "Who... who gave you this?"

"Some bloke. Some bloke who owes me."

"This man owes you?" She lit another cigarette, forcing her hands not to shake. "Good God! What have you done that I don't know about? Do you seriously know this man?"

"Erm... No, Diana. Not actually know him. He gave me the card though. I'd remember his face if I saw it, probably."

"Do you know his number?"

The brothers looked puzzled. "You mean the one on the card?"

She said nothing, just fixed Al with a stare.

"I haven't memorised it. Is that what you mean?"

She kept staring.

"Or got it in me address book. Or saved it on me phone." He sat back.

"Nor me," said Dubs, sitting back too. "What is it? Some kind of devil number, like six, six, six?" He laughed.

She pulled out another cigarette and made ready to light it. "This devil is for real, Dubs. You've hit the nail right on the coffin lid there."

They both looked puzzled again, then glanced at each other, seeming slightly unnerved, like they thought she was batty, but she ignored it. Al put his hand out for the card, but she tucked it under the strap of her watch and pulled her sleeve down to cover it. She wasn't giving this little piece of treasure back.

"I'm serious. Trust me, boys. You don't want this number in your life if you're planning on having a long one. People who get involved with these kinda killer sharks end up in a dark alley with their throats opened up."

"Oh. Right. Right," stammered Al as if the weight of everything he'd convinced himself he was hoping for had suddenly hit him and he realised what a fool he'd been.

"It's best you forget it," she said.

He nodded dumbly.

"And let's forget our chat, too."

"What chat is that?" said Dubs.

Likely Di tried to laugh but only managed a smile. "Don't worry about that. You did the right thing coming to me. I'll see you both right too. Just keep shtum."

*

"That went well," said Dubs once they were outside.

"Yeah. Sorry, bro. Think we've had a lucky escape though, so it's not all bad. Thinking about it, I don't really mind us not being 'King of the Road'."

"Nor me. Race you to the next pub."

THIRTY

July

It was nearly two and a half months since the fateful race day. A smouldering Docherty was still no closer to working out what had really happened or, much as it grieved him, no nearer to punishing anyone for it. He had visited Lorraine and Nancy's stable with his neanderthals, but despite threats of beating, or far worse, nothing was forthcoming. You can lead a horse to water and make it drink, but not if there's a drought.

What bugged him more was that it was also over one month since the bizarre LP cover had arrived with the message about McQueen. Whenever he phoned the number some plebs had sent with it he couldn't get any answer, and no amount of pressure on DHL got him any accurate information about the sender – they just didn't have it.

He was certain it all tied up. Who had put that dosh on his horse? How? Who had sent the LP cover and message? He wasn't going to let it go.

There was a rap on his door. It was his next in command, Dave Acheson.

"Any news, Archie?"

"Yes, Mr Lennox. Hearsay on the street in London, Birmingham and Liverpool says that a flash puss and his runners plundered over seven hundred and fifty thousand, paid out on a first past the post, on the quick in and out raid."

"Got any names?"

"Not so far. It seems like a detailed, well-planned operation."

Docherty poured them both a drink.

"Ideas, Archie?"

"It's surely gotta be that Cockney tosser, McQueen, behind it."

Docherty cracked his knuckles when Archie mentioned him.

"I know your niece, Elspeth, swears blind it can't be him, and she did a grand job there, sorting out that Herd Ringer threat, so I guess she knows."

"Aye. She did a good job, you're right. But if it's nae him, that just the leaves the frog."

"You always say it can't be her. So does Elspeth. Perhaps Elspeth protests too much about it? Do you think she might have got a bit too fond of things there?"

"She liked that rat of a dog, that's for sure. But my niece does what I say. Got that?"

"Got it."

"Good. Just remember, it's a million to one chance that Mrs T could have come up with my nag."

"You really think she'd definitely not have found Lorraine and Nancy and tipped people off? Tipped off Le Manx Gang, perhaps?"

Docherty cracked his knuckles again and looked at Archie, on the verge of tearing him off a strip and more, for questioning what he firmly believed. He valued Archie's opinions though and let him challenge him, even though he wasn't a Scot. It was good to have someone who wasn't afraid, to bounce ideas off. Archie might be right to have doubts about Françoise. "Mibee ye should pay her another personal visit," he said.

"Nah. I think you're right, boss. The odds are too high. I've got one of our boys dating someone who uses the stables. He's there a lot, snooping round while she rides. Disabled girl. Big arse, I'm told. They can't refuse him access cos she's in a wheelchair and he drives her there. No hint of the two you're after there, he says, or anything out of order. Girl after your own heart, she is."

"Eh?"

"Won't let him in her house. Likes having it in hotels, Callum says, and so he obliges." Docherty got his drift, and they laughed together like the dirty dogs they were.

"And I've still got my boys round and about in London, circulating our target's photos. Their heads will pop up over the parapet soon, and that will be that."

"Good. Good. I'm glad that we're on the same page."

"We are, sir. You can be sure of that."

"Talk to yer contacts in the Midlands and north-west and try to locate the other conspirators."

"Will do, sir."

"I want them all, ye ken?"

August

Country life suited McQueen and Gabby, but he admitted there were things to get used to, much of it for the good. Without a kebab house on the doorstep, or any other house for a mile or more, in no time he'd lost half a stone and instead of smoking her roll-ups, Gabby was on twenty organic carrots a day. The local farm-shop owners viewed them with suspicion at first, but they soon became good buddies. Even so, in arguments Gabby often remarked, "So we should be! Considering the amount of produce we purchase there."

"Well, you could go to the supermarket in town, Gabby."

"So could you. Anyway, I had enough of supermarkets and towns when I was in London."

McQueen knew he'd better not press his point today because Gabby was preparing brunch, and he wanted his full share. He got on with shaving and kept quiet. The letterbox clunked. He heard her footsteps in the hall, then her raucous laughter.

"What is it, love?"

"It's a postcard from Likely Di. She's on a nine-night cruise around the Med, lucky thing. She says, 'Hi, you two. Wish you weren't here! Having a delightfully boozy cruisey. Seen all the sights. Currently in Rome. Even got an audience with the Pope and, even better, nicked a few quid off him after a few rounds of seven card brag! Take care and will give you a bell on my return.' She's given us each a kiss."

"Glad she made time to get away," he said, coming down the stairs. "It'll do her a power of good, all that sea air."

"Can you imagine the clothes she took with her?"

He raised his eyebrows, horrified by the thought. "Does it say if she's gone on her own? Or is she with a friend?"

"It doesn't say. She's always been on her own though, hasn't she?"

"Dunno really. Dark horse is Likely Di. If she's on her own, perhaps we should ask her to come and live with us? There would be plenty of room if you discarded all your old horsey stuff."

Gabby threw an olive at him and laughed. "Not on your nelly!"

That evening with a salt and vinegar Hula Hoop for a ring, he knelt on one knee and proposed.

"No," she said, without hesitation.

He flinched, frozen on the spot, thinking he'd misjudged everything. What a fool. But then Gabby added, "I am not marrying a Cockney dwarf. Get up, you soppy bugger," and perhaps there was still a chance. He took her hand, Hula Hoop poised, his eyes gazing into hers. He hoped and he waited.

"Oh Mac! Course I will. I wanted to the first time I saw you when we were 'shopping'."

That night they held hands in the garden, counting shooting stars and making wishes.

Maurice Pasternak stood in Long Acre then meandered towards Covent Garden. It was a muggy summer's day. London streets swelled with sweaty, spellbound tourists. He detested them: tourists were both the bane of his life and the hands that fed him. Instinctively, he noted anyone heading vaguely in the direction of his pub, The Salisbury. He was heading in the opposite direction in no hurry. He always looked forward to his Wednesday afternoons off. They gave him time to unwind and take it slow. The morning had been quiet, and as his assistant manager was experienced enough to deal with any issues that may arise, he'd take the chance to down a few pints. Outside his own pub he was known as Maurice, but in his boozer, he was always called Mo, except by Simon. Even though he hated it, his locals persisted, as did his staff. He was to blame for it, they always said, because of the number of times he told them he'd be with them in a mo.

The Cross Keys, his regular Wednesday destination, was busy and loud, with mainly locals. He ordered a light and bitter and located a free space at the far end of the bar then settled down to attempt the *Daily Telegraph's* cryptic crossword, his usual ritual there. He'd almost run out of ale before even getting as far as two across: '*Angry report on dirty duck*'.

He chewed over the baffling clue as he waited for service at the bar.

Eight letters.

Fourth letter: D.

Was it pigeons? Naah. Wrong spelling and too easy. Anyway, pigs weren't dirty, despite their reputation.

"Same again, Maurice?" said the barman.

"Yes please, Dave. How's trade?"

"Not too bad. You?"

"Yer. Last couple of weeks have been good."

Mo ready for his crossword and a cross word at the bar

Reflected in a pub mirror to his left he could see a couple with heads down, ignoring their two pints of Guinness on their table, too engrossed in sketching something out, making lists and laughing. He managed to overhear that they were in London for a *Mamma Mia!* matinee at the Prince Edward Theatre. *Nice to see a happy couple*, he thought, returning to the crossword.

Widgeons?

Duck, yes, but why dirty?

The chatty loved-up Guinness pair distracted him. He tried to block them out, not hear what they were saying, but their excitement cheered and intrigued him as they discussed music, a party, catering, transport, hotels, practicalities, an invitation list, and the specific wording they'd use to invite them all. It sounded like some bash. He shifted from accidentally overhearing to actively listening. Did he recognise those voices? Old customers probably. Nice to hear Cockney accents, not tourists from afar. He couldn't see without standing up and making it obvious he was gawping. He'd leave them to their joy and get back to his other two-across problem.

Why was the duck dirty? He racked his brains on both counts, scribbling ideas on a beer mat. "Bother," he muttered, shifting on his seat to reach for a pen he'd dropped. One more stretch should do it. He stretched and had a double result: now he could reach it and see the couple as well. *What?* He came up for air, flabbergasted, and shuffled back to where he could be hidden, convinced it was that wannabe author babe. She couldn't have been doing well as an author. He'd always been convinced she would have brought him in a signed copy of her book if she'd ever made it big – after all, she'd sat in his pub writing and bending his ear about plot lines enough times.

But wait. It wasn't just her; it was him too. She was with that vanished-into-thin-air record dealer. He was stunned. She was actually with that con artist? She was his girl? His mind raced. His whole body fumed.

Three letters.

Starts with D.

Sounds like 'hell'.

Although deep down he'd suspected it, once he'd found the cover was a fake, it all fell into place, finally confirmed. Yes.

They'd been working together! His trembling hand gripped his pen so tightly, the plastic cracked. *Bastards. Bastards!* Dirty ducks, the pair of them. He felt ashamed that he'd sometimes tried his best to convince himself that he hadn't seen her again because she might have died, and she'd not told him that she found out she was ill after that blood test she'd fussed about. Bogus bloody blood test, more like. What a trusting naïve fool he was.

What to do? He should go and say hello. Should he? Then what?

All thoughts of the plans he'd once made with Simon were forgotten. He was in such inner turmoil. Confront them? They'd just deny it. Call on his mates to rough them up? That wouldn't look good in a public place and anyway they would be off and away by the time the heavy mob arrived. He grew wilder and wilder, burning with fury and humiliation. The cheating charlatans were right near him, and yet again there was nothing he could do about it. Did that make him a coward? he asked himself, deflated, as he watched them drain the remainder of their stouts and leave the pub together, arm-in-arm, still giggling.

He stood up and stared at their vacant table, feeling sick. *You'll be facing your Waterloo soon*, he thought.

Suddenly it hit him: 'dirty' meant 'wild' not 'pig shit'. It was wildfowl. A tiny victory in the circumstances. He was about to return to his table to fill in the answer when his bartender habits kicked in and he checked the ashtray for smouldering ends. No butts: that wasn't like the author babe he'd known, but they'd left behind two lumps of discarded notes, screwed up tight. *Well, relight my fire*, he thought as he picked them up and flattened out the papers. He gasped. Would you Adam and Eve it? At that moment he felt more joyous than he would have if he'd found a winning lottery ticket.

Mac and Gabby cordially request your company for
A day and night of bangers and crash

Saturday 3rd November

B+B accommodation has been reserved for you at xxxxx Hotel
tba (Gabby to sort)
with minibus transport courtesy of your hosts to and from
Gabby 'n' Mac's
3pm for
house-warming buffet and afternoon fun
evening: hot food, hot drinks, cold bar
fireworks
live music from two of our very own
followed by 9.30pm bonfire and midnight surprises
Bring a rocket or sparklers!
*TOP TIP *(and we're not talking horses!)* Wear warm layers
and countryside footwear.

RSVP to The Rambles...

Mo couldn't read anymore. He was welling up with excitement. He had their address! And he had their names too. *So, that's what you're really called, punks,* he thought. He had 'em! They'd moved to Suffolk, the London sell-out luvvies.

"You all right there?" called Dave, polishing a glass between customers.

"Yeah. Yeah. I'm good, thanks. I've just solved a puzzle. Bit of an adrenaline buzz going on." He waved the crossword in Dave's direction, then sat down.

"You old crossword junkie." His barman friend laughed. "Another pint?"

Mo didn't answer. There was more to excite him! On the second crumpled paper was a scribbled list of guests. He scanned it. Two names jumped up with treble clefs doodled alongside them: Al Dennett, Dubs Dennett, the Dennett brothers. His Al and Dubs? His Friday band, The Substitunes? Could it be them? It had to be. He had their card at home, so he hurried back to St Martin's Lane to find it in his flat above The Salisbury.

*

Half an hour later, Mo was talking on the phone to Al in the guise of checking The Substitunes dates for the next month. Then he asked if he and Dubs were going to be at McQueen's party, and would they be all right for the Friday night gig before it?

"I should hope so!" said a cheery Al. "Me and Dubs will be playing for them. Just us two, calling ourselves, The Substi-Two-Tunes. Get it?"

"Very clever."

"I didn't know you were friends with Mac."

"Let's just say we've met before. I know Gabby better." Staring at the crumpled invitation draft in his hand, the hurt he'd felt at her betrayal and his urge for revenge resurfaced. At the very least, he wanted his money back, with interest. What the hell? He told Al the whole story and read out the phoney business card he'd been given.

It wasn't long before he was back behind his bar in an unusually affable mood. Al had promised to get his grand back in spades and thanked him profusely, as ever, for the ongoing pub bookings.

"Maurice? Is that you?" a voice called from downstairs. "Can you nip down for a second?"

"Sure thing. Your wish is my command," Mo replied. Simon was back early. Things were looking up. He'd love this news.

Thirteen down. 7-2-4

Begins with R.

Clue: '*A dish best served on a cold and smoky night, all yours*'.

There were thirteen stone steps down to the cellar. He trod heavily on each one, muttering letters to himself as he made his way down.

"R – E – V – E – N – G – E – I – S – M – I – N – E.

"Simon, listen to this…"

THIRTY-ONE

October

Likely Di lined up the grapefruits and straightened the courgettes. She was like McQueen in that way. "Tidy as you go," she'd once heard him mutter, and she knew what he meant. She liked the way he kept everything ordered and well-planned. Today she was applying it to her mate's veg stall, minding it for the day as a favour. He'd owe her one after this. Tidy goods were important on any market stall, but she always felt immaculately set out fruit and veg were more appealing to buyers, and she wanted to prove it. Reg-the-Veg was a bit slapdash, and she warned him he'd go under unless he paid more attention.

It was a good day to be working outdoors. Sunny blue sky, crisp air with an early autumnal feel. The market trader chatter was buzzing round her, and the place was busy but not hectic. She loved it on Borough Market. She was near the river, not far away from the fuzzy hum of traffic, yet in a historic oasis. Mike the Pike was on his fish stall. Today, a gang of giggling schoolboys were hovering near, taking it in turns to look at the shark head he had out front. They were armed with clipboards, pencils, and pages with things to tick off for their teacher, but they weren't interested in any of that. They were interested in the shark's eyeball, and they'd dared each other to touch it with their bare finger. Mike the Pike didn't mind. He even turned his back now and again so they could sneak up in turn and claim glory. *Marvellous whippersnappers*, she thought.

Sandi and her fresh bread and bakery items made up for the smell of the fish. Vikram was there as usual, with his army of salamis, and her favourite stall, run by Shakila and Rhona, was crammed with their homemade chocolates. Likely Di knew for a fact they'd bought them from the cash and carry and just added extra chocolate blobs or doused them in syrup and then rolled them in coconut, but she admired their gall, and presentation.

She greeted the brothers as they approached the market stall. "Hello, Al, Dubs. Nice to see your kissers again. The linen game's a bit quiet and Reg is a man short today, so I'm lending a hand. What'll it be, gents? Half a dozen St Clements or a coupla pounds of King Edwards?"

"No. You're all right," said Dubs. "But thanks. We're more meat men than broccoli heads." She would have sworn he looked scared at the thought of consuming vegetables, and she waved a bunch of watercress at him, teasingly.

"You're looking sharp, as always, boys. Right pair of fashion victims aren't yer?" she said, tapping the toes of her favourite shiny Jimmy Choos on the ground.

"That's right," said Dubs. "From our Tommy Hilfiger sunglasses down to our black leather Chelsea boots. The boys of summer we are!"

"Don't mention lucky Chelsea! They beat my beloved Millwall on the last game of the season."

"Proud to say we have never owned a pair of jeans between us."

"That's right," said Al. "With this dapper clobber and our saucy chat-up line, it's a doddle to pull a bit of skirt."

"Not sure about the blond streaks though. Not turning poofta on me are ya?"

"Never!" they shouted in unison.

She ruffled Dubs's hair. "I'd still love you both if you had. It don't bother me, loves. Each to their own. Just enjoy yerselves." She winked. "Must cost you a pretty packet to fund these new styles. Don't know how you can afford it."

"Too right," said Al. "But our new fast one helps."

"Go on."

"We pick a crowded city pub on a Friday lunchtime, posing as charity workers, speak to the landlord to get his permission. We flog raffle tickets fiver each or three for a cock and hen. Prize is a gorgeous giant panda. All the secretaries want it, and all the blokes want to buy it for them. There's a couple of bottles of Prosecco for the runners-up. Once a few have a go, the whole thing snowballs and with a few drinks inside them, they're queueing up to stroke the Peter Panda. They part with their lolly, the raffle gets held, winners presented and we're off. Last week in the Slug and Pitcher we took nearly eight hundred quid. The bubbles cost us three quid a go, wholesale, and then we pick up the bears from some geezer in the Blind Beggar pub in Whitechapel for a tenner."

"Know it well, love."

"Thought you might."

Dubs finished off. "And to keep our consciences clear, we send a few quid to the charity. Happy days!"

"Yep. Impressive, boys. But if you don't know your history, keep your visits to a minimum in that boozer. I had some very unprincipled friends in there once upon a time."

Al was suddenly distracted by the fish stall. "Cor! Look at that shark head!" he said, eyes wide, face beaming.

"You big kid! What you after from me, then, if it's not a pound of bananas, or a manager for your band?"

"Sorry, Diana, just wondered if you have a spare five minutes? We need to have a quick chat."

"Yep, okay, providing it's none of that Mac nonsense."

"Well," said Al, "it is in a way, but please hear us out."

Three minutes later, Likely Di was armed with news of McQueen and Gabby's party plans and how she would be getting an invite, so she should keep the date, and the secret. They waited for her to answer while she served a customer – yuppie type wanting courgettes for her spiraliser.

"So, from what you've told me, it looks like Mac and Gabby are going to invite us all to their November bash. Nice. Thanks for the heads-up. I might buy a new frock. And you'll be playing. How could that not be nice?" She laughed.

"Well, yeah. It's just us two, as The Substi-Two-Tunes, not the full Substitunes, Danny and Dennis can't be there. But we're good as a duo."

"I'll bet you are. You know I'm a big fan. Of course you'll still be good. Better, actually. I always thought that other guitarist was a show stealer. Dennis? Is that him?"

Al waited for Dubs to explain.

"I may be the band's drummer, but when we're a duo I dump the drumkit and I ain't half bad on a Rickenbacker guitar." Al nodded and beamed with pride. Another customer turned up, wanting broccoli and late-season samphire. Once she'd dealt with that, she turned back to them. "Boys, I can't help thinking there's more to this story. Am I right?"

They leaned in, checked that no one was within earshot, and told the story of McQueen and Gabby scamming Mo. She felt like a priest hearing a confession, even though it wasn't their crime.

"What's bothering me," said Al, "is what if Mo turns snake in the grass, and gatecrashes the party with Simon, and they bring along a tooled-up clique. It could have serious repercussions."

"Are you talking fisticuffs or percussion? Only joking, boys. Don't mind me."

Another customer to serve. Elderly gent. Potatoes for mashing, three carrots and a swede. Likely Di slipped him some sprouts for free. They were on the turn. "There you go, ducks. Got to balance it out with some greens or you'll never get to pick up yer telegram from the Queen."

She thought on the story about Gabby, McQueen, and Mo for a while, saying not a word. She knew it unnerved people when she was silent. Sometimes silence was the only thing that got her brain working. Silence and vitamin C, that is. She looked at Al and Dubs and slowly peeled a satsuma. The smell of oranges in the air helped attract customers.

"Thanks for enlightening me, boys. You certainly did the right thing. I'll sort a powwow with Mac and Gabby and get this sorted." As a parting treat, she gave them both a juicy Victoria plum. "Now, on yer bike, lads. I've plenty to mull over and another gent to serve. What'll it be, sir? Satsumas? Certainly."

An idea started to take root.

*

McQueen and Gabby sat on shiny poppy-coloured plastic chairs, four to a table, in a greasy spoon. Likely Di had chosen it. McQueen shuddered. It wasn't his type. They put their coats on the other two empty chairs. A loud red and white gingham tablecloth covered their table. It was home to the usual suspects: there were red and brown plastic sauce bottles with obligatory congealed blobs of gunge breeding heavens knows what around the spout; a stainless-steel ashtray crammed with discarded butts from a previous customer; chipped, discoloured salt and pepper pots; a half-blocked all or nothing dispenser for white sugar. Despite what seemed like gross failings to McQueen, the fabled Old Ma Kelly Café was heaving; they were lucky to secure a table. He had never eaten there before but knew it was thought to be one of the best in London. Today's specials were scrawled on a blackboard in pink chalk.

- *Full English (just for you builders) – two eggs, two sausages, bacon, beans, fried bread, mushrooms, tomatoes, bubble and*

squeak, black pudding, toast, and, to wash it all down, a
mug of tea or coffee.
- *Roast Lamb, with spuds, mint sauce and all the trimmings.*
- *Cheese and Onion Ommelet – with chips and mushy peas.*

McQueen laughed to himself over the spelling mistake. With the regular menu too, the choices seemed endless; endless but not overly appealing.

Covering the wall were photos of B-list local boxers and footballers, all signed '*To Ma, xx*'. There was one of Henry Cooper, youthful and trim, before he made it big, and Joe Bugner too, looking like a clean-faced, shy teenager. The nicotine discolouring the ceiling must have lasted longer than many of its forty-a-day patrons. A roly-poly waitress, with excessive eyeliner and a shiny, greasy forehead, came over. She pulled a pencil and pad from her nylon apron pocket and stood poised to take their order. She was chewing gum in time to the record playing on the radio, tuned in to Capital Gold.

"Yes, loves?"

Gabby explained they were waiting for a friend who'd be with them shortly. She ordered two coffees to tide them over until Likely Di arrived. McQueen feared they would be getting Maxwell House's finest. Or might it be Camp?

Their sticky laminated menu smelt of stale ketchup. McQueen left it on the table. He'd been trying to work out what this summons was all about since Likely Di had phoned two days ago. Her manner had been curt, most unlike her, unless you'd done her wrong and she wanted to have it out with you. What wrong had he or Gabby done Likely Di? None that they could think of.

"Not got much of an appetite," said Gabby.

"Me neither." He tapped his watch face.

*

Likely Di was fifteen minutes late. She knew that no amount of her designer labels could bring any class to this place, but she liked it. Catching the eye of the waitress as she walked in, she asked for tea, strong, with milk, then made her way to the table where McQueen sat with Gabby. There was no spare chair for her because of their coats, so she stuffed McQueen's on top of Gabby's and left his sleeve dragging on the floor. That would probably bug them as much as not having a chair sorted for her had bugged her.

No matter. The waitress had arrived with her tea. "Your tea, Diana," she said, setting it down. "And your usual to follow?"

"Thanks, Shakila."

"And for you, loves?"

"Just a round of toast with marmalade please," said Gabby.

"Same for me, but Marmite," said McQueen.

It seemed no one wanted to break the silence, and Likely Di was happy to drink her tea. In the end Gabby spoke.

"Well, Diana, what's this all about? Is there a problem you need us for? Are you ill?"

Likely Di eyeballed them both. "I'm not ill but thank you for caring. A little birdie told me you had a nice pub touch a while back. Gotta say, an admirable flanker you pulled there. And I have to admit, I laughed when I heard who it was you stung."

"So?" said McQueen. She knew very well that she could have been referring to any number of cons from his past. She thought he should sweat a bit. To his credit he stayed cool. "How did you discover all of this?"

Likely Di offered Gabby a cigarette, lit them both and told the story of Al and Dubs's market meet-up, and the possible ramifications that could ensue if Mo was left fuming. McQueen said nothing. She sensed that he didn't like being called to order. Gabby stayed smoking, silent too.

"Mac, I'm old and ugly enough. I need to speak plainly to you both. It was a schoolboy error to leave the invitation there. If Mo turns up on the night with his mob, which he might, gawd knows how it might end."

"I'll cancel the party then."

"Mac, don't you bleedin' get it? He's got your address! Going to move home then?"

Neither of them had ever heard her as brusque as this before.

*

Gabby needed another cigarette. This whole Mo business had been her idea, and McQueen was taking the rap for it. She picked up her Tintin. It was stuck to the tacky PVC tablecloth and made a soft tearing sound as she pulled it away. Trying not to grimace, and not wanting to insult Likely Di more than the coat error already had, she beckoned to the waitress, Shakila, for a cloth, and they waited while she came over to wipe the sticky table. Gabby nodded thanks, then passed one of her ready-rolled Likely Di's way.

"Mac," said Likely Di, filling the air with smoke, "I'm not your mum but please heed my advice. In all my fifty-odd years, I have had two premonitions. First was West Ham to win the FA Cup in 1980, which I won a nice few quid on. And more recently, the killing of a very close friend – a great loss. I have a foreboding about this, Mac. Call me an old soothsayer if you like, but my honest counsel to you is to return Mo's money, with interest."

"But you know you can't cheat an honest man. He fell for it."

"Yes, I know, my dear. But he's not a bad man. Just maybe a bit of a dimwit." She looked at Gabby. "And a pain, I know. I guess you needed to see if you still had the pluck and mettle, after your break. Am I right? And you have. Give him his money, Mac. And get that monkey off your back."

They sat in silence for a short while then Likely Di went on. "Just listen. Stay at mine tonight, I've got some knocked-off cognac. Right up your street. I want to hear what LPs you had. Any by The Who?" she said, laughing. "Then in the morning, you can decide what to do."

McQueen looked at Gabby, asking without words if she was okay with that. She nodded.

The waitress brought the food to the table. "There you are,

loves. Toast and spreads and yours, Diana: liver and bacon, onions, spaghetti hoops, two poached eggs, gherkin and a banana milkshake."

"Yum," said Likely Di. "Thanks, hon."

Gabby looked at her plate, then caught McQueen's expression. He looked as if he was repulsed.

*

They discussed the situation late into the night, while Likely Di snored, finally agreeing that her fears were probably hokum – they weren't convinced that Mo had it in him to get revenge, but they both knew revenge was a powerful driving force and decided to take Likely Di's warning as good advice.

"Anything for a quiet life," said Gabby.

THIRTY-TWO

The next morning McQueen visited his bank: half an hour later, he arrived as it opened, this time minus a copy of *Shindig*. Mo had his back to him, fiddling with the top shelf.

"Morning, Mo."

Mo turned around. When he saw McQueen, he took a sharp intake of breath. "Get off my premises, you mountebank, before I call the police. I've a button here. All I need to do is press it, and they'll be all over this place in a trice."

McQueen held up both his hands. "No, Mo. I'm here to give you something." He slid his hand into his inside pocket.

"No!" shouted Mo. "We both know Al 'n' Dubs. And I'm too young to die. Don't kill me!"

"I'm not here for that, Mo. Don't be ridiculous. Look." He pulled out a roll of banknotes. "There you are. A thousand notes. Plus, a monkey for your inconvenience." He placed the money on the table next to Mo. Mo looked at it suspiciously. He looked at McQueen, then back to the glorious pile. He picked it up, turning it over as he scrutinised it.

"It's all there, Mo, with my sincere apologies."

"Why? What? How the hell?"

"Sorry. Can't really go into details. Let's just say it was part of a greater plan. Look, you know where the party is. Please come along."

"Thanks for the invite, but I'm away sea fishing in Weymouth that weekend."

"Of course you are. Of course." McQueen couldn't resist adding, "Well, don't get reeled in again."

Mo smirked, then laughed. "You sod, Del!"

McQueen laughed with him. "Listen, gotta chip off soon, but before I go, how about I buy you a beer for old times' sake?"

"I tell you what, I remember you had a penchant for a decent ale. Pedigree, if memory serves. I've a barrel in the cellar with a new ale I might introduce. Fancy coming down there and doing a taster? I'd appreciate that. I can get someone from upstairs to watch the bar for half an hour." Mo pulled out his phone and texted someone.

"Really? You want to test out my seasoned taste-buds, do you?" said McQueen, stalling for time while he figured out how long it might take and whether to accept the offer. Gabby would be waiting.

There was an instant ping from Mo's phone. "That's settled," he said with a bright look on his face. "He's on his way down. Come on, mate. I can't make my mind up about this. It's from an up-and-coming microbrewery. Ooooh, there's a cider too you might be able to give an expert opinion on."

"Cider?" Instinct was telling McQueen not to go. It seemed too close to the Hansel and Gretel children's story. *Be guided by your inner self. Trust your feelings,* Grandad would be saying. But Grandad wasn't there, and McQueen thought his childish suspicions were ridiculous, so he said, "That sounds great, Mo. I'll be honoured."

Mo unbolted the bar flap and lifted it so McQueen could walk through. He beckoned him round to the other side of the bar and signalled for him to follow down the stone cellar steps. Instantly McQueen regretted it; his leather-soled loafers were slippy on the stone, so he held the railing as he walked. How could anyone carry a crate of beers up these steps? They were lethal. It struck him that he'd never been in a pub cellar before and the idea of seeing a new underworld was growing on him. He imagined a Dalek, or some Cybermen skulking among the rows of barrels.

A phone rang. It wasn't his.

"Damn it," said Mo. "I left my phone upstairs. You stay here. I better get it. It could be the brewery." He turned and took the stairs two at a time, speedy and sure-footed.

The cellar went dark. There was a loud echoing thud as the door in the ceiling slammed shut, and a final clink that made McQueen realise this was deliberate. He'd been locked in.

He stood in the beery blackness and cursed his own foolishness. He reached for his phone. No signal.

"Mo? Mo? Can you hear me?"

*

Mo and Simon stood together, clutching their phones. In perfect synchrony they closed them up and put them away. Simon took Mo's hand and they walked together to the cellar door, then danced on it like two roguish elves.

"We could be auditioning for parts in Michael Flatley's *Riverdance*," said Simon, laughing and holding his arms straight by his side as he bobbed up and down. A customer applauded.

Between bouts of laughter, Mo shouted to the cellar door, "There's no phone signal down there, mate, so don't waste yer battery trying to call for help."

And, "Watch out for the rats. The last one I saw was as big as a fox. If they bite, they don't let go."

And, "Try to keep calm. There's no ventilation down there. Don't waste air."

And, "I expect Miss Smarty Pants will turn up at some point

to rescue you. In the meantime, all you can do is—" He nodded at Simon and they chorused together, the way they'd planned to, should this unlikely day ever arrive: "All you can do is shout for 'el. P! El. P! El. P!"

Mo straightened up and turned back to the bar where a customer stood waiting for a refill. He shrugged. "New staff. It's a little initiation ceremony they all go through. Same again?" he said as he took the glass and poured a fresh pint.

"Training," said Simon, rolling his eyes at the customer and tutting in an exaggerated way. "You should have heard the words I came out with when it happened to me! I didn't even know I had such an extensive vocabulary."

"It's a harsh way to get used to working with the barrels in the down belows, but no pain, no gain, eh?" Mo smiled across the bar. "Have this one on the house."

The customer looked amused and, as Mo had hoped, he was unperturbed by McQueen's banging on the cellar door. Mo signalled to Simon, who turned up the radio, almost blocking out the noise. Mo congratulated himself, remembering his fury on the day Del had conned him. Things were going to plan. *Let the bugger sweat down there. Rat or no rat, he'll be bricking it before long. Even with a light on his phone, if he has one, that cellar's truly spooky. I'll release him when I get what I'm really after.*

Thirteen down. 7-2-4. Begins with R.

He'd worked out that revenge was a dish best served cold. But here he was, on a bright sunny morning and for once in his life, he was up. It felt good.

*

What was keeping McQueen? *Bloomin' typical! He knows I get stressed when he keeps me waiting.* In truth, he rarely kept her waiting. Not since the time... Gabby stopped her train of thought. Now was not the time to go over the day they'd fled from Docherty in Edinburgh. She tried McQueen's phone again. Still no answer.

She peered up and around Soho Square, the place they'd picnicked years back. No sign of him.

Maybe he was in deep debate with Mo. *Good luck to him there.* As far as she'd worked out there was nothing deep at all about Mo. Money talked to him though, and her Mac had gone to him with money, so there should be no problemo.

What? What was holding him up? Then she knew. *Ha! He's getting me a new crimson dress. That'll be it.* Twenty minutes later she dismissed the stupid, romantic idea and hailed a passing London taxi to The Salisbury. It was not much more than ten minutes on foot, but she couldn't wait that long.

"I'm extremely late for an important appointment," she said as she got in, exactly as McQueen had done in Edinburgh. "So, if you wouldn't mind stepping on it."

"Certainly," said the cabbie.

*

"Hello, stranger," said Mo as she walked through the pub door. "Lost something, babe?"

Babe? That was something she hadn't heard in a while, and she hadn't missed it. She let him have his say; best he gets it out of his system; best she lets him feel superior. Well, technically he was.

"Box of LPs perhaps? Notebook and pen to write another bestseller? Or have you come here to phone a friend?"

She felt sick, hearing his feeble taunts. "Very funny, Mo. Where is he? I know he's been here. He's seen you, right? So where is he?" She stopped in her tracks. Savoy Simon was behind the bar. *Oh hell.* Had Simon remembered McQueen's cool Savoy exit last year? What was going on here? She shot glances round the pub. As far as she could see, there was no sign of him, and so far, only three customers. None she recognised.

"Mac. Mac. Are you there?" she shouted.

There was a burst of knocks from somewhere behind the bar

and a muffled voice that she recognised. "Gabby. Is that you? I'm in the cellar. Door's stuck. Get me out of here."

She strode over to Mo. "Let him out! Let him out now, or I'll call the police!"

"I don't think you'll do that, babe." He winked at Simon. "They know that this cellar door often jams, and if some idiot customer insists on wandering down there, it's hardly a crime, is it? You don't want to be done for wasting police time. Do you?"

Gabby tried to gather her thoughts and work out what to do next. She didn't want the palaver of police turning up. What would McQueen do? Should she text Al? Or Dubs? They'd sort this out, wouldn't they? Or Likely Di? She'd always got a heavy mob to hand when she needed one.

"Your face, babe. You've gone very pale." Mo looked like he was enjoying this. He was laughing. Simon, too. "Given blood this morning, have you, up at the hospital?" She felt helpless. "Oooh. Hold up." He put his hand to an ear. "I think I heard something from the cellar." Mo screwed up his face as if he was listening hard. "What was that, Del? Sorry. I mean, what was that, Mac? Is that you, calling for help?" He nodded at Simon, and they went through the LP/help routine together. "El. P! El. P!" Turning back to Gabby, he said, "Get it, babe? Get it? El. P. Get it?"

She said nothing but knew the change in her posture would have told him that he was pissing her off and yes, she'd understood.

Mo pulled down a straight pint glass and focused on polishing it. He smiled reassuringly across at his customers and waited.

Gabby tried to read him. Had he called in his own heavies? Had he harmed McQueen? Or was he planning to? What would it take to get him to set McQueen free? Surely, now he'd got his money back, and more, things were settled between them all?

He cheerily served a new customer then got back to his glass polishing as if he was waiting for something and didn't mind how long it took to get it.

Then it struck her. How could she have been so dumb? This

was Mo she was dealing with. Nothing was complicated. Nothing was deep. She put her elbows on the bar, rested her chin on her fists and looked into his eyes.

"I'm sorry, Mo. Truly I am. What I set you up for was wrong. But you've been repaid now, and rewarded, so let's please not blow this out of proportion."

He looked away and took another glass.

"Mo. Please." She touched his arm softly and he turned back.

"Yes, babe?"

"I. Am. Sorry. Please forgive me."

He fixed her with his eyes. This could go either way, she thought, half expecting to be thrown down there with McQueen. Should she call for help now? Appeal to the customers? Nope. She'd ride this one out.

"Finally." He started laughing and stood back, puffing his chest out, looking powerful and smug. "Open Sesame."

Simon went over to the cellar door, slid back the bolt to unlock it; he pulled it up, hooked it to the wall to secure it, and switched the light back on. McQueen's head appeared. He stopped near to the top step. She felt frightened, and impatient to know what was going on. Was he injured? Probably checking himself for cobwebs, she assured herself. Once he was out, she knew he'd spotted her, but he was playing it cool and made nothing of her being there.

"Well. Thank you for that cellar tour, Mo," he said, sounding unflustered. How did he do it? "I'll be on my way if it's all the same with you." He brushed past Simon, acknowledging him with a "Simon," and a curt smile.

So, it was Savoy Simon; she'd been right. Had Simon recognised McQueen? What might happen if he did? Time to do a legger while they still could, she thought. *Hurry up, McQueen.* She studied Simon's reaction. He'd looked at McQueen quizzically, but the penny didn't seem to have dropped and he lifted the bar flap so Mo's prisoner could walk free.

McQueen held out his arm for Gabby to link. "Come along,

my dear. I think we're done here." He turned back to Mo and Simon. "Nice doing business with you today. No hard feelings, guys. If you want to come to our party, please RSVP. You've got the details. Al 'n' Dubs will be pleased to see you, I'm sure."

Mo walked towards them looking sterner than Gabby had ever seen him look. Once he was close enough for no one else to hear he said, "I've no gripe with our mutual friends, but you two: don't come back. You're both barred. If you step into my gaff again, don't expect to be leaving. Do you follow?"

The instant they were outside Gabby heard Mo and Simon hooting with laughter and the customers too.

"Christ, Mac. You're a cool-headed bastard sometimes. You didn't flinch once. What the hell happened in there? I was crapping it when you didn't turn up. I knew I should have gone in with you from the off. Wait till I tell Likely Di what she put you through."

He started laughing.

"What? What, Mac?"

"It's just that down in the cellar I left Mo and Simon a nice warm pint of hell pee to add to his LP collection."

*

Docherty's phone rang. He snatched it from his desk, flipped it open and glowered at the screen before pressing the keypad to accept the call.

"Ye've withheld yer number. I dinnae appreciate numbers being withheld. This better not be someone wasting my time an' it better be good."

He listened.

"So, it's you. Nice touch wi' the LP cover you sent. Impressive artwork." He didn't let the caller speak. They'd only deny sending anything; say they didn't know what he was talking about. He'd had enough of that. "I've never been a fan of The Who but if this matter turns out well, I might be tempted to try 'Getting in Tune'." He was pleased with his off-the-cuff pun and the way he'd recalled a track from the album. Quick wit. He liked that about himself.

He had more to say; he had a major gripe.

"I've been phoning yer number – the number on yer anonymous message. I think ye'd better get it checked." He ignored the caller's bleating protests and forged on with what he wanted to say. "If ye've been deliberately wasting my time, I'll make sure ye have nae time left tae waste. Ye get what I'm saying? Ye can fool me once, but I 'Won't Get Fooled Again'." He was enjoying this. Let them squirm. Let them wonder, whoever they were. He'd find out. Their time would come.

He listened, absent-mindedly doodling on his notepad. Whenever they returned to protesting ignorance about the LP cover and the message, he reprimanded them. "Dinnae play the 'I don't know what ye're talking about' game wi' me," he said, near to growling. "Get to the point." Then he'd let them speak, taking in every detail, noting every anxious nuance, turning over every possible flaw.

"Remote location sounds tae perfect. Dinnae forget who ye're dealing wi'. If what ye're telling me is in any way inaccurate, ye'll nae be too perfect ever again."

He went to shut down the call but paused instead. Why miss a chance to issue another of his famous Docherty threats?

"And be sure nae tae post me anything more, or ye'll be hunted down by my infantry and when they find ye, which they will, I shall personally carve ye up and get ye posted to each and every one of yer so-called friends."

He held the phone to his ear. He always found the monotonous tone of the telephone satisfying, after he'd cut someone dead, so to speak. He knew they'd be in pieces at the end of the line. He knew they'd do their best to make sure everything went like clockwork.

When he looked at what he'd drawn he saw it was an axe. He smiled at his clever subconscious.

THIRTY-THREE

Saturday 3rd November

"I think we're good to go, Mac."

"Sorted things out for your sister? Ramps in the garden being done?"

"Yep. All arranged. Still no word on why her boyfriend isn't coming. If it wasn't for Françoise, I'd never believe she even had one."

"Leave her be. She'll tell what she wants to tell if she wants to tell it."

Gabby ignored him; she hated being told what to do regarding her sister.

"Toto is with Noel and his dogs for the day."

"Just as well. Your vol-au-vents would have him begging everyone for crumbs."

Gabby ignored him; she hated it when Toto was criticised. "D'you reckon we've covered all the bases?"

"Yes. I reckon we have, Gabby."

"This has been worse than planning Herd Ringer's race! I don't know how you did it."

"There's one important detail we mustn't forget."

"What's that? More advice from Grandad?"

McQueen smiled at her, nodding his head.

"Go on then, Mac. Hit me. I'm ready."

"We mustn't forget to enjoy it."

She gave him one of the smiles he loved. "I'll wear my crimson dress. It still fits. Likely Di will be green with envy."

*

"Hey, Woollyback! Hey, Wacker! You've ironed your denim and put white shirts on," said McQueen as he opened his front door. "I'm honoured. You look amazing. Been up the gym?"

Wacker didn't want to go into details there and then, and confess that there was no gym involved, just rehab, AA meetings and along with all that, church matters. They were off the booze, off the drugs and trying to eat healthy food. Eating food at all seemed like a novelty after years of self-neglect. McQueen knew some of their struggles and he'd been supportive, insisting they come along to the day of fun.

"Come in and catch up with Tonker and Blaggit. Blaggit's had a makeover too. Check out his straight teeth. And when he hugs you, your eyes won't water!" Wacker wasn't sure if he should laugh at this revelation. He wanted to but held back.

McQueen didn't seem to spot his anxiety, or maybe he was covering it up. He knew McQueen could read people. "Come and see everyone, Wacker. Likely Di's here, but be sure to call her Diana, and Gabby's sister's here too. You've not met them before. And Binky and Phil. You know them, of course. Shame you missed the lunch. Al 'n' Dubs were around for a bit, but they had something to sort. It's good to see the both of you. Really it is. We can do you a plate if you're hungry."

They stood on the doorstep as their cab drove away. McQueen gave them each a 'welcomed-by-an-uncle'-type hug. Wacker had felt uneasy about going to the party for days, dreading it even, but it was wearing off, now he was actually there. He was more confident than he had been at their first meeting with McQueen. This time he and Woollyback were fuelled by nothing more than Werther's Originals, and massive doses of builder's tea. He stroked the winter jacket he was carrying, and it calmed him.

"Thank you for the invitation," he said, modestly shifting his eyes from McQueen to Gabby.

Woollyback joined in. "Lovely place you both have here. We thought we would drop in to see you and the old gang, but we probably can't stay long as we have to be back tomorrow in time for a meeting. We'll maybe catch a train back tonight. Erm, probably, or first thing tomorrow."

"Yeah," said Woollyback, looking down at the doorstep boot scraper made from horseshoes welded together. "It's just. We're… er…" Wacker wiped his shoes on it and cast a glance around McQueen's oak-panelled entrance hall as he and Woollyback stepped inside.

"Whatever's right for you, guys," said Gabby. "Come in. Come in."

"My grandad's been a warrior against alcohol and drugs too," said McQueen. "He even had to be watched with the communion wine." Gabby whacked him and Wacker laughed, feeling more at ease. "Seriously, I get it," McQueen went on, quietly and sincerely. "I get it, and I'm proud of you."

"There's a room at the hotel booked for you if you decide to stay. I hope you do," said Gabby. "I see you've no bags, but there'll be a toothbrush at reception."

McQueen and Gabby's welcome was just what Wacker had needed. He'd never liked being pressed or rushed, it made him seize up. Woollyback too, but in their company he, and it seemed, Woollyback, were starting to relax.

"Well, well. Lord, Lord!" said Binky, coming over and smiling as he greeted them. He'd obviously overheard, or already knew about their lifestyle change. "Good to see you both looking so well."

Wacker shook his hand. "They say sin and religion go together."

"Oh, yes. God loves a sinner," said McQueen, winking at them.

Woollyback nodded. "He's always there for us."

It shouldn't have been a shock to Wacker when Binky started to sing, 'I'll Be There For You' by The Rembrandts, but it was.

Binky's voice sounded good. Everyone spilled out of the living room into the large hallway to join in with the song. He looked at Woollyback and in his heart he was glad to be with friends.

"Oh, I love this one," said Gabby, dancing on the rug.

Wacker had missed Binky, this wonderful singing nutter from his hometown, Liverpool. He liked both him and Phil. Phil was fiercer but meant well. He had their interests at heart. They'd been like older brothers to him and Woollyback. Without Phil and Binky who knows where they'd have ended up? *Who knows where?* He laughed to himself at what he'd just thought. *Who* knows! Ha! Binky's happy vibes were rubbing off on him already.

When Binky's singing was done everyone shook his hand, then shook Woollyback and Wacker's hands too. What a welcome. Gabby led her guests back into the living room. She introduced the two newcomers to her sister. Wacker had spotted her watching Binky sing from a wheelchair in the doorway. By the time Binky joined them, Gabby was off doing hosting duties with her sister wheeling after her, offering to help, followed by Tonker. Binky beckoned Phil over. "Hey, bro. You're the only one who hasn't shaken these two's hands. Come and make friends."

"Phil!" said Wacker, trying to sound more like the trooper he wanted to be, not the weed he felt he was. "I want to thank you. And you, as well, Binky. You brought me... us... I mean, me 'n' Woollyback, to our senses and because of you, we saw the light."

Phil hugged them both and shook their hands firmly. "Well done, you pair of scallies. You're a lesson for all of us. I'm really moved. And sorry I nearly strangled—"

"Say no more, mate," said Wacker, holding up his hand to

silence Phil. "There's no need to apologise for that. I was out of order." Wacker hated dwelling on the dark place he was in when they'd last been together, or how ashamed he felt about it. He made a stab at a joke instead. "But don't expect me to turn the other cheek, Phil – you might hit me!"

Phil laughed and shook Wacker's hand again. "We're solid, mate. Solid."

As they joined the others in the living room Phil turned his attention to Woollyback's shoes. "Oh my! You've ditched your winkle-pickers!"

"Just for the day, Phil!"

Gabby returned, just as Wacker was saying, "Contrary to what people think, Woollyback's pickers aren't welded on!"

He wished he hadn't said it because Gabby laughed so much she snorted, but she didn't seem to mind. "I certainly hope his winkle *is* welded on," she said, laughing even more.

*

Standing near, with Likely Di beside him, Blaggit let out a low grizzled laugh and handed Gabby a tissue which she took, graciously. "Such a gentleman, when he's all scrubbed up nice, don't you think, Diana?"

Diana acted as if she hadn't heard Gabby. Blaggit stepped in, keen to cover for the rudeness. "It's all a matter of moisturising," he said, smoothing his cheek and flashing his new teeth with a smile. "Lovely house they've got, isn't it?"

Gabby looked pleased. "Let me get you two a drink Wacker, Woolyback. Alcohol-free punch? Or fruit juice? Or Coke?" She tapped her forehead. "Cola, I mean. Not coke. Coca-Cola. Pepsi, I mean. Oh God. Sorry. Oh God. Now I've said oh God! Sorry."

Blaggit felt her embarrassment. Flustered, she flushed pink. Cute.

"Sorry. I'll bring you some of the punch. It's nice. And some nibbles. And beers for Phil 'n' Binky. Nothing for Diana, and I'll fill your glass, Blaggit. More Perrier? Back in a tic."

Never mind refilling drinks, being with Likely Di was tough tonight. Blaggit couldn't work out what he'd done wrong. She was never like this when they'd been together over the past few months. Good job he was sticking to sparkling water; apart from wanting to keep a cool head to deal with her mood, since he'd been with her, he'd tried to keep a check on his weight, but he was still as big as a bull. Next to him, Likely Di came up to his shoulder. He thought of her as a Barbie doll with her vast wardrobe of deluxe clothes. If he was honest, she was an aging Barbie doll. He liked that. And he liked having Tonker as a friend because Tonker had a body that was larger than his. Fitter, of course, but Blaggit was working on that. Woollyback and Wacker were doll thin too. He remembered when he first met them in Stoke and they'd all laughed about the way the two skinnies, combined, didn't even make up one Tonker, and then they'd messed around with making up what they'd called 'Tonker equations' on McQueen's flipchart.

$$W + W \neq T$$
$$W \times 2 > T$$

And many more. But that was maths, and this was a party. And Gabby was back with drinks and bits.

*

Wacker took his glass of punch and lightly touched his neat moustache, admiring Blaggit's sleek, soft-looking ponytail. Very Vidal Sassoon! He was certainly smarter this evening. Wacker thought he'd have a ponytail when he was Blaggit's age, but he'd opt for less of a hanging gut. He'd definitely have his teeth done though, before they got to the state Blaggit's had once been. Blaggit looked great with his new, white, straight gnashers.

He couldn't think of anything more to say to Binky and Phil, so acted distracted by the outside crackles of early fireworks from distant displays. "Oooh! Fireworks! Look." He grabbed Woollyback and Phil, guiding them towards one of the living room leaded windows, feeling like an excited child.

"Oooooh! Aaaaah!" they said.

"Go outside and watch. I'll find you," called Gabby, balancing another loaded tray. Waitressing didn't seem to be her thing.

THIRTY-FOUR

McQueen pulled down the two sturdy locks on his patio doors and opened them for guests to move onto the exterior loggia. They stepped outside. There was a ramp for Gabby's sister and Tonker steered her through the double doors, then fussed to make sure her glass was filled. For November it wasn't an overly chilly evening, but Likely Di went back in and got her coat, turning down Gabby's offer of another drink. Something was definitely not right about Likely Di. She wasn't what he'd been expecting. Was it that Blaggit was constantly with her? Wacker wasn't sure. McQueen seemed happy with Gabby though. They made a good couple. He'd bet they'd risk anything for each other.

"Woah! Wacker! Look at the size of that bonfire," said Woollyback, pointing.

At the end of the expansive garden, far from the house, was a well-constructed bonfire. Beyond it, and all around the house, Wacker had learned, were fields and woods. Long-trunked Scots pine grew in a cluster on the left, with branches spreading out at their crowns like heads of thick, bountiful broccoli. One gnarled old oak had thrown down a harvest of acorns for delighted squirrels, and beyond that stood six massive fir trees, standing tall and wide, like elegant green velvet-clad crinoline ladies watching over them as if for centuries they had been guardians of the garden. This was a wonderland: a far cry from the damp-riddled viewless bedsit Wacker rented in Tranmere.

"That bonfire's for later, mate. First there's a full-on display at the village hall grounds," said McQueen as they watched the early evening sky pop with faint glows and fizzers.

"Yow worried about yower thatched roof, Mac, and rogue rockets? That why we're being shipped over there?" said Tonker, lighting up a cigarette and offering one to Gabby's sister.

"Naah! Never mind the rockets," McQueen laughed, "I'm just worried about London rogues!"

Gabby laughed too. "Village life happens in the village hall. Believe me, that's the place to be! Think of it as your induction to Suffolk."

Gabby's sister tapped Tonker for a light, flashing Gabby's Tintin tin as she pulled it from her pocket and got out a ready-rolled.

"There's no pub here is there, Mac?"

"That's right, Tonker."

"Oooh. Your kind of place, you Woolly Wacks!" said Gabby's sister, knocking back another Suffolk Aspalls cider.

Wacker raised his fresh Pepsi can and smiled feebly.

"Ignore her," said McQueen.

Wacker was getting used to this kind of comment, although he'd noticed that Tonker was another one sticking to soft drinks, on account of driving the minibus he guessed, and Likely Di still had no drink at all, just a constant supply of cigarettes. He was glad they were outside, and he imagined McQueen was too. Cigarette smoke would have played havoc with the flowery chintz soft furnishings inside.

*

Tink, ting, ting! Gabby tapped her glass with a fork to get attention. "In a bit we'll all go down to the village hall for the display. Me 'n' Mac did warn you on the invite. Team McQueen likes a walk, though, doesn't it!"

Everyone groaned while Gabby laughed at her own joke. Why not? She liked her jokes. If no one thought they were funny, they were wrong.

"As long as you're not expecting us to stop at a ton of bookies on the way," said Binky.

"You'll be lucky," said McQueen. "There's nothing round here but fields."

"What? No wolves?" Phil laughed and Binky howled like one. Gabby was relieved that nothing answered back.

"We've wellies to lend if you need them for the walk, but you all look sorted to me," she said, checking their footwear and throwing Woollyback a smile.

"It's the best village display in these parts by all accounts."

"Don't big it up too much, Mac. It's not gonna quite be Ally Pally. There's a bar though, and burgers, and fish 'n' chips. Oh, and village hall champion, Doris, will serve hot drinks too. Make sure you pick up one of her cakes. All of it's on me 'n' Mac. Enjoy!"

"So that's how you get friends in Suffolk, is it? You buy them?" said Binky, laughing. "It puts another spin on getting by with a little help from your friends, doesn't it!"

Gabby shook her head and laughed too, hoping she wasn't going to snort again in front of everyone. "No, Binky. It's more complicated than that. You have to get a dog; more like six dogs, actually, and keep your garden in order, and do village voluntary work. That's what you do if you want to make any Suffolk friends!"

"You forgot to mention the panto at Christmas, Gabby," said McQueen. "You have to audition for the local panto, too. She's only Puss in Boots, isn't she?"

"Oh no she isn't!" said Binky and Phil, right on cue.

Gabby felt proud and embarrassed, but she mimed preening

imaginary cat whiskers, and running her paw over an imaginary cat's ear.

"I'd stick to pyrotechnics if I were you," said her sister. "Everyone loves a sparkler."

Not nice, sister, thought Gabby, knowing they'd loved sharing sparklers as children. She stayed calm. "There'll be lots of them tonight. And a late surprise."

Binky piped up: "The surprise that you can sing, do you mean? You secret little panto queen," said Binky. He slapped the front of his thigh like an enthusiastic Prince Charming.

"I think there's enough singers outed in Team McQueen already," she said, laughing.

"The surprise! I spotted it," said Blaggit. "I reckon you've stopped smoking. Maybe you could give Diana here some tips."

"Yes. But that's not the surprise. The surprise is that Dubs and Al are playing after the display is done. Oh. Bother. I've told you now!"

Binky drained his beer glass. "What? The Substitunes are playing?"

"That's them. Well, The Substi-Two-Tunes for tonight."

Phil spoke fast. "Me 'n' Binky saw them in a pub a while back. Good, weren't they, Binks?"

"Sound," said Binky, nodding fast. He gave a yowl of joy. "Cheers, Mac. Cheers, Gabby, for arranging that. And all the other things too. I wondered why Al 'n' Dubs had disappeared after the lovely buffet. It was bugging me."

"Not like them to bail out of a good lunch with good company, eh?" said Gabby, trying to hide how pleased she was over Binky's excitement.

"I expect they're setting things up," he said, face bright and fingers twitching.

*

Everything that had happened so far meant that Wacker thought the night was looking up. Should he and Woollyback stay? Were they both up to it? He passed Woollyback the plate of food Gabby had brought over for them. She was right: it was delicious. Between them they scoffed the lot.

Finally Likely Di piped up. "I'm all for getting off to the village hall right now."

Wacker had heard about her from Phil and Binky and imagined her as sparkly, funny, fair, up for a verbal spar, someone to have on your side but not someone to cross. Seeing her for real, she seemed reserved, disappointingly dull, mild and agreeable, despite her very classy pale-pink diamanté denim trouser suit.

"Which way is it, Mac? Better leave soon if we're walking, eh? Busy night ahead. You'll want us to keep to your plan, if I know you, Mac."

Wacker was very aware that after making her point Diana seemed to disappear back into herself. He noted the way she stayed with Blaggit, as if she was shielding behind one of the largest men in the group. Maybe she was uncomfortable not being on her own London patch. Maybe she was unwell. Maybe he'd been expecting too much of her. She was another one he'd spotted not drinking alcohol. Perhaps she was struggling with his complaint too?

While the rest of Team McQueen clad themselves in coats, scarves and gloves, and armed themselves with torches, McQueen pointed out how easy the fifteen-minute walk would be. He signalled to Tonker who turned his back on Gabby's sister and spoke to parka-jacketed Woollyback and Wacker almost in a whisper. "Any time yow feel yow want to bail out, just let me know and I'll drive yow back to the hotel or to the station, if yow want. Yow'll be waiting till Wednesday for a cab in a place like this."

"Too kind," said Woollyback.

"Otherwise, stay to the very end. Everyone wants yow to, especially Mac and Gabby. I'll drive everyone back to the hotel in the minibus at the end of the night."

Wacker looked at Woollyback before saying, "Thank you, Tonker." Phil had been right. McQueen and his team were solid.

"Do what's right for you," said McQueen, joining them. "Just see how it goes."

Wacker felt very moved by their kindness and support. He knew it meant a lot to Woollyback too. He was glad when McQueen changed the subject. "Gabby will go with the walkers, and I'll grab a lift with Tonker, show him the way."

On the mention of her name, Gabby came over. She'd put on a waxed navy Barbour jacket, red scarf, with matching hat and gloves, and sturdy walking boots. "Okay. We'll race you!"

McQueen turned to address everyone, as if they were his audience. "And Françoise will be here later. That's Noel's partner and Herd Ringer's amazing trainer. She's with her horses right now, over in Newmarket, briefing her stable hands, as we speak, I'll wager. It's not far away."

"If you're in a car," said Gabby, hands on hips looking at McQueen.

"Or on a horse," he retorted. "Horsepower really does mean horsepower here!"

"That's impressive," said Wacker, feeling more relaxed.

"It's a different world in this spot, Mac. I can see why you love it. A new start for you 'n' Gabby and a new clean start for me 'n' Woollyback, eh? And one for Blaggit too, like you said. It's amazing what a new bathroom can do for a man!"

To Wacker's relief, Blaggit laughed, then everyone laughed with him.

"The stars are enough for me," said Woollyback wistfully. "The sky here is amazing."

"We do our best! One night I counted twenty-four shooting stars. That's my record so far," said Gabby. "We can stargaze as we walk." She looked at her sister. "And wheel."

"Oh, please walk to the hall with everyone too, both of you," said Gabby. "And stay long enough for the firework display. Even if you can't to see the band afterwards."

"We-ell..." Wacker couldn't finish. He didn't know what

to say. He could feel eyes on him waiting for a decision that he couldn't make.

"In the summer, one of the times I walked down to the hall from here, I followed a badger almost all the way!"

"Really, Gabby?" he said, feeling suddenly moved by the firmament above him and the thought of following a badger.

"Yeah, really. Badgers. Mac doesn't believe me. He says it's a badger con."

McQueen groan-laughed and she kept going. "Sometimes it's pheasants, sometimes hares, or rabbits, deer – muntjacs or bigguns – barn owls too."

"Yeah? You'll be saying there's friggin' wombles on the village green next," said Likely Di. "Come on. Let's get going."

"Barn owls?" Phil shuddered. "Some people think hearing an owl's cry signals a pending death. Did you know that any of you?"

"Rubbish," said Gabby with a laugh before anyone else could reply. She'd never heard that before, and never wanted to hear it again. "But just in case it's not rubbish, earmuffs anyone?"

"Never mind blocking out owl hoots, I'll 'ave some earmuffs to wear when the band starts, in case they aren't any good!" said Blaggit.

*

"I'm walkin' it," said Likely Di. "Got me trainers on, like the invitation said to. It'll give me a chance to light one up 'n' all!" She wanted to get the next bit over with and she didn't want to say why.

"I'll be your chaperone, Diana, if you'll allow," said Blaggit.

"Hurry up then all of you," she said, taking his arm. "Me 'n' Blaggit are ready for the off."

"Yow seem keen for another ciggie, Diana!" said Tonker staring up at the sky.

"Just don't want things to go wrong. Wrong for Mac and Gabby, I mean."

"Well, I'll follow on in a bit, driving the minibus, like Mac said. I'll give yow all time to get there. I'll rest up my leg that way. And I'll bring us all back here after for Gabby's final surprise, whatever that is. Then a lift for all of us back to the Newmarket hotel when it's all done."

"And Gabby's sister's all wheeled up for it,' said Likely Di. "Let's not keep her waiting. Me 'n' Blaggit will keep with her."

"If you can keep up with her, you mean!" said Gabby as she tied the laces on her walking boots. "She's down at the gate revving up now! If her battery runs out, you'll have to come and pick her up, Tonker. Her chair folds up. That okay?"

Tonker nodded.

"Or someone can give her a push?"

"We will," said Binky. "This is gonna be great."

*

"Hey!" Binky shouted. "Now, hurry up, everyone."

Wacker liked the way he chivvied them all to get ready. He saw how it made Likely Di happier. Binky was like an excited sheepdog rounding everyone up and when they were finally ready and as he wanted them, they set off.

The ground sounded crisp under foot and wheel. Binky not only led the way, but also led them in a rousing version of 'Follow the Yellow Brick Road'. A misty stream of breath, lit by moonlight, snaked along with them as they sang.

Wacker didn't miss the powdery white stuff, or the endless beers he'd shared with everyone in the past, but he had missed their banter and to his surprise, he realised how much he'd been missing Binky's songs. "C'mon, Woollyback," he said, sensing his loyal friend felt the same. "We'll watch the fireworks, grab a burger, and we'll hear Al 'n' Dubs's opening number, then decide what to do. Step at a time, like we promised ourselves, eh?"

Woollyback looked pleased. Turning to McQueen and Gabby, Wacker added, "Hope to see you both later."

Then they follow, follow, followed into the torchlit darkness.

"Woah!" said Wacker. "I can see Orion already. His belt's so clear."

THIRTY-FIVE

Al and Dubs were in the village hall car park to greet them when they arrived.

Gabby saw that everything was as she and McQueen had planned and paid for. On either side of the village hall entrance there was a van: one serving gourmet burgers to the left, and to the right another serving top grade fish and chips, which delighted everyone after their short star-spangled hike. Woollyback started a queue for burgers, and Wacker a queue for fish and chips.

"You two in a race?" She laughed as she walked over to Al and Dubs.

Binky and Phil shook hands with Al and Dubs. "Hold on, mate," said Dubs, laughing. "Don't shake it so fast! I've got to strum with this hand in a bit."

Binky apologised and got them to sign his shirt.

"Sorry about Binky. He's a fan. Gets excited."

"Ah! The singing Binky. I've heard about you and your musical improvs. Nice to have that skill," said Al. Gabby was sure that Binky blushed.

She insisted on taking a picture of the four of them in front of

275

the Substitunes van. Al beckoned Likely Di over to join in, but she gave a soft wave and stayed near to Blaggit and Tonker. Her sister scooted across the gravelly car park to offer artistic advice.

"Get the bullseye in shot. And get the band name too," she insisted.

"You do it," said Gabby, handing over the camera and trying not to snap. She'd known since childhood to let her sister do the things she was good at. She introduced her to Al and Dubs and left them to it.

Never-to-be-crossed Doris, from the village hall committee, came out. She greeted Gabby then looked across at the photo shoot, still going on in front of the Substitunes van. "We haven't had targets like this in the village hall grounds since we had the local archery club here to do a display, three summer fêtes ago. Your photo would make a nice spread in the village newsletter, dear."

"Archers?" said Binky. "Archers? Here? I love a bit of dum-dee-dum-dee-dum-dee-dum. You must introduce me to Walter Gabriel and Joe Grundy."

"Oh, you teaser," said Doris with a twinkle in her eye. "Cup of tea, anyone?" she added, leading the way into the hall. Everyone followed. It was Doris, and they instinctively knew they must obey.

Inside was a makeshift bar, set up and staffed by Andy and Elaine, two more stalwarts from the village hall committee. Through the kitchen serving hatch was Doris's domain. She was ready with homemade cakes and hot drinks.

Loaded with food and drinks of their choice, the new village friends of Gabby and McQueen mixed with the rabble of out-of-towners they'd brought along. Once well mixed, they went back outside to watch a top-notch fireworks display, enthralled and wowed by it all, just as Gabby and Mac had hoped.

"Who needs Ally Pally when we've got this?" he whispered into her ear. She'd never felt so happy. Hand in hand they led everyone back into the hall where Al and Dubs were waiting for McQueen's cue to go on stage.

Gabby mingled, encouraging everyone to get more drinks then make ready for the music. She nodded at Doris who was serving Woollyback.

"Thank you, Doris," he said, picking up two refills. "I never thought I'd get such a buzz from village hall coffee."

"You should try it with sugar, dear," she said, winking at Gabby.

There was a rumpus at the bar. As Gabby rushed over, she could hear Andy's irritated voice. "Elaine. I told you to slice the lemons," he said. "There's no lemon ready for Emily Cobbold's gin 'n' tonic. It's a disaster."

Before Gabby could step in, Likely Di was there.

"Give me a knife, love and I'll slice them for you."

Andy slid over the lemons on a cutting board. Gabby watched Blaggit wince as Likely Di picked up the sharp knife and make the first incision. Seeing his reaction Gabby knew that she wasn't the only one who had heard rumours about Likely Di being able to end a life with a knife. Was it true?

*

Likely Di was sorry not to be as buoyant as usual in front of her favourite band. She envied Binky and Phil's enthusiasm for Al and Dubs. Tonight, she just couldn't be excited, despite Blaggit's best efforts. She knew that Gabby would blame her unsociable behaviour on her occasional low moods which she knew from past years crept up on her at this time of year. That wasn't helping her cope with the situation tonight, but Gabby would surely never suspect what it was really all about; Likely Di knew she'd be done for if Gabby worked things out. The only pain she had was heartache and the reason for that she'd always kept to herself.

*

The lights went down, and a spotlight lit the makeshift stage. Everyone ooooed, and McQueen stood in front of the centred microphone. He tapped it and looked at Al who nodded for him to carry on.

"Welcome everyone," he said. "Thank you all for coming." He looked out at the audience, trying to imagine how anyone was ever brave enough to sing in front of a crowd.

"Some of you are locals!" Locals whooped and Doris's waving tea-towel caught his eye.

"Some have come further afield, from Liverpool." Binky and Phil whooped, with Woollyback and Wacker joining in.

"Some have come from Birmingham." Tonker and Blaggit raised their glasses and took their turn to whoop.

"And there's a few motley folks here from London." Likely Di whooped from the audience but then seemed to hold back, while behind him, setting things up on stage, Al and Dubs gave a cheer.

"Me and Gabby are pleased you enjoyed the fireworks and insist that you keep replenishing your glasses, your cups and saucers. Be sure to send the food vans away empty; they're here till the end. And please stuff your faces with Doris's lovely cakes. Thank you, Doris," he said, signalling towards the kitchen hatch. Whoops came from everyone.

McQueen went on. "I started this speech saying, 'Me and Gabby'. What I should have said was, 'My future wife and I'."

There were instant whistles, cheers and more whoops. He looked at Gabby. She was beaming with encouragement for him.

"We'll be tying the knot in April, on the anniversary of a special day that got us where we are today. And you'll all be getting an invite."

Whoops and a few woo-hoos.

"The first time I saw my future wife's face, deep down I knew I didn't need to search anymore for a rainbow with a pot of gold at the end. I had everything I wanted right there. I'd found my very own Emerald City in her beautiful eyes. Gabby is the only one for me." He paused and looked right at her, hoping she knew he meant every word he said. "No one else is my type. And I know I'm backing a winner."

Everyone awwwwed and McQueen wiped a tear from his eye. "To Gabby," he said, urging them all to raise their drinks in a toast as Al and Dubs positioned themselves on stage.

Once composed, McQueen introduced them. "Now, for all you *guys* out there—" He paused to register the groans from the audience.

"I give you a band that's a right pair of twit-two-who's! Let me hear a big village hall welcome please, for the best The Who covers duo you'll hear this side of West London. Take it away: The Substi-Two-Tunes!"

He left the stage to applause. Al and Dubs stepped forward. There was an alarming electrical weeeee, a fizzzz, and a pop, but it wasn't fireworks. Andy from the bar rushed over to help.

*

"Diana, you look pretty in pink, tonight. Very bling. New outfit?" said Blaggit, fired up by the atmosphere and buzz of Adnams in the air. He managed to hold back from saying her outfit was fit for a princess – his own Princess Di. That's what he genuinely thought but saying so would have blown things for him. Instead, he blurted out, "How about filling in for your London friends, The Substitunes, with a number from Queen?"

Likely Di rolled her eyes and turned to Phil, who turned to Binky. "Hey, Mr Rent-a-Voice. Did you hear that? Blaggit's got a request for something regal. While them two on stage fiddle with their wires, get this party started, will you?" Phil said.

Binky did exactly that. In one leap he was on the stage blocks. Lifting the lid of the ancient-looking piano, he introduced himself as a friend of tonight's sponsor, then bashed out a tune, singing Queen's 'We Will Rock You'. Next, he told the story of the starry, starry night sky he'd just seen en route to the village hall, and slowed things down, wowing everyone with his version of Don

Binky's key moment

Maclean's much-loved song. Even Doris stopped clanging her saucers and listened, clutching her apron. She had tears in her eyes when he looked directly at her as he sang the words, 'as beautiful as you'. He reckoned no one had said that to her since the war. By the last verse, Al and Dubs were up and ready but they abandoned all things The Who, and followed Binky's lead which turned into a Chas 'n' Dave Cockney knees-up medley starting with 'Rabbit', dedicated to Gabby on account of her being the lady of the moment, and her telling him earlier about rabbits invading their garden.

"Join in, if you've got rabbit raiders too," he hollered, like a man dreaming he was playing to a packed stadium at Wembley Arena, instead of no more than Team McQueen and thirty Suffolk locals in a tatty village hall. But it didn't matter. The new trio were well and truly in sync and the audience loved them. They played on and finished their improvised set, then took requests. They should have expected 'Combine Harvester' by the Wurzels to come up, being among farming folk, but it visibly shook Al when Binky got straight into it without flinching.

"They're not bad," said Tonker, swinging Gabby's sister round in her chair. "Maybe they could get a summer season in Lowestoft," he said with a wonky wink and a wonky smile.

Phil led the clapping for encores, keeping it up until McQueen tapped his watch to signal it must end.

*

One of the things that struck Gabby when they'd moved from London was that nights at the village hall always ended early, compared to what she was used to. By nine thirty people were usually yawning, no matter how good the entertainment was. Farmer families went to bed early, up at dawn for a bright start with their pigs, sheep and crops. So, unlike her guests, Gabby wasn't bemused when Doris and Andy bundled everyone out of the hall pretty quick as if they were orchestrating an emergency evacuation. And she hadn't been surprised when Elaine had started stacking chairs before the encore was done.

"There's a yoga class in here early in the morning. Vicky has to clean tonight and check it again before they arrive. Shoo, all of you!" said Doris.

They stood in the car park putting on coats, hats and gloves. Hungry stragglers queued for the last offerings from the food vans, but everyone in Gabby and Mac's gang were well and truly stuffed. And there was more back home to be had if they wanted.

McQueen and Gabby stood chatting to their new local friends, thanking them for coming, and being congratulated on their engagement. Binky appointed himself as honorary roadie, helping Al and Dubs stack the speakers and instrument kits into the unmissable van. They joked together, glowing in the glory of their night's work, enjoying the praise laid on them by their new, drunken fans who weebled away into the Suffolk dark.

Tonker helped Gabby's sister back into the minibus, then

folded her nifty wheelchair in too. Everyone piled cheerily on board, and they headed back for the last few surprises of the night.

Likely Di, with attentive Blaggit by her side, remained sullen but Gabby pretended not to notice and tried not to take offence.

THIRTY-SIX

There was usually no one on the road at night. Occasional Saturday night cars were parked in passing places, shaken by the exertion of what was going on inside. Tonight, Tonker's headlights caught a black Mercedes parked in one. Binky started a chorus of, "We know what you're doing!" and they chanted like gleeful, jeering ten-year-olds.

They were silenced by Gabby's cry. "There's a fire, Mac! It's at our house, I think!"

Everyone looked to where Gabby was pointing. Darkness shielded the silhouette of a house in the distance. There was a fire, yes. It seemed small. Why the panic? And why be surprised? It was a night when pubs, clubs and families were having fireworks and bonfire parties, after all. Tonker assumed there must be some of those around in this no man's land of an isolated rural oasis.

"Step on it, Tonker, but watch out for deer," said McQueen.

Tonker was a careful driver, but Suffolk country lanes needed extra focus on a pitch-black night. They were narrow too, which could be a challenge for city drivers. He assured himself that he'd see headlights if a car approached, heaven forbid a farm vehicle, and he was thankful for regular passing places to let drivers from the opposite direction get through, as long as they weren't all bunged up by fornicating couples in black Mercedes cars. Despite what Gabby had said about stepping on it, he maintained a steady speed. There were no other cars about. Nothing. No one. He sensed a change in his passengers. They were quieter, notably tense.

McQueen lightened the mood. "Of course there's a bleedin' fire! Lots of people are doing bonfires tonight cos it's the Saturday before the fifth of November. We're not that out of touch in the sticks."

Exactly, thought Tonker. He wanted to look in the direction of their house but couldn't risk taking his eyes off the road. As he pulled into McQueen's drive Gabby lifted her head. "I'm right! See there? Someone's lit our fire."

"I feel sick," said Likely Di. "Can you open the window?"

*

McQueen snapped to when Tonker pulled up on the drive. "No alarm going off and no security lights have come on, so the house is okay. It'll be local kids, that's what it is. We've all done it." He laughed.

"Stay safe," said Likely Di.

Her reaction made him uneasy, and he was taking no risks. "Tonker, Blaggit, Phil, come with me. We'll do a check. Got your torches? The rest of you, stay in here. We won't be long. Tonker will lock the van." And he duly did.

They scoured the large garden, its crevices, clumps of bordering trees, sheds, and hidey-holes. They looked out at the surrounding fields and copse of trees, walked round the outside of the house, and checked inside. Nothing. No one was down by the trees or the garden edges. McQueen looked for tracks by the fire, but there were no giveaways. He knew it would be idiot kids, scarpered on their bikes and well away by now, but just in case, he called out, "Mo! Are you out there?" He waited. No answer. Nothing stirred.

"Mo! Simon! If you're out there, come and have a drink, mate.

We're all friends here. Join us. Al 'n' Dubs are here. Come and join us as friends."

McQueen tapped his watch. All was still and silent.

A few minutes later they were back, announcing the coast was clear and claiming to have slain a dragon. The mood brightened as everyone piled out of the minibus. Tonker went to help Gabby's sister.

Al and Dubs turned into the drive and parked.

"Hi, fans," said Dubs as he slammed his door. "Have we missed anything, Binky?"

"I need a wee," said Al, striding towards the Scots pines, not waiting for an answer.

"Me too," said Binky.

"Just don't start singing 'Rivers of Babylon'."

*

The garden was now a wonderland, flanked on all sides with fairy lights. Gabby led them down it like she owned the place, which she did. McQueen prickled with pride watching her.

"Bloody hell," said Phil. "This garden's so vast you could get a nine-hole golf course in here."

"If you walk on the grass, watch out for rabbit holes, not golf holes!"

Likely Di was last to follow, walking arm-in-arm with Blaggit.

McQueen was happy. When they were planning the evening, he'd felt it was worse than engineering a long con, but now he was pleased they'd taken so much trouble over the details. There were still a couple more surprises in store for them. They'd love the last one.

*

"That fire'll roar for a while yet," said Tonker. "Whoever built it did a good job." He winked at McQueen. "If yow want a fire chief, I'm your man."

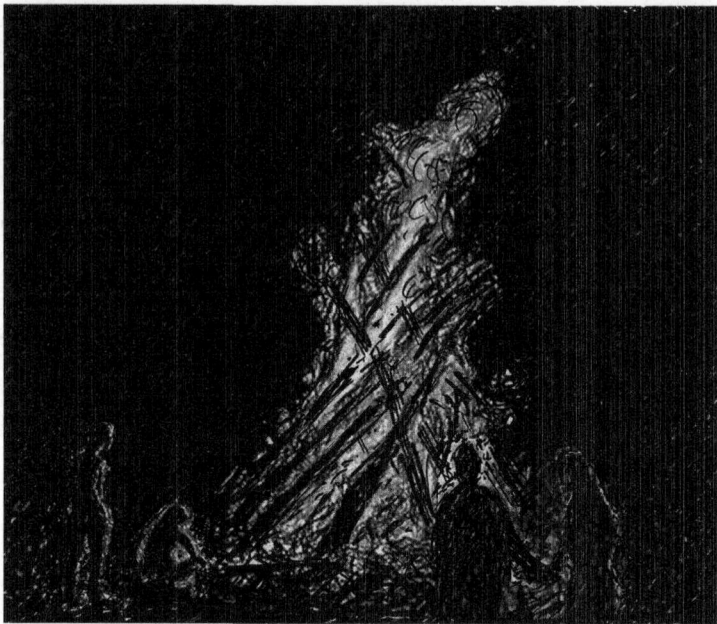

Remember, remember the fifth of November

"Cheers, mate. I'll need it low before midnight. Water buckets are there." He pointed to three hidden by the chalet wall. "And an outdoor tap with hose there."

Tonker nodded. "It's fantastic here, Mac; light years away from Spaghetti Junction. I heard a fox. Think it was a fox. Hope it was a fox. It sounded like a real old bugger, whatever it was. Proper nature, this."

McQueen reserved hugs for his finest troops and Tonker was now one of those. The rugby hulk of him was broad and he held on like an ant clinging onto a discarded Jelly Tot. He coughed and pulled away, changing the subject. "What's going on with Likely Di and my mate Blaggit?"

"Search me," said Tonker.

McQueen shook his head. "She's not herself tonight. I'm not sure why." He checked his watch.

Tonker looked thoughtful. "Hmm. Women!" he said, tutting and shrugging. "I'll be back to check the fire, Mac, once I see Gabby's sister is settled right where she wants to be."

"Good man."

*

Gabby watched her guests through the garden chalet's French doors as she and McQueen set out the mulled cider they'd prepared earlier, and non-alcoholic cocktails, complete with umbrellas and cherries. She was happy too but bursting to share her fears.

"Did you really think it might have been Mo, Mac? Al was thinking it might be."

"It crossed my mind at first, but he's too spineless."

"Yeah."

"And what would he have got out of it? It'll just be kids on a night bike ride, mucking about. Forget it, Gabby."

She spied something she'd forgotten to tidy away: Toto's red slipper, the one he loved to carry around. She picked it up, hoping McQueen wouldn't tease her about it. "It's going all right, isn't it?" she said, suddenly anxious.

"I think it's going grand. Thanks to Binky for saving the day."

"Likely Di's not her usual, is she? She wouldn't even comment on Al's idea about Mo."

"Off her own patch, I guess. Just let her be. And don't go saying she's turning into the Witch of the West!"

"As if I would," said Gabby, putting the slipper in a cupboard. "Only a munchkin would do that," she mumbled, knowing he'd hear but ignore it.

"We've got the big surprise, later. She'll love that, you wait." He checked his watch. Less than an hour and a half to go. "Come on. Let's serve these drinks."

THIRTY-SEVEN

"You 'n' Al should do this," said Gabby's sister. "Me 'n' Gabby wrote our names in sparklers every fireworks night when we were children. Have a go."

Quickly, before her sparkler died and desperate that no one saw, especially Tonker, she flicked her wrist and wrote '*Callum*' in the air, wishing he was there; wishing she could show him off. It wasn't just Gabby who had friends.

Al and Dubs, then Woollyback and Wacker joined her in filling the darkness with words, not all of them polite. Binky came over, lit his sparkler from hers and wrote '*ABC*' in the air, then he danced like a young Michael Jackson and sang The Jackson's alphabet song by firelight. His new fans looked on and swayed their sparklers at him.

Phil was off again, sky-watching and talking about Jupiter's giant red spot. Dubs told a Uranus joke that everyone must have heard before. She certainly had. Gabby's friends were nice. She was having more fun than she thought she would. "Hey, Binky," she said. "Do me another marshmallow, will you?"

"Have mine. I haven't blown on it."

"Thanks. Ooooh! Brace yourselves. It looks like Gabby's about to release this year's Mr Guy Fawkes."

Heads turned to see Gabby carrying what looked like a body in need of more sessions at a gym than a human lifespan could offer. Gabby sat it on a chair.

It wouldn't have been any effort to have told her sister that she'd done a good job. Gabby had always led the guy-making when they were children, and she'd made some good ones. Did she bother to compliment her tonight? No. Gabby was getting enough compliments from everyone. She didn't need more from her. Gabby had Mac. And a lovely house. And working legs. What did she have? Her cast-off Tintin tin. She opened it up. Why should she praise her? She lit another cigarette.

She liked Binky. Binky was a laugh. And Tonker had been kind to her. But she'd never let on to Gabby that she was glad to have met them all.

Binky prowled around the mystery guy like a sprite. He pointed to Al and Dubs, taunting them and laughing. "Who? Who is it? Come on! Guess who. Get it? *Who?* You two. You're The Who!"

No one laughed as much as she thought they should. She tried to make up for it but got cut off when Gabby ceremoniously snatched the hood from the guy's head for a big reveal.

"Arrh! What an ugly son of a bitch you've come up with this year, sister. Where did you get that kilt? I'd not like to meet him in a dark alley. I might shit myself."

"Lovely," said Wacker. Woollyback sniggered.

"Hey, Tonker. He's uglier than you!" said Blaggit. Tonker shrugged, laughing.

Al looked horrified, and cast a glance at Dubs, then at Likely Di.

"Anyone you know?" said Phil, helping McQueen to throw it on the fire.

"I'm saying nothing. You know what Gabby's like, with her pranks."

"Look at you, scaredy cats!" said Binky. He obviously thought he hadn't sung enough that night and had an idea. "Ha! Let me do Smokey Robinson's 'My Guy' for you all!"

She wished she could get up and dance. It had felt nice when she was wheeling around with Tonker earlier, but not the same as having her feet on the floor and grooving the way she'd like to.

Tonker had told her that Blaggit's downfall was fast women and slow horses. Then they'd watched Blaggit trying it on with Likely Di. Moody cow, she seemed. What was Blaggit playing at? And why had Likely Di been invited if she was such a sourpuss?

Anyway, regretting not being able to dance on her own two feet to Binky's song was a waste of time as he only managed the first four lines. Dubs had put a stop to it because he reckoned the burning guy had made the air too smoky to sing, and he didn't want Binky damaging his voice. Well, that's what he said. He was quite protective, Dubs. They all were in their way. She mustn't be mean about Gabby. Gabby and Mac had made sure she got to see Herd Ringer whenever she wanted, and Françoise was helping her get the confidence to ride. She had all the equipment at her special stables to get her on and off horses. And Callum liked taking her to the stables and hanging around there, and spending nights in hotels with her. *Whoop!* Perhaps life wasn't so bad these days.

*

Gabby had spent hours creating the guy. She'd told McQueen she wanted it to resemble an old adversary of theirs and he'd said, "No guessing who that is!"

Tonker had loaded up the bonfire and they stood back watching the orange flames crackling and dancing in the night. It felt like a place of sanctuary. No wonder Wacker and Woollyback had stayed. The flames grew higher and hotter. McQueen whispered to Gabby, "Let's hope this burns away the spirit of Docherty forever."

Faces glowed. Smoke choked them as the guy caught, flames rising, flicking and swirling around its torso. Wacker started off the clapping when the first flame reached the guy's ugly head, until they roared round it, engulfing it completely. Woollyback led the retreat back up the garden when the bangers that Gabby had stashed in the head went off. Shocked, McQueen and Tonker jumped into action. They threw the buckets of emergency water onto the fire and McQueen turned on the hose, attached to the chalet's outdoor tap.

"I said that I wanted it out by midnight, but I wasn't expecting this."

McQueen poked the hissing fire as it faded. A light breeze took away the smoke. "Come back, everyone. Gather in," he said, holding up a box of Doris's toffee apples and rustling it. "Anyone?"

Gabby took the box and passed it round. They all dipped in. She offered blankets, but no one was owning up to being cold enough for one.

"One more surprise left," she said. "Just wait."

McQueen screwed up the toffee apple bag and threw it into the dying embers. "It shouldn't be long now," he said. "Watch the garden. It'll be here round about midnight when everyone's fireworks have stopped." He looked around and pointed to his right. "I reckon from this direction. It's someone I've been wanting you to meet for a while. Since our epic race day, actually."

Likely Di stared into the distance, then at her watch. She looked as if she was mulling over what McQueen had said, giving it serious thought.

McQueen turned to his left. "Hold on. Hear that? That's not right. Someone's coming and the security lights haven't come on." Three torches were heading their way, from the direction of the house.

"Kids back?" said Tonker.

As they got nearer, McQueen made out the shape of three bodies. "No. Looking too big for kids. Adult, I reckon. Not who I was expecting."

They were heading straight towards them, across the grass.

Gate crashers

"Mo? Is that you?" called McQueen. "Simon? You out there too? Come on. Stop messing about, mate. Come and have a drink with your friends Al 'n' Dubs."

Al and Dubs peered into the darkness, and then everyone was trying to make out who had turned up, uninvited. Tonker walked across to Gabby's sister and turned her chair to face the new visitors. The garden lights helped them see but it wasn't enough to get a clear view. Phil shone his torch but that was feeble. McQueen couldn't make out who was approaching. What was going on? "Oi! You! Get off my land! This is private property!" he called. "Who goes there?"

Three heads looked up, two in full-face balaclavas. McQueen blinked as their bright torchlights blinded his eyes.

"Really, Mr McQueen? Private property? Is that a fact?"

*

It was a voice Gabby had heard before. Not Simon's. Not Mo's. The balaclava'd bodies moved closer. Gabby swallowed hard and gripped McQueen's hand. As her eyes adjusted, she made out three

292

men; two wielded butcher's knives and carried ropes, the middle one held a double-headed axe. They came clearly into view beyond the dregs of the fire.

"Well, well, McQueen. Ye're even prettier than yer beach photo."

"Beach photo? This is November. What are you on about?" he said, cool and calm.

His eyes briefly searched for Gabby's, then back to the three imposters. Gabby watched his face change as it dawned on him who he was dealing with. She knew McQueen would be noting their every move. Taking in every detail, and so cross with himself that they'd been tracked down; he'd think he should have known. And they'd been watched tonight. She shuddered. Watched for how long? And to what purpose? She blamed herself for this. Yes. It was all her fault. In the corner of her eye, she saw Likely Di clinging on to Blaggit as her knees buckled. This was serious.

*

The intruder spoke again. "Y'know something? I might seriously interfere with ye before ye meet your maker. Yes? Yes, I think that's a good idea. What do you think, boys?" He looked at the toady stooges either side. They both sneered and nodded. "But the night is young, plenty of fun to come."

Team McQueen closed in. Tonker stayed near to Gabby's sister.

"McQueen. What the hell's going on?" said Tonker.

Phil backed him up. "What do you want us to do?"

"Stay calm," said McQueen, trying to take his own advice. "This one's mean." He tapped his watch.

"What a loyal band of merry men, oh, and women, ye have here. Or do ye? Eh? Are you sure they're all loyal?" He paused and looked along the line. "For those who dinnae know me, allow me tae introduce myself. Mr Lennox Docherty is my name. I am the owner of a horse ye all did well on. Lorraine and Nancy. Ring any bells?"

Gabby looked at McQueen. No one spoke. Docherty went on.

"Tonight, I'm nae fixing horse races. Ooh no. I'm fixing ye. Tonight, killing is my game."

Gabby's sister started laughing. "Nice surprise, Gabby," she said. "And yeah, yeah. I nearly shat myself. Very funny."

"Shut it, wheels," snapped Docherty. "I dinnae want to know about yer movements." Her laugh changed to a whimper. She looked across at Gabby who wasn't laughing. She tried to turn and move away but her wheels jammed on a misplaced piece of wood, and she was stuck.

"More trouble with yer movements, eh, hen? If ye know what's good for ye, ye'll stay right where ye are."

Tonker made to bend and free the wheel, but Docherty brandished his axe and warned him off. "One to watch, boys," he said, looking left then right to his balaclava'd henchmen. Tonker stood up and put his hand on Gabby's sister's shoulder while Docherty carried on. "Well, hen, I'll be sure tae tell Callum he has a replacement. He was supposed tae be here today, by my side, not yours, but he got himself intae a bit o' trouble, so he's nae a pretty boy anymore. Still, it seems ye like them ugly."

Gabby's sister looked more wounded by the words than by anything Docherty's axe could have done. She dropped her head low. It was hard to tell what she was feeling but McQueen guessed it was grim. Could she ever have imagined that Callum was working for an oaf like Docherty? Could Callum ever have worked out there was a link between Gabby and her sister, and the Newmarket race day? McQueen thought not; their paths never crossed in his company, and Gabby's sister liked horses purely for the love of them, not for financial thrill or gain. What had Callum been after? Was he watching Françoise for racing tips? Or was he watching her to find him and Gabby? McQueen stole another look at his watch and tapped it softly.

"All of ye," said Docherty, in a more sinister voice, "all of ye, bar the traitor in yer pack, won't be 'remember, remembering the fifth of November' ever again. But which one of ye could go free? And why is that?"

Wacker walked towards Docherty as if propelled by an invisible force. "This is not the Lord's way. This is *not* the Lord's way," he said. Woollyback tried to pull him back, but Wacker wouldn't stop.

This wasn't the Lord's way: this was McQueen's worst nightmare.

"Oh, here we go. 'Onward Christian Soldiers', I suppose. Time for ye tae turn the other cheek, son. I am your Lord now," said Docherty, bending slightly to line his eyes up with Wacker's. "Tie them up. That big tree'll do nicely. Over there." He waved his axe at the oak tree. "And be sure tae mark the lippy one."

The henchman on the right cut into Wacker's cheek with the tip of his knife. Woollyback wilted as he watched, helpless. Their thin, slight bodies offered no resistance as they were dragged away towards the ancient, gnarled tree. Woollyback and Wacker were submissive and did not struggle. That was the best way to handle Docherty for now, thought McQueen.

"You bastard," said Phil, touching his own scar.

"He's lucky I didn't say 'an eye for an eye'."

They'd fixed a torch in the tree as a warning, McQueen guessed, so everyone could see Wacker's bloody face as he was tied up. McQueen thought he heard him mutter, "And deliver us from evil." Woollyback let out a groan, confused and bound.

This was hopeless. McQueen felt helpless. What to do? Was submission really the best thing? He looked at his watch.

*

Woollyback whimpered quietly to himself; Wacker wouldn't give in to it. These were surely no ordinary bindings; they were tied by experts, tightly, with no wriggle room; no chance of escape. One set of bindings under the armpits and round the tree trunk, another round the waist; ankles bound together; knees bound and wrists too. No twisting could untwist the fastenings. At least they weren't gagged; at least they had no crown of thorns, no nails in their hands and no nails in their feet fastening them to the cross they must bear. And it was somehow comforting to be bound to a solid trunk, possibly rooted fast for centuries – more like a companion, or protector, than a jailer. They must have faith. With faith they would be delivered from evil.

"Please, Lord. Let us not die. Let us not be left out bloodied in the cold. Help us, oh Lord. Save us, Lord and forgive those who do these wrongs."

Docherty turned to Wacker. "Shut that praying up, or I'll cut off yer lips."

"This is our beef," said McQueen, loudly. "Let these people go. This is between you and me, Docherty."

"Oh no. This is a beef between ye, me, your bitch-slag there, and all of you." As he spoke, he used his axe to point out people, but it was poised in the air when he said, "Including that traitor in yer pack."

There was a buzz of "What?" and "Who?" Confusion spread. Gabby's sister cried all through it.

McQueen tried to think; tried to come up with a plan. He glanced at his watch. *Tick tock.*

"Let me tell ye a wee yarn," said power-crazed Docherty. "Up in Edinburgh, yer hero and his tramp tried to fleece me and unfortunately, the rest of ye too, in a roundabout way, with yer April run-around. And that's unforgivable, in my book."

Tonker stepped forward and stood tall and wide. "Yow won't get past me, yow whoreson."

"I think I will. Have ye nae seen this axe?" Docherty waved it in menacing swipes. "See it? This will make ye even more hideous, big ugly boy."

"Bollocks," said Tonker. He took one step forwards, squaring his shoulders, standing straight, looking big, strong and ready for a fight, but he remained at Gabby's sister's side.

Docherty laughed. "That's right. Stay with Ms Wheels." He turned to McQueen. "So, how did I manage tae track ye all down? Hmm?" He waited. "Well, McQueen, ye never guessed ye had a snitch in your midst, did ye?"

"Never!" he said.

"Afraid so, sucker. Come tae Daddy, my Judas. Come get yer thirty pieces of silver."

Woollyback and Wacker looked over to see who moved. Everyone waited.

The dying embers crackled.

An owl hooted.

Gabby let go of McQueen's hand and took half a step forward. She dropped to the grass, fumbling. Docherty and his men braced. McQueen held his breath. For the first time in his life, he felt he might faint. *Not now. Not now. Stay alert.* He tapped his watch. *Oh, Gabby.* What was she doing? Was she in shock? Was she bowing down to Docherty? Was she a traitor? What had she done? Gabby's sister cried louder.

Gabby popped back up. "Dropped it. My friendship bracelet. Can't live without it," she whispered.

"Christ!" he whispered back. "Your sense of timing sucks."

The ranks stirred again. To Gabby's left, Likely Di moved forward. After three yards she turned to McQueen. "Sorry, Mac. Really, I am. I had to."

Gabby burst out, "How could you, Diana?"

Stunned, McQueen's mind raced, desperate to recall every detail of the day, and the recent months. What had he done to Likely Di to make her do this?

The crestfallen Dennett brothers looked on. "Why?" called out Al.

Blaggit shook his head in disbelief.

THIRTY-EIGHT

Likely Di continued walking slowly in Docherty's direction.

He smiled a sickly smile. "Thank you, Di. Without yer help, this would nae be possible."

He'd called her Di. But she knew he'd done far worse. It was best not to think of that. She looked at him and returned the grin.

"Well, I did say I owed you one," she said. As she moved closer her demeanour changed. She walked with an assertive stride and when she spoke her voice was clear and strong. "You killed my Len, you motherfucker."

The diamantés on her pink denim caught the torchlight and flashed as she launched at Docherty with a knife: a knife she had pushed into flesh before. She was confident; so confident that she hadn't hired her heavies for the night. Look how she sparkled; she had no need for heavies tonight; she was Likely Di; Likely Di was good with knives; everyone fled if Likely Di held a knife. Before she could land her strike, one of his oafs intervened. He kicked the knife out of her hand, caught it, and pushed her to the ground. Turning to Docherty he gave a polite bow, but Docherty was busy boring a fierce gaze into Likely Di's eyes to keep her in order.

Diana sank to her knees. Docherty pulled back her head and looked down at her with contempt. Her sense of triumph evaporated. Her only comfort was that now McQueen and Gabby would understand the reason for her betrayal. And Blaggit too, dear Blaggit. She'd heard Tonker call him 'loved-up *Likely Blaggit*' when they were dancing. That wasn't a name he'd want to keep now, or was it? Surely anyone who'd heard the rumours about Docherty and Limehouse Len would understand why she'd done what she'd done. Until that moment no one had known that Len, although he had a wife, was Likely Di's one and only true love. Now everyone would know the truth and surely, they would forgive her and think: *Oh, Likely Di. All these years you were shielding a broken heart, poor love.*

"Thank ye for yer assistance, Di," said Docherty. "Yes, I know all about ye. Did ye nae think ye might be likely to die tonight, eh? Ye're sealing yer own fate. I promise, if it comes it will be swifter than that o' yer loverboy, Limehouse. Aye, he was begging for death."

"Don't say that about my Len! No, no, no!"

"Aye, 'fraid it's true, hen. And I ken all about yer fling with him; winners in an ugly bug ball, both of ye were." He laughed mockingly.

Likely Di struggled to get to her feet, but Docherty pushed her back. "And stay down, Cockney scrubber." He aimed a string of spit at her. "That's the price of adultery. Tie her up," he said.

*

"Leave her alone!" shouted Al, with Dubs looking ready to back him up if he launched himself on Docherty. "I said *leave her.*"

Likely Di was touched by Al's support. Blaggit remained silent. What did he make of it? Did that matter now? Did anything matter? She had failed. Should she let that break her?

This wasn't how it was supposed to be. Likely Di looked beseechingly at Al and Dubs. She shook her head trying to warn them off upsetting Docherty and Docherty's men. Did Al still know she was on their side? Did he remember her warning him and Dubs to stay away from killer sharks like this one? Dubs was right: the number on Docherty's card was the devil's number. But she'd had to take the risk, to get revenge for her Len.

"Ouch. Not so rough," she said as she was thrown against the tree and the ropes went on.

Docherty watched. "Scots pine. Very appropriate, do ye nae think?" He looked across at Al with scorn. "Ah. I never forget a voice. Ye're the one who kindly kept look-out for me once, and for that I thank ye. Ye're the one with the arse I fancied. Doctor Who, is it now? And are ye the one who sent me that LP cover? I know it wasn't that traitor. So. Who's next?"

"What?"

Gabby's sister sobbed out loud. She stared at Gabby. Gabby stared at McQueen. McQueen stared back.

"I don't know what you're talking about," said Al. "All we do is play songs from that album. Is that what you mean? If that's a problem for you, we'll stop. And you can let everyone go."

That's right, Al. Good lad, thought Likely Di. *Say it as it is.*

Docherty wasn't moved. "It dinnae bother me. Ye're the one who'll be the first and quickest tae die," he said.

"Oi!" shouted Dubs. "He doesn't know what you're on about, mate." His voice was quivering. "And nor do I." Likely Di willed him to stay brave and not to lose his head.

"And ye must be… Doctor Who's assistant, I'm guessing. Let me see. Are ye Mr Drums, or Mr Bass? Either way, ye're nae good tae me. And if ye mess wi' me I'll cut off yer fingers then ye'll be nae good tae anyone as a musician, will ye, even if I did release ye? I'm good at cutting off fingers. Tie them both up."

They were dragged off, each to their own Scots pine, just within Likely Di's vision. She watched them, determined to be a model of bravery for their sake. That was all she could offer them, but at least it was something.

"So ye see, McQueen, Lennox Docherty never loses, however long the odds are. Tonight, there is tae be a house bonfire. See? I'm getting them all lined up. I'm so pleased tae see it's a thatch. 'One rogue rocket'. That's what people will say. 'Foolish Londoners having fireworks onsite with a thatched roof'. But before that, there will be one last insult for ye tae hear, McQueen. But I will get tae that shortly."

Likely Di surrendered to the inevitability of the moment. All she could do was act brave to the last. She hoped that would be her legacy. She would keep an eye on the two at the tree and her boys, Al and Dubs. She'd tried to rid the world of Docherty. Len would have been proud of her. At that moment she hoped Blaggit was proud too.

*

Gabby didn't think she could take any more. The mention of the LP really shook her. It was just a joke between her and Mac. Gabby's sister had the skills to make the LP cover, so they asked her, and she did such a good job that after a few cocktails one afternoon they'd sent it off to *Mr Docherty, Cockburn Street. Edinburgh*. They didn't have his number so they never thought it would actually reach him, but obviously it had. How could they have been so reckless? She felt sick. Could her sister have worked out who it was for? Surely she couldn't have, could she? She was making designs all the time for people. Her sister would be safe, wouldn't she? She cursed herself; she should never have persuaded Mac it would be a laugh to goad Docherty further, after his humiliation on race day. This wasn't funny. This was a living hell. *Let's get it over with,* she thought. How much longer was Docherty going to drag things out? And now the brute had gone and ruined their last surprise: the real point of their party. How would things resolve? As she fretted on all this, headlights flashed in the distance. Cars rarely went down their road. No one else seemed to notice them, certainly not Docherty. Had

McQueen spotted it? Did it mean what she thought it might mean?

She sensed something coming up behind her. Before she could react, a hand reached over her shoulder and spread across her mouth. There was a gun pointing at her head. Panic pulsed through her. She was roughly nudged forward, but not in a way that hurt her.

What was going on?

McQueen would be at his wits' end. Why was she worrying about that? She had a gun at her head. There was nothing McQueen could do about that. Gabby, the love of his life, his future wife, was being led away at gunpoint. She caught a glimpse of her captor – slight, dark clothes and balaclava'd, dressed like Docherty's men. Was this another of his henchmen? She thought not. Docherty looked far too surprised.

Just past the bonfire, the balaclava hood came off.

Docherty gasped. "Elspeth, my darling niece. Is that you?"

"Yes, Uncle Lennox. It's me."

Of course. That was why Elspeth stopped working for Françoise. She'd forgotten. It all fell into place.

"Oh. My Elspeth. This is over and above your brief, but very welcome. Bring that rent girl tae me. Let's have some mirth."

He ran his finger over the blade of the axe, goading McQueen. "What shall we cut off her first? Fingers? Toes? Or how about... a nipple or two? But not before my boys have their rightful shaggage."

Phil and Binky rushed to restrain McQueen before he lunged at Docherty. *Yes. Keep him back,* thought Gabby, fighting against being overwhelmed by anxiety. A gun, an axe-wielding maniac, and two yes-men with knives were too much for anyone to take on. Elspeth led Gabby closer to Docherty. It wasn't the gun at her head that sickened her and made her unsteady. It was the memory of the last time she'd seen Docherty up close, in Edinburgh – the perverted sadist that he was.

Elspeth held Gabby, but not in a threatening way; with one hand she was supporting her, helping her stand. With the other, her aim shifted and she pointed her gun at Docherty.

"Tonight, I have come for my own revenge, Uncle," she shouted.

Gabby felt Elspeth's grip loosen and then was pushed gently away. Disorientated, Gabby ran. *Mac. Mac.* Where was Mac? She saw him and melted into his steadying arms. Blaggit gave her water to sip. Her sister tried again to come over, but Tonker set his hand on her arm to stay put.

"We did this, Mac. This is our fault," she said, quietly sobbing into his shoulder.

*

"Right, everyone. On yer knees, Uncle."

"Elspeth. What's happening, hen?" said Docherty.

She fired a bullet into the sky.

"How dare ye?" he cried, enraged. "Ye little—"

"There's plenty more where that came from. On yer knees, Uncle."

No one moved. She fixed her aim on Docherty. "I will nae ask again."

Docherty and his sadistic sidekicks lowered themselves to the ground, looking at her resentfully.

Is this what it was like being Uncle Lennox? Such power. *Stay brave, Elspeth. Stay brave, hen,* she told herself. You're related to this mean, monstrous man. You can do this.

"Now, let me tell ye all about my wonderful Uncle Lennox, who beat me black and blue and abused me in my teens and used me tae spy on people, some of them good people and you ruined them. So tonight, Uncle, ye die. No one else here. Just ye."

She strode towards him, hands trembling, and pulled the trigger. A few inches to the left and he would have been a goner, but the bullet barely grazed his bicep. He didn't even drop the axe.

He hissed out a bitter laugh of fury and pain. Before she could get in a second shot, he rolled forward, screaming. He kicked her, then sprang to his feet tearing the gun from her hand. He shoved her down on the grass as he took out the bullets, one-handed, tossing them nonchalantly behind him into the darkness. He threw the gun hard at the ground beside her. Before she could reach for it, he dragged her to the trees, throwing her down in a patch of mud close to the crushed, defeated others. "Family ties," he ordered, as his men moved in with ropes. There were many Scots pines to choose from and they got busy.

"Elspeth, I am so disappointed with ye, girl," he snarled. Blood dripped from his wound and spread across his fingers. He shook it at her and specks spattered across her face.

Elspeth was disappointed with herself too. She was broken, desperate, and more afraid than she had ever been. In a daze she succumbed to the grabbing hands of her captors.

"And tie up anyone else who moves," he said, skulking near the trees to catch the eyes of each hostage in turn. "They can blink and breathe, but that is all."

He stood over Elspeth, tutting and shaking his head. "Ye stay still, with that Cockney witch by yer side. I expect Cheeky Boy and his chum will pray for ye. We'll be back tae sort ye later."

She looked at him, defiantly. Tears gathered in her eyes as the binds went on, but she fought them away; she knew tears or pleas would make no difference to her fate, so what was the point? She would not let her uncle see her cry or get a sense of her deep despair, discomfort and self-loathing. These goons of his were friends of Gabby's lost Callum and they all knew her as Docherty's niece. How could they do this to one of their own?

Once secured to Docherty's satisfaction, the thugs left her and moved in on the garden towards McQueen and the rest of his crew.

THIRTY-NINE

The ground she'd been set on was hard and damp. Tree roots dug into her butt and a lump of bark jutted out just where her shoulder blade was, but at least she could lean her head back. She was cold and shivering, but not just because of the temperature: she was in shock. And there would be insects on this tree. She was sure she could feel them, crawling all over her. Or was that shock too? She didn't know. All she knew was that she wanted to get away, but the ties were tied so tight, and everything was hopeless.

Being so close to a tree made everything look different, as if she was seeing the world anew, as if she were at one with the woods and the wildlife and that was all she had to rely on. There was no one to help her, she knew that. There was no one but herself – her pitiful, less than competent, failure of a self. She was less than animal, less than insect, less than worthless. Everyone had seen that. Like a tree she had no sense of hope, no dreams, and there was no longer any point in wanting to be free. And yet. And yet, she still had a strong sense of fear. It was not death at her uncle's hands that she feared, rather it was being spared and never escaping his world of horror. That had been the fate of so many in his employ. It wasn't what she wanted. One way or another he would fell her, like a tree. She was no more than a discarded autumn leaf, spent and left to decompose, like rotting compost.

"Well, this is a bind," said the woman next to her, with a jokey air. How could anyone be like that when they're tied and bound just as she herself was? Elspeth tried to focus on this extraordinary woman. "That was a brave thing you did, sweetheart."

Elspeth could not answer. The kindness stunned her.

"I'm Diana. People call me Likely Di. They think I don't know, but I'm not stupid. Well. I'm stupid enough to be tied to this bleedin' tree. But I'm in good company."

Elspeth surprised herself with a half laugh.

It was strange not being able to see the other captives, but a comfort to hear encouraging words.

She tried to pull herself together. "Ye... ye are brave too."

"Shame we both missed our chance. How the hell did you know he'd be here tonight?"

"My cousin Callum's one of his heavies. Bullied into it, like me." She went back to hiding her Scottish accent, ashamed to have one, ashamed to be associated with Docherty. Callum was ashamed too. "He was due to be here with Uncle tonight, but he got beat up recently on another of Uncle's gigs, and then Uncle punished him. Now he's disappeared. I'm so worried. Callum told me he'd had enough too. He wanted him stopped."

Elspeth stopped talking. She could hear two voices from another tree. Were they? Yes. They were reciting alternate lines of a psalm.

"...*Yea, thou I walk through the valley of the shadow of death, I will fear no evil...*"

"Chin up, boys," said Likely Di. "Safety in numbers, eh?"

Elspeth couldn't stop herself shaking and snivelling. It hit her in waves. "You don't... you don't think he'll torch these trees, do you? With us as guys?"

"He might try, love, but McQueen'll no doubt have sent in the cavalry by then. For now, try to be like Woollyback and Wacker here. Have faith, dearie. I personally have faith in Mac, though I'm not one for the Lord."

Elspeth wanted to believe Likely Di but what were the odds that she was right? Everything was hopeless. The comforting words could just be bravado. Elspeth knew Docherty and his ways. They'd get knocked out one by one, dumped inside the house, a whoosh, up they'd all go in a blaze. She tried again to loosen the ties round her wrists and feet, but it was no good. All she could do was sit and wait.

"*Thou preparest a table before me in the presence of mine enemies...*"

*

Docherty stopped in front of McQueen. He fondled his axe.

"Are ye all ears? I want ye tae hear this. A word in yer shell-like, as ye say."

He leaned towards McQueen and whispered, "For yer ears only, while ye've still got them. *Let me lie beneath the ground, where earthworm, beetle can be found.* The words of a dying man I once met. Mean anything tae ye?"

McQueen faltered. Suddenly he was back on the allotment, sifting stones for his grandfather and watching him dig and turn the soil, muscles flexing, laughing to himself contentedly as he muttered a poem, his blade cutting through the earth forcefully on the start of every new line. When he was strong enough to manage a full-sized spade of his own, they dug together, both happily chanting the poem as they worked the soil, or as Grandfather preferred to say, 'worked their souls'.

"Let me lie beneath the ground,
Where earthworm, beetle can be found.
Let me rest at peace below,
To aid the plants and help them grow.

And there I'll hear the word of God:
'*Beneath this sod there lies a sod*'."

It was then that McQueen understood the truth of things.

It was then that McQueen knew what he should have done long ago and never managed to: track a killer down and avenge the death of his grandad.

Regret ravaged him and drove him on.

Docherty was the killer. He was sure of it.

Oh, Grandad.

Docherty's next words seemed far away, but they hurt deeply.

"Caught him with a real corker. I still remember the echoing sound of bone against porcelain. Ouch. Even managed tae kick him in the balls before he went tae hell. So, there ye have it. No happy ending for him. Or ye."

Docherty signalled to his henchmen. "Tie them."

*

"Stop it! Stop it!" screamed Gabby.

Docherty stood above her. "What are ye saying, ye vile bitch? Oh. I get it. Ye're going tae declare yer undying love an' sacrifice yerself tae set him free? How sweet."

"Yes. If that's what it takes. Yes. It was all my fault. It was me who humiliated you in Edinburgh, and it was me who sent the LP, and it was me who made tonight's guy."

"Well, well. What a confession. And what a guy." He stared at the embers of the fire. "Ye walked all over me. Some of it was nice, as I remember. I've an idea that might help ye out of this." He swirled his axe. "D'ye want absolution? Take yer boots off, hen. Get down tae bare feet. Now. Hurry."

She ripped her laces apart and pulled off her boots, then socks. He sneered at her manicured toenails. "Red varnish. Ye're still into that I see, hen." He strutted to the fire, beckoned her to position herself opposite him, then picked up a discarded stick to turn over

308

the hot ashes of the dying embers. It glowed red and spat out occasional popping flashes.

"I'm waiting. We're all waiting. Time tae walk over hot coals. Ye burnt me and now I'll burn ye. Then we're quits. I'll leave ye be."

"No, Gabby. Don't trust him," yelled Tonker.

"Shut it," said Docherty, axe ready.

She could do this. If this would make things right. It was all her fault. She deserved to suffer for wrongs she'd brought upon Mac. She crept over to the fire, snivelling and trembling, grass soft beneath her feet. Was this the last time she'd feel it? She lined herself up, looking down at her beautiful, perfect feet. She lifted her head to face Docherty.

"And this will make you happy, will it? This will set Mac free?"

"Och, yes. Hot-foot it over here. Come intae my arms and be a brave bonnie lass. Come tae Daddy." He shot a glance at McQueen. "I wonder if he will still fancy ye as a stunted burnt-out freak. Or perhaps he will move in on yer sister? Hmm… even share the two of ye. After all, two halves make a whole, they say, don't they? Come this way. Come, come tae me."

Swaying from both heat and fear, Gabby bent down and rolled up each leg of her jeans. One of Docherty's men shone a torch on the ashes to light her way. She took a breath and shifted, readying herself to take the first step.

*

"Nooo! Nooo, Gabby!" screamed McQueen, struggling to free himself from the hold of the brute securing him. Her sister was screaming too.

"Over my dead body," roared Tonker.

Docherty fixed him with a wild, demented look. "Aye, and that. It makes nae difference tae me if ye die oot here before ye all end up tossed inside this tosser's gaff and toasted. Ashes tae ashes."

With no warning, Binky picked up the hose and sprayed it

on Docherty as Tonker, fast on his feet, charged at him, swerving round the fire, head forward, bent at the waist, in full rugby tackle mode. Enraged, Docherty swung his axe making to decapitate him. Skilful Tonker twisted and dodged the blow. It missed him by inches thudding into the mud. Diving forward to grab it, he slipped on the sodden grass, landing with full force on his knee. He cried out as it crunched on impact. Docherty retrieved his weapon and stood over him, primed, ready to deliver the coup de grâce.

The pain unbearable, Tonker could do no more than act as a distraction. "For Mac!" he bellowed, rolling over and urging Phil and Binky forward. As if suddenly unfrozen they stormed towards Docherty. Blaggit joined them and they tried to get through the minders, smashing low into their bodies, dodging knife swipes, then falling back, windless. Docherty lost his balance but held onto the axe. Quickly back on his feet he sneered down at the three of them, as they lay stunned, fighting for breath.

"Stay down," he said as if they were pet dogs. He turned to Tonker. "And ye too, ye slab of a has-been rugby forward, if ye ken what's good for ye."

Injured, Tonker stayed down, whispering to Phil and Binky to breath in through their noses and keep calm. How could anyone keep calm when it seemed that Docherty's boys were moving in with knives, ready for a final bloodbath?

Gabby's sister cried out, "*It was me! I made the fucking LP cover. I didn't know it was for you but I'd make it again because it's you who's gonna be next!*" Frantic, she tried to free her wheel, hands fumbling and failing.

In the darkness a voice shouted loud and commanding, "Woah there! Hold! Hold! Hold!"

Everything and everyone stopped. Docherty and his two brutes looked up, startled.

Gabby broke away and rushed over to her desperate sister. "I'm sorry. I'm sorry," she said and they held each other, sisters sobbing together.

"Bonjour, tout le monde!" said Françoise, bursting out of the copse astride a horse with a star on its forehead. Noel rode beside her on one of his charges, directing a shotgun squarely at Docherty's heart. His henchmen released McQueen.

"Docherty, remember me? Last time we met, you called me Joan d'Arc." She called across to McQueen. "Your surprise is here, Monsieur Mac. You wanted your guests to meet a real winner tonight. He is here: Herd Ringer." She patted his mane, softly saying, "Se calmer. Se calmer," as Noel spoke.

"Docherty, remember me?" said Noel, steadying his horse. "Last time we met you called me a toerag." He put two fingers to his lips and whistled for his dogs. Five bounded over: two of Noel's gundogs running with his favourite bull terrier, Usher. Sweet Pierre and Toto followed at the rear. No longer in their usual carefree, friendly dog gait. One whiff of Docherty and their primeval core took over. Efficient and alert, they sniffed out the evil one, intent on getting revenge on he who dared challenge their pack leader, he who had once harmed one of their own. Like wild wolves they advanced, their hackles up, focused, working together; they were going in for a kill. "Stay!" commanded Noel and they stopped running instantly but growled and barked resentfully, straining for destruction.

*

"Fuck ye, ye half pint!" shouted Docherty, livid and loving it. "Fuck ye, and yer performing canine circus! Ye havenae enough spunk tae get hold o' frog legs here, let alone discharge that popgun o' yours." He turned to his men. "Hey, ye! What's with the walking backwards? Get back here, ye pair of jellyfish. Afraid o' a couple o' whippets and a crippled bronco are ye? Fuck ye." His threatening, low voice stopped them in their tracks. "Rest assured that I will come back for ye when I am done here and I shall castrate yer bits, just like I did wi' that Callum, but I'll be feeding yours to these mongrels here. Ye best stay loyal to me. That's a final warning."

He didn't need to watch their response. No one who valued their life refused a final warning from Lennox Docherty. Fired up and joyously insane, he faced Noel again, eyes on the barrel of his gun. "Bring it on, will ye? *Bring it on!*" he said, gurning.

Noel took aim. He squeezed the trigger.

What was that? Wood pigeon in the trees? Something flapping.

Docherty was unsure whether he was disappointed or delighted that it had distracted Noel, and the bullet missed its target, whistling over his head. There was no time for taunting the gunman, he had to focus on holding his ground as Herd Ringer cantered forward. He swung the axe as if the sail of a broken windmill were an extension of his arm – alternating speed, direction and swing style. It felt good. He was an expert with a hatchet and had no doubt he could deliver a fatal axe blow when it was needed. He'd play for a bit first. The horse snorted and eyed him, guided by the French bitch in the saddle. She was no threat. He'd soon have her down and begging for mercy and a clean cut, if he could hear her over the frantic yapping dogs. Suddenly one broke rank; a furious salivating bull terrier headed towards him. It dodged under Herd Ringer and spooked him. Docherty saw his chance.

"Sweet Pierre!" called a frantic Elspeth. "Stay back!"

"Toto! Stay back," shrieked Gabby.

Docherty sneered as the dogs disobeyed orders and launched themselves at him. Yelping, they snapped at his ankles, drawing blood. "Bad dogs," he said and kicked them, Toto first, into the hot ashes. "Burn yer paws, ye whingeing beasts! This is a night tae burn, burn, burn."

Usher sidestepped his blows and wasn't giving in. As the dog crashed into him, Docherty railed. "I'll slaughter humans and animals alike. Bring it on!" He lined up his axe and let it fall. In an instant Usher's decapitated body lay at his feet, spraying him with blood. It quivered and jerked as the last shreds of life departed. Docherty felt the world slow. He surveyed the scene with the pride of wreaking carnage and adding another death to his toll: he, and the turf where he stood, enveloped by blood and dog snot; he a demi-god of the underworld; he a master warrior of the decapitation blow. He could hear the preacher boys wailing in the trees, reciting the Ten Commandments. Blood-washed, he shouted back, "Thou shalt not kill?" He laughed, manically. "For *mine* is the Kingdom! The power and the glory. For ever and ever! *Bring. It. On!*"

No time to think of future glory. From the corner of his eye Docherty spotted Toto and Sweet Pierre, fire-damaged, hostile and vengeful. Before he could recover the axe and turn to face them, they were on him, the stench of dog breath overpowering. He grappled for the gun in his pocket, but it slid from his muddied hand. Toto went for his neck and Sweet Pierre worked on an arm. Sharp canines set about the business of annihilation. The hounds showed no mercy. He fought to hold back screams, in excruciating pain, as Toto's incisors sunk deep into his lower neck and the dog tore through muscle and bone while a revenge-hungry claw ripped at his cheek and tore away his ear. Toto held it, shining red in his mouth, splattering blood as he moved away and began to devour it.

He would not cry for mercy; he would rise above all pain.

He pushed at Sweet Pierre as if he was wiping away a bothersome fly, and partly shook the dog off, but it quickly returned to the manic mauling of his left hand. Desperate, Docherty tried to pull his hand away, but the angered dog grew more frantic and clung on with locked teeth. Moments later he wrenched the hand off at the wrist, exposing Docherty's veins and his fear. "Noooooo!" he cried in a pitiful wail that shamed him.

He must not cry for mercy; he must, he must rise above all pain; he must let slip these dogs of war.

Where were his men? He needed his men. How dare they

abandon him? Cowards and curs. He would make them pay. Oh, how they would suffer.

Listless, he watched Toto feasting, fascinated and amused, the way the Docherty of yesterday may have been, as the dog half choked and spat it out, shuddering with distaste. How he wished he could taunt the rabid creature and say, 'Revenge is mine, you dog', but all he could do was gurgle and mutter through blood. His puncture marks haemorrhaged gore and the two baying dogs left their treasures to circle him as he lay in the mud, helpless, trying to hide his despair, his fear and his yearning to surrender. He stretched out his right arm and fondled the handle of his axe. Hope grew inside him.

*

Docherty's actions lit the blue touch paper in Françoise. Excited, outraged, and struggling to control the spooked Herd Ringer, she dug her heels in. Bring it on, he'd said. Bring it on she would; a plea sure to grant Monsieur Docherty his last wish. This was for Noel's dog; for her dog; for McQueen, for McQueen's team, and for McQueen's grandad too. It was for Elspeth, for Herd Ringer, and for all the horses she'd lost at the hands of Le Manx Gang, and it was for her. This was from the heart. *Bring it on.*

"Allez! Allez! Allez!"

*

Herd Ringer bolted forward, head low. He dodged a clumsy, misjudged swipe from the desperate, bloody man with the axe. He reared up onto his hind legs with his beloved Françoise holding firm. He sensed revenge pulsing through her veins. He felt it transfer to his veins. He knew what was required. Nothing would stop him. But then he felt it. Pain. Pain. Unbearable pain. Pain like he'd never known before. Pain in his shoulder. Blood everywhere. His own blood, flowing like a river. He'd been struck. His own flesh flailing out of him, free from skin for the first time, and the blood of revenge seeping away. Blood and more blood, smothering the evil one who threatened him, washing over the two halves of the dead dog. He would not let this pain weaken him. He would see it through to the end, like a race. He must not fail. His front hooves danced in the air above a cowering Docherty before they crashed down on his skull, trampling it into the mud. Then Herd Ringer fell to the ground, his work done.

*

The life of Edinburgh's most evil was over. His two associates threw down their knives, fleeing like hyperactive, hapless startled deer, with the bloody dogs in chase, verging on feral, growling, snarling, drooling at their heels. Noel shouted after them, "They're hungry for more blood. You'd better keep running."

Everyone's eyes were on the scene of the massacre. Noel dismounted. He turned towards McQueen and shrugged while patting and calming his horse. He handed over the reins, signalling that it should be led away and tied up safely.

Noel paused before covering the body of his beloved terrier with his jacket. He shook his head. "Good boy, Usher. Good boy. Be at peace," he said, fighting back tears. He sidestepped the remains of Docherty as he threw his keys to Binky. "First aid kit. Back of the trailer. Hurry." Binky shot away and Noel flew to the mess that was Herd Ringer and his broken-hearted loved one, Françoise.

FORTY

Two minutes later

McQueen left them all to it and studied Docherty's trampled, mangled body. It wasn't a good time to note details, but he couldn't miss what he assumed was brain matter smeared on the dead man's sleeve. He wasn't sure whether it was dog brain or Docherty's brain. He wanted to laugh, thinking how much Docherty would hate to be less than immaculate. There, looking back at him, a bloodshot eyeball had popped out of its socket. It was staring menacingly at him. McQueen stared back. "I've a spade in the shed," he said to it. "Looks like I've got some digging to attend to. You can watch me, you sod."

Two hours later

Free from the restraints of their ties and the threat of Docherty or his henchmen, Team McQueen sat in the house, supporting each other, dazed.

No one mentioned that Herd Ringer might not survive.

No one mentioned the dead and damaged dogs.

No one mentioned Docherty or what had happened.

No one mentioned why McQueen had been digging.

Two weeks later

It was good to be back at McQueen and Gabby's without any crowds, and without… Françoise didn't want to think about it.

"So, what's the latest?" asked McQueen. "Although we've been in touch about Herd Ringer a few times, I wanted to hear it direct from the horse's mouth, so to speak."

Noel rocked back in his chair, looking at McQueen square-on. Françoise listened as he calmly gave an update on Herd Ringer's progress. She loved his professional approach to all things animal and the caring way he explained the facts to their owners. It showed he had a heart, and that heart belonged to her.

"I'd say that from now Herd Ringer will never be any more than seventy-five per cent fit. That's the best we can expect." He rested his hands on his knees. "Be assured, my friend, he will continue to have a happy life, which is a good outcome, given all that he's been through."

"Yes. Yes. C'est très bon," said Françoise, nodding and hoping to add reassurance.

"Thank you," said Gabby, trying to hide her disappointment. "You've done wonders."

Françoise handed her a tissue. "Dry your tears, Gabrielle."

She gulped back her sadness. "I can get my sister over soon to see Herd Ringer, can I? Is that okay, Noel?"

"Thank you both," said McQueen before Noel could answer Gabby's question. "From the bottom of my heart. I know that without you two and Elspeth doing her bit, Herd Ringer would have been good for nothing but the knacker's yard."

Françoise left Noel to talk visiting details and Herd Ringer's care routines with Gabby, and led McQueen round the garden, pointing out new shrubs. As they walked, he asked the question she'd been expecting from him long ago.

"One thing that's always bugged me, Françoise, is why anybody would name a horse Herd Ringer?"

She moved close and whispered, for effect, "It is an anagram."

McQueen stopped walking and to her amusement looked cross with himself. "I should have thought of that!"

She let him tut for a bit before adding, "First, of course, I picked him on merit as a good horse, but the name, Herd Ringer, unscrambled, summed up everything we were plotting."

The pleasure in watching McQueen's puzzled face eventually break into a large grin was worth the long wait. She had known it would happen one day. "Bloody clever that. Bloody clever! And you clocked it straight away? Bloody clever." He beamed, shaking his head as he walked away. "Wait till Gabby hears this!"

She called after him, "Thank you, Monsieur Mac. I really thought you would have… what is it you say? Sussed it out much sooner!"

Two years later

"I never thought you'd get me into this gardening lark, Mac. But I s'pose it saves going to the gym every day. What shall we plant here, next to the runner beans?"

"Sweet cicely, of course."

"Oooh, yes. That'll do nice-erly!" It amused and baffled him that she still found her joke funny.

McQueen pulled an unwanted thistle from the middle of their newly laid turf. He waved it at her. "And what do you think Docherty would say about planting something here?"

Gabby thought for a bit, watching their chickens strut around, pecking, posing and enjoying a chance to be out of their pen, ruling the roost while Toto was out on a shoot with Sweet Pierre and Noel. She tapped the side of her forehead. "Lemon squeezy, Mac. Docherty would say, 'Over my dead body, hen!'."

McQueen hid his laughter and pretended he hadn't heard. He walked towards the trees. "I always think we should have had a scarecrow round about here, dressed in a kilt," he said, laying the thistle down to rest.

Little Albert toddled over, waving his hands at shoulder height as he gleefully wobble-walked across the grass. The hens scuttled off, flustered.

McQueen picked the young boy up. "Ooooh, Bertie. How Grandad would have loved you."

Bertie wriggled and laughed.

"That's right. Great-Grandad Albert would love you, Bertie!"

McQueen lifted him high and sat him on his shoulders.

"Daddy dig more. Daddy dig more. Find verms an' beedles," said Bertie.

McQueen galloped round with little laughing Bertie jiggling on his shoulders.

"Clip-clop, clip clop," said Gabby, beaming.

Flower of Scotland

The End

La fin

GLOSSARY

Aintree irons: *gay persons.*
All around the Wrekin: *the long way round.*
'ampsteads: *Hampstead Heath (teeth).*
Arrête: *French for stop.*
Badger con: *a specific confidence trick usually undertaken by a woman luring single men at a bar to her hotel room, getting them into a compromising position and then working with an accomplice who bursts in to blackmail them.*
Baked bean: *Her Majesty, The Queen.*
Bag of sand: *a grand, (one thousand pounds).*
Barlinnie drumstick: *lead pipe studded with nails.*
Barnet: *Barnet Fair (hair).*
Big folding: *paper money, notes.*
Bilk: *fraud/con.*
Bizzies: *a derogatory term for police officers.*
Bostin days: *brilliant days/happy days.*
Brass bands: *hands.*
Callards: *callard and browsers – trousers.*
Carey Street: *bankruptcy court.*

Chookies: *young persons/sweethearts.*

Cobb on: *bad mood.*

Costermongers: *fruit and veg sellers on a market stall.*

Cozzers: *cops.*

Cuddy: *buddy/friend.*

D'accord: *French for all right.*

Dasachtsh: *an epitath given to Donald II of Scotland 900 ad*

Devil's dandruff: *cocaine.*

Dew beaters: *feet/thickly soled shoes.*

Dog-eye: *someone who keeps watch.*

Écoute attentivement: *French for listen carefully.*

Épineux dealings: *French for horse profile dealings.*

Getting the babby a frock and pinny: *an endeavour that generates financial reward.*

Giraffe: *laugh.*

Gregory Peck: *cheque.*

Grifter: *con artist.*

Hank Marvin: *starvin'.*

Haymaker: *hard punch, likely to knock someone out.*

Hen: *term of endearment for woman or girl.*

Hergé: *pen name of Georges Prosper Remi, Belgian cartoonist, most famous for creating The Adventures of Tintin series.*

Je t'ai eu: *French for got you.*

Kite: *cheque.*

Layers: *a betting term for someone who offers odds and accepts wagers on the outcome of an event.*

Lowie: *money.*

Lucky Last: *last race of the day.*

Malky: *slashing someone with a razor.*

Mark: *target.*

Méchant: *French for villain.*

Merde: *French for shit/damn. (Oh shit.)*

Mick Jaggers: *pints of lagers.*

Mon pauvre cheval: *French for my poor horse.*

Monkey: *five hundred pounds.*

Moon-shot: *such a grand plan it's unlikely to succeed.*

Mountebank: *fraud, deceiver, trickster.*

Mutton: *mutton Jeff (deaf).*

Natch: *naturally.*

Nous avons flambé notre argent: *French for we have burnt our money.*

Paperback writer: *all nighter.*

Pauvre: *French for poor, as in 'poor dear'.*

Pica pica: *Latin name for magpie.*

Pint of wallop: *pint of beer.*

Pished: *drunk.*

Plazzy Scouser: *plastic Scouser – not a true Liverpudlian.*

POETS: *piss off early, tomorrow's Saturday.*

Pot-valiance: *courage (as a result of drinking alcohol).*

Purple Edward Elgars: *twenty-pound notes.*

Purple patch: *lucky times.*

Revanchism: *seeking to retaliate to recover losses.*

Ruby Murray: *curry.*

Sassenachs: *derogatory Scottish term for an English person.*

Schindler's: *Schindler's list – pissed.*

Scotch-walloped: *hit with a bottle of Scotch.*

Sherbet: *alcoholic drink.*

Shill: *a plant/stooge.*

Shrapnel beano: *wildly spending money in the form of coins.*

Skyrocket: *pocket.*

Slàinte Mhath: *Scottish Gaelic toast of 'good health' (pronounced Slanj-a-va).*

Spanker: *spirited horse.*

String: *a group of horses owned or used by one individual.*

Tilt at the layers: *attempt to win money from bookies.*

The splits: *a wager placed on two numbers.*

Toper: *someone who drinks alcohol a lot.*

Tosher: *scavenger/thief – can be a term of endearment.*

Trabs: *trainers/running shoes.*
Trojan: *condom.*
Un plan de secours: *French for Plan B.*
Vantardise: *boastfulness.*
Welshed: *go back on your word.*
Winnie Mandela: *pint of Stella.*
20 to 1 bar: *odds not quoted are 20 to 1 or bigger.*

ABOUT THE AUTHOR

Odds & Sods is Andy Catling's first full-length fiction. His work is usually short stories, many of them imaginary meetings with celebrities, past and present, written with humour and comment on contemporary issues. In between shifts for the NHS as a former ward clerk, and his earlier work in the murky waters of estate agency, double glazing sales, and managing rock bands, he has always loved to write.

Born in 1957, Andy was involved in horse racing and gambling from the age of eighteen when he chalked up odds and results on a blackboard in his local North London bookmakers. Over the years he devised scores of madcap betting systems. Ever eager to explain his rationale to punting buddies, they nearly always ended with a hard luck story and made very few visits to the payout window. As a diehard Cockney, racehorse owner, form student, and weekend punter, Andy has yet to take much money from the bookmaker's deep satchels. Older and perhaps only a little wiser, he still has pipedreams about landing the jackpot.

He lives with his wife in Bedfordshire and is conveniently located only a minute's walk from a Paddy Power shop, but these days he is usually spends his time at a desk, writing.